THE WAY OF THE SAMURAI

Yoshi Matsuhara's eyes widened. Three Messerschmitts were dead ahead and closing fast. As the lead enemy fighter filled the first ring of his rangefinder, Yoshi pushed down hard on the rudder pedals and glanced at his airspeed indi——— T———— ————y-five knots—and he was

York's cockney ——————————— "Edo Leader this is Edo ——————————— arse. Slow 'er down a bi—————————

Willard Smith's ——————————— ggest you throttle back a bit, Edo Leader. You're uncovering your tail."

"Roger," Yoshi said and grudgingly eased back a notch on the throttle. "I will take the leader. Engage your opposite numbers. Individual combat after first pass."

Yoshi would have preferred to maintain the three plane section, but against three of the enemy's best he could very well keep his own tail safe. If his Englishmen died, he preferred they die fighting for their own skins, not his. That was the warrior's way—the way of the samurai. In a few brief moments the sky would be filled with snarling, tumbling fighters, and young men would die—the smart, the proud, the brave, the clever.

Death would make them all equal.

THE SEVENTH CARRIER SERIES

By PETER ALBANO

THE SEVENTH CARRIER   (2056, $3.95/$5.50)
The original novel of this exciting, best-selling series. Imprisoned in a cave of ice since 1941, the great carrier *Yonaga* finally breaks free in 1983, her maddened crew of samurai determined to carry out their orders to destroy Pearl Harbor.

THE SECOND VOYAGE OF THE SEVENTH CARRIER   (2104, $3.95/$4.95)
The Red Chinese have launched a particle beam satellite system into space, knocking out every modern weapons system on earth. Not a jet or rocket can fly. Now the old carrier *Yonaga* is desperately needed because the Third World nations—with their armed forces made of old World War II ships and planes— have suddenly become superpowers. Terrorism runs rampant. Only the *Yonaga* can save America and the Free World.

RETURN OF THE SEVENTH CARRIER   (2093, $3.95/$4.95)
With the war technology of the former superpowers still crippled by Red China's orbital defense system, a terrorist beast runs rampant across the planet. Outarmed and outnumbered, the target of crack saboteurs and fanatical assassins, only the *Yonaga* and its brave samurai crew stand between a Libyan madman and his fiendish goal of global domination.

QUEST OF THE SEVENTH CARRIER   (2599, $3.95/$4.95)
Power bases have shifted drastically. Now a Libyan madman has the upper hand, planning to crush his western enemies with an army of millions of Arab fanatics. Only *Yonaga* and her indomitable samurai crew can save the besieged free world from the devastating iron fist of the terrorist maniac. Bravely, the behemoth leads a rag tag armada of rusty World War II warships against impossible odds on a fiery sea of blood and death!

ATTACK OF THE SEVENTH CARRIER   (2842, $3.95/$4.95)
The Libyan madman has seized bases in the Marianas and Western Caroline Islands. The free world seems doomed. Desperately, *Yonaga's* air groups fight bloody air battles over Saipan and Tinian. An old World War II submarine, *USS Blackfin*, is added to *Yonaga's* ancient fleet and the enemy's impregnable bases are attacked with suicidal fury.

TRIAL OF THE SEVENTH CARRIER   (3213, $3.95/$4.95)
The enemies of freedom are on the verge of dominating the world with oil blackmail and the threat of poison gas attack. *Yonaga's* officers lay desperate plans to strike back. Leading a ragtag fleet of revamped destroyers and a single antique World War II submarine, the great carrier must charge into a sea of blood and death in what becomes the greatest trial of the Seventh Carrier.

Available wherever paperbacks are sold, or order direct from the Publisher. Send cover price plus 50¢ per copy for mailing and handling to Zebra Books, Dept.3631, 475 Park Avenue South, New York, N.Y. 10016. Residents of New York and Tennessee must include sales tax. DO NOT SEND CASH. For a free Zebra/Pinnacle catalog please write to the above address.

REVENGE OF THE SEVENTH CARRIER

PETER ALBANO

ZEBRA BOOKS
KENSINGTON PUBLISHING CORP.

For Cynthia and Drew who signed aboard for their first voyage.

The author makes the following grateful acknowledgments to Master Mariner Donald Brandmeyer for his generous help with maritime and ship handling problems; Patricia Johnston, RN, who assisted with medical problems; Dale Swanson for advice concerning the North American B-25, "Mitchell," medium bomber. Mister Swanson also gave freely of his expertise in helping solve the variety of problems besetting bombers on long, arduous missions; Mary Annis, my wife, for her careful reading of the manuscript and thoughtful suggestions; Robert K. Rosencrance who so generously contributed his technical and editorial skills in the preparation of the manuscript.

ZEBRA BOOKS

are published by

Kensington Publishing Corp.
475 Park Avenue South
New York, NY 10016

Copyright © 1992 by Peter Albano

All rights reserved. No part of this book may be reproduced in any form or by any means without the prior written consent of the Publisher, excepting brief quotes used in reviews.

If you purchased this book without a cover you should be aware that this book is stolen property. It was reported as "unsold and destroyed" to the Publisher and neither the Author nor the Publisher has received any payment for this "stripped book."

First printing: January, 1992

Printed in the United States of America

Chapter One

Oberleutnant Ludwig von Weidling eyed the blood-red Messerschmitt Bf 109 of Major Kenneth Rosencrance, his leader and commanding officer of the *Vierter Jager-staffel* (Fourth Fighter Squadron). Rosencrance was throttling back. Measuring Rosencrance's right elevator, von Weidling eased back on his own throttle, his tachometer dropping to nineteen hundred rpms, air speed to 170 knots, manifold pressure 146 centimeters of mercury. A red light glowed low on his instrument panel. His auxiliary fuel tank was empty. Leaning forward, the fighter pilot threw a switch, bringing his fuselage tank on line. Then he pulled back hard on a toggle-release. There was a slight jar and the fighter felt suddenly slightly tail heavy as the three-hundred liter *Rustsatz 3* drop-tank fluttered away from its crutches and tumbled toward the vast blue-gray expanse of the Western Pacific. Grunting, Ludwig cranked the tail trim handwheel which was mounted on the left side of the tiny cockpit just beneath and below the throttle quadrant and mixture control. The drag vanished.

Quickly, Ludwig glanced at Rosencrance and then to his left at his counterpart, Rosencrance's other wingman, Wolfgang Vatz. The black and white "Zebra" striped ME of Wolfgang Vatz kept perfect station, riding easily, exactly opposite von Weidling's colorfully painted fighter and only fifty meters off the leader's tail. Ludwig disliked the elderly Vatz who was the son of an ordinary iron worker from Cologne. Only World War II and enlistment in the *Luftwaffe* had pulled Wolfgang from the streets where he had run for years with a gang of Hitler's Youths. Vatz claimed he had lied about his age and had entered flight training at the age of fifteen. Serving with such a common, vulgar guttersnipe brought feelings of revulsion to von Weidling's aristocratic stomach.

Born in Buenos Aires thirty-five years before, Ludwig von Weidling was the only son of a proud Prussian family. His father, Helmut von Weidling, who had held the rank of generalmajor in the *Wehrmacht* when World War II broke out, had been a staff officer serving Field Marshal Fritz Erich von Manstein. Helmut von Weidling was also one of only a few Prussians who had joined the Nazy Party in the thirties and became a rabid supporter of the Fuehrer.

Von Manstein had been given credit for the brilliant German breakthrough at the supposedly impenetrable Ardennes Forest. This brilliant stroke led to the collapse of the French and British armies in May of 1940. Actually, Generalmajor Helmut von Weidling conceived the plan and argued its merits over the old Schlieffen plan that failed so miserably in the first months of World War I. The debate was held in Hitler's presence at Berchtesgaden in the Bavarian Alps and the Fuehrer ruled in Weidling's favor over the objections of Commander in Chief Field Marshal von Brauchitsch and the Chief of Staff, General Halder.

Four years later after the failure of Operation Citadel — the German attempt to erase the Soviet Kursk salient — and subsequent withdrawal of German forces behind the Dnieper River, Hitler sacked von Manstein and promoted von Weidling to General and put him in *ehemaligen*

command of the Eleventh Army. Ludwig's father remained in command to the bitter end, finally donning civilian clothes in the ruins of Berlin and managing to elude capture. He was smuggled out of Germany with forged papers, taking the famous "main route" from Memmingen to Innsbruck and across the Brenner Pass to Italy with the help of ODESSA, an acronym for *Organisation der SS-Angehorigen* — Organization of SS Members. Then a steamer to Buenos Aires. Here he was given a position as an accountant for a German-owned importing firm and married Hilda Rosenberg, his employer's daughter and a woman of pure Aryan stock.

Ludwig was born in 1955. Although he was an Argentinian by birth, he was never allowed to forget his proud Prussian heritage. He was constantly reminded that, "Germany lost the war because of traitors at home and because of the efforts of international Jew bankers." Incessantly, he was indoctrinated with the article of faith, "German first, Argentine second." German was the language of his home and he was sent to German schools.

When he grew into manhood, he met many furtive strangers who called on his father, usually at night. Only years later did he learn he had met some of Nazi Germany's most famous and distinguished fugitives Martin Bormann, Walter Rauff, Klaus Barbie, Heinrich Mueller, Doctor Josef Mengele, Adolph Eichmann and many more. All had been proud in his part in *Endlösung* — the final solution to the Jewish problem — and spoke of the resurgence of Germany and the establishment of the Fourth Reich after the Russians and Americans annihilated each other.

Ludwig grew into the ideal Nordic type exalted by the Nazis. Blond with clear blue eyes, his fierce competition in sports gave his short, compact build a burly, solid look. True to his Junker lineage, his forehead was broad and intelligent, nose straight, jaw square and strong, neck thick as a young tree. Inevitably, his appearance could cause women to stir with excitement while men cast him uneasy looks.

Ludwig fell in love with flying at an early age and with the encouragement of his father joined the Argentine Air Force at the age of twenty-one. He flew *Super Etendards* against the British in the war over the Malvina Islands (the English called them the Falklands) and put an Exocet missile into the British destroyer *Sheffield* before he was shot down by a Sidewinder AIM 9L missile fired from a Sea Harrier. From this moment on, his hatred for the English knew no bounds.

He was recuperating from a broken leg, four broken ribs, internal injuries and still smouldering from the humiliation of defeat when the great carrier *Yonaga* broke loose from its Arctic trap and devastated Pearl Harbor. Everyone had a big laugh on the hated, arrogant Yankees. Ludwig convulsed until his broken ribs threatened to puncture his lungs.

Then, the Chinese orbited their laser satellite system. It was an incredible achievement—twenty deuterium-flourine particle-beam powered weapons platforms orbiting at 1,500 kilometers and three command modules in geo-synchronous orbit at 36,000 kilometers. Proudly, Beijing proclaimed an end to the threat of an ICBM nuclear exchange. However, the technology was faulty. Immediately, the system malfunctioned, not allowing a single jet or rocket engine to operate. Ignition meant instant destruction by lasers striking like lightning bolts. The whole world changed in less than a minute. Then the frantic scramble began, the return to the old reciprocating engines and the mad search by all powers for the old fighters and big-gunned ships of World War II. And Japan, Israel and America were drawn closer together in the face of growing Arab unity.

Finally, Moammar Kadafi gave leadership to the men of good will all over the world who would fight the Israeli, American and Japanese tyranny. When hostilities broke out between the Arab coalition and the Israeli and Japanese allies, Ludwig was eager to join Kadafi's air force. But his wounds were slow to heal and it was not until 1987 that he was sufficiently recovered to fly a Messerschmitt Bf 109. Now he was a wingman to Kadafi's greatest fighter pilot, the American Kenneth Rosencrance, and was earning a million a year American plus fifty-thousand dollars a kill. He had earned a quarter of a million dollars in "kill" money and the enviable position as one of Kenneth Rosencrance's wingmen. It was a good life, flying out of Saipan with all the liquor a man could drink, an Arab woman especially trained to please a man and over two-million dollars in his Swiss bank account.

His eye caught a movement of the red Bf 109. Rosencrance was banking. With radio silence, you had to be alert for changes in course, hand signals and the waggling of wings that could signal danger. He pressed right rudder and balanced with aileron and elevator as the aircraft bounced up on a tropical thermal and then dropped its right wing into the turn. Continuing the turn, the lieutenant glanced at a chart tacked to a board, strapped to his knee. They had reached the twentieth parallel, the northern end of their leg. Time to turn and head south on the one-hundred-fiftieth meridian. They were 650 kilometers northeast of Saipan, bucking the northeasterly trade winds and burning fuel at an alarming rate. But with the wind on their tails, the run south would require less fuel.

Watching his compass swing to a southerly heading with one eye and monitoring his section leader's turn with the other, he centered his controls as Rosencrance settled on the expected new course of 180. Ludwig glanced at his fuel gauges. If they did not meet the enemy and go "balls out" to full military power, he had another 1450 kilometers of fuel left in his wing and fuselage tanks, adequate for the swing to the east and then west on the sixteenth parallel for the return to *Jihad* Field on Saipan. The German snickered. The Americans had called it Isley Field after one of their heroes killed during the invasion many years ago. My, how things had changed in less than fifty years. The Yanks had paid a bloody price for the place and now it was an Arab base menacing Japan their current ally and former enemy. What irony! Von Weidling laughed out loud.

He reached up and adjusted his goggles which were up. The cold air must have tightened the strap and the rims were digging into his forehead. He pushed the goggles higher over the leather of his helmet and tucked an annoying tuft of blond hair under it. The air at nine thousand meters (29,520 feet) was very cold. He coughed into his oxygen mask. Oxygen made his throat raw. He wished they could drop to a lower altitude but with the great Japanese carrier *Yonaga* prowling somewhere to the east, enemy patrols were probably in the area.

Altitude was the one supreme advantage of the fighter pilot. With airborne radar outlawed by the spineless *Glasnost* hungry great powers at Geneva, a man had to be alert to survive. He sighed and rubbed the stiffening muscles of his neck. He felt hair and corded muscle. He snickered. Funny how his thick neck and hairy body excited women. Once they ran their hands over his matted chest and muscular, hairy arms, their hunger seemed to flame as if they were transported back to a primal level where the only thing that counted was animal lust and carnal satisfaction. Like a hot wave, the sultry sexiness of Nada Muhahili suddenly crowded into his thoughts.

10

She was the best piece he had ever had and would be waiting for him on Saipan in her small apartment just outside Garapan. She was an animal, a clawing, squirming screeching animal. Long, boring patrols always brought her back. He could never get enough of her firm, hard body. Strange, he always needed her the most after a kill. He squirmed uneasily with his own arousal. With a conscious, painful effort, he pushed the girl from his thoughts and brought his mind back to his work.

Automatically, he searched the sky with the short jerky movements of the experienced fighter pilot. No staring at any particular spot. No, indeed. Avoid the sun and the fan with its hypnotic power to deaden a man's concentration. Keep your eyes moving and depend on your peripheral vision to pick up spots that could materialize into the deadly Mitsubishi A6M2 Zero with its powerful new engine. He was acknowledged as having the best eyes in the Arab Air Force. "Combat vision," they called it. He was capable of focusing out to infinity and back with the precision of a zoom lens, searching a section of sky each time. His ability to see at a distance was astonishing and inexplicable. Once he had actually spotted enemy fighters at the impossible range of eighty kilometers. It was no wonder Rosencrance had wanted him as a wingman.

A movement of his stick dropped the starboard wing. From this great height, the sea appeared as flat as a steel-blue disk. When it caught the sun, the reflection glared like polished silver, overpowering his retinas and flashing afterimages when he looked away. Four thousand meters below, legions of small puffy clouds as wispy as bridal lace drifted lazily toward the southwest, the brilliant sun imprinting their flat shadows on the sea like black ink. In the distance, far to the west, the usual scattered thunderheads a man learned to expect in latitudes south of the Tropic of Cancer soared into the heavens; a single imperious giant rearing its anvil-like head up above all the others to at least ten thousand meters. Surrounded by a near perfect circular cloud, it looked as if it were wearing a halo. It was stunning and arty and unreal as if created by some overzealous Hollywood special effects man. However, Ludwig von Weidling saw no beauty there. Today and every day was a day for killing. He looked for possible concealment, possible traps. Death could hide anywhere, in the clouds, the sun, under the unwary pilot's fuselage.

He brought up his wing and studied Rosencrance's red Messerschmitt for a brief moment. The BF 109 was an aerodynamic beauty from its needle-nosed propeller spinner to its rounded vertical tail fin. It was a much more graceful aircraft than the club-nosed Zero with its huge radial engine. Its "Galland type" canopy was low and blended in a perfect line with the fuselage unlike many of the bulbous greenhouses of fighters of its time. With an inverted V-12 engine, the Messerschmitt was designed with perfect rounded symmetry. Even the radiator, oil cooler and supercharger intakes, exhaust manifold fairing strips and ejector exhausts were streamlined, blending into the sleek design. With the new three thousand horsepower Daimler-Benz DB 605 Valkyrie engine, it was capable of 420 knots and its range had been increased to over 2000 kilometers. And it had a killing sting; two wing mounted 20 millimeter Mauser cannons and two cowling mounted 13 millimeter Rheinmetall Borsig machine guns. Although the ME could not turn with the Zero — nothing on earth short of a hummingbird could cut a sharper turn — the ME 109 was rugged, fast and could outdive the Japanese fighter. Ludwig smiled to himself. He would like to earn another fifty or hundred thousand dollars today. "Come on, you *verfluchte scheisse*," he said to himself.

"Schnell!" He was urging those damn shits to hurry.

Ludwig sobered with a new thought. Commander Yoshi Matsuhara was out there somewhere. Carrier *Yonaga* had been spotted putting to sea the day before. Matsuhara and his two despicable Englishmen. A souped up Mitsubishi A6M2 Zero with two Supermarine Seafires off its rudders. A snipe and two killer hawks. A comedic trio at first, but it was rumored the trio had shot down at least twenty Arab fighters and bombers in the last battle alone. And the Seafire was fast, durable and equal to the ME 109. No one laughed anymore. Matsuhara! Yoshi Matsuhara, *"Yonaga's* Butcher," they called him.

The man was a legend, a hateful, despicable relic of the past. A renown scholar and poet, the world's media had drooled over the man's past. An original member of *Yonaga's* air groups, Commander Yoshi Matsuhara had been frozen-in in the Arctic with the great carrier for forty-two years. The man had to be well over sixty-years-old, but fought with the bloodthirsty instincts and lightning reactions of a great white shark. It was said he had over thirty kills. There was a million-dollar bounty on his head, half a million each for the two Englishmen; Captain Colin Willard-Smith and the cockney, Pilot Officer Elwyn York. Ludwig von Weidling hated Matsuhara who had killed his best friend six months earlier during the great carrier battle in which *Yonaga's* air groups sank carrier *Ramli al Kabir* and damaged carrier *Al Kufra.* It had been a terrible, bloody defeat and Kadafi's forces thirsted for vengeance.

Ludwig was particularly hungry to kill the Englishman Captain Colin Willard-Smith. It was rumored the Britisher had fought in the Malvinas, had been a Sea Harrier pilot. Von Weidling reserved a special venom for Sea Harrier pilots. He would kill the Englishman and gain a double revenge in one swoop, perhaps one burst. He licked his lips. "Come on," he said. "Where are you hiding, you Jew-loving *schweinhund?*"

"Where are you hiding, Rosencrance?" Commander Yoshi Matsuhara muttered into his oxygen mask, scanning the pristine, eggshell blue sky above and the throngs of small gossamer clouds below. Despite the low clouds and a strange anvil-headed thunderhead nearby to the west that wore an eerie circular ring of clouds like a halo, the day was a fighter pilot's dream. However, at ninety-five-hundred meters (31,160 feet) it was very cold — minus fifty-seven degrees centigrade. And he felt the cold despite wool underwear, two pairs of wool socks, padded brown flying suit, fleece-lined boots, jacket, and his leather lined helmet circled by his *hachimachi* headband — a white cloth covered with ideograms proclaiming his determination to die for Emperor Akihito.

Adding to the commander's irritation, his face itched. Before a long patrol that could last eight hours or more, he always shaved close to avoid any stubble that would chafe under the tight-fitting oxygen mask. But his fast-growing whiskers refused to cooperate, and the persistent, maddening itching had begun. And the worst was yet to come. Soon, he would begin to sweat under the mask. Then the itch would become unbearable. However, the crowning discomfort would come from his bladder. It was almost full and it was useless to reach for the elimination tube. At this altitude it would be frozen solid as usual. Gritting his teeth, he hoped he was not forced into a full-throttle power dive. The "gs" of the pull-out would most certainly force him to wet his flight suit. That occurrence would bring a smile to his crew chief, Chief Teruhiko Yoshitomi, and the entire ground crew.

He pounded his padded combing in frustration. The Marianas were just over the horizon, less than 180 kilometers to the west, and he had not even sighted a sea bird on the long patrol. He wanted to push on, making strafing runs on the enemy airfields on Saipan and Tinian. But these attacks were out of the question. He was to make a high-altitude reconnaissance of the airfields on Saipan and Tinian, patrol east on the sixteenth paralel for a one hundred kilometer and then turn for home.

Yoshi breathed an oath. This was a job for the slower, two and three man Aichi D3As and Nakajima B5Ns, but the bombers had been decimated during the last battle. Now most of the air crews were green, far too inexperienced to send on such a dangerous mission even with fighter protection. Old Admiral Fujita had cautioned all section leaders that this was only a fighter sweep, a sweep designed to sniff out Arab fighters and destroy them before slower reconnaissance aircraft were sent in. Had the enemy squadrons in the Marianas been reinforced since the great Japanese victory six months earlier? The CIA and Israeli Intelligence had both reported strong reinforcements by submarine and by two freighters that had docked in Saipan's Tanapag Harbor while *Yonaga*'s battle damage was being repaired. It made sense. The opportunity was there and the Arabs must have grabbed it.

The section leader glanced to the right and then to the left. He grunted with satisfaction: Pilot Officer Elwyn York was off his starboard side, Captain Colin Willard-Smith his port. They were holding their Seafire F.47s on station with their usual precision. They were a strange, mismatched pair.

The son of a prominent barrister from Barmston in Humbersideton, Captain Colin Willard-Smith was so British that he appeared stereotypical. He was not a young, lean John Bull or Colonel Blimp, but, instead, a cool, resolute fighter with the urbane sophistication of

15

Anthony Eden and the dogged obduracy of Winston Churchill. Raised on a family estate outside Barmston, young Colin had every advantage English society could provide, but the heart of a rebel beat in him. After enrolling in Eaton when only seventeen, Willard-Smith defied his father, left school and joined the Royal Air Force at eighteen.

He flew every fighter in the British inventory. A true professional, he spent thirteen years in the cockpits of fighters. His favorite was the V/STOL, (Very Short Take-off or Landing), Sea Harrier which he flew in the war in the Falklands from carrier *Illustrious*. He shot down two Skyhawks and a *Super Etendard*. He was awarded the Distinguished Flying Medal by the queen, herself, and was made a Member of the British Empire. He was so "British" that the first time Yoshi Matsuhara saw him, a scrap of a poem by William Ernest Henley had immediately come to mind. "Ever the faith endures, England, my England: Take us and break us; we are yours, England my own." If there had been English samurai, Yoshi was convinced Willard-Smith would have had more *damashii* or spirit than any of the others.

Yoshi pivoted his head to the starboard side. No poetry came to mind when you looked at Pilot Officer Elwyn York. A tough cockney, he was as pragmatic as a twenty-millimeter shell. The air group leader was sure his wingman was grinning despite the oxygen mask and goggles that almost concealed his face. York always seemed to be chuckling as if he found life one great macabre joke. Despite the disarming smile, he was a ruthless killing machine and Yoshi suspected the man smirked at the moment of the kill.

York was the antithesis of Captain Colin Willard-Smith. One would believe that they came from different countries. They even seemed to speak different languages. Yoshi Matsuhara had been born in America

16

and English was the language of *Yonaga,* yet with his thick cockney accent with its rolling, rhyming slang, York seemed to be speaking another language. He differed from Willard-Smith in every way. Short and compact, he walked with a simian-like roll, muscular arms hanging low. His skin was dark for an Anglo-Saxon, hair black, eyes flashing with alertness and a practical intelligence honed in the gutters of London's East End, the heart of cockney London.

Born in the great loop of the Thames just south of Bow Common, Elwyn York grew up running the narrow back streets surrounding the West India docks. His father had been a costermonger, a fruit and fish peddler. His mother did piece work in a sweatshop where shirts were manufactured. Elwyn discovered she also did "piece work" with men in some of the back rooms of the innumerable pubs that crowded the area. Both parents died before Elwyn reached his twentieth year.

The cockney grew up on potatoes and jellied eels, living in a nineteenth century tenement with a single outdoor toilet serving twenty families. At sixteen, after his mother's death, he decided to run as far away from the East End as he could, finally ending up in Africa as a mercenary, fighting in the endless wars that broke out after France, England and Belgium pulled out and left the emerging third world countries to founder and bleed on their own.

In Africa York discovered flying, the one true love of his life. He learned to fly making supply runs in old Douglas DC-3s, Curtis C-46s, Douglas C-54s, Lockheed Constellations and then made the switch to single engine in the old North American AT-6. His first modern fighter was the Dassault MD.452 Mystere which he flew for Chad in its interminable war against Moammar Kadafi's aggressions. Here he saw entire villages massacred by Libyan troops and his best friend, a young

Frenchman named Andre de Lattre, was shot down and tortured to death in the presence of Kadafi, himself. The man was skinned, blinded, fingernails pulled and genitals slashed and jammed down his throat. York was consumed with hatred and now sought his own personal cockney brand of vengeance with *Yonaga*'s air groups.

Commander Yoshi Matsuhara had flown with Japan's best, beginning in China in 1940. However, he was forced to admit the Englishmen were the best wingmen he had ever had. He had never seen men fight with such tenacity, panache and verve. Perhaps it was the same bulldog determination of their race that had carried them alone through the darkest days of their war against Hitler. His Englishmen had shown the most exalted qualities of the samurai in every battle, surprising everyone, including their enemies. In a way, they were samurai with white faces. The thought brought a smile to Yoshi's face. The pair was so fair, flying daily above the weather the sun had burned ovals around their eyes, imprinting the outlines of their oxygen mask, goggles and flying helmets. He chuckled out loud. They looked like raccoons. He had made the same joke about his dearest, closest friend, Lieutenant Brent Ross who had burned even more on long patrols in the rear cockpit of his bomber. The Englishmen and Brent had roared with laughter at the quip.

The gunner-observer on an Aichi D3A and Admiral Fujita's most valued junior officer, Brent Ross was back on *Yonaga* with the rest of the bomber crews, three hundred kilometers to the northeast and waiting impatiently for the results of the sweep. The Aichi D3A dive bombers and Nakajima B5N torpedo bombers would not take off for their reconnaissance patrols off the Marianas until the fighters had completed their search.

In the traditional Japanese manner, the twenty-seven aircraft had taken off in "three threes of three," and then

18

split off into nine groups in order to patrol nine separate sectors. However, the sectors were not so widespread that any one group could not receive support from at least two other groups within three minutes. In a major encounter, all twenty-seven fighters could concentrate within fourteen minutes. Of course, you can lose an entire section in fourteen seconds. With the exception of the two Seafires, all fighters on the sweep were Zerosens, the carrier's twelve American-piloted Grumman F6F Hellcats acting as *Yonaga*'s Combat Air Patrol.

Yonaga! Yonaga, the world's greatest carrier. Built on a *Yamato* hull and over one thousand feet long, the behemoth could operate 150 aircraft. She had had an incredible, tragic, yet glorious history. The seventh carrier of the Pearl Harbor stroke force of December 7, 1941, she had been the flagship and sent to a remote anchorage on Siberia's Chukchi Peninsula two months before the attack. Here a sliding glacier trapped her for forty-two years. Yoshi thought they would all go mad during those four decades. Some did. There were suicides, bloody fights to the death. Senior officers died in droves. But somehow the ship and its surviving crewmen endured, breaking out in 1983, starved for battle and revenge. Nobody believed the radio reports of Japan's surrender. Was not surrender incomprehensible to the samurai? Then the attack on Pearl Harbor and the return to Japan to discover the impossible . . . Japan had indeed surrendered! Then the Chinese laser system was orbited and the madman Kadafi and his terrorists went wild. From that day on, the fighting had been incessant. Yoshi smiled. That was why he had been born, trained, lived, breathed. Fighting, killing, dipping his sword in enemy blood gave meaning to his life. He was the Emperor's sword, the embodiment of the Code of Bushido. Only death could sheathe him.

He glanced at the noon sun which was farther north

than it should have been. Another glance at the chart strapped to his right knee confirmed his suspicions. Dropping his starboard wing and banking slightly to the north to counteract the set of the northeasterly wind that he knew was pushing his aircraft south, Commander Yoshi Matsuhara stared down over his right wing tip.

He could see the glistening blue sea through breaks in the patchy clouds. Weird how the whole world seemed to be revolving while the fighter hung stationary in the sky like a stuffed bird suspended from a taxidermist's ceiling. One of the many phenomena a man found when pressing close to the realm of the gods. Man was an interloper here, a feather on the wind who clubbed his way into the heavens for a brief moment, glimpsed the awesome delights reserved for the sun goddess Amaterasu-O-Mi-Kami (Heaven Shines Great August Deity), the storm god Susano (Imperious Male), Tsuki-Yomi (Moon) and their entourage of lesser gods.

Although Yoshi had been born in America, he had been imbued with Shintoism, Buddhism and the Code of Bushido by his father and then sent to Japan as a teenager for his education. He was a samurai to the marrow of his bones and loved flying and dogfighting. He was born to the sky and knew one day he would die here. Years crammed into the cockpit of the Zero-sen had given him the feeling he was an extension of the control column, the throttle, rudder pedals. He knew his aircraft better than any woman he had ever "pillowed," flying the Mitsubishi on a fine, feathered edge with a feel for his fighter that allowed him to push it to the limits of its design.

Sometimes, he pushed the aircraft so close to the limits, firing the guns forced a high-speed stall or a half-roll into the torque led to a power dive without moving his controls. He felt the great new Sakae 43, thirty-two hundred horsepower engine in his bones, in his heart. Felt it when the Mitsubishi flirted with a stall; felt it when "balls to the wall," brutally forced the fighter into maneuvers and stresses that would have horrified its designer Jiro Horikoshi. He knew precisely how to turn the plane, riding the edge before the Zero waffled out on him. Maximum power, lift and maneuverability were found mostly by instinctive flying, not by an arcane rationale and inner debate. Concentration was total and man remained focused, ignoring fatigue, strangling oxygen mask, anger, fear, a full bladder. No static was allowed to enter a man's mind up here. He could only connect with himself or die, his tiny cramped cockpit his coffin.

He loved to dogfight. This was the ultimate challenge, man against man, plane against plane, gun against gun. Battle gave meaning to a samurai's existence, the Code of Bushido. Brave, bold conduct in battle polished a man's karma and, of course, everyone knew death in combat guaranteed entrance into the Yasakuni Shrine where his spirit would dwell with those of countless heroes for eternity.

Matsuhara always fought with his engine in overboost despite the thirty-two hundred horsepower Sakae 43's tendency to overheat. The commander was a confident hunter and his trigger finger was always steady. He liked to approach from slightly below with minimum deflection. He would lead his target a little like a game bird and squeeze off a short burst from his two twenty-millimeter cannons and two 7.7 millimeter machine guns. Then he would veer off to avoid flying metal when his enemy disintegrated. If the enemy blew up, it was a thrilling, beautiful sight and inevitably he felt a hot surge of pleasure deep down like being with a woman. He had been told many times that the object of combat was to destroy the enemy's machines. However, he wanted the kill. He wanted to know his enemy was dead.

Only death could bring him the satisfaction, the gratification he craved. And he knew when he had killed the enemy pilot in his cockpit. He could tell by the way the machine began to gyrate wildly, windmill, tumble and then plunge straight down into its final twisting dive. Yoshi loved to follow the dying aircraft down, savoring every moment of the kill.

His tactics were basic, predicated on his fighter's performance and pilot limitations. He drilled them into his men incessantly: always seek the advantage of altitude and approach out of the sun if possible; once an attack is started, always carry it out; fire only at close range and only when your enemy's wingspan fills two rings of your range finder; fire short bursts, long bursts overheat your guns, causing them to jam; attack from behind, every plane has a blind spot; never dive with an ME 109; never fly straight and level; stay alert to stay alive, the man with the better eyes wins; the good pilot knows the best survival tactic is to check his tail constantly and to stay in top physical condition.

Yoshi constantly warned dogfighting was hard work, requiring strong arms and shoulders. All pilots were required to train with weights and run at least five kilometers a day. With no hydraulics or power boost, a fighter's controls became very heavy. In fact, after a few minutes of dogfighting at four hundred knots, a man began to fatigue as if he had been lifting boulders for hours. And clouds could be treacherous, especially cumulus where an enemy could hide and lash out in ambush. Good pilots — live pilots — avoided flying below thin cirrus. The enemy could look down through the cover while it was difficult to see up through the white, hazy glare.

Sighing, Matsuhara rubbed his thumb over the safety cover shielding the red button at the top of the control column. He looked around in his usual jerky movements, taking a small sector of the sky at a time. He depended on his peripheral vision to detect the dimmest specks. His vision was better than ever and had contributed more to his survival than any other factor. In fact, his ability to spot tiny specks in the distance seemed to improve with age. "Hyperopia," the ancient Chief Hospital Orderly Eiichi Horikoshi had complained once. "Farsighted," Yoshi snorted to himself. But he could still read small print up close without the aid of glasses. He had eyes that made men a third his age stare in envy. However, new aches and pains crept into his body with every passing day. No one was immune to time.

His neck and back were sore and the irritation seemed to grow with every patrol. Despite his extraordinary vision, black hair and unlined face, he was quite old now, but would not admit it to anyone. Not even Brent Ross and especially Eiichi Horikoshi. He could rub his neck, but could only push against the padded seat in futile efforts to relieve his aching back. He glanced at the sun. Amaterasu-O-Mi-Kami was watching. And, indeed, they would need the help of all the gods if they met the killer, "Rosie" Rosencrance and his wingmen.

It was rumored the renegade American now boasted over thirty kills. And his wingman, Captain Wolfgang "Zebra" Vatz, at least twenty. There had been reports of a new German fighter pilot named Lieutenant Ludwig von Weidling, a Prussian aristocrat, who had run up a quick score of five victories. A skillful and merciless killer, von Weidling had been quickly claimed by Rosencrance as his other wingman. The young German flew a solid purple Messerschmitt with a yellow propeller boss and yellow and black stripes painted across his wings much like the stripes painted on the wings of Allied aircraft during the invasion of Normandy. Perhaps, soon, they would meet. Yoshi dampened his suddenly parched lips with the tip of his tongue.

Watching his compass carefully, he centered his controls when the compass card swung to 280. He marked his chart and spanned the distance to the island chain with his experienced eyes. They should hit the still invisible Saipan dead center within minutes. He glanced at his wingmen. They clung to him as if tied by invisible cables.

The Seafire was a beautiful aircraft. Adapted from the land based Spitfire F.24, the Seafire F.47 was a graceful bird, its silhouette altered distinctly by a cut down rear fuselage and bubble canopy. Four wing-mounted Hispano-Suiza twenty-millimeter cannons gave it a lethal punch. It was fitted with a tail-mounted sting-type arrester hook, catapult spools, a strengthened undercarriage, slinging points and extra tankage that gave it a respectable range of over two thousand kilometers. Mounted under the nose was a tropical air filter that had been specially designed and fitted for service on *Yonaga*. It was crescent shaped like a quarter moon. The big elliptical wings had been clipped and provided with wingfold gear so that the fighters could fit into *Yonaga*'s nine-meter lifts. Without a doubt, this modified wing resulted in a small loss in torsional rigidity, increased wing-loading and, perhaps, caused a fall-off in performance. But the Seafire had been sent to sea to honor the fabled Supermarine mystique and had more than held its own. And the British had kept apace with the horsepower race by upping the horsepower of the Rolls Royce Griffon 88 engine from 2550 to 3050. This great power plant drove the six-bladed, contrarotating propellers that pulled the fighter in level flight at more than four hundred knots. It could climb, dive and turn with Kadafi's best. In fact, York had six kills, Colin Willard-Smith eight. Six more Seafires were on the way from England. They would be a welcome addition to *Yonaga*'s fighter group.

Something on the western horizon caught Yoshi Matsuhara's eye. A peak, shrouded in mists. Mount Tapotchau, Saipan's highest point, over 474 meters (1554 feet) above the sea. He waggled his wings and pointed. Both of his wingmen nodded. Everyone scanned the sky anxiously. Arab patrols should be up, seeking them out. Most certainly enemy radar on Saipan and Tinian had been tracking them. Now all of Saipan's eastern coastline and the flat contours of Tinian, which was only three kilometers south of Saipan, were visible. Still no enemy fighters. Had the Arabs lost so heavily they could not afford to protect their most valuable bases? Perhaps he was flying into a trap. Maybe his other groups were engaged. But all he could hear in earphones was the hiss of the carrier wave. Not one section leader was engaged, calling for support. He forgot his stiff neck, flipped down his goggles and glanced back over both shoulders. The Messerschmitt had a service ceiling of at least eleven thousand meters. They could be up there. "Watch out for the enemy in the sun!" his old instructor at Kasumigaura had drummed into him over and over as he had done himself to generations of his own pilots. But he saw nothing at all. He needed a closer look below.

Now he could see all of Saipan, Tinian and Aguijan — an impregnable small citadel-like island south of Tinian which was still occupied by a company of Japanese infantry. Again he waggled his wings, made a circle with his thumb and forefinger and waved the signal over his head. Willard-Smith and York returned the signal. Yoshi raised his goggles, unsnapped his seat belt, loosened his six-point shoulder harness and pulled a pair of powerful binoculars from their case attached to the side of the fuselage. Carefully he lowered his starboard wing, balancing with rudder and brought the binoculars to his eyes with his right hand. This was a terrible way to conduct a reconnaissance and he hated every minute of it.

He was completely vulnerable in hostile skies, the proverbial sitting duck. Never had he ever been so completely dependent on his wingmen for his safety, his life. Quickly, he focused the glasses out to infinity and studied Saipan first and then Tinian. Both islands were now just off his starboard wing tip. He strained against his harness.

Suddenly, he saw fearsome flashes on both islands. Leaping upward. He knew them well. Eighty-eights. His mind reviewed the enemy antiaircraft like a computer: maximum ceiling fifteen thousand meters (49,215 feet), rate of fire twenty 9.4 kilogram (20.73 pound) rounds a minute. A vicious, deadly weapon especially when geared to radar control. Parts of the islands seem to be burning with their fire. At least a dozen batteries. Far more than he had expected. They had been reinforced. Then the first explosions; ugly, black smears in the pristine sky like a loathsome pox. Short. But the gunners adjusted as good gunners always will. The bursts moved up, blending into a black, rolling carpet that seemed to hang in the sky below as the fighters raced over it. Then they were bracketed with bursts above and below. Yoshi tightened his jaw and ignored the fire. He had no choice, anyway. He studied the islands.

He saw two airstrips on Saipan and two more on Tinian. Revetments could be seen clearly lining the runways. But he could not make out any aircraft. The Zero rocked as two shells burst directly below the fuselage almost knocking the glasses from his hand. He cursed. He had called on Amaterasu for help. He tightened his grip and raised himself even higher, straining against the harness. He felt terribly vulnerable like a target in a shooting gallery. Then he saw them, five four-engined aircraft parked off to the side of one of Tinian's runways. Lockheed Super Constellations. Unmistakable. And at least six black fighters at the end of one of the runways on Saipan. Two were taking off and the other four were taxiing into take-off position. However, he did not concern himself with those fighters. They were not an immediate threat. No indeed. Where were the rest of them? Certainly, Arab radio must be screaming. Patrols must be up. ME 109s must be vectoring in on him now. That was where death lurked. If he made a diving attack, he most certainly would be jumped from behind. It was an old trick and he had seen it work many times. He had used it himself in two wars. He dared not linger. He had seen enough.

He returned his glasses to the case, but the top would not snap and lock in place. Without hesitation, he threw the binoculars over the side. "No loose cannons in this cockpit," he told himself. Quickly, he locked his seat belt and tightened his shoulder harness. Pulling back on the stick, he kicked right rudder and watched the horizon wheel below his cowling as he brought the fighter around for its easterly heading on the sixteenth parallel. Without even glancing at his point option data he knew he was to make a one hundred kilometer run on this heading and then north to *Yonaga*. At least to the point where it was supposed to be. The Seafires clung close.

The antiaircraft (AA) bursts trailed behind them and he noticed some huge bursts intermingling with the eighty-eights. They were 105s and, maybe, 155s with new gun mounts and special ammunition. In the name of the gods, the Arabs had some big artillery down there. And no doubt they were dual purpose (DP) and could be depressed to engage any attempts to land on the islands. Yoshi bit his lip and his stomach suddenly felt hollow and empty just as it did when he had drunk too much sake and was about to vomit. He choked down the rancid acid taste and switched on the microphone in his oxygen mask. He must report to *Yonaga*. He could be

27

blown to bits in the next instant and his new intelligence would die with him. *"Saihyosen* (Icebreaker), *Saihyosen,* this is Edo Leader," he called.

"Edo Leader, this is *Saihyosen,*" a voice came back in his earphones. "Go ahead."

"Saihyosen this is Edo Leader. Sighted five four-engined aircraft on Tinian, six fighters taking off from Saipan. Heavy AA fire—eighty-eights, one-oh-fives and possibly one-fifty-fives. No other aircraft sighted. Turning onto leg four of my patrol."

"Roger, Edo Leader. Well done."

Commander Yoshi Matsuhara dropped his hand from his mask and sank back into his padded seat. He scanned the skies with his machinelike search. He saw nothing but scattered clouds below and that strange thunderhead with the vaporous halo behind. He slapped his bulletproof windscreen. "Where are you Rosencrance?" he shouted into the slipstream. "In the name of the gods, where are you?" Only the roar of the engine and the hiss of air streaming past his canopy answered him.

Holding a tight "V," the three fighters droned off to the east.

Chapter Two

Captain Kenneth Rosencrance went to full throttle and began to climb when Radio Saipan reported the three intruders; a red, green and white Zero accompanied by two Seafires. Matsuhara and his two Englishmen at last and they were reported on an easterly heading on latitude sixteen. A collision course.

Lieutenant Ludwig von Weidling choked back the excitement that churned up from his stomach and focused an eye on his leader's elevator. Pulling back his stick, he pushed his own throttle forward, enriching his mixture at the same time. The Prussian watched his tachometer zoom to twenty-eight hundred rpms, manifold pressure increase to 150 centimeters, airspeed to 380 knots, altimeter passing ten thousand meters. He cursed. As usual, the ME's control surfaces had become extremely heavy at the new high speed. He knew in the dogfight that seemed imminent, it would take all of the power of his muscular arms and legs to avoid high speed stalls and to prevent the wing slats from flicking open and shut, causing a disastrous loss of control.

And the left rudder felt heavy as if a drag had been attached. It always happened at full throttle. Maybe it was the weight and torque of the new Daimler-Benz Valkyrie engine, but the aerodynamics of the aircraft had not been changed externally, anyway. He did not understand. No one seemed to understand. His crew chief had never been able to correct it. And he had heard other pilots complain of the same defect, but, strangely, not all. It was an idiosyncrasy confined to only a few aircraft. He cranked his trim wheel an eighth of a turn and felt the rudder pedal lighten slightly. Good enough; it had to be good enough. Grimly, he held his station off his leader's right elevator, his nose pointed west on the sixteenth parallel.

Von Weidling narrowed his eyes. Something was far to the west just south of the great thunderhead. Seabirds? An optical illusion? No! It had to be Matsuhara and his two renegade Englishmen. He spoke into his microphone, "Caliph Leader, this is Caliph Three. Three aircraft at twelve o'clock, range fifty kilometers, high and closing."

Rosencrance acknowledged and immediately clawed for more altitude. The American's calm voice filled the Prussian's earphones, "Intercept and blow their fucking asses out of the air. Hold your positions until I release you."

Von Weidling heard Wolfgang Vatz acknowledge and then made his own acknowledgment. Then he heard Rosencrance report the contact and call for support. Thirty more Messerschmitts were on patrol, but the closest were, perhaps, four minutes away. No doubt Matsuhara was calling in his own support. Von Weidling was sure of that. The German licked his lips. Soon the sky would be filled with fighters. He had a chance to earn big money this day. Real big money. "Come on you slant-eyed yellow *schwein*. A few more kills and I will retire." Von Weidling chuckled into his oxygen mask.

The approaching trio was pulled up hard. He, Rosencrance and Vatz were above ten thousand meters and climbing, too. He had heard of the great new Sakae and the powered-up Rolls. Now he was seeing them in action. The two formations were closing at an incredible speed, perhaps a combined closing speed of nearly nine hundred knots. It appeared neither group would have an advantage in altitude.

Now Ludwig could make out details. A gleaming white Zero with a red cowling and green hood leading two Seafires. Matsuhara, *"Yonaga's* Butcher,"* leading his two ice-cold British killers. Von Weidling felt an amalgam of excitement, anticipation and fear rush through his veins, sending his heart to hammer wildly against his ribs and a rock to lodge in his throat. He swallowed hard. Flipped up his Revi 16B reflector sight and threw a switch. Immediately, a hundred millimeter orange reticle glowed on his ninety-millimeter armorglass windscreen. He brought the red dot of the "pip" in the center of the reticle to the three approaching aircraft and flipped the safety cover off the red button on the top of his control column. Running his thumb over the red button, he felt new confidence. There was a million-dollar bounty on Matsuhara. He wanted him more than anything else on earth. He could retire on one kill. He leaned forward and skinned his lips back. His mouth was suddenly filled with saliva.

Yoshi Matsuhara's eyes widened. It was Rosencrance, Vatz and Weidling. No doubt about it. Dead ahead and closing fast. Both flights were at 11,500 meters. There would be no advantage in altitude for either flight. He had called in all sections when he had first sighted the enemy flight just minutes before. He was certain Rosencrance had done the same thing. But no other aircraft were in sight. Only the three fighters growing in his range finder. He gently caressed the red button with his thumb, but the lead plane did not even fill his first ring.

31

He stole a look at his new American instruments. With his giant new thirty-two hundred horsepower Sakae 43 *Taifu* (Typhoon) engine in overboost, the water-methanol injectors were spraying their mixture into his cylinder heads and the superchargers were whining and whistling their strange high-frequency song. His cylinder head temperature showed a disquieting 265 degrees and creeping upward, oil temperature 220 degrees, oil pressure eighty-seven pounds, manifold pressure fifty-eight inches of mercury, airspeed 410 knots and climbing. He corrected for the great torque with a slight touch of right rudder.

Originally designed for an engine with one-third the horsepower, the Mitsubishi A6M2 vibrated its objections to the brute in its nose. With two banks of nine closely packed cylinders around a circular crankcase, the Sakae 43 only weighed one hundred kilograms (220 pounds) more than the old Sakae 42. Two turbo-superchargers pumped in air at high pressure, boosting the amount to be ignited with gasoline in the cylinders and giving the fighter increased power in the thin air of high altitudes.

When Yoshi Matsuhara first announced his intention to install and test fly the monster in his fighter, Mitsubishi engineers threw up their hands in disbelief. When he went ahead with his project, anyway, they claimed he was bent on committing *seppuku*, ritualistic suicide. Before the engine was installed, Chief Teruhiko Yoshitomi and his crew stripped the skin from the fighter and rebuilt it in accordance with plans drawn up by Commander Matsuhara. The light aluminum engine mounts were removed and new steel engine mounts put in their place and two more added. All were equipped with anti-vibration rubber pads. New titanium-aluminum alloy members replaced the main wing spars, ribs, longerons and formers. The fuselage ribs and stringers were also replaced or strengthened. All control cables were removed and heavy-duty lines installed. Control surfaces were strengthened and even the aileron, flaps, elevator and rudder hinges replaced. A larger self-sealing fuselage tank was installed which helped counterbalance the weight of the new engine and increased the Zero-sen's range at the same time.

Yoshi did not worry as much about his airframe as he did the engine. Built under license by Nakajima, the Sakae 43 was based on a revolutionary power plant, the Wright Cyclone R-3350, that had been originally designed by the Wright Corporation for the old American Boeing B-29. Magnesium was extensively used in place of aluminum in order to save weight. Magnesium is one-third lighter than aluminum. However, magnesium could not withstand the stresses and heat as well, and the engine had a nasty habit of overheating and bursting into flames. Despite extensive modifications including the replacement of the magnesium crankcase with one of aluminum, American engineers never completely solved the problem and the new engine still ran hot and when in overboost the cylinder head temperature always crowded the red line at 280 degrees.

Twice Yoshi had overheated, the first on his maiden flight when climbing vertically like a rocket over *Yonaga* at full throttle and the second time in a dogfight. He had been forced to break off the engagement and run for home at reduced throttle. Only the cover of York and Willard-Smith saved him. He was determined not to order the engine installed in the rest of his Zero-sen fighters until he was completely satisfied the R-3350 was operationally safe. All of the remaining Zeros and bombers of *Yonaga's* air groups were powered with the Nakajima Sakae 42, two thousand horsepower engine. It was low powered by today's standards, but reliable.

The lead enemy fighter now filled Yoshi's first ring.

He gripped the stick and pushed down hard on the rudder pedals but the vibrations continued. He glanced at his airspeed indicator; 425 knots. He was pulling away slowly from the Seafires.

York's completely undisciplined cockney voice filled his earphones: "Edo Leader this is Edo Three. You're showing us your arse. Slow 'er down a bit or be buggered by them three MEs."

"Roger, Edo Three," Matsuhara replied. "Put the spurs to the old horse or eat my prop-wash."

"There ain't no more in this ol' 'orse, guv'nur."

Willard-Smith's cultured voice broke in. "Edo Leader, this is Edo Two. I suggest you throttle back a bit, Edo Leader. You're uncovering your tail."

"Roger," Yoshi said. Grudgingly, he eased back a notch on the throttle, but kept the mixture at full rich. His air speed indicator dropped to 390 knots. The Seafires crept up slowly.

Yoshi stared intently into his range finder. The lead Messerschmitt's wingspan had grown through the first ring. They would be in range in seconds. He spoke into his microphone, "Edo Flight this is Edo Leader. I will take the leader. Engage your opposite numbers. Individual combat after the first pass."

Yoshi would have preferred to maintain the three plane section. However, against three of Kadafi's best, he could very well sacrifice one or both of his wingmen in an effort to keep his own tail safe. If his Englishmen died, he preferred they die fighting for their own skins; not his. That was the warrior's way—the way of the samurai.

Even with all of his concentration on the red Messerschmitt, Yoshi picked up the specks with his peripheral vision. Aircraft were closing in from the east, north and south. And he was sure they were coming from the west, too. All points of the compass. Soon the sky would be filled with snarling, tumbling fighters. And many young men would die this day — the smart, the proud, the brave, the clever. Death would make them all equal.

Lieutenant Ludwig von Weidling heard them in his earphones: "Caliph Leader this is Caliph Green. Have you in sight. Closing from the north and low." Then, "Caliph Yellow," " Caliph Orange," and at least five other sections reported visual contact with Rosencrance's section. But von Weidling could see Zeros streaking in. They seemed to be coming in from every point of the compass. However, his total concentration had to be on the Seafire boring in off Matsuhara's Zero's port side. His range finder showed one thousand meters. He flexed his big biceps, pulling back slightly on the control column and just touched left rudder which still dragged despite the increased torque of the Daimler-Benz at full military power, supercharger shrieking. Staring through his antiglare gunsight screen, he smiled as the enemy's wingspan filled the lighted orange circle and the red "pip" blended with the enemy's propeller boss. He punched the red button.

All six aircraft opened fire at the same instant. Von Weidling felt the fighter tremble, buck and slow as the two thirteen-millimeter Rheinmetall Borsig machine guns and his pair of twenty-millimeter Mauser cannons ripped and stuttered to life. Brass cartridge cases streamed out of their chutes in both sides of the hood and popped out of the ejectors in the wings, bright and shiny, glinting in the slipstream. Brown smoke streaked back.

Fire motes winked red on the enemies' wings and the Zero's cowling as the enemy opened fire. Tracers ripped past each other like deadly fireflies. His tracers seemed to be eaten by his enemy's propeller. Nothing happened. He cursed. His damned controls seemed to be fighting him. And twenty-millimeter shells stormed past from the

Seafire's four cannons. One hit and he could be a dead man. But the high speed apparently spoiled the Englishman's aim, too. None of these fighters were designed for the power plants they carried. They were all heavy in the controls and the ME 109s and the Zero were twisted by enormous torque. Only the Seafires with their contrarotating propellers were free of the gyroscopic pull of the engines. But they, too, appeared to be suffering from sluggish controls.

Rosencrance dropped his nose and banked slightly to the left, not daring to expose his radiator and oil cooler intake to enemy fire. Following his leader, von Weidling saw the Seafire rocket so close to his canopy, for an instant, he thought he would be scraped by his enemy's radiator. The Prussian fought his controls as the ME 109 twisted and bounced in his enemy's wake.

Immediately, Rosencrance pulled back hard, rolled to the left, dropped his nose to pick up speed and turned toward the enemy. Vatz and von Weidling held close to their leader's rudders. Von Weidling knew turning with a Zero was all but forbidden. But Matsuhara's Zero was not an ordinary Zero. It was equipped with a huge new engine and, obviously, Rosencrance felt the Japanese would have trouble swinging the great pendulum of the twin-banked power plant around. And the Seafires could not turn any faster than the Messerschmitts. Everyone knew that.

Now ME 109s and Zeros were pouring in from every direction; some from above and others climbing up fast from low altitudes. "Caliph Flight, this is Caliph Leader. Individual combat! Kill the motherfuckers. But that yellow-assed Matsuhara is mine!" Rosencrance shouted.

"Greedy *schwein*," von Weidling screamed, punching his instrument panel. He increased his bank. But the sharp turn cost him eighty knots and he felt the juddering that warns of a high-speed stall. Easing his turn, he twisted his head until his neck ached and stared up through the perspex of the head panel. The Seafire? Where was it? He had something to settle with the Britisher.

Then he saw it. He screamed with joy. The Englishman had dropped at least three hundred meters, trailing a white mist. He had damaged his enemy and had the advantage of altitude. A sure kill. A half-million American dollars in the bank. Let Rosencrance try for his million. He had a better shot than the American. He chuckled at a corrupted old bromide that flashed through his wildly spinning mind: "I will make a corner of a foreign ocean forever England with one burst." He laughed maniacally at his clever paraphrase.

The Prussian licked his lips, rolled out of his turn into a shallow, speed-gaining dive. He brought the nose of the ME to the Seafire.

"Individual combat! Individual combat!" Commander Yoshi Matsuhara shouted into his microphone.

His earphones were filled with the frantic, near hysterical voices of combat. He winced as he heard one of his section leaders, Takashi Shigatomi, scream a warning at one of his new men, Yasujiro Arii.

"Arii this is Shigatomi. One-oh-nines above you. Can you see them?"

"Negative Shigatomi. And your radio is terrible. Where are you?"

"A hundred meters off your starboard side and low. Open your eyes. Break right Arii!"

"Shigatomi, this is Kuruma. One-oh-nines at nine o'clock low. Closing fast."

"See them Kuruma. Engage! Engage! One on your tail Arii. In the name of the gods, break right, toward me! Turn! Turn! They can't turn with us."

Matsuhara caught a flash in the corner of his eye and a Zero curved toward the sea, a plunging torch on the end of a ribbon of black smoke running down the sky behind.

"Arii is a dead man," came through his earphones.

A yellow-white explosion filled the sky like a blossoming gray flower with arching black petals. An ME 109 and a Zero-sen had collided head-on. Locked together, the two engines spun out far to the side of the raining, burning debris and tumbled downward. The great billowing gray cloud took on a spider shape, its ever-lengthening gray legs formed by smoking debris falling to earth.

Heavier and with a slight advantage in speed, the Messerschmitts' usual tactic was to make one pass, shoot and break off. Sometimes they pulled up again and sometimes they half-rolled onto their backs and dived steeply out of the fight in the reverse direction. But not this day. They stayed to fight, probably believing the new, heavier Sakae 42 engine encumbered the Mitsubishi's ability to maneuver. And the Japanese fighter was slightly slower in its acrobatics, but still faster in its turns than its adversary. The battle took on a classic matchup between quickness and maneuverability versus speed and ruggedness.

Quickly, the dogfight took on a frenzied fury, both sides killing with swift, cold efficiency. Planes twisted, spun burned, disintegrated. A Messerschmitt, caught in the wing root by a burst of twenty-millimeter shells, lost its port wing, and tumbled across the sky like a teal at full speed blasted by a shotgun. Another Arab aircraft with a headless pilot, twisted downward through the dogfight, barely missing two fighters before crashing into the sea. Two Zeros followed it. Both were burning. One parachute blossomed behind one of the Mitsubishis. A burning Messerschmitt shot into a roll, canopy open. A black figure tumbled out, cannoned off the wing and slammed into his own stabilizer before bouncing away, spinning seaward, arms and legs spread-eagled.

Commander Matsuhara ignored the horror surrounding him and took a quick look around for his wingmen. All dogfights are a matter of turns, feints and rolls. But hard turns cost speed and speed is regained by diving. Thus air battles tend to drift lower and Yoshi Matsuhara looked downward to find most of the combatants. York and Vatz were locked in a personal duel to the south while Willard-Smith had vanished. The slaughter had been fast and furious. Five pillars of black smoke marked the graves of fighters while at least four parachutes swung far below as they drifted toward the sea.

Bringing his huge engine around, Yoshi saw the red Messerschmitt which was trying to turn with him. But he was turning faster than Rosencrance and was above the American. He blocked out the savage spectacle filling the sky, his concern for his wingmen, ignored the cries in his earphones, his instruments, and focused his total concentration on the red fighter. He had altitude and altitude meant speed, the fighter pilot's most priceless possession.

Quickly, Rosencrance saw his disadvantage and whipped his fighter brutally into a high-G barrel roll and curved downward to regain speed and put distance between himself and the pursuing Zero. A Messerschmitt could outdive any Zero except Matsuhara's.

Pushing his stick grip forward, Yoshi plunged after Rosencrance in a shallow dive that intersected the geometry of the ME's evasive maneuver. The red fighter filled both rings of the gunsight. A perfect deflection shot from three-quarters above. Gently he triggered the red button, felt the gun-camera pressure, pushed through it and then the guns' recoil kicked the airframe. He shouted with joy, seeing his strikes like tiny red blossoms on his enemy's fuselage and port wing. Rosencrance whipped his aircraft again into a gut-wrenching turn and pointed his nose into a vertical dive. Yoshi laughed, followed his enemy's maneuver, pushing his own stick forward and ruddering back onto his enemy's tail.

At that moment a frantic cry jarred him. It was Elwyn York who was still fighting the Zebra striped Messerschmitt far to the south. "Edo Leader. Willard-Smith's in a bad way. 'E's 'it. Von Weidling's got 'im, low an' at your ten o'clock. I got me 'ands full o' this kraut."

Captain Colin Willard-Smith's voice broke in. "I can handle my own problems, old boy. Take care of your own and send Rosencrance west."

Yoshi pulled back on the stick and then rolled to the left, staring down over his port wing. He saw a Seafire streaking off to the northwest trailing glycol. A flamboyant purple, yellow and black ME 109 was in pursuit — Lieutenant Ludwig von Weidling. Yoshi cursed. Ruddered to the northwest while Rosencrance curved off to the west and south. He would lose the renegade killer, but he must try to save his wingman.

He horsed the stick to the left and split-essed into a dive, bringing his cowling to von Weidling's Messerschmitt. The vast expanse of the Pacific Ocean filled his windscreen. He stole a glance at his instrument panel. His dive was accelerating the fighter to an enormous speed. His air speed indicator was doing frightening things, the white needle chasing around the clock with a speed he had never seen before, catching up with the slower red danger line, passing five hundred knots. His controls stiffened like they were freezing and the aircraft began to shake. Yoshi gritted his teeth until his jaw hurt. He knew the laws of aerodynamics well, and they were taking control of his aircraft away from him. He knew air travels faster across the top curved surface of a wing than across the flat bottom, and this anomaly produced lift. In the Zero's full-throttle steep dive, turbulent air was ripping past the fighter's wing at six hundred knots or better, producing shock waves that slammed against the control surfaces. The commander was experiencing the feared buffeting pilots called "compressibility" and he fought the fighter's stiff controls with all of the power in his arms and legs. And his cylinder head temperature was crowding 280. A few more minutes at this speed and he would burn up his engine. But he had no choice. Von Weidling was closing in on the damaged Willard-Smith. The German had his killing angle and was almost in range.

The commander's speed and dive angle had closed the gap on the Seafire and the pursuing ME 109. Time to pull out. He said a prayer for his reinforced airframe and strengthened wings and pulled back hard on the grip. He thought the stick would bend; so hard he feared it would break off. Slowly, the nose came up and the horizon dipped down and crowded out the sea. He felt the great forces hammer him down at least with the power of 6-Gs; perhaps, more. He weighed nearly twelve hundred pounds.

There was a dull pain in his stomach, his legs became lead. He was forced down into his seat until he thought his spine would snap. The corners of his mouth pulled down and saliva streaked off his chin. His head lolled to one side as if his thick neck had suddenly become a wet string. He felt the skin of his face sag down, tears run from his eyes and his nose ran. Centrifugal force was draining the blood from his head, his peripheral vision vanishing and he was staring down a tunnel filled with a red haze. He could lose consciousness, already he was "graying out." He fought the encroaching gray clouds by shaking his head, screaming and breathing in short hard gasps.

After an eternity, the horizon came up and he cried "Amaterasu!" over and over into his mask, trying to relieve the pressure that still pounded his guts down, pres-

41

suring his bladder and his bowels. For a horrifying moment, he feared he would lose control of both. Then his flight suit was wet in the crotch and he cursed himself. But he managed to maintain the rest of his sphincter control.

The aircraft bounced, vibrated at the bottom of the dive and the wings actually flopped up and down like a fledgling bird just out of its nest and trying the sky on its own for the first time. He shook his head, screamed some more. His face tortured him; sweat and stubby bristles of his beard cloying and pushing against the tight fitting rubber; itching, tingling. He longed to push it aside and wipe and scratch, but dared not. Shaking off the dark clouds, he fought his controls until he had brought the fighter back. His airspeed indicator dropped to 490 knots as he streaked down on von Weidling. The German had turned hard to starboard after the desperately maneuvering Seafire giving Yoshi a terrible one-half deflection shot from the starboard side.

The German opened fire. Yoshi kicked hard rudder despite a red haze that lingered just back of his eyes and a head that felt rock heavy. He would take what von Weidling had given him. Willard-Smith would be dead before he could position himself on the ME's tail. Maybe, Willard-Smith was a dead man, anyway.

Obviously, the German had not seen him, so intent was he on his kill. Yoshi had heard there was a half-million-dollar bounty on the head of the Englishman. Maybe the German's greed had caused a momentary lapse into carelessness. He most certainly should have seen Matsuhara by now.

Lieutenant Ludwig von Weidling grinned as his guns shook the airframe. This would be a leisurely, sure kill. Zero deflection and at two hundred meters. His tracers streaked past the Seafire's starboard side. Then the starboard wing flashed shiny like silver coins had been sprinkled on it, thirteen-millimeter bullets punching holes into the aluminum. Bits of metal ripped off like leaves in a gale. The damaged Seafire banked to the left out of the stream and the Prussian released the red button. The Englishman was having trouble with his controls. Von Weidling could see large rips in the enemy's right wing just forward of the aileron. The aileron was not working and the holes served to make the wing an air trap. Left rudder balanced by elevators and ailerons brought the orange circle back to the target.

Von Weidling chuckled. The range was down to 150 meters and the "pip" was on the canopy. He thumbed the red button. But the Englishman snapped rolled to the right, cleverly using the damaged wing's drag to whip him over sharply. The Prussian released the button, punched the stick to the right and down. The Englishman had no chance. Cat and mouse. It was only a matter of time. The Britisher would die and von Weidling would be a half-million dollars richer. "A corner of a foreign ocean . . ." he muttered to himself.

Then he saw it and the happy muttering stopped abruptly. Something streaking in from five o'clock high. He only had time to turn his head and scream in horror when the first shells and bullets struck. The fighter bucked as a shell blew off a cowling panel. Another shattered the cooling intakes and ruptured the oil tank. Oil and greasy black smoke instantly streaked back over the gaudy paint job and blackened the windscreen. Then the canopy dissolved and he shouted with pain and fear as a hundred needles ripped his oxygen mask. Bullets punched into his instrument panel, smashing it to junk and spraying the inside of the cockpit with red hydraulic fluid. He screamed, thinking he was being sprayed with his own blood. Then the red-hot pokers struck.

A 156 grain 7.7 bullet hammered into the right side of his back close to the spine, angling down, ripping the upper and middle lobes of his right lung and knocking him forward against his restraints. After six inches of travel, it began to tumble, exiting in a huge wound and breaking the ninth and tenth ribs. Another struck his shoulder, shattering his clavicle and rendering his right arm useless. The pain knew no bounds. When he tried to scream, he only sprayed blood.

Von Weidling had time to gurgle *"Gott! Nein!"* through the blood before the killing round hit. It slammed into the chest cavity by fracturing the seventh rib and striking downward through the left ventricle of the heart. In its passage, the slug stretched and displaced the heart muscles, valves and chambers, forming a cavity the size of a tennis ball. Continuing its sanguineous rampage, the bullet tumbled and yawed. It crashed into the sternum, ripping a huge hole in von Weidling's chest and spraying the wreckage of the instrument panel with gouts of blood, shattered bone and cartilage. Then charged with adrenaline, the heart pumped furiously, squirting blood from the hole in its wall. It filled the pericardium and poured into the chest cavity itself at a rate of five quarts a minute, leaving no pressure to carry blood through the aorta and the network of arteries to von Weidling's brain. With no blood, there was no oxygen. With no oxygen, no functioning body cells. Almost immediately, cerebral and neuromuscular activities stopped.

Four more bullets struck the Prussian, but they only punched holes into a corpse.

"Banzai! Banzai!" Commander Yoshi Matsuhara shouted, watching the burning purple, yellow and black Messerschmitt 109 tumble into wild right-hand rolls, hemorrhaging black smoke into the sky. He could see von Weidling's limp body slammed from side to side by centrifugal force as the fighter tumbled and gyrated beneath him, the rolls gradually flattening into the last fatal spin. Eyes riveted to the plunging fighter, he at last ripped the oxygen mask to the side and felt sheer joy as he scratched the sweaty, itchy stubble with long luxurious strokes. The rarefied air smelled sweet after the harsh pure oxygen.

"Good show! Good show, Edo Leader," Willard-Smith's voice came through the earphones. "Thanks awfully, old boy," the Englishman continued. "I'd thought I'd bought the farm."

Yoshi secured his mask and looked around. Incredibly, the sky seemed almost empty of fighters. It was like a miracle. He had seen this happen before. One moment the sky would be filled with snarling, spitting, spinning, burning aircraft. The next moment it would be all but empty. Two MEs were to be seen. Wolfgang Vatz had broken off his fight with Elwyn York and was streaking off far to the west, giving the damaged Rosencrance cover. Yoshi could just make out the two specks of the ME 109s on the far horizon obviously headed for the Marianas. No other Messerschmitts were in sight.

Every Zero had vanished. Only Willard-Smith's Seafire directly ahead and Elwyn York's Seafire ten kilometers to the southwest could be seen. Yoshi glanced at his altimeter. Three thousand meters. Sacred Buddha, the dogfight had devoured altitude.

Yoshi called York, "Edo Three, this is Edo Leader. Take Edo Two's starboard side, I'll take his port. Escort him back to base on this altitude."

"Right-oh, Edo Leader," York answered. "We'll give 'is nibs an umbrella fit for the Queen-Mum, guv'nur."

Willard-Smith's voice: "Dash it all lads. Just took a nick in the cooler."

"Coolant temp?" Yoshi barked into his microphone.

"It's one-one-eight Celsius."

"Too hot. In the red?"

"Not quite. Holding, old man, below the red."

"Oil?"

"Oil temp one-one-two, pressure forty pounds, Edo Leader."

"Too hot and your oil pressure is down by half. Reduce speed to one-five-zero knots, thin your mixture and keep your prop on full fine. Maintain current altitude. If she heats up more, reduce throttle and give up altitude."

"Roger. Reducing speed, thinning mixture and don't get your wick up, old chap. I can jolly well make it."

Yoshi glanced at the chart taped to the small clipboard strapped to his right knee. "You won't on this heading. According to my point option data, you should steer zero-three-five."

"We've been set south by the northeasterlies, Edo Leader."

"Not that much. Your vector is zero-three-five."

York's voice: "Edo Leader, I'll bet a quid to a pinch of rat dung, you ain't right, guv'nur."

Yoshi chuckled. "I'll take your bet Edo Three. I have flown these latitudes for years. I know the set. The course is zero-three-five."

"Zero-three-five," the Englishman answered.

The three fighters banked to the right, straightened out on their new course and droned off into a faint haze on the north-east horizon.

Chapter Three

High on the flag bridge of carrier *Yonaga*, Lieutenant Brent Ross raised his binoculars and rolled his thumb over the focusing knob. With the most perfectly ground lenses in the world, his personal pair of MIV/IT Carl Zeiss 7x50 glasses quickly brought a pair of the eight Grumman F6F Hellcats patrolling over the carrier into vivid focus. True to American tactics, the fighters flew in two plane elements; a leader or "top gun" and a single wingman forming an element; two elements a flight. The lieutenant sighed, feeling the wellspring of pride surge up. Those were his countrymen up there; young, highly skilled fighter pilots who had resigned their commissions in the US Navy to fight for *Yonaga* and the cause of free men all over the world. Six of the best had died in the last carrier battle and had been replaced by six more bright, intelligent young men brimming with life. "War always claims the best," old Admiral Fujita had said after the terrible losses of the last battle. "The best are always the first to fight tyranny, and the first to fight are the first to die." How true.

Brent Ross was a giant. Six-feet-four-inches tall and nearly thirty years old, he still carried his 220 pounds like the all-American fullback he had been at the Naval Academy. His blond hair had been bleached by the sun to the

47

color of straw, his fine skin deeply tanned. His nose was straight, face broad, jaw square and hard as granite. It was a visage that inevitably turned female heads.

Although he was devoted to his friends and capable of great warmth, his blue eyes gleamed with a perpetual cold watchfulness. It was a look that warned everyone that Brent Ross could unleash the savage that lives in every human being; the genetic ghost capable of ripping the reins of civilization and destroying with atavistic fury. With most men, the ghost was deeply rooted and bound securely by the chains of civilization. With Brent Ross, the savage dwelled much closer to the surface and could be triggered by an insult, a moment of fear, and especially, an ambush.

He had lost control on at least six occasions since reporting aboard *Yonaga* in 1983. He had killed three Arabs with his hands, shot a female terrorist between the eyes while she lay helpless, shot two assassins and an imprudent hotel security guard to death in the dining room of the Imperial Hotel, and blinded two other assassins; one with a broken bottle in a Tokyo alley, the other with a wrench after an ambush on Oahu. Several other men, including three proud, arrogant samurai of *Yonaga*'s crew who had been foolish enough to challenge the giant, had been badly injured by his rocklike fists.

His own countrymen would have condemned him. However, *Yonaga* was a different universe. In fact, the Japanese regarded his actions as typical of the highest ideals of the Code of Bushido and the teachings of the *Hagakure*. Translated as "Under the Leaves," this was the bible of the samurai. "Those who have won are invariably right, and those who have been defeated are wrong," the philosopher Arai Hakusaki had written three hundred years earlier. To the samurai, this aphorism was a self-evident, eternal dictum. Consequently, the samurai crew of *Yonaga* found a fulfillment in Brent; a fulfillment of

Hakusaki's sagacity, the ancient codes of *Dai Nippon* in which they still believed, and the highest qualities of the fighting man. With admiration and respect, they called Brent "The American Samurai," and the sobriquet had been pounced upon and spread by the world's media.

A communications expert, the young lieutenant was officially on loan to *Yonaga* by Naval Intelligence Service (NIS) as a specialist in computer generated codes and ciphers. However, old Admiral Fujita had found many uses for the young American. "You have the best eyes on the ship," the old man had said many times and demanded his presence on the bridge whenever the admiral took the con. Brent's ability as an aerial gunner was astonishing. He had shot down a Douglas DC-3 in the Mediterranean and three Messerschmitt Bf 109s fighters in the Western Pacific and damaged three more. Every bomber pilot wanted him in his rear cockpit. In all, he was a valued deck officer, communications expert, and gunner.

Brent lowered his glasses. They were on a northerly heading, breasting a force five wind and a mounting swell. They were only 180 miles northeast of the Marianas and must open the range. In the past, Junkers JU 87 Stukas, Heinkel 111s and North American AT-6s had operated from Saipan and Tinian in squadron strength. There had even been a sprinkling of Douglas DC-3s, DC-6s and Lockheed Super Constellations. True, most had been destroyed in the recent fighting, but still there were bound to be survivors and the threat of sudden, fanatical attack remained. Despite this threat, soon they must reverse course and close the range on the returning fighter group, give the aircraft the best possible chance. Some must be damaged, some low on fuel. Combat devoured gasoline.

The sun was declining in the west and patchy clouds were beginning to "mackerel" the sky, dappling the sea with sunshine and shadows. In the distance it was dark and brooding while nearby the swells looked like molten steel. Weirdly, in some places with the sun's rays filtered by the clouds, the sea might have been surging masses of dark blood. Suddenly chilled, Brent dropped his glasses to his waist and jammed his hands into the pockets of his windbreaker.

Where were the Zero-sens and the two Seafires? Twenty-seven fighters had taken off nearly five hours earlier. They had picked up the frantic shouts of pilots locked in aerial combat on the ship's radios. It had been exhilarating and horrifying. He had even heard his friend Commander Yoshi Matsuhara shout "Banzai!" He must have made a kill. But was Yoshi-san still alive? *Yonaga* was steaming with all electronics equipment shut down, including the receivers. There could be Arab submarines about, old diesel-electric *Whiskies* and *Zulus* armed with the new lethal Russian 533 torpedo tipped with Semtex warheads and every boat was equipped with Electronics Support Measures (ESM) that could pick up and track radio and radar emissions. The carrier could take no chances. And the returning fighters were also observing radio silence. Enemy radio direction finders (RDF) could track their signals and, perhaps, home in on *Yonaga*. War was a maddening profession, especially this war that seemed to feed on itself and have a life of its own. Then a truth struck the young officer like a flash of light in a dark room. *All wars must seem that way to the men who fight them.*

Restlessly, he pushed the troubling thoughts from his mind and ran his eyes from the bow to the stern of the carrier, over a rectangular flight deck which stretched like a steel plain, cleared to receive aircraft. Thirty-two five-inch, forty-caliber dual purpose cannons and 186 twenty-five-millimeter machine guns in triple mounts thrust their muzzles skyward like rows of young trees and clusters of saplings. With the ship at Condition Two of readiness, half were manned, their helmeted crews dressed in Number Two green battle fatigues. Although the cannons were evenly divided with sixteen to a side and mounted in the galleries that lined the flight deck, the machine guns were everywhere. Batteries were spotted between the cannons in the galleries, mounted in platforms below both the bow and the stern, three mounts were overhead in the foretop and one on each side of the single great stack which tilted twenty-six degrees outboard in typical Japanese fashion. Brent sighed. It was like surveying a great estate, three football fields laid end to end, the great heads at Mount Rushmore, the pyramids. A man could never adjust himself to the size of the behemoth nor truly comprehend it.

When she was completed, carrier *Yonaga* was the largest floating man-made object ever conceived, 1,050 feet long and displacing eighty-four thousand tons. What was truly amazing about the leviathan was the fact she was a converted battleship, designed and built in the thirties. Built on the same hull as the super-battleships *Yamato* and *Musashi*, her conversion and construction were planned by Admiral Hiroshi Fujita with the aid of the dean of Japan's naval architects, Vice Admiral Keiji Fukuda who was the head of Kanpon. That is the Imperial Naval Technical Bureau.

The hull with a triple bottom was completed up to the main deck when the Navy General Staff finally gave permission and Fujita began the conversion. The admiral's clever plans retained the barbettes of the main battery the ship would have mounted as a battleship, fitting them with high speed armored elevators to carry bombs, shells, and torpedoes from the magazines to the flight deck. The original magazines were kept for ordnance and extra fuel tanks built-in for aviation fuel. The hull was divided into five decks, 1,176 watertight compartments with a double bulkhead dividing her from stem to stern.

Because of her battleship genesis, *Yonaga*'s protection was extraordinary for a carrier, never matched by even the giant American nuclear carriers built decades later. Large bulges or "blisters" below the waterline minimized the impact of torpedoes by detonating them before they reached the main hull which was plated with an eight-inch armor belt. With steel varying from four inches to 7.5 inches, her main deck became her hangar deck and her great flight deck, nearly four acres in size, was built on top of it. Fujita and Fukuda decided the flight deck and its two nine-meter elevators should be able to withstand one thousand-pound aerial bombs. A layer of 3.75 inches of steel covered the flight deck and thirty-three inches below this deck, another layer of one-inch steel was installed. Not satisfied with this armor, the two admirals sandwiched box beams between the two layers and then filled the intervening space with cement, sawdust and latex. The admirals estimated *Yonaga*'s flight deck could withstand five times the punishment of *Taiho*, the only other Japanese carrier with an armored flight deck.

For added protection, Fujita designed what he called the "Citadel," an armor plated structure as wide as the ship and extending from frame sixty-eight to frame 190. Made of eight-inch steel plate, this great box protected the very heart of the carrier, housing the boilers, engines, steering equipment, electronic and communication gear and the magazines. In all, 19,600 tons of steel was installed in *Yonaga* for defensive purposes. This, alone, was more than the weight of a heavy cruiser.

Because of a carrier's great vulnerability to fire, the admirals devised special protection. All ducts of her ventilation system were protected with 1.5 inches of armor.

Wherever possible, wood was eliminated and fire-resistant paint used throughout. The first foam system built in Japan was installed.

Unlike her sisters which were two hundred feet shorter and ten thousand tons lighter, *Yonaga* was powered by sixteen Kanpon boilers instead of twelve. Her four geared turbines developed two hundred thousand shaft horsepower and could drive her through the sea at thirty-two knots while *Yamato* and *Musashi* could only make twenty-seven. She was a stable platform; her clever planning assuring a low metacenter, the center of buoyancy of a floating body. She answered her forty-five-ton rudder quickly, took the seas with the solidity of Gibraltar and offered her pilots a large, stable deck from which to operate.

Shifting his eyes to the northeast, Brent Ross could see endless rows of combers advancing from the great birthing place of storms in the North Pacific. Once a storm stirred up the seas in the northern latitudes, the swells swept unimpeded across the vast wasteland of the greatest ocean on earth, not stopping until they crashed and died on islands and continents. Arrogantly, the great carrier slashed through them. She tossed the riven seas aside and sent blue water and spume as white as eggwhite flying so high that rainbows flashed gloriously for brief milliseconds. Terrified flying fish flew off in every direction, pectoral fins working furiously like wings, their fluttering tails leaving twin tracks to dapple the surface. As if to remind Brent that the mighty carrier was still a creation of man and a puny thing, indeed, in the grasp of nature, a clifflike swell bore down on the carrier. It took her on the starboard bow with a shock that sent tremors through every frame and plate and a booming sound through the hull like a great temple bell that had been struck by a giant. Instinctively, Brent Ross's hands shot to the rail that crowned the windscreen. He smiled as an old thought crept in. *Man could war with nature with all his ingenuity and clever, powerful machines, yet his defeat was inevitable.*

The lieutenant swept his glasses over the five World War II *Fletcher* class destroyers escorting the carrier. Five hundred yards directly ahead, Captain John "Slugger" Fite's DD Number One led. Then two *Fletchers* to port and two more destroyers to starboard, carefully maintaining their stations five hundred yards off the carriers' sides. All were painted a deep gray and all wore their pennant numbers in white paint on their bows. Brent always admired the flush-decked grace of the sleek warships. With two stacks, five gun houses blending into a low superstructure, the old destroyers were top-heavy with guns and depth charges.

Not nearly as good at sea-keeping as the huge carrier, the narrow *Fletchers* rolled and yawed, crashing into the swells and dropping into the troughs. Sometimes, their hulls would disappear and only their upper works were visible. In extremely heavy weather, Brent had seen destroyers dip down so low into the valleys between seas, the entire ship would disappear with only the masthead, radar antennas and directors visible. Many times he had held his breath, wondering if the doughty little vessels would ever stagger up from the troughs. Inevitably, the rugged ships, rolling and pitching, shot up through the seas, blue water streaming from their scuppers and shaking off water like drenched hounds.

A soft rasping voice that rustled like dry bamboo rubbing in a strong wind turned his head. Brent recognized the voice of Admiral Hiroshi Fujita. "Stay alert Mister Ross. You have the best eyes on the ship." He waved a tiny hand to the south. "They should be returning soon."

"Aye, aye, sir," Brent said. He looked down at the withered old sailor who had crept to his side as quietly as a wisp of fog. Over a hundred years had worn and shrunk the ancient Japanese, his deeply riven flesh tanned and drawn like cured leather. The lips were smothered with wrinkles, drawn tight as if slashed into his face by a sharp blade. One was reminded of the mummies on display at New York's Metropolitan Museum.

But the black eyes were remarkable. Sunken into dark hollows and surrounded by deep wrinkles and sagging lids, they could take on moods as quickly as a chameleon can change color. They could be the warm eyes of the altruist, benign, filled with compassion. They could be the cold, ruthless, pitiless eyes of the predator who knew not of the human world and cared nothing for the pain and death he inflicted so casually. At this moment they were warm and concerned, looking at the young officer for the power they had lost so many decades ago. They also had a distant look; the enigmatic look of a man who could lose himself in his own dim past.

Everyone knew of the ancient admiral's unbelievable background. The son of a mathematics professor at Nagoya University, Hiroshi Fujita entered Japan's Annapolis, Eta Jima, at the turn of the century. The training was brutal and rigorous. However, with a brilliant mind and powerful body, young Hiroshi was one of only twenty-five percent of the class that survived the four year curriculum. Because the Imperial Navy was modeled on the British Navy—even the bricks used to build Eta Jima were brought from England—Fujita learned English and the English system of measurements, becoming equally at home in the metric and the English systems. It was here he met Isoroku Yamamoto, the future Commander-in-Chief of the Imperial Navy. Classmates for four years, they became very close friends.

Fujita's first seagoing assignment was to the British-built battleship *Mikasa*. In 1905 Fujita fought the Russian Navy at the massacre at Tsushima as a turret captain, commanding two twelve-inch guns in the aft turret. His friend Yamamoto lost two fingers in the battle while serving on cruiser *Nishin*.

After the war, Fujita rose rapidly through the ranks. Because the navy believed its key officers should be exposed to graduate study in western universities, Fujita enrolled in the University of Southern California in 1919 while Isoroku Yamamoto enrolled in Harvard. Fujita was awarded his Master's degree, summa cum laude, in 1921. After commencement, Fujita hitchhiked to Mexico where he met Yamamoto who had thumbed his way from Cambridge, Massachusetts. The pair got drunk on tequila, played poker with Mexican and American thugs, and picked up Mexican girls.

Returning to Japan, Fujita was assigned to carrier *Akagi* and fell in love twice the same year. His first love was the airplane and he consummated the courtship at the Kasumigaura Air Training School when he earned his flyer's patch in June of 1924. Then he met and married the beauteous Akiko Minokama. It was true love, unusual for the marriage of a man of Fujita's station. In fact, unlike Yamamoto and the rest of his peers, Hiroshi never took a geisha as a permanent courtesan. Both of Hiroshi's great loves soared his spirit heavenward. Akiko was the consummate lover, bearing him two sons, Kazuo and Makoto; the airplane carrying him into the realm of the gods.

Hiroshi Fujita became a specialist in dive-bombing and torpedo tactics and in the late thirties was assigned to the planning of the greatest carrier on earth; carrier *Yonaga*. Then, in 1940, Admiral Yamamoto, now Commander-in-Chief of the Combined Fleet, assigned Hiroshi Fujita, Kameto Kuroshima and Minoru Genda to the planning of a surprise attack on the American fleet at Pearl Harbor. The trio came up with the famed "Plan Z" which led to the destruction of the American battle line on December 7. Ironically, Fujita did not participate in the shocking victory. Instead, he was trapped with *Yonaga* in the isolated cove on the Chukchi Peninsula called Sano Wan. Here he would remain until the breakout in 1983. Only after *Yonaga*'s return to Japan did he learn of Japan's defeat and the vaporization of his wife and two sons at Hiroshima. His mourning was short, the vicious war with Kadafi's Arab *jihad* engulfing Japan and sending *Yonaga* into an unending series of bloody battles.

Brent stared down at the little oriental who was studying the horizon through his glasses. The young American gestured over the stern. "Respectfully, sir. We're still putting distance between ourselves and our own fighters. Shouldn't we come about?"

Lowering his glasses, Fujita glanced forward on the narrow platform of the flying bridge which surrounded the carrier's huge conning tower, sandwiched between the navigation bridge and the flight control bridge. Three lookouts leaned onto the windscreen and peered intently into their binoculars. Forward, over the pilothouse, a talker, the reliable Seaman Naoyuki, wearing the headpiece of his trade, stood by a bank of voice tubes. The old admiral turned to his executive officer Captain Mitake Arai who currently headed the navigation department.

Fujita did not trust loran, the pulse signals transmitted by pairs of radio stations, and other modern computerized methods of navigation. Instead, he still relied on the old-fashioned pencil-and-paper methods predicated on a good hand with the sextant, an accurate estimated position, exact Greenwich civil time and precise plotting by dead reckoning (DR). To insure staff proficiency, Admiral Fujita rotated the duty through his senior deck officers bimonthly. Arai, with still a month of tenure left, had his pencil in hand and was leaning over a small chart table attached to the bulkhead opposite the talker.

"Captain Arai, distance to Tinian?" Fujita asked.

"Distance to Tinian, Admiral," the navigator repeated, picking up a pair of dividers. Mitake Arai was an Eta Jima graduate and a former destroyer captain of the old Imperial Navy. He had survived the sinking of his destroyer *Rikokaze* when he had tried vainly to screen battleship *Yamato* with his AA fire when the great battleship was sunk by American planes south of Kyushu in 1945. In his late sixties, he was still a tall and straight man, highly intelligent and competent. Measuring the gap between the points of his dividers on the chart's latitude scale, he announced, "Three hundred thirty kilometers, sir."

"Still within the coordinates of our pilots' point option data?"

"Yes, Admiral. But we are approaching the twenty-second parallel — the northern limit. I suggest we steam our reciprocal course — two-one-five."

"Very well, navigator." Fujita walked haltingly forward to the bank of voice tubes and took a place at the windscreen far forward and next to the talker. Staring over the bow, he spoke to Naoyuki, "Signal bridge, bend on the hoist. Course two-one-five, speed twenty-four."

Naoyuki repeated the commands and within seconds flags and pennants whipped from the halyards, but still short of the yardarm. Brent swept his glasses over the escorts. With their usual efficiency, every destroyer had answered *Yonaga*'s hoist almost as fast as the carrier's signalman had bent on the bunting. "All escorts answer at the dip, Admiral," Brent reported.

"Very well." To the talker: "Two-block!"

Immediately, the carrier's hoist was snugged up to the yardarm and every destroyer followed suit. "All hoists are two-blocked, sir," Brent said, staring into his glasses.

"Very well." The admiral turned to Naoyuki, "Execute! Execute!" Naoyuki spoke into his mouthpiece and the flags and pennants whipped down.

"All escorts answer, sir," Brent said.

"Very well." The admiral was already leaning over the bank of voice tubes. "Pilothouse!"

"Pilothouse, aye."

"Right standard rudder. Steady up on two-one-five."

Brent heard the helmsman repeat the command and the great carrier began a wide sweeping turn to starboard. Fujita shouted into a voice tube. "Speed twenty-four."

"Speed twenty-four, sir," came back. Immediately, Brent felt the pulsations of the engines pick up and vibrate through the perforated steel floor plates. Casting an anxious eye over the escorts, he found them holding station still in perfect alignment like fawning courtiers following every whim of their queen. Slowly, the great carrier straightened on her new course with a new smooth ride, the seas now following instead of breasting her bow.

"Steady on two-one-five, sir."

"Very well."

"Speed twenty-four, one-hundred-twenty-eight revolutions, sir."

"Very well."

The old admiral turned to Brent Ross. "Mister Ross. How long have our fighters been in the air?"

Brent glanced at his watch. "The air group commander took off five hours and thirteen minutes ago." The air group leader had taken off first and would probably have the greatest consumption of fuel. But fuel consumption depended on length of combat as well as distance flown.

"Very well. If they are following their point option data, with the benevolence of the gods they should be visible within thirty minutes."

The admiral's estimate was off by four minutes.

59

Twenty-six minutes later a lookout in the foretop shouted, "Aircraft, bearing three-three-zero, elevation angle twenty!"

A half dozen pairs of binoculars swung to the sighting as if choreographed. At the same time four F6F Hellcats of the CAP streaked down the same bearing.

"General quarters, Admiral?" Arai asked.

The old admiral glanced at Brent who was studying the approaching aircraft, low on the horizon. "Five Zerosens, Admiral Fujita. One just fired a red flare."

Everyone knew the flare meant a damaged aircraft or wounded pilot. They would be receiving aircraft within minutes. The rumble of approaching engines could now be clearly heard. Fujita turned to Arai. "Negative on general quarters. Wind?"

"It has dropped to force three and shifted to zero-four-four, sir."

Brent's mind worked quickly. Force three on the Beaufort Scale meant a wind of eight to twelve knots. This was a weak breeze but much better for carrier operations than the nineteen to twenty-four knot gusts of the force five wind they had just experienced.

"Very well." Fujita gave the orders for the force to turn into the wind and within seconds flags and pennants were flapping overhead. Then the hoists were jerked down and the carrier and her escorts came about on the new course.

"Steady on zero-four-four," came up from the pilothouse. "Speed twenty-four."

Fujita glanced at the battle ensign ironed out by the wind at the gaff and then shifted his eyes to Captain Arai. "We'll maintain this speed."

The old captain nodded agreement. "I agree, sir."

The admiral spoke to the talker, "All handlers and flight deck personnel prepare to receive aircraft."

Naoyuki's voice could be heard giving the order

through the ship's PA system. Promptly, colorfully clothed handlers were seen scurrying across the flight deck and the yellow-clad control officer with his bright yellow wands took his station on a raised platform at the end of the island on the ship's starboard quarter. Then the fearsome steel mesh barrier was cranked out of its well amidships. Any aircraft that missed the five arresting cables stretched across the ship's aft part would be caught and possibly crushed by the barrier like a moth snagged by an iron net.

"All stations manned and ready," Naoyuki reported.

"Very well. Two block 'Pennant Two'."

Already bent on by an expectant signal crew, the blue pennant with the white oval raced up the halyard, announcing to all eyes the great carrier was ready to receive aircraft. With the same pennant at her yardarm, one of the *Fletchers* dropped slowly behind *Yonaga*, finally taking the lifeguard station five-hundred yards directly astern.

"More Zero-sens," Brent reported. "Eleven in sight and another red flare."

"The air group commander? Seafires?"

"Not in sight," Brent answered, heart sinking. Were Matsuhara, Elwyn York and Colin Willard-Smith all lost? Maybe there had been some damage and the section had been forced to throttle back. *There are still a lot of stragglers out there,* he told himself.

Now the roar of the big Sakae 42 engines filled the sky and seventeen gleaming white fighters were visible, flying low and quickly overtaking the carrier. The first two, the two that had fired the flares, were already approaching the stern. In fact, the lead aircraft already had its landing gear and flaps locked down and was on its approach, hook extended like a stinger. The other was veering to starboard followed by the remaining fighters to begin the usual counterclockwise orbit of the ship. The control officer raised his wands.

At that moment Brent heard a step behind him. A petty officer lookout announced, "Admiral Whitehead on the bridge."

Brent turned and brought his eyes to Rear Admiral Byron "Deep Six" Whitehead. "As you were, as you were," the admiral said to Brent, Arai and the lower ranks who turned and began to stiffen at attention.

A short, round man in his late sixties, Admiral Byron Whitehead was so singularly round and firmly packed into his uniform he gave the impression of a big man who had been pounded down into a compact mass by repeated blows to the top of his head. Despite a uniform that appeared to be a full size too large, the man's big barrel chest pushed against his shirt and his paunch hung over his belt. Size was in his head and visage, too; nose broad, forehead wide, jaw as massive as a boulder. His white hair was streaked with yellow that still hinted at the full shock of blond hair he had brushed back so proudly in his youth. Now it was long and disheveled and tufts of it hung down under his cap. The isolated gold strands reminded Brent of the tips of ripe corn in an Iowa cornfield.

And, indeed, Whitehead had been born and raised on an Iowa farm and despite attending Annapolis and a career in the navy that spanned almost a half century, the Midwestern antecedents clung to him like lint; could be heard in the slight lilt and roll of his diction. It was in his eyes, too; his slow smile, the high IQ that hid behind the misleadingly naive stare that almost seemed blank at times.

A classmate of Brent's dead father, Ted "Trigger" Ross and of the late Admiral Mark Allen, Whitehead was a veteran of fourteen carrier battles in World War II and earned the sobriquet "Deep Six," and, sometimes, "Sinker," by being sunk on carriers *Lexington*, *Yorktown*, *Hornet*, *Wasp* and *Princeton*. His frequent misfortunes earned him the Purple Heart and the Navy Cross. It was said dozens of officers would request transfers when Byron Whitehead was assigned to a ship. However, no one could deny the man's brilliance. He worked his way up to chief of staff to Admiral Marc Mitscher who commanded Task Force 58 and his crowning achievement was planning the attack that sank battleship *Yamato*. This delicate topic had never been discussed with Admiral Fujita or any of the Japanese, for that matter.

After the war, he served with Ted "Trigger" Ross and Mark Allen in Japan on the staff of Admiral Samuel Eliot Morison and did the key research in the preparation of Morison's fifteen volume, *History of the United States Naval Operations in World War II*. Eventually, he found his niche in NIS where he worked closely with Admiral Mark Allen in the hectic cold war of codes, ciphers and counterintelligence. After Mark Allen's fatal stroke and massive heart attack, Byron Whitehead came out of a short retirement and volunteered to act as Allen's replacement. Admiral Fujita was quick to accept the experienced old warrior as the NIS liaison officer in his communications department, and although the old Japanese would never admit it, his unofficial adviser in carrier warfare tactics.

Whitehead's battle station was at Admiral Fujita's side on the flag bridge and he usually found his way to the same place during the launching and landing of aircraft. This was not required, but the old American rear admiral was new to the ship and felt a pressing need to familiarize himself with procedures and personnel. In addition, he seemed to find nostalgic pleasure in watching the old World War II fighters of three nations race across the deck. He had been particularly thrilled when the first dozen Grumman F6F Hellcats came aboard. The loss of six pilots, including the brave popular squadron commander, Commander Conrad Crellin, had devastated him.

Brent focused on the approaching fighter. There was a

huge hole just aft of the cockpit. The Zero had been hit by a twenty-millimeter shell and the skin of the rear part of the fuselage sieved by machine-gun bullets. In the past, without self-sealing tanks and an armor plate mounted behind the pilot's seat, the hit by the shell would have destroyed the fighter twice over; exploding the fuselage fuel tank and riddling the pilot. But now, with two thousand horsepower packed into the new Sakae 42, the fragile old Mitsubishi A6M2 was quite a different aircraft.

Brent glassed the markings. The usual single blue stripe behind the cockpit identified the aircraft as belonging to *Koku Kantai,* First Sir Fleet, the force that attacked Pearl Harbor and Fujita insisted on retaining the marking. On the vertical tail fin was the letter "Y," identifying carrier *Yonaga* followed by a three digit number, 141, to identify the type of mission and individual aircraft. "Fourth section, number one pilot, Admiral," the American lieutenant said.

The old admiral's remarkable memory could recall every man, every name. "That is Lieutenant Tani Toojoeiwa. One of our best section leaders. He is a fine pilot."

Anxiously, Brent studied Toojoeiwa. Sitting erect, he seemed to be unwounded; canopy locked in the open position, gear down, flaps down, hook extended. Brent nodded and heard Whitehead sigh his relief, "The boy looks all right."

Brent nodded and watched as the white fighter cleared the stern, dropped as the throttle was reduced, and caught the first hook smartly. Gracefully, the Zero dropped to the deck in a perfect three-point landing, stretching the cable like a rubber band. Lieutenant Tani Toojoeiwa cut his throttle. Then with a scream of tortured, ripping metal, the entire tail assembly all the way to the shell hole ripped off. Free of the restraining hook, the forward part including the cockpit, wings and now dead engine, spun around and dropped on its belly like a

64

game animal with its rear legs shot off. Ground looping hard to the right and balanced only on its right wheel, the fighter lost its starboard wing and skidded sideways forward and diagonally across the flight deck. Crashing into the barrier, the other wing ripped off and Brent saw Toojoeiwa hurled against the side of his cockpit.

Before the plane hit the barrier, rescue crews were already racing across the deck. New American foam was sprayed on the engine and gas tank from a pair of motorized carts and two men in white fire-resistant clothing clambered up on the wreckage, freed the unconscious pilot and pulled him from the cockpit. Brent could see Chief Hospital Orderly Eiichi Horikoshi and two of his medical orderlies racing across the flight deck. One had a collapsed stretcher over his shoulder. Within a minute, Lieutenant Toojoeiwa had been pulled from the cockpit, strapped to the stretcher and was being carried at a trot to the island. The control officer frantically waved off the next fighter.

"Clear the junk off my flight deck!" Fujita screamed at Naoyuki. "Throw it over the side. Clear the stern first. We can continue landing with the wreck in the barrier." He pointed skyward at the circling aircraft. "Sacred Buddha, that wreck cost us another orbit."

Gangs of men crowded around the wreckage. Quickly, the tail was unhooked and dragged to the side by a small but powerful rubber-tired vehicle. It was pushed over the side while another gang of men and a similar vehicle disengaged the forward part of the fighter and began dragging it to the port side. In the event of another mishap, these men would be in mortal danger. The next damaged fighter banked unsteadily onto its final leg.

Brent brought the fighter in close with his Zeiss lenses.

"Read me his numbers, Mister Ross," Fujita ordered.

"One, two, two, sir."

"Second section, pilot number two. Ensign Ikemi

Harasawa," Fujita said, staring through his binoculars.

The plane's flaps were down, hook extended, but one wheel appeared to be at an unnatural angle. The fuselage and wings had been riddled, canopy shattered, and the pilot's head seemed slumped to the side, *hachimachi* head band bloody. "Port wheel appears to be unlocked, damaged, sir. The pilot is wounded."

"Wave him off, two-block 'Baker'!"

The talker shouted into his mouthpiece. Instantly, the red flag shot to the yardarm and the control officer waved his hands over his head and pointed to the bow.

"You've ordered him to ditch, Admiral. You'll kill him," Rear Admiral Whitehead said, staring at Admiral Fujita. "He appears to be badly wounded."

The black eyes held Whitehead like lasers. Again, Fujita showed his astonishing memory, "Ensign Harasawa is twenty-years-old. Inexperienced. But, he is a samurai. He can understand if you cannot."

"I resent that, sir."

"Resent anything you like. We have already had one wreck on this deck." He waved. "No one, nothing will peril my ship, jeopardize the recovery of the rest of my fighters," Fujita snapped back. "You should understand this, Admiral."

The roar almost directly overhead of a Sakae being throttled up drowned out the exchange. Banking clumsily, the damaged Zero veered over the ship's port side, headed for the *Fletcher* holding station off the carrier's port bow. Ensign Harasawa never came close. Banking too sharply, the Mitsubishi stalled, lost all lift, and plunged straight down into the sea from a hundred feet. Shot full of bullet holes, the wreck sank with the speed of a crash-diving submarine. Everyone searched the sea frantically, but no head bobbed to the surface. In fact, there was no wreckage at all to mark the grave; only turbulent water and a little spreading oil. Quickly the sea washed the human tragedy from its face as it always does and within a minute not one trace of Ensign Ikemi Harasawa remained on the surface of the earth.

"Haul down 'Baker'! Resume landing operations," Fujita shouted at the talker. The next Zero began its approach.

"No marker for that grave," Whitehead said grimly, gesticulating at the spot where the fighter had vanished.

Fujita threw the American an irate glance. "Ensign Ikemi Harasawa died the death of the samurai. He died as well as Sato Tsugunobu."

"Sato Tsugunobu?"

"A great warrior who gave his life intercepting arrows aimed at his master, Yoshitsune. Harasawa did the same."

Whitehead stared at the admiral incredulously. "My God, that's ancient history."

"Twelfth century."

"You still believe?"

"Of course, Admiral Whitehead. The truth of the way of the samurai is inviolable. It cannot be changed by the years." He waved a hand at the sky. "Ikemi Harasawa's karma now glows with the purity and brightness of the morning sun and his spirit has found nirvana in the Yasakuni Shrine where it will dwell with the spirits of countless other heroes for eternity. What greater marker could a samurai earn?" There was no answer. Instead, Whitehead turned toward Brent Ross, a disconcerted, unbelieving look on his face.

The third Zero landed without incidence and was pushed at a trot to the forward elevator and immediately struck below. Then the fourth and fifth landed and the sixth was making its approach when Brent saw a glint of the sun off airfoils on the far southern horizon. Staring, squinting, toying with his focusing knob, he prayed, promised a half-dozen gods—Christian,

Shinto and even Buddha—filial devotion if the shining airfoils belonged to two Seafires and a Zero.

Then he shouted with joy. The consortium of gods had listened. "A Zero-sen and two Seafires bearing one-seven-zero, low, range twenty-two kilometers."

Fujita, Whitehead and Arai all swung their glasses to the sighting. "Sacred Buddha," Fujita muttered. "It is my air group commander and the two Englishmen."

"They're very low, sir," Brent offered. "And a Seafire's leading. He must be damaged." At that instant, a red flare arced up from the leading Seafire.

"Correct, Mister Ross!" Fujita looked around quickly. He shouted at Naoyuki, "Take aboard that Zero." He pointed at the sixth fighter that was almost over the stern, "And then instruct the control officer to wave off the others." He turned to Whitehead. "All the pilots should have seen the flare. They are trained to watch for them."

Whitehead nodded. "I know, sir."

The damaged Seafire swung slowly into the landing pattern and began its approach on the carrier's stern. Brent studied the aircraft. A faint white haze trailed it. "It's Captain Colin Willard-Smith, Admiral. He's losing coolant." Fujita remained silent.

Brent continued, "Gear's down, hook extended, right flap down full, left flap only showing about ten degrees." He straightened rapidly. "The end of his hook has been shot off, sir, and the lower half of his rudder is gone!"

"Wave him off! Two block 'Baker'! We cannot take him aboard!"

Instantly, the red flag shot to the yardarm and the control officer waved his wands overhead and pointed to the bow. There was a deep throated roar and a whine as the supercharger cut in, the big Rolls Royce pushed to at least three-quarter throttle. The sleek fighter shot over the flight deck. Brent felt a fine mist rain down. He wiped coolant from his face with the back of his hand.

Colin Willard-Smith was actually leaning over the combing and waving gaily.

Brent felt terribly sad and depressed. Perhaps another pilot consigned to a horrible death, trapped in his cockpit in two thousand fathoms of water. And the Englishman was one of the best. Confident, capable Willard-Smith with the droll sense of humor, ready quip and disarming smile. Soon to join the young Ensign Ikemi Harasawa and the numberless legions of young warriors strewn across the bottoms of every ocean on earth. Again, Brent called on the gods, this time even including Allah.

"Execute 'Baker'!" Fujita shouted as the Seafire cleared the bow with its landing gear retracting. Carefully, it banked toward the destroyer patrolling to the carrier's port side. "Resume receiving aircraft!" was the order. The next Zero began its approach.

Wide-eyed and with his knuckles white on the bridge rail, Brent watched the Seafire. Expertly piloted despite the damage, the graceful fighter throttled down and then the engine was cut completely. Gliding gracefully, it passed the destroyer's bow and caught the tip of the first wave at least a hundred yards ahead of the warship. Then the expected huge splash as the sea reached up and caught the plane with greedy fingers and pulled it down. Not ready to surrender, the plane bounced like a flat rock thrown by a boy across a pond, freeing itself for the last time and then plopped down hard in a welter of churned water and sheets of spray.

"Amaterasu, be with him," Brent heard the admiral whisper. Whitehead glanced at Brent Ross. The rear admiral's eyes were narrow and sad, jaw sagging.

There was a cheer from the foretop. "Dinghy! Dinghy!" was the call. Brent searched frantically before he finally found the small inflatable boat that all the pilots stored as part of their seat packs. It was just behind the fast disappearing tail. A minute yellow craft with a man in it, waving a small piece of pink cloth. Brent focused on Willard-Smith. The Englishman was on his knees, grinning and waving a pair of women's panties. Brent laughed until tears streamed down his cheeks. All the other men joined the laughter. Finally, he turned away. Admiral Fujita and the young lieutenant avoided looking at each other.

Slowly, the destroyer approached the downed pilot.

Chapter Four

Returning to Tokyo Bay, Admiral Fujita cut a course close to Japan, running just a few kilometers off the southeast coast of Honshu. Although this course gave a clear view of the magnificent coastline, Brent knew the old man's motives were pragmatic, not esthetic. The course took *Yonaga* inside the one hundred fathom line where submarines would be reluctant to operate in the shallows.

It was early morning when the volcanic island of O Shima was sighted. Then the Shima Hanto, the island peninsula which dominated the southeast coast of Honshu, came into view. Silently, without command, Brent found his way to the flag bridge. He knew Admiral Fujita would be there although the capable Commander Nobomitsu Atsumi was Officer of the Deck (OD).

Atsumi, an Eta Jima graduate and *Yonaga* "plank owner," was a tall, sparse man still showing a wealth of black hair through incursions of strands of gray and white. Typical of the old hold-outs who had sailed *Yonaga* into her entrapment in 1941, he appeared much younger than his seventy years. True, incipient lines and tiny wrinkles had crowded around his eyes and dropped off from the corners of his mouth like commas. But his hair was full, skin fine and tight under the deep tan, posture erect and physique tapering down from broad shoulders to his narrow waist. "It was as if time was put on 'hold' with these men," Admiral Mark Allen had said when he and Brent Ross had first come on board in 1983. "No cigarettes, no booze, no women, an austere diet and plenty of exercise. I saw this phenomenon when I debriefed Sochi Yokoi and Hiroo Onoda. They looked like thirty-year-old men," Allen recollected, referring to Yokoi who had held out on Guam for 27 years and Onoda who had done the same on Lubang in the Philippines for 30 years. And then he had added, "*Yonaga's* crew is no different. It's like a miracle."

Brent watched Atsumi adjust his binoculars and sweep the sector ahead of the ship. Brent liked the man and had great confidence in his competence. He was probably the best gunnery officer the Imperial Navy had ever produced. "Having the deck," his usual station would have been the navigation bridge. However, with Admiral Fujita on the bridge, Atsumi moved his watch to the flag bridge, standing well forward next to the voice tubes. His Junior Officer of the Deck (JOD), a young lieutenant junior grade named Tokuma Shoten, maintained his watch on the navigation bridge. Here the young junior officer, aided by a quartermaster, took continuous bearings and piloted the vessel up the coast on the course plotted in advance by Admiral Fujita.

Brent was in high spirits. Although eight Zero-sens had been shot down, four of the pilots and an enemy fighter pilot had been picked up by two Consolidated PBYs and a single Martin Mariner of the Self Defense Force. And Captain Colin Willard-Smith had been recovered by DD Number Two. The unflappable Englishman had not even wet his boots in escaping from his sinking Seafire.

Everyone rejoiced when Commander Yoshi Matushara reported killing that butcher of a Prussian, *Ober-leutnant* Ludwig von Weidling. Colin Willard-Smith and Elwyn York confirmed the kill. Seven other Messerschmitt Bf 109s had been shot down and five damaged. The pilots were gleeful in the spirit of victory and many *sakazukis* were downed in toast after toast in the officers' mess. The hot sake was greatly appreciated.

But Yoshi Matsuhara had not been riding this crest of good cheer. Utterly weary, he had led Brent into his cabin after a full hour of debriefing and quickly downed three double shots of Chivas Regal. "They were tough, professional pilots, Brent-san. Gave as good as they took," he said grimly.

"You killed von Weidling, Yoshi-san," Brent had reminded his friend.

Yoshi smiled and called on an ancient Shinto messenger of death for his epithet. "May his nazi soul spend eternity between the loins of the foul old woman of the underworld, my friend."

Brent stared at the tired face over his drink. "He was a Christian, Yoshi-san. He'll burn in hell."

Yoshi raised his drink. "Either will do, Brent-san." They touched glasses and drank. Then the big pilot had begun to nod off, exhaustion fogging his mind and cramping his muscles. Long combat patrols were taking a heavier toll of the aging pilot and they both knew it, although it was never mentioned. Brent had helped him to his bunk and left.

Now on the bridge at Fujita's side, Brent Ross stared to the east where the sun was rising in a cold translucent sky of palest ethereal pinks and mauves. The water was flat and a dark blue, nearly cobalt, and the track of the sun was a brilliant beam of solid light, glistening like the shaft of a highly polished sword pointed directly at Lieutenant Brent Ross. All around the compass the sky was clear except to the northeast where distant cumulus nimbus piled like snow-clad mountains, threatening to rush down on the sun and obliterate it. The sun played tricks with these haughty giants, brushing their tops with electrical fire of silver and gold, leaving their great billowing bases for the darker hues of royal blue, purple and dense grays.

Brent sighed as he drank it all in. He was contented. Certainly, the return of Yoshi had bolstered his spirits. But there was more to it than that. He loved the sea. Clutching the windscreen and gazing at the delights nature reserved for only those who plied the great liquid wasteland, Brent felt a unique warmth. It was a feeling of fulfillment he found only at moments like these. The cold air was clean, the salt spray on his lips a tonic. Maybe, someday, the sea would claim him as it had countless thousands who had dared challenge her before him. But it would be like dying at the hands of your lover—your courtesan. Perhaps that was it. The sea was a man's most demanding, yet most irresistible, mistress. She could be denied nothing.

He swept his glasses over the coast of Honshu. The steep mountainous silhouette appeared blue-purple in the morning light. He knew magnificent stands of pine, beech, ash, spruce, and oak covered the rugged slopes, but he could not yet distinguish them. Brent smiled. The strange shape of the mountains reminded him of a crouching tiger in ambush. The *tora* was the most revered animal by the Japanese because it traveled far, made its kill, and always returned home.

The smile vanished, Brent's mind casting back to a recollection that would forever bring anguish to Americans. *"Tora, tora, tora,"* were the code words Air Group Commandeer, Commander Mitsuo Fuchida had shouted into his microphone on December 7, 1941 to triumphantly proclaim complete surprise. Most certainly, *Kido Butai,* the Pearl Harbor strike force, had traveled far, surprised its prey and would make its kill. The thought always left Brent with an empty, wrenching feeling in his guts. The British had their Somme, the French the Ardennes, the Italians Caporetto, the Russians the Pripet Marshes, the Germans Stalingrad, the Japanese Guadalcanal, and America would live forever with the chagrin and humiliation of Pearl Harbor.

Brent Ross tore his mind from the painful thoughts and concentrated on the shoreline. Despite its elysian beauty, he was looking at a harsh land, a cruel land. Its jagged topography yielded up less than twenty percent of its surface for cultivation. Natural resources were meager, most metals and practically all petroleum imported. The stern realities of living in such an inhospitable land had bred a hearty, courageous, yet contradictory and ruthless people who yielded easily to autocrats and the rigorous, austere dictates of Buddhism and Shintoism.

Many times Brent had heard his fellow officers discuss and often argue about the origins of the islands as described in the sacred books, the *Kojiki* and the *Nihon Shoki.* In addition to the *Hagakure,* Admiral Fujita had given Brent leather-bound copies of the *Kojiki* and the *Nihon Shoki.* The young American spent many long nights studying the two ancient volumes which not only explained the origins of Shintoism, but the Japanese people and the Japanese islands as well. *"Genesis.* The Japanese Adam and Eve," Brent had chuckled to himself, reading the first pages of the *Kojiki.*

But Brent did not find the story anymore fantastic and unbelievable than the scriptures believed by Christians and Jews. Similar to Adam and Eve, the ancestry of the people could be traced to a primeval divine pair,

Izanami and Izanagi, who first inhabited the islands which they had formed out of drops of mud from Izanagi's spear. At first, the pair was not aware of how to produce children. However, they soon solved that problem and numerous offsprings were born, the last being the deity of fire. Tragically, while giving birth, Izanami was fatally burned and passed to a nether world of death.

As Izanami passed into the nether land, the old woman of the underworld broke free from the land of the dead and pursued Izanagi. She was loathsome and foul-smelling. As he fled, Izanagi dropped his headdress which turned to grapes, then discarded his comb which became bamboo sprouts. The old woman paused to eat the grapes and bamboo and Izanagi escaped.

Izanagi stopped at a stream to cleanse himself of the foul smell of death that clung to his body. Here the supreme deity, Amaterasu-O-Mi-Kami, the sun goddess and the divine ancestress of the Japanese imperial line, was born of his left eye. From Amaterasu-O-Mi-Kami sprang the myriads of gods of the Shinto faith and the intricate mythology which finally spawned the Code of Bushido. This was the code that ruled the samurai, this was the code which was followed so rigorously by *Yonaga*'s crew, and this was the code that had gradually crept into the mind and psyche of Lieutenant Brent Ross. This code displaced some of his Christian beliefs, but, inexplicably, lived side-by-side with most. Brent had learned to suffer these contradictions with the help of a peculiar Japanese rationale. *The greater the number of contradictions with which a man can live, the stronger the man.*

Brent always chuckled at this thought. He had become a strong man, indeed. He was "The American Samurai," a ruthless, merciless killer, a powerful swordsman who had actually beheaded three men with his fabled Konoye blade.

76

Brent swept his glasses over the shoreline which was about eight miles away. Now, with the sun climbing higher in the sky, he could make out details. He could see a small fishing village. The hamlet crowded the shore around a tiny inlet. Every structure was made of wood and thatched so that in the event of collapse during one of the frequent earthquakes, the inhabitants had a better chance of surviving. Strips of sand dunes like white ribbons stretched to the north and south of the village, undergrowth breaking through almost to the sea in places. Behind it all the typical rounded mountains of Honshu dominated everything. His lenses picked up two lights swaying erratically, masthead lights. It was probably two fishing boats working lobster lines.

"Two small boats, Admiral Fujita," Brent reported. "Bearing three-one-zero, range twelve kilometers."

"Seven-point-four-four miles," the old admiral said, slyly showing his ability to move from one system to the other almost instantaneously.

Touching his focusing knob, Brent brought one of the boats into focus. It was a typical two-man boat. One man was at the tiller while the other stood with his feet braced on the thwarts and did the backbreaking work of hauling in the line, pulling in one pot after another and emptying their contents into the boat. While he watched, the man at the tiller gesticulated wildly and the other man stopped his work. Then they both stood and waved at the carrier. Brent chuckled, "Well, someone loves us."

"As long as we provide fuel for their Toyotas they will love us," Fujita muttered, staring into his glasses.

Brent, the three lookouts, the talker Seaman Naoyuki, and the OD, Commander Nobomitsu Atsumi, all dutifully laughed at the admiral's quip. But there was truth in it and they all knew it.

Brent dropped his glasses and eyed his companions. With the power of British tradition so prominent still on *Yonaga*, the appearance of her Japanese crew could be misleading. He had lived with them, known mortal peril with them, fought some of them with his fists or any weapon available, adopted many of their ways and attitudes, yet still found them enigmatic and often inscrutable.

He had seen the short tempered rashness of the samurai and could not excuse himself from the same. He had seen the frenzied reactions when confronted with frustrating situations; the Buddhistic reverence for life juxtaposed with wanton killing when seized with panic and fury; the belief in fantastic illusions; the perception that all foreigners were unclean vermin. He had learned in teeming Tokyo, and especially the commuter trains, the Japanese were dangerous when crowded. They were probably the hardest workers in the world with a broad sense of humor, but, sometimes appeared eccentric and stubborn. Yet, fatalistically, they accepted life as it was, regarding the conceptual world as unnatural, unworkable and distorted.

He had heard many Japanese claim foreign minds could not understand them, that the behavior of the Japanese was "unscientific," and that they thrived on ambiguity. This Brent could understand; he had found it growing within himself. And he understood this proclivity for the ambiguous, the contradictory which even leads to two kinds of *seppuku:* one to purge feelings of guilt, the other to deny guilt.

Repeatedly, Brent had heard the tale of *The Forty-Seven Ronin* who avenged their martyred lord's honor in an eighteenth century vendetta and then committed mass *seppuku.* An entire literature including a timeless play had been written about the famous forty-seven. Brent had seen the play, the *Chushinguru,* in Tokyo in a packed house. And the magnificent disembowelment of General Nogi and his wife was another story on which the samurai doted. After Emperor Meiji died in 1912, Nogi, the victor over the Russians in 1905, dressed in white robes and kneeled with his wife. When Emperor Meiji's funeral procession left the palace, the couple slashed out their intestines with vicious double-edged, nine-inch *wakizashis. De rigueur* for such occasions, a brief poem was found next to the general's body: "My sovereign, abandoning this fleeting life, has ascended among the gods; with my heart full of gratitude, I desire to follow him." This bloody, tragic gesture became a venerated event that was taught with awe in all Japanese schools.

At first, Brent considered this reverence for *hara-kiri* savage and ludicrous. Then, over the years, he had finally come to terms with it and had even served as a second or *kaishaku* at the *seppuku* of Lieutenant Nobutake Konoye. To the delight of the Japanese witnesses, he had beheaded Konoye neatly with a single powerful stroke after the suppliant had disemboweled himself. "Banzai! Banzai!" Admiral Fujita and a hundred officers had shouted. However, Admiral Mark Allen and the Israeli intelligence officer, Colonel Irving Bernstein, had been horrified. Allen, his face crossed by a storm of anguish and rage, had railed, "Why? Why did you do it?"

Brent had looked at his oldest friend with eyes as cold as blue ice and answered matter-of-factly, "Because it was right."

Now he was called "The American Samurai." Brent laughed to himself. To admit the absolute truth, this was quite impossible. The samurai and his laws of Bushido had evolved over centuries of incessant warfare and was typically oriental. In fact, Bushido's roots dated back to

79

pre-feudal times and the patriarchal relationship between vassal and feudal lord, samurai and his *daimyo*. Brent had quickly learned his samurai companions were guided by two basic principles upon which the whole structure of Bushido rests: *giri* and *chugi*. *Giri* was a moral obligation that bound the warrior to the Emperor, his superiors, equals, inferiors. *Chugi* or loyalty defined its nature. However, one absolute imperative emerged above all else; loyalty to one's lord.

Brent had heard his friends discuss the necessity for wisdom, benevolence and valor in the makeup of the samurai. But he soon learned wisdom did not mean knowledge. Instead, the drive was to live by supreme and eternal ethical principles. Consequently, it was only natural the samurai would turn to Zen Buddhism. Brent had found it in Admiral Fujita, Yoshi Matsuushara and all of the others. Differing totally from all other varieties of Buddhism, Zen repudiated all work of the intellect and the teachings contained in books. Finding the ultimate truth was not found by the mind working in isolation, but was something a man had to live with with his whole being. Yet, with the usual Japanese ambiguities, the old admiral and Matsuhara loved books, and were inveterate readers. Another contradiction which built stronger men and sharpened karmas.

Standing above all of the mysticism and dogmatic trappings, one universal persuasion glared. The supreme measure of a samurai was his courage and valor which must be combined with serenity and composure. "True courage is to live when it is right to live, and to die only when it is right to die," was one quote from the *Hagakure* Brent had heard repeatedly. Despite his skepticism about some of the mystical legends at the roots of Bushido, he felt the adage spoke the truth. He lived by it and was convinced someday he would die by it.

Brent shook the musings from his head and moved his eyes over the hulking land mass. On the other side of the mountainous spine was the great city of Osaka at the head of the Inland Sea. He had seen it once with the young, exquisite Mayumi Hachiya. Hand-in-hand they had walked through acres of the strange keyhole-shaped burial mounds just outside the city that dated back to the fourth century. Then awed, they had strolled through the magnificent castle built by the warlord Toyotomi Hideyoshi in the sixteenth century.

As with all men who spend long hours on watch at sea, Brent's subconscious could evoke erotic memories that jolted with their reality. Abruptly, Mayumi was back like a phantom drifting off the bridge just out of reach. Vividly, he could see her shoulder-length hair, glossy black and luxuriant; her sculpted body with thrusting, taut breasts, tiny waist, slender hips and legs like carved marble. She was dressed, or undressed, as he liked her best; lacy, silk brassiere and panties, on her bed, arms upraised, black eyes glazed with passion.

He closed his eyes to shut off the torment, but she remained burned into his brain; into his being. He felt her. Smelled her. He twisted uneasily, remembering the heat of the fierce lovemaking in her apartment in Tokyo. But he had lost her forever to Japanese tradition. Pledged through *yuino,* an arranged betrothal between families, she was now married to her second cousin, Denko Yunoyama, and lived just over the peninsula in Osaka.

He shook his head, refocused his glasses but could not banish the torturous thoughts from his mind. The parade of women began. Pamela Ward came back, sleek in her satin blouse and slacks, inviting him into her bedroom in Seattle when he was only a twenty-two-year-old ensign on his first assignment. Fifteen years older than

81

Brent, she had been a marvelous teacher. In fact, all of the other women had been older than Brent. Sarah Aranson, the Israeli intelligence officer, had consumed him with her passion in her Tel Aviv apartment. Although she told him she loved him, Brent always suspected she used him in place of her dead lover, Ari Weitzman. He had been blown to bits with his Mystere fighter by a surface-to-air (SAM) missile over the Sinai. Then came the traitor and terrorist, Kathryn Suzuki, and her maddening dance and exhausting sexual gymnastics in her condominium on the north shore of Oahu. Finally, Dale McIntyre, terrified of the big "Four-oh" birthday, who loved him with the desperation of a woman drowning in her own years. But she had ended it, appalled with herself for bedding a man so much younger than herself — a boy almost as young as her son.

"Damn! Damn!" Brent mumbled to himself, aroused and punished by the stream of memories that spooled through his mind like a broken film.

"Sight something, Mister Ross?" Fujita asked, shocking Brent from his reveries.

"No, sir."

"Troubling thoughts, Lieutenant?"

The old man had been to sea since 1904. He knew everything, missed nothing. He seemed to have access to a man's mind. Brent flushed.

"No, sir." He patted his stomach. "Too much coffee, Admiral. Just a touch of heartburn."

"Heartburn or heartache? Brent-san," the old man almost whispered into the young officer's ear, using the familiar form of address usually reserved for private conversations in his cabin.

"Perhaps a little of both, sir."

"You have disturbing memories, persistent memories, Brent-san." It was a statement of fact, not a question.

Brent smiled. It was like having a genie in your head who blabbered all your thoughts into the admiral's ear. "There are some," Brent admitted simply.

The old man nodded. "I, too, was troubled by *those* visions when I was young. But they vanished decades ago. Apparently, the gods have reserved some blessings for the aged."

Silently, Brent raised his glasses and swept the area off the port bow. *How true,* he said to himself.

The admiral reduced the speed of the task force so that landfalls on the two peninsulas, Izu Hanto and Boso Hanto, which flanked the Uraga Straits and the entrance to Tokyo Bay like bookends, were not made until early the next morning. Although radar search was resumed, the navigator Captain Mitake Arai was on the flag bridge, plotting the ship's track while Quartermaster First Class Ryo Rokokura peered through the gunsight on the bearing ring mounted on top of the gyro-repeater, shouting out bearings and tangents on points of land and islands. Slowly, the force left the string of islands that pointed like an arrow at the Uraga Straits to port; Mikura Jima, Miyake Jima, Nii Shima, To Shima and O Shima all dropped off close aboard. Then, with DD-One leading and four escorts in her wake, the great carrier entered the entrance to the enormous bay. The special sea detail was posted.

Taking his station on the flag bridge between Admiral Fujita and Rear Admiral Whitehead, Brent swept the entrance with his glasses and found nothing but DD-One and the channel markers. Slowly, he brought his binoculars to the magnificent Boso Peninsula, falling off to starboard. He scanned the mountains. He loved this place. It was like a piece of the nineteenth century. He and Mayumi had motored over it several times. It was a pristine sanctum that possessed in miniature nearly all of the greatest beauties of the Japanese landscape: lush valleys with villages and farmhouses hidden by thick stands of trees and surrounded by garden-like rice fields; streams shining in the sun; wooded mountains; a sharply indented coastline; tiny offshore islands, thick with grotesquely twisted pine strike roots.

He lowered his scan and the Zeiss lenses brought the shoreline into precise focus. Here the mountains plunged steeply into the sea, forming high rocky headlands. He could see narrow roads skirting precipitous promontories. Every inlet harbored a fishing village. Big boats—perhaps twenty and thirty tons—were pulled up on the steep beaches by lines attached to huge capstans. The usual nets and seaweed were spread out to dry on the narrow beaches. Anchors, cables, supplies of food, buoys, and tools were piled and stacked near the boats.

The voice of Talker Seaman Naoyuki turned Brent's head. "Radar reports many small boats approaching the channel, Admiral Fujita."

"Secondary battery, Condition Two of readiness!"

Brent dropped his glasses and stared as Whitehead whirled in alarm. "You're manning half your twenty-five-millimeter guns."

"Quite right, Admiral Whitehead."

The old American waved at some gaily decorated specks visible in the channel directly ahead. "They are welcoming you. Do you respond with gunfire?"

Brent Ross smiled to himself while Fujita thumped the windscreen impatiently. "You have heard of Sabbah?"

"Of course. Fanatical followers of Kadafi. They prefer the knife, but will kill with any means at hand, are quite willing to sacrifice their own lives. Assassins who took their name from Hasan ibn-al-Sabbah, 'The Old Man of the Mountains.' He lived in a fortress in Persia in the eleventh century, I believe," Whitehead said. Warming to the subject, he appeared pleased to show his knowledge. Brent and Admiral Fujita studied the florid face as the American rear admiral continued, "They would get sky-high on hashish and attack anyone with suicidal fury."

"Death on one of these missions guaranteed eternity in paradise," Fujita said.

"I know."

"And the sect still exists. Most are Shi'ites and they are directly under Kadafi's control."

Whitehead nodded understanding. "Shi'ites! Much more belligerent and dangerous than the other two Muslim sects, the Druze and Sunni. I understand you have had some problems with them, sir."

Fujita's laugh had no humor in it. "Some problems?" The rhetorical question was acid with sarcasm. "Why, they are Arab kamikazes. They have tried to ram *Yonaga* three times. Even tried to destroy her with a truck bomb in drydock."

Brent winced with a cruel memory. He envisioned Kathryn Suzuki ramming a truck loaded with twelve tons of plastique through the gate house leading to the great graving dock at Yokosuka where the damaged *Yonaga* rested on her blocks. The truck, ripped by a Nambu, crashed into a shed, and turned over. Kathryn spilled out on the pavement, badly injured, and stared up at him, imploringly. Her beautiful face in the "V" of his sights. The scream of "No! No!" The Otsu bucking in his hand. The small blue hole between her eyes; the

85

gush of brains and gore splattering the pavement, the flat-nosed, nine-millimeter slug flaring and tearing out the back of her head. Limbs jerking, convulsions and then the stillness in the embrace of death.

He had loved her, but she had tried to destroy *Yonaga*. She had used him like a randy schoolboy drooling over her body. Nothing but a terrorist, she had earned death many times over. Her execution was mandatory and he had carried it out with the spirit, the *damashii* of a samurai. She had expected it, yet denied it at the end. She still haunted him and always would.

Byron Whitehead bit his lower lip, but remained silent while Fujita continued. The ancient Japanese waved a tiny hand over the bow where the boats were now quite clear. "They could be there, Admiral Whitehead. They tried ramming us with a speedboat earlier this year." A tiny, tendril-like fist struck the windscreen. "I take no chances." He stabbed a finger at the approaching boats. "They had better stay well clear."

"Use fire hoses."

"We tried that. The range is too short."

Arai's voice interrupted. "Suggest course zero-one-zero, Admiral. One point should do it, sir. Put us right in the center of Uraga Straits."

"Very well." Fujita leaned over the voice tubes. "Pilothouse."

"Pilothouse, aye."

"Right one point."

"Right one point, sir."

Brent saw the bow swing slightly as the great carrier changed course eleven degrees. "Steady on zero-one-zero, sir."

"Very well."

"Passing the sea buoy hard to starboard, sir," a lookout shouted.

Brent shifted his glasses and found the huge black buoy bobbing in the seas a hundred yards off the starboard beam. A string of red buoys extended into the channel in a line and bearing off their starboard side. "Exactly where they belong," he said to himself. Then he mouthed to himself the old maritime phrase that had been drilled into so often, it always came to mind when entering port. "Red, right, returning."

The carrier left Kurihama and Uraga to port, Tateyama to starboard. As usual, crowds lined the two peninsulas flanking the straits, cheering wildly and waving gaily colored paper streamers. Some released colorful balloons trailing tails of colored paper. "They love you," Rear Admiral Whitehead said.

Admiral Fujita laughed. "As I said before, they still have enough petrol for their Toyotas. Their affection fluctuates with their petrol gauges." Again the obligatory chuckle at the admiral's wit.

Entering the enormous bay, the carrier seemed to glide over the serene waters. Speed was reduced and Brent could see the sprawl of Yokohama to port. Tokyo, which was still twenty-two miles to the north, was not visible. An ugly brown blanket of foul air hung over Yokohama like a shroud. Fujita waved. "Perhaps, Moammar Kadafi and the rest of his OPEC friends are a blessing, too."

Whitehead and Arai turned, eyebrows raised quizzically. But Brent knew where the old man's mind was. "Burned petrol fouls our air." He turned to Whitehead. "When I was a youth, you could see," he stabbed a finger in the direction of Tokyo where an ugly brown haze hung over thirty degrees of horizon, "across the bay, and Fujisan reared up all the way to the heavens. Now we have this progress and we are blinded by it," he added with loathing and disdain.

Captain Arai pointed at his chart and said, "Admiral, I suggest we make our turn. Left to one-nine-seven. We are in the basin. Yokosuka is just abaft our port-beam."

Brent moved his glasses to the port-beam and brought the huge naval base into his lenses. Rows of docks, gantries, warehouses and machine shops were visible. A half-dozen cargo ships were tied up. Two flew British colors; one Israeli. DD-One had already turned and was headed for the base.

"Very well, Navigator," Fujita said. And then into the voice tube, "Left standard rudder, steady up on one-nine-seven."

The command was repeated and the great ship turned slowly onto her new heading. The boats arrived. Hundreds of gaily decorated craft swarmed around the carrier. However, all remained at least a discreet six hundred yards from her sides. Whitehead pointed at the streamers, balloons, and hundreds of small colored paper objects lining the gunwales. They glowed like lamps. "They've really gone all out to welcome you, Admiral Fujita," he said.

Fujita answered while he stared through his glasses. "It is more than a welcome. It is the *O-bon*, the festival of the dead."

"Festival of the dead?" The American rear admiral said in surprise. "Why, they appear happy. They seemed to be celebrating."

"Why of course. It is a happy occasion and is celebrated for three days. Death puts an end to our brief life which is as ephemeral as a wave of the sea. But, remember, rebirth awaits us." He pointed to a large boat of at least thirty tons that seemed to lead the others. It was an old craft of wooden construction and was steered by a man at a large wheel on a small poop deck on the stern. However, it appeared to have a powerful engine and moved at a good speed. "Look in the bow of that boat, you will see a Buddhist priest casting small objects into the sea."

"I see," Whitehead said. "They look like paper lanterns on floating wooden bases, like small boats."

"Very good," Fujita acknowledged. "That is exactly what they are. The lanterns are called *chochin* and they are of the Gifu design. Each is inscribed with *'samkai banrei tsuizen-kuyo'* which translates into 'funeral service for the myriads of souls of the three worlds.' Each has the name of a dead person on it."

"A floating memorial."

Fujita chuckled. "Far more than that, Admiral Whitehead." He raised a hand imperiously and his voice dropped. He spoke to the horizon, "The *chochin* light the way for the dead to return to this earth and to their homes." The hand dropped. "There, more *chochin* are lighted, tables set with the departed ones' favorite food, pipes, paintings, musical instruments, books, flowers; whatever the dead had liked and enjoyed. Even pails of water are set by the doors so that they can wash their feet before entering."

"But why the lamps here at sea?"

"Because the sea is the cleanest, purest place." Fujita waved at the shore. "The dead can find their way from here." He stared at Whitehead. "Now do you understand why this is a happy occasion?"

The American nodded. "Of course."

Now hundreds of *chochin* floated on the smooth surface like enchanted glowworms. But the enchantment ended abruptly as the old lead boat with the priest still in the bow turned toward the carrier. "Boat closing off our starboard beam," a lookout shouted from the foretop. Dozens of heads turned toward the starboard side. Brent could see the barrels of dozens of Type 93 twenty-five-millimeter guns cranked onto the bearing.

"Starboard battery, commence tracking vessel closing on starboard beam," Fujita shouted at Naoyuki.

"You're not going to open fire, Admiral?" Whitehead said sharply. He waved. "He's having trouble with his steering gear."

Brent stared through his glasses. There was bedlam on the decks of the small boat. Men, women and children scurried around like a nest of disturbed insects, staring at the threatening guns of the carrier. Two men appeared to be working furiously on the lines leading from the wheel to the rudder. The bow continued to swing toward *Yonaga*'s stern. "He's out of control, Admiral Fujita," Whitehead said.

"He would have us believe that," Fujita said grudgingly. And then to Naoyuki, "Stand by to open fire!"

"My God! No!" Whitehead pleaded, pointing. "He's carrying women and children."

Brent studied the boat. It was only four hundred yards off the starboard side and closing on the ship's stern, the carrier's most sensitive and vulnerable area. Two men at the wheel seemed to be pulling and pushing the wheel hard aport and slowly there seemed to be a slight change in course to port.

Fujita turned to Naoyuki, "Starboard battery prepare to—"

Before he could complete the command, a triple mount amidships stuttered into life, three machine guns each firing four hundred rounds a minute.

"No! No!" Fujita shouted. "Cease fire! Cease fire!"

But the command came too late. The sea around the boat boiled with spouting water, colliding expanding circles of ripples. Hundreds of shells loaded with high explosives raked the decks, harvesting corpses the way reapers cut wheat. The storm of hellfire blew out huge chunks of planking, lashed billows of dust and storms of wood splinters. It swept the celebrants into bloody heaps, hurling some over the sides, dismembering most. Some ricochets bounced and exploded above the deck while others whirled off with the sound of tearing silk.

Immediately, the deck became a charnel house; limbs, entrails, heads, brains littering the torn planking. Blood ran to the sides of the tapered deck and stained the sides of the vessel as it poured out of the scuppers. The small deckhouse was smashed to splinters by a dozen hits. Blasted at the base, the mast toppled crazily over the starboard side, still held to the boat by its stays. The poop deck and the two men struggling with the wheel were flung into the air by a rain of shells and blown over the stern. The priest exploded as if he had swallowed a grenade. His arms, legs, and head all blossoming out separately from a central red gory core of blasted intestines, organs and shattered bone.

Completely out of control and listing, the boat swung around on its own axis like a bloody pinwheel and dropped off astern of the carrier. Mercifully, the guns stopped.

Brent had never seen Fujita's face so contorted, so twisted with rage. The parchment-like flesh actually showed a purple-red hue and the black eyes burned with a fury so great it was a palpable force felt by every man on the bridge. Looking into those eyes, Brent felt icy fingers climb up his spine and clutch the base of his skull. The young American looked away.

The old admiral spoke to Naoyuki in a chillingly calm voice. "The officer in charge of the battery that just fired on the boat is to report to the flag bridge immediately!" While the talker spoke into his mouthpiece, Fujita turned to Arai. "Captain, you have the deck. Con her into Berth B-Two."

91

"Berth B-Two," the navigator repeated. He waved at Quartermaster Ryo Rokohura who peered into the sight of the bearing circle and began to shout out bearings.

Glowering at the deck and apparently oblivious of everyone, the old admiral paced back and forth, glancing periodically over the stern where the wreck of the boat drifted, slowly settling by the bow with a severe list to starboard. Three other boats crowded around her, removing survivors. Not one boat remained near *Yonaga*, all racing away with the exception of the brave trio that had gone to the aid of the stricken vessel.

The silence on the bridge was heavy. It seemed to bend Brent's shoulders like the weight of a boulder. Incessantly, the admiral paced, breathing hard, staring at the deck and throwing quick glances astern. The only sound heard was the soft thump of the engines turning at slow speed and the exchanges between the navigator and quartermaster.

After an interminable wait — actually only four minutes had passed — a tall, powerful lieutenant stepped onto the bridge. Brent recognized Lieutenant Jimpei Yashiro, an original member of *Yonaga*'s crew. The newcomer walked stiffly onto the deck and stopped at attention in front of the admiral. He saluted, but the admiral, standing as rigid as an iron beam, only stared back; his eyes as black as the bottom of a grave.

A native of the Bonin Islands, Yashiro stood out from the other officers with a face that curiously reflected both the east and the west. Born on Chichi Jima, the largest of the Bonins six hundred miles south of Tokyo, Yashiro was truly a child of two worlds. He traced his mixed ancestry back to an American family with the surname of Gillman which had arrived with the Savorys, Gilleys, Robinsons and Webbs in the early nineteenth century to colonize and establish a fishing village on the uninhabited island. All were from Massachusetts and all were hungry for a new beginning. Chichi Jima with its magnificent, heavily wooded interior and sheltered Futami Bay seemed ideal. Immediately, a small village was built on the bay and a small fishing industry began to thrive.

However, the Bonins were annexed by Japan in 1876 and Japanese colonists began to arrive in great numbers. Inevitably, there were intermarriages and Jimpei Yashiro descended from one of these unions when his grandmother, Matilda Gillman, married Gessen Yashiro. Consequently, Jimpei's eyes were rounder, nose larger, skin the color of ivory. He stood out among the Japanese and had paid for it.

Early in Jimpei's career, other young officers attempted to taunt him with cruel jokes about his "Filthy Yankee pig-eating ancestors." However, Yashiro was of tough fisherman stock and possessed the muscular physique of a man who had begun hauling nets and lobster pots from the sea when only eight-years-old. He had left a trail of broken noses, split lips and shattered teeth behind him as he slowly and haltingly climbed the ladder of command to lieutenant senior grade. Without the fights, he would have attained the rank of at least commander. However, he had been put on report so often, his record looked more like the history of a fighter than a naval officer.

Now he was sixty-eight-years-old and, similar to most of the other original members of the crew, appeared at least twenty-years younger. Besides the fighting, only one other thing marred the man's efficiency; it was rumored he was losing his hearing and had actually learned to lip read to compensate and fool his superiors.

A dozen pairs of eyes stared as Admiral Fujita asked in a low voice as stinging as dry ice, "Who gave you the order to open fire?"

Jimpei swallowed hard as if his Adam's apple were a steel ball bearing stuck in his throat. "You gave it, sir." A dozen men gasped.

The admiral responded with remarkable calm. "The command was 'Stand by to open fire'."

"That is not what I heard."

"Do you hear?"

"Yes, sir. My ears are perfect."

"Did your talker make an error?"

"No, Admiral. And it would make no difference, would it, sir? I was the senior officer present in command. I know now I caused a terrible tragedy."

"Your hearing is failing, Lieutenant, and I know it. I should have removed you long ago."

"Not true, sir."

For the first time, the admiral's voice showed heat and his face twisted and contorted like a sheet of red-hot metal struck by a hammer. "Do not contradict me!" he bellowed.

Jimpei Yashiro tried to work the steel ball down his esophagus, but failed. "I request that I be allowed to commit *seppuku*."

The admiral's voice softened. His response shocked Whitehead, but no one else. "Perhaps, that is a worthy suggestion."

"No!" Whitehead shouted. He looked at Brent for support, but found nothing but a flat, unreadable stare.

Fujita silenced the American rear admiral with a wave. He said to Yashiro, "When would you like to perform the ceremony?"

"Immediately, sir. I cannot wait."

"You must wait until we dock."

"Then I request the Shrine of Infinite Salvation and that all senior officers be my witnesses."

94

"Of course. It will be arranged."

Rear Admiral Byron Whitehead could not contain himself. "You're going to let him kill himself, Admiral Fujita?"

"This is the only way he can salvage his honor and redeem his karma."

"He did a terrible thing, that is true. He killed innocent people. But to kill himself?" Whitehead leaned forward, eyes boring into Fujita's. "Why don't you strip him of his commission? Dismiss him from the service?"

"You miss the point, Admiral Whitehead."

"Miss the point?"

"Yes. His dereliction was in disobeying orders, not in firing on that boat." He waved astern where the boat had sunk and the rescue vessels still hovered about, looking for survivors. "I would have ordered the destruction of the boat if it had closed another fifty meters."

"Women and children and all?"

"Of course."

Whitehead sighed. Took another tack. "You said Lieutenant Yashiro's hearing was failing."

"True."

"Then there is a reason . . ."

Fujita interrupted, unquiet shadows clouding the black eyes. It was obvious his patience was wearing thin. "Not according to the Code of Bushido." He stabbed a finger at Yashiro and continued, "He has dishonored the Emperor, this ship, his fellow samurai and me. Only his blood can wash away this stain. He understands this, his fellow officers understand." His wave encompassed every man on the bridge including Brent Ross. "Why can you not understand?"

Whitehead's voice rose, lips pulled back in a rictus of determination. "Because it's self-murder; a stupid practice that should have died with feudalism and a terrible

95

waste of a valuable officer."

"Would you like to be relieved of this duty?"

The American's jaw twitched and worked as he ground his teeth. "My duty is here. I have never turned my back on that. It would be dishonorable." Then with a hint of irony that bordered on sarcasm, "We Americans have a sense of honor, too, even if we don't cut our guts out."

Fujita's eyes smoked with resentment and his voice was hard. Each word was enunciated slowly and precisely as if his lips were a chopping block severing one word from the next. "Then, as a senior officer, I will expect you to be present at Lieutenant Yashiro's *seppuku*. If you cannot stomach the idea, leave my ship immediately! You are dismissed." He turned his back and raised his glasses.

Grimly, Whitehead stared first at Fujita's back and then Yashiro who returned the stare with wide eyes as blank as glass. Finally, he squared his shoulders and strode from the bridge.

Chapter Five

Berth B-2 was located next to the great graving dock at Yokosuka. One of Japan's greatest naval bases since the inception of the Imperial navy in the nineteenth century, the facility had been largely destroyed by B-29s during World War II and then expanded and improved by occupying American forces. Great new warehouses and machine shops had been built, channels dredged, docks added, powerful new cranes brought from the United States and mounted on special tracks. Four rode a pair of gantries built on B-2 while two more floated on wide steel barges moored nearby. Offices, commissioned and noncommissioned officers clubs, and enlisted men's recreation facilities were built on the perimeter, most next to the twelve-foot chain-link fence crowned with barbed wire that surrounded the entire facility.

There was one armored gatehouse and a single entrance, flanked by pillboxes. Concrete barriers like irregular dragon's teeth prevented any vehicle from accelerating above five miles per hour. Twenty Nambu Type 92 heavy machine guns were spotted on the perimeter and among the barriers in sandbagged emplacements. Seaman guards under the command of Admiral Fujita manned the posts even when the carrier was at sea. Actually, the positions should have been the responsibility of the Self Defense Force. However the admiral, with Emperor Akihito's support, took all security into his own hands. No one could ever forget Kathryn Suzuki and her fellow terrorist crashing through the then flimsy gatehouse with their explosive-laden attack. Only an alert Brent Ross and a single Nambu stopped the attack. The terrorists had come very, very close to success. Now such an attack could not make it past the gatehouse.

As the great carrier was warped into Berth B-2, Brent could see a huge crowd outside the chain-link fence. It was a somber crowd, the usual boisterousness dampened by the tragedy of the slaughtered boat. Word had spread fast. Brent guessed the media had been present and had witnessed the destruction of the boat. There had probably been television cameras on the scene, telecasting every detail of the bloody event. He hated reporters. "In time of war, truth is the first casualty," Fujita had said many times. Never had Brent heard a truer statement. Sometimes he suspected the media was dominated by *Rengo Sekigun,* the Japanese Red Army.

As two tugs nudged the great carrier into her berth and the first "monkey's fist" sailed over to the dock, he focused his glasses on the crowd. Most were well-mannered civilians carrying signs of welcome. However, on the edge of the crowd, he could see Red Army members parading in long lines. His lenses brought them very close; filthy, unkempt men and women in ragged clothes, the men bearded, the women with stringy disheveled hair. They carried the usual signs: "Japanese Die For Yankee Imperialism," "Blood for Oil," "Power to the People," "Deformed, Greedy Bourgeois," *"Yonaga* is Imperialistic Materialism," *"Yonaga* Back to the Ice."

Then, Brent noticed a new sign had been added: "Fujita Murders the Innocent."

Brent reserved a special kind of hatred for the *Rengo Sekigun*. He had learned to know them well over the years in Japan. Supported by Kadafi's worldwide network, their headquarters were actually in Paris, not Tokyo, with smaller cadres in Zurich, Frankfurt, London, Amsterdam, Brussels and Milan. Similar to the Popular Front for the Liberation of Palestine (PFLP), the PLO, Naif Hawatmeh's Democratic Front, Abu Nidal's *Fatah* Revolutionary Council, the Italian Red Brigade, the Rejection Front and a whole alphabet of other Kadafi backed terrorist units, it was a highly sophisticated organization with codes, weapons procurement and exchange, courier routes, frontier getaway points, and safe houses. Brent soon learned the front of poverty, sacrifice and revolutionary altruism was nothing but a hypocritical facade. Money was the drive; money, power and lavish living for the leaders provided by a flood of oil dollars. Naive young zealots were persuaded by liquor, drugs and sex to carry out suicidal attacks to keep the money rolling in.

The Red Army had assassinated dozens of businessmen, diplomats and politicians all over the world. One ambitious member had even thrown a grenade into the Japan Air Lines offices in Zurich. Their supreme accomplishment came in 1972 with the massacre of twenty-six innocent bystanders at Israel's Lod Airport. This slaughter was done by only three Japanese fanatics armed with Czech automatic weapons and shrapnel grenades. And it was believed at least three members of *Yonaga*'s crew had been murdered by Red Army assassins while on liberty in Tokyo. The police, who Brent suspected were fearful of the Red Army, had never solved the murders.

Brent heard Admiral Fujita mutter grimly as he studied the filthy pickets, "What has happened to Japan that she can breed such vermin?"

"Vermin should be exterminated, Admiral," Brent said, lowering his glasses.

"The Diet is nothing but a bunch of women," the admiral snorted. "The Self Defense Force is impotent and the police are cowards."

"Respectfully, we don't need any of them, sir."

Fujita looked up at the big American and the weathered parchment cracked with a smile. "Said like a samurai, Lieutenant."

"Thank you, Admiral." Brent brought his binoculars back up and found the Red Army protesters again. He had clashed with picketing Red Army members outside the gate twice. On both occasions he had beaten one of the picketing "soldiers" senseless. But the Red Army had exacted its vengeance when he, Mayumi Hachiya, Yoshi Matsuhara and his fiancee, Kimio Urshazawa, had been ambushed in Ueno Park by four *Rengo Sekigun* killers who attacked with the rabid abandon of Sabbah. Although Brent and Yoshi had killed all four attackers, Kimio had died instantly when hit by a six-round burst from an AK-47.

Yoshi had never recovered. He became *shinigurai* — crazy to die — and fought like a madman. Yoshi then devoted himself almost entirely to the teachings of Bodhidharma, an Indian monk and the first patriarch of Zen who lived in the sixth century. Bodhidharma's austere philosophy rejected ceremonies, scriptures and the trappings of other Buddhist groups. As a follower, Yoshi sought his enlightenment through intuition. Brent knew, under it all, the pilot searched for a rationale that could justify the death of his beloved. This was impossible and Brent knew it. The guilt remained. To Brent Ross it was a backbreaking burden that forced Yoshi deeper into his own personal "Slough of Despond" like John Bunyan's pilgrim, Christian, weighed by his own sin. Similar to Christian's plight, the ultimate, final release could only come through death.

Brent had spent long hours with his friend, trying to talk him out of his reckless search for release. The young American would think he was breaking through and then Yoshi would make a ridiculous statement. "What is the sound of one hand clapping?" he asked one time when comparatively sober. Brent had shrugged helplessly. If Yoshi had not been so concerned with his new green pilots, Brent knew the air group commander would have found his niche at the Yasakuni Shrine long ago.

Brent leaned over the windscreen and stared down at the dock where the ship's lines were being heaved in. It was like looking down from the World Trade Center. Vehicles were toys and the men ants. Slowly, the great vessel was winched in and finally secured to the dock. Two gangways were put over and the colors at the gaff struck while another ensign was raised at the stern. "Secure the Special Sea Detail," Fujita ordered, placing his binoculars in a leather case attached to the windscreen. And then almost casually, "We have some business in the Shrine of Infinite Salvation."

Brent followed the admiral off the bridge.

An hour after *Yonaga* docked, Lieutenant Brent Ross was summoned to Flag Plot. Immediately, he learned Lieutenant Jimpei Yashiro would be forced to wait for his *seppuku*. Officials of the Self Defense Force, the Cabinet and reporters had been clamoring at the gate since the destruction of the boat. Emperor Akihito had even designated Lieutenant Commander Tadayoshi Koga of the Maritime Self Defense Force as his representative. The meeting could not be denied and Brent was summoned to the large conference room an hour after *Yonaga* docked.

Located in the aft part of "Flag Country," Flag Plot was almost as large as the fighter pilots' briefing room. Long and narrow, it contained an oak table that had been polished thousands of times by generations of tireless hands. It reflected a row of wire-shielded overhead lights like a mirror. A dozen chairs surrounded the table. At the far end the picture of Emperor Hirohito astride a white charger had been replaced by a painting of Emperor Akihito in civilian clothes. Next to the single door a rating manned communications gear. Two burly seaman guards with Otsu — "Baby Nambu" — automatic pistols on their hips flanked the door.

A paulownia wood shrine occupied the space next to the emperor's picture. Looking much like a small log cabin with an entire wall removed to expose the interior, it was filled with icons, talismans and holy relics. Brent saw many new icons; some strange, some familiar.

He recognized Inari the goddess of success in worldly affairs. And "The Seven Gods of Good Luck," especially prized by sailors, had found a place. Two other seagoing gods, Ebisu and Daikoku, who brought good luck and wealth had been placed in a corner. Brent smiled as he spotted a huge egg-shaped monk who at first looked like another Buddha. But closer examination revealed the new figure was that of Daruma-san, a famous patriarch of the sixth century A.D. who lost the use of his legs as the result of remaining motionless for eight years. Yes, indeed, Fujita believed in arming himself with all the pantheonic help available. Brent knew he would need it this day.

Seated at the far end of the table with Commander Yoshi Matsuhara on one side and Rear Admiral Byron Whitehead on the other, Brent stared the length of the gleaming surface to Admiral Fujita who sat at the head. The implacable brown face was as expressionless as the Buddha in the paulownia shrine. Executive Officer Captain Mitake Arai was there and the ancient scribe, Commander Hakuseki Katsube, was in his usual place next to Fujita.

Another "plank owner," Katsube was so old and withered by the years he looked like an Egyptian mummy that had been unwrapped. Eyeing the doddering old man hunched over his pad and pencil because Fujita and Katsube disdained modern recorders, Brent nudged Yoshi and whispered into his ear. "If Katsube is ever hooked up to monitors in intensive care, all his vital signs will show straight lines right off. Right now."

The pilot laughed softly. "I think he died years ago and no one noticed, my friend."

Brent's eyes moved to the dive bomber commander, Commander Takuya Iwata. Young and haughty, Iwata was huge for a Japanese. He was over six-feet tall and easily two hundred pounds. Iwata had shown an instant dislike for Brent Ross. Perhaps it was because Brent was an American, or, perhaps, it was Brent's friendship with the Negro submarine commander, Lieutenant Reginald Williams, that had incited the hostile feelings. A follower of Yukio Mishima and nineteenth century in his attitudes, Iwata was an insufferable bigot and had not even appeared for the memorial services at the Yasakuni

Shrine for Williams and the crew of his submarine *Blackfin* which had been sunk with all hands after it destroyed tanker *Jabal Nafusa* off Tomonuto Atoll. Brent had served on *Blackfin* and had become very close to every member of her crew. The loss was like having an entire branch of your family wiped out at one stroke. He despised Iwata even more after the snub.

Brent stared at Iwata and the flyer glared back unflinchingly. Of pure samurai stock, he had been recommended by the Emperor and immediately accepted by Fujita. However, no one could argue with the man's ability as a pilot and his courage. Without question, he was the best dive bomber pilot on the ship and deserved his command. Brent had flown a combat mission with Iwata as the gunner in the commander's Aichi D3A. On this mission Brent had shot down a ME 109 and damaged another while Iwata had hit carrier *Ramli al Kabir* with his entire load of three bombs. Yet, despite experiencing this mortal danger together, the hostility between them had never faded. In fact, once it had erupted into a fist fight in the hangar deck. Brent had beaten Iwata senseless. However, in doing so, the American had discovered just how powerful the flyer really was. Brent had emerged from the fracas with a black eye, lacerated lip and innumerable bruises. But Iwata had been beaten into unconsciousness. Coming from the filthy hands of a round-eyed foreigner, this was the ultimate humiliation to the proud samurai. Takuya Iwata hated everything about Brent, some of the venom spilling over to the American's best friend, Yoshi Matsuhara. The score would be settled one day. Brent knew this. Brent was ready.

Next to Iwata sat Lieutenant Tadayoshi Koga of the Maritime Self Defense Force. Officially designated the liaison man to *Yonaga* by Chief of Staff Admiral Shuichiya Higashiyama, Brent had seen the short, obese officer many times. With most of the Self Defense Force ships sunk in a surprise Arab raid, the timid officer actually had little liaison to occupy him. In addition to some amphibious craft, frigate *Ayase* and destroyer *Yamagiri*, two combat vessels, had survived. However, both had been originally armed with useless rockets and cruise missiles which had to be stripped and replaced with AA machine guns. The pair had been useful as radar pickets only. Fujita did not trust their crews, any Defense Force crews, for that matter. The Japanese Red Army had infiltrated the entire force. In fact, it was suspected most of the force's submarines had been scuttled by their own crewmen during the Arab raid.

However, today Lieutenant Tadayoshi Koga represented the Emperor. This gave him new stature and his usual shrinking, apprehensive look had been replaced with a confident new expression of near bravado. He sat erect, his huge belly sagging over his thighs. Next to him was an empty chair.

Fujita spoke to Lieutenant Tadayoshi Koga, "You were to bring a member of the Cabinet; the Minister of Agriculture and Forestry, Mister Shizuki Kaushika." He gestured at the chair.

The officers exchanged worried looks. In order for the Diet to support *Yonaga* under the stringent strictures of Article Nine of the Constitution which forbade offensive weapons and renounced war, *Yonaga* had been declared a national park and put under the minister of Agriculture and Forestry. As far as Brent knew, no member of the crew had ever met Minister Shizuki Kaushika who headed the department. Now he was coming aboard. The boat destroyed by Lieutenant Jimpei Yashiro was

105

at the bottom of it and everyone knew it.

Koga placed both hands on the table and pushed himself to his feet, his stomach forcing him to take a step backward. He spoke in a high, reedy voice that always grated on Brent like fingernails on a chalkboard. "Sir, I would like to convey the Emperor's greetings."

"Long live the Emperor! *Tenno heiko banzai!*" scribe Hakuseki Katsube shouted, trying to push himself to his feet but failing. Arai and Iwata contributed their "Banzais!"

Fujita's rootlike fingers drummed the table until silence returned. "Extend my deepest respect and affection to the Mikado, but where is Mister Kaushika?" he asked.

The fat little officer squirmed as if his underwear were attacking his ample bottom with a hundred sharp teeth. "Ah, sir, he was to be here—"

He was interrupted by a knock and a seaman guard opened the door. The Minister of Agriculture and Forestry, Shizuki Kaushika, entered. He was an impressive man with a strong rugged face and a proud bearing, his every nuance exuding the confidence of the consummate politician. The visage was dominated by a big flat nose, gaunt-boned cheeks and a heavy square jaw. Not a single strand of hair graced his head. His bald pate gleamed under the lights as if it had been polished by the same numberless hands that had waxed the table. Beneath his unlined forehead and bushy black eyebrows, his narrow eyes sought out each man, evaluating and weighing just like a gambler about to sit down for a hand of poker with a group of strangers. Set in deep cages of bony sockets, they were underlined with dark plum-colored smears as though they had been bruised by fists. Either the man drank too much or read too much. Perhaps both. He was wearing what appeared to be an exact duplicate of a Brooks Brothers three-piece suit.

All politicians look alike, Brent said to himself. Immediately he felt a pang of disquiet and he could see his apprehension mirrored on Yoshi Matsuhara's face. The newcomer, following Fujita's gesture, strode across the room and seated himself next to Koga. The pair clasped hands, smiled at each other and mumbled greetings. They were obviously well-acquainted.

Fujita's black eyes drilled through the newcomer. He hated politicians. The antagonism had grown throughout his career as he and Isoroku Yamamoto had fought to enlarge and strengthen the Imperial Navy for the war they both knew was coming. Always some politicians were in opposition to their plans. Funding was never adequate. The culmination came when the cabinet made the foolish decision to send *Yonaga* into hiding at Sano Wan in the face of Fujita's and Yamamoto's objections. Here it was ultimately trapped and assumed destroyed. Only a few responsible for the decision survived the war and by now they were all dead. Fujita never forgave and still hated their memory. Brent was sure the old man prayed to the gods that the spirits of those long-dead politicians languished in the arms of the foul old woman of death.

Squaring his thin shoulders, Fujita introduced his officers and then spoke to the civilian in a factual tone, "You are the Minister of Agriculture and Forestry." He thumbed a dossier on the table before him, but did not open it.

"That is correct, Admiral," the minister concurred in a basso profundo strident enough to fill the Imperial Kabuki Theater. He stared at the dossier under Fujita's fingers where his name was clearly visible.

Without glancing at a single note, Fujita recited in startling detail Kaushika's career. "You were born in Hiroshima in 1930, the son of a rice importer. You are *hi-bakusha,* an atomic bomb survivor."

"That is correct, Admiral." Kaushika stole a baleful look at Brent Ross and Byron Whitehead. "I was burned, lost my hair." He ran a hand over his head. "The rest of my family was not so fortunate. They were vaporized." The timbre of his voice turned acid with sarcasm, "Thanks to the *Enola Gay* and her gallant American crew." Whitehead stirred uneasily. Iwata snickered and threw Brent a sidelong glance. Brent felt a hot pang of anger rise like a sudden flame.

Fujita thumped his tiny fist on the table. His dislike erupted. "That is unacceptable. You will not insult the American members of my staff. Of course they were responsible, but so were we responsible. Our esteemed ancestors were responsible, all of mankind was responsible." The fist came to rest. "I lost my wife and two sons at Hiroshima, too. The French have an expression, *'C'est la guerre.'* Remember it. Fighting men never forget it."

"I meant no affront to your aides, Admiral." The minister moved his eyes to the two Americans. "I apologize." The tone lacked sincerity, but the Americans nodded back.

Fujita seemed placated. He fingered the dossier but still did not open it. He spoke to Kaushika, "You were well-educated by your uncle Tozao Suyeisha who was a chamberlain to Emperor Hirohito. You graduated from Tokyo University with a law degree in 1955, practiced law for five years and went into politics. You were first elected to the Diet in 1960, the House of Representatives. You served three terms, twelve years. Then you were elected to the House of Councilors in 1972."

108

"You know me well, sir."

Fujita ignored the acknowledgment and proceeded like a recording. "You served as a Councilor for three terms. Four months ago you were appointed by the Prime Minister to your current cabinet post." He drummed the table. Brent knew the old man despised Shizuki Kaushika and everything he stood for, but was not prepared for what followed. "Your career has been marked by a remarkable ability to avoid conflict. You have an ability to compromise and promote your own career at the expense of others. You have even tried compromising with *Rengo Sekigun*."

The Councilor came erect, eyes wide and glaring. "I resent that, sir."

"Resent what you like. It is the truth." Fujita hunched forward, eyes burning into Kaushika's. "Why do you, a civilian and a politician presume to enter my Flag Plot, insult two members of my staff, and then sit smugly with samurai who have dedicated their lives to Nippon and the Son of Heaven?" His face was twisted as if the words had been rotten food, spat out in revulsion.

Every eye moved to the politician. He drew himself up and suddenly seemed much larger, sanguine face twisting and contorting like a torn sail whipped by the wind. "I am here on the Prime Minister's business. Let me remind you, sir, the Meiji constitution was abandoned in 1945. Our sovereign power is no longer vested in the Chrysanthemum Throne. Emperor Akihito is nothing more than a symbol of our state and the unity of the people. He is no longer *Kokutai*." He glanced at the Americans, explaining, "The word means the Emperor is Japan, the essence of our nation." He turned back to Fujita, "But no longer. The Emperor has no political power."

Brent heard Iwata growl with anger. Katsube reacted as violently as his arthritic old bones would permit. "Treason! Blasphemy!" the old scribe screeched, spraying spittle over his notes and Commander Iwata who wiped his face with a handkerchief. Katsube half-rose and gasped, "Off with his head!" He waved a fist threateningly and the effort almost toppled him to the deck. Iwata caught him with a single hand to the neck and lowered him into his chair like a dead chicken dropped by a butcher. Sagging to the side, he breathed in short hard gasps from the exertion.

"He cannot be serious," Kaushika demanded, concern sweeping across his face.

"A worthy suggestion," Fujita answered. "However, your neck is safe."

The minister hunched forward, fingers interlaced on the table, thumbs warring. "We support you. You know that."

"You support your own greed. Without *Yonaga* Japan would be an Arab puppet."

Kaushika had courage. He shouldered the insult aside with the aplomb of an experienced politician and came on hard with is own attack, breaching the subject everyone expected, but hoped to avoid. "You killed twenty-seven innocent people, today," he said in a voice that singed.

Fujita sighed and turned his thin lips under. "An unfortunate by-product of war. Sometimes the innocent, your own, are killed by your own weapons." He ran his fingertips back and forth on the polished surface as if he were searching for a hidden imperfection he could never find. He continued, showing his vast knowledge of World War Two. "During the Greater East Asia War, battleships *Hiei* and *Kirishima* bombarded both Ameri-

110

can positions and our own men on at least two separate occasions on the island of Guadalcanal. Innumerable times our own bombers punished our own men as severely as they did the enemy. Incidents of our own troops being killed by their own artillery are too numerous to count."

He gazed at Brent Ross and Byron Whitehead and startled them both with his knowledge of Allied blunders, too. "During the invasion of Sicily, twenty-two American transport planes loaded with paratroopers were shot down by their own ships off Sicily. Scores were killed. At Saint Lo, American bombers pulverized the German lines and they also dumped hundreds of tons of bombs on their own troops. And it was not uncommon for the RAF to miss its targets. In fact, they often bombed the wrong cities. Bomber Command did not discipline the errant crews severely. After all, the cities were all filled with Germans. However, on April 1, 1944, American B-17s bombed Schaffhausen, killing fifty people." He looked around at the raised eyebrows. Even Brent Ross and Rear Admiral Whitehead stared quizzically.

The Admiral explained, "Schaffhausen happens to be in Switzerland." The Americans exchanged an awkward, disconcerted look. They should have known, but American military histories rarely mentioned the tragic error.

Fujita raced on, "In the Pacific, the American submarine *Guardfish* sank the *USS Extractor,* a salvage ship. And two submarines, the *Tang* and the *Tullibee,* were sunk by their own torpedoes." He leaned forward and pushed the bony hands forward on the table. "All armies, all navies have suffered these tragic accidents. It not only is a risk of war, it is an inevitability of war."

111

"Perhaps, Admiral. But what happened today goes beyond an accident of war. A boatload of innocent people who were greeting you with joy and love were butchered. It was all recorded by television cameras and has been running constantly all day on every channel. The officer responsible should be . . ."

"You do not tell me how to run my ship," Fujita bristled.

The tone was conciliatory. "I would not presume, Admiral. Japan could not survive without *Yonaga* and your leadership, but *Yonaga* is not a sovereign state. Justice cries out for some kind of action against the perpetrators. Some kind of disciplinary action, sir." The man was pleading.

Fujita's eyes ran over his officers and a silence filled the room, broken only by the sounds of blowers and auxiliary engines. "That has already been decided. Appropriate action will be taken when this meeting is concluded."

"You will discipline the personnel responsible?"

"I said the decision has been made."

"Then the men responsible for the destruction of the boat will be punished?"

"A single officer was responsible and his punishment will be appropriate. He has selected his own form of retribution." The old admiral pounded the table with a single fist. "But keep this in mind, he will be punished for disobeying my orders, not for sinking a boat and killing the occupants." A finger jutted from the fist and stabbed at Kaushika. "Orders are sacred. They must be obeyed." He spread the fingers and swept a hand grandly over his officers. "Discipline and the inflexible, unquestioning obedience to orders give meaning to our existence."

Iwata, Arai and Katsube shouted, "Banzai!"

Kaushika looked at them with wonder in his eyes.

Waving them into silence, the admiral palmed a leather-bound copy of the *Hagakure* which was always on the table before him. Then he raised his eyes and quoted it, " 'If one has not mastered his own mind and body, he cannot defeat his enemy'." He sank back and turned to the minister. "Do you understand?"

The minister nodded. "Yes. A single officer was responsible. He will punish himself?" He gesticulated at the book.

"That is correct."

"But how will he do this? I do not understand." The tone was suspicious.

"You will see for yourself. I insist that you witness this supreme act."

"Not suicide?"

"You shall see."

"I am sorry, Admiral. I have a meeting with the Prime Minister in forty-five minutes." He began to rise.

Fujita smiled. "I just cancelled the meeting."

"What do you mean?"

"You are to remain."

"I cannot." Kaushika came to his feet. Takuya Iwata, Brent Ross and Yoshi Matsuhara rose slowly from their chairs and the two seaman guards came erect, staring at Admiral Fujita expectantly.

Minister Shizuki Kaushika ran his eyes over the formidable array of muscle, sighed, and sank back into his chair like a punctured balloon. The officers returned to theirs. "This is illegal," the minister said.

"I am the law here," Fujita shot back. He turned to Lieutenant Tadayoshi Koga. He reverted to the honorific, a form of address which the Japanese reserved only for the Heavenly Emperor. "You said *Tenno* has a special

113

communication for me." *Tenno* was a reverential reference to the Heavenly Emperor.

Brent knew Koga would respond in the peculiar form of address. He had heard him use it before. It was a unique, clumsy form that always confused Brent Ross because it avoided the usual three forms of politeness of speaking down, or up, or on a level of equality. Instead, the Japanese created a fourth level of ultra-subservience for the Emperor where every noun and verb changed form and the passive voice dominated. Fortunately, Fujita and the Maritime Self Defense Force officer remained in English, only alluding to the honorific form.

Koga, obviously flustered at occupying center stage, rose and said haltingly, "Yes, Admiral." He glanced down at Kaushika. "*Tenno* has been wishing to assure you he has faith in your judgement and was aware today's unfortunate incident must have been an accident. You can be assured of his unwavering support."

Arai, Iwata, Brent Ross and Katsube all shouted, "Banzai!" Wide-eyed, Whitehead and Kaushika stared at Brent. The minister showed shock at the American's reaction.

Koga continued. "*Tenno* has a request."

"My command," Fujita acknowledged.

Koga took a deep breath and blurted it all out in one sentence, "*Tenno* wishes to see you tomorrow and he has suggested that you allow reporters on board to interview you and to witness whatever actions you take to discipline those who were responsible for the destruction of the boat." His eyes sought refuge by searching for his feet which were concealed by his stomach.

There was shock on the face of every officer. Everyone knew Fujita despised reporters almost as much as he hated politicians and Kadafi. A cold silence poured

114

through the room like an Alpine avalanche, the iciness enveloping everyone and everything, flowing into every corner, every niche. Brent shuddered, staring at Fujita's glacial eyes. The old man was in an impossible situation. He had no choice. The man he believed to be a god directly descended from Amaterasu, one-hundred-twenty-fifth in line, had spoken. It was the ultimate command. His voice was cold and dead, "How many?"

"Only three, sir. United Information, Nippon Press Service and International Reporting. These reporters represent pools."

"No cameras."

"No cameras, sir."

Fujita nodded and sighed resignedly. "Very well. At least we will not be overrun by these jackals." He smiled incongruously. "We will soon discover if they have strong stomachs to match their big mouths."

The officers looked at each other and smiled at the admiral's tension relieving jest. Fujita said to Koga, "Where are these reporters? If I must see them, let it be as soon as possible." He waved a hand. "There is much to do. Reports to read, a war to fight, and a ceremony to attend in The Shrine of Infinite Salvation."

"They are at the gate, sir." Koga nodded at the communications man. "A phone call will have them here in minutes."

Fujita sank back with the expression of a driver who realizes a head-on collision is inevitable. "Very well. I will see them immediately." He stared down the table. "Lieutenant Koga, Lieutenant Brent Ross and Commander Yoshi Matsuhara please remain. Admiral Whitehead, Captain Arai and Commander Iwata please show our guest Minister Shizuki Kaushika to the wardroom." He nodded to the minister. "Mister

Kaushika, you can have a libation and something to eat there, if you wish, before you witness just how strong, how alive the Code of Bushido is on *Yonaga*."

Minister Shizuki Kaushika began to rise, but Fujita halted him with a raised hand. He stared at the minister and spoke slowly and deliberately. "You have heard of Tachibana Akemi?"

Kaushika stared back. "A poet, I believe. He lived long ago."

Fujita gestured at Brent Ross. The American took his cue and spoke with a taunting smile on his face. "He was a great poet, a traditionalist who hated modernism. He lived during the nineteenth century."

Fujita was obviously pleased with Brent's response and Kaushika's discomfort at being upstaged by a round-eyed American barbarian. Commander Takuya Iwata, too, appeared disconcerted, glaring at Brent.

Watching the minister with an amused glint in his eye, Fujita continued, "Tachibana Akemi wrote, 'It is a pleasure when in these days of delight, in all things foreign, I come across a man who does not forget our Empire'." He drummed the desk. "Keep in mind, Mister Kaushika, these words reflect the beliefs of every samurai on this ship."

"These are old-fashioned beliefs, sir."

"We are old-fashioned men, Mister Kaushika."

Commander Takuya Iwata, unable to restrain himself longer, leaped to his feet, obviously determined to show his own patriotism and depths of knowledge. Every eye was on him as he addressed the admiral. "Sir, may I say a word?"

Fujita nodded his assent. The commander's eyes moved over every officer, finally stopping on Minister Shizuki Kaushika. He spoke with the superior air of a

116

college professor lecturing a freshman. *"Taiko Tenno,* 'The late Emperor,' has found nirvana and now dwells in the clouds with his fellow gods. He gave us these honorable words in 1946 — Nippon's darkest hour." He paused dramatically, raising his eyes to the overhead as if he were searching for a deity in the maze of conduits and pipes. He spoke slowly and deliberately as if his words were precious gems being dropped from his lips into a pool. " 'Under the weight of winter snow, the pine tree's branches bend, but do not break'." He brought his eyes to Kaushika and stabbed a finger for emphasis, "While others break, sir, samurai do not even bend!"

"Banzai!" old Katsube sprayed. Fujita nodded approvingly and Iwata seated himself, staring at Brent Ross with gloating self-satisfaction. Brent stared back, lips turned down with disdainful amusement as if he had just witnessed a small boy showing off a new trick on his bicycle.

Fujita seemed pleased. Yet, he was not finished. He seemed determined to show off the talents of his officers. Brent knew he would turn to Yoshi Matsuhara and the old man did precisely that. "Commander Matsuhara," he said. "You are the best poet on the ship. Would you give us one of your haiku verses to conclude this meeting?"

The air group commander rose slowly. Staring above the minister's head at a spot on the bulkhead, he spoke as if he were addressing someone from another place, another time. The timbre of his deep voice was grim and determined. "What do men think, I care not, Nor for my life, For I am the sword of my Emperor."

Brent, Arai, Katsube and Iwata all came to their feet shouting, "Banzai!" Kaushika stared in wonder. Fujita smiled. Over and over again the shouts resounded in the

117

room. Finally, the officers settled into their chairs, Katsube again aided by Iwata. Brent pounded Yoshi on the back. Fujita, with a contented look on his face, sank back, hands clasped on his chest. "You are dismissed, Mister Kaushika," he said to the overhead.

Minister Shizuki Kaushika, Rear Admiral Byron Whitehead, Captain Mitake Arai and Commander Takuya Iwata left.

Only minutes passed before there was a pounding at the door. A seaman guard opened it and the three reporters entered. Two of the three were women.

The first woman was stunning. She caught all eyes. Brent Ross, Tadayoshi Koga, Yoshi Matsuhara and Hakuseki Katsube all stared transfixed as the girl walked into the room. It was like looking at a polished gem, an exquisite glistening diamond reserved only for the eyes of a fortunate few. The old scribe grasped the table with both hands, leaned forward, eyes gleaming from their bed of wrinkles. He actually drooled. It had been over a half-century for the old man. Brent felt sorry for him.

Fujita saw the reaction of his men, and then stared at the beauty with undisguised hostility. Women were not welcome on board *Yonaga*. In his nineteenth century mind, they were made to serve men, bear children and maintain a home. Nothing more. It was inconceivable that they could shoulder responsibility in the business world and the military. Their sex along with politicians and reporters completed the triumvirate of pariahs the old man strove to bar from his ship. He held all of them in contempt. They were troublemakers; they disrupted his crew.

The girl stiffened in the glare of the hungry stares as

beautiful women are wont to do; slightly embarrassed, yet deep down enjoying the obvious desire her presence provoked. Clearly, she was not adverse or unaccustomed to playing center stage.

Tall and young, her profuse mane of sun-bleached hair streamed to her waist in luminous folds like shimmering gold lace, streaked with copper, silver and platinum. Perfectly ordered, her face was delicate yet strong, skin radiating that waxy plastic glow of youth and good health like the skin of a ripe peach. Remarkable blue eyes, with full-lashed eyelids cut straight across, gave her an intense, reproachful look. Her cheek bones were high and classic, lips full and pouting, lending her mouth a near prehensile quality. It was a face that encouraged a man to search for a word to describe it. Brent thought of *"stunning," "magnificent,"* but quickly rejected them as too commonplace. And then he realized there were no words, just metaphors that would require the poetic genius of a Byron or Keats.

Although she wore a business suit and flat heels, the heavy clothing could not disguise the slimness of her body. The ample mounds of her breasts were pointed and jutted out like ripening fruit. The waist was tiny, flaring gently into the curve of her trim hips. Her tight skirt revealed the well-turned calves and slim ankles of a dancer, glistening under the sheen of expensive panty hose. She was sensual, sexy, and dangerously beautiful.

Brent stared with the hunger of a sailor too long at sea. The strength of his desire for her shocked him with a physical jolt. Aroused by the sheer sexuality of the young woman that filled the room with a palpable force, his body stiffened; a hot fist clenched in his groin and his heart banged furiously against his ribs as if he were experiencing an onanistic rite. It had been nearly a year

119

since Dale McIntyre. He was not cut out for a celibate life. He stared at the girl like a starving, shipwrecked sailor suddenly finding a gourmet meal spread on the beach.

The second woman was the antithesis of the first. She could have been thirty-five or forty-five. She was one of those women who aged too quickly or very slowly and left men guessing. Although she was tall, her body was thick, almost burly, waist as large as her narrow hips. Although the skirt of her business suit was cut unfashionably low, it still revealed stubby, muscular calves. *Legs by Steinway,* flashed through Brent's mind.

Without cosmetics, her face was plain, nose straight, lips a thin gash across a jutting jaw. Short brown hair was styled in a masculine fashion. Her eyes were a strange gray-green, and they searched the faces of the officers who, with the exception of Fujita, were coming to their feet. They found Brent and the arousal he had felt from the first woman was squelched abruptly. They were jaded eyes that gave the woman the air of someone who had seen everything twice. They were brooding eyes, hinting at a ruthlessness; an awful look that cared little for the human world. Especially the male world. This was a woman to be reckoned with. This was a woman to be feared.

Dyke ran through Brent's mind. He glanced back at the first woman and felt near panic. Not these two together! Not the beauty and the stereotypical bull-dyke. The usual male reaction to suspected female pairings tortured his mind. *Good Lord, she can't be wasted on that bull dyke.* He tore his eyes from the women and concentrated on the man.

Dressed in a baggy suit that looked as if it had been bought in one of the Ginza's nondescript shops, the man

120

appeared to be about fifty. Tall and gaunt enough to be slightly bent by an accommodating stoop, he had a long bloodhound face with a beak of a nose, brown restless eyes and receding gray-streaked hair. He could pass for a football coach or, with more pronounced sartorial accents, an aging professor. His eyes probed like searchlights in the dark; the look of a man who seemed to know something glorious, something awful, about everyone in the room. Perhaps he did. That was the man's business.

Lieutenant Koga gestured and began the introductions. It was a miserable start. "This is Ms. —"

"Ms.?" Admiral Fujita spat. "It is Miss or Mrs. on this ship."

The older woman's eyes flared. Her voice was low, harsh, and cut like a file. "It's Ms. today, sir. This is the twentieth century."

Fujita's eyes fixed on the woman with an intensity that could melt. "Do you wish an interview?"

The woman glared back, square jaw twitching. "Yes," she managed as if she were choking on the word.

"Then it is Miss or Mrs." He nodded at Koga.

Koga sighed, obviously uneasy with the charged atmosphere that permeated the room. His eyes darted over the furniture, avoiding everyone like a frightened ferret. He spoke to the table while gesturing at the young beauty, "Miss Arlene Spencer of the Nippon Press." Then he raised his head and introduced the older woman, "Miss Lia Mandel of The United Information Service." Finally, he introduced the man, "Mr. Alistair Cunningham of International Reporting." And then he added, "These reporters represent a pool including *Tass,* Reuters, Associated Press and most of the world's major news services. The ladies are American and Mr. Cunningham is a British citizen."

Fujita nodded at the empty chairs. While the reporters seated themselves, he introduced Commander Yoshi Matsuhara, Commander Hakuseki Katsube, and Lieutenant Brent Ross. The officers found their own chairs.

Brent was startled when Arlene Spencer found her way to the chair next to him which had been vacated by Rear Admiral Whitehead. He felt an almost forgotten tingling sensation deep down in his groin when her thigh brushed his as she seated herself. She turned with a dazzling smile of perfect white teeth and said, "Pardon me, Lieutenant. Clumsy of me."

"My pleasure," Brent managed in a forced casual tone. He caught a hateful stare from Lia, or was it jealousy. He felt a surge of triumph. Perhaps, Arlene Spencer was sending a message to everyone.

He saw Katsube glare with the same kind of look in Lia's eyes, Yoshi smile and Fujita stare implacably. The old admiral spoke bluntly. "You are here by special request of the Mikado. State your business."

Lia Mandel removed a pad, pencil and recorder from a huge purse as big as a picnic basket and placed them on the table. Her gray-green eyes, dull like stagnant swamp water, caught and held the Admiral's. Evident to all, she was smarting from the admiral's rebuke. She moved aggressively with an astonishing lack of tact like a boxer who had just been jolted by a hard right to the jaw. "You murdered twenty-seven people. We want to know why."

Brent saw the admiral's jaw tighten, eyes narrow and he knew the fuse was burning. Luckily, before the admiral could explode, Arlene Spencer interrupted. "Lia! Don't be so blunt. We can't accomplish anything that way."

Alistair Cunningham joined in with a Welsh accent that gave his words a soft, lilting edge. "Quite right, old girl. We shan't accomplish anything if you make a sodding muck of it right off."

"I'm not making a muck of it," Mandel shot back.

Fujita took over. "Speak cordially, madam, or I will order you off the ship immediately!"

The big woman swallowed hard and stared silently at Fujita. Brent knew she was trying to douse her own fuse. She tapped her pad with the eraser end of her pencil and then nudged Arlene Spencer. Arlene took the cue immediately. Her voice was soft and respectful. "Ah, Admiral. The whole world would like to know the circumstances of today's incident."

Avoiding Mandel, the admiral spoke to Arlene Spencer and Alistair Cunningham. Slowly and with careful detail he explained the incident, the misunderstood command. He did not identify the offending officer.

"You will punish him?" Lia Mandel asked, finally showing a modicum of control.

The admiral sighed and turned his thin lower lip under. "Yes. In accordance with the Code of Bushido the officer responsible will be punished immediately after the conclusion of this meeting."

"May we witness it?" Mandel asked, hunching forward eagerly.

For the first time, Fujita smiled. "I insist upon it."

"What is the punishment?"

"Why they'll bloody well keel-haul the cad and then draw and quarter him," Cunningham offered. No one laughed. The Englishman sagged back, tugging on his long nose, annoyed that his tension-relieving quip had not relieved anything.

123

"Let me just say, the punishment will, indeed, fit the breach of discipline."

"You consider the murder of twenty-seven people a breach of discipline," Lia Mandel injected, suddenly. "Nothing more?"

Fujita maintained his remarkable control. "That is correct. The offender will pay for disobeying my orders, not for destroying the boat."

"You won't reveal the form of punishment?"

"I have already discussed that matter, madam."

"You want to surprise us?"

"Perhaps." The admiral turned to Arlene Spencer. "You represent Nippon Press?"

"Correct, sir."

The old man turned palms up. "But why you? You are an American."

"True, Admiral. But I've worked for the *New York Times, Wall Street Journal,* the Associated Press and several smaller news services. I am fluent in Japanese, Korean and Chinese. My major was not journalism, it was actually Asian languages. I learned journalism on the job. Actually, writing the stories is quite easy. I was exactly what Nippon Press needed." She looked at her fellow reporters. "Getting the story is the tough part. Right partners?"

"Hear! Hear! Jolly right!" the Englishman concurred. Lia showed her agreement with a nod.

Arlene turned to Brent. "Speaking of stories, you're known as 'The American Samurai', Lieutenant. Correct?"

Brent stared down into the blue eyes that reminded him of a pristine mountain lake reflecting the sky. Despite being slightly flustered, he managed to answer in an even timbre, "I have been so honored, Miss Spencer."

124

Fujita beamed, Yoshi Matsuhara smiled.

Then the words that promised an opportunity to see the wondrous creature again caressed his ears. "May I arrange to see you again?" She suddenly reddened, flustered. "I mean to interview you? My editors insist on it."

"I think that may be arranged," Brent said, completely failing to master a matter-of-fact tone.

Yoshi smiled in amusement at Brent's discomfort. Both officers looked at the admiral. Fujita said, "Tomorrow you have liberty, Mister Ross. You have my permission."

Arlene said, "Thank you, Admiral Fujita," and handed Brent a business card. "Can you give me a ring at my office? I can see you in the afternoon or early evening."

"I think I can make it," Brent said, pocketing the card. He felt heat on his face as Yoshi Matsuhara chuckled into his hand. Fujita looked away.

Lia Mandel spoke to the admiral. Her voice was businesslike, hard-edged, but not disrespectful. "Six months ago you engaged Kadafi's battle group in the Western Pacific."

"That is well known."

"You sank carrier *Ramli al Kabir* and damaged carrier *Al Kufra*."

"The engagement was thoroughly reported in all of the world's media."

"You took heavy losses in air crews."

The old Japanese drummed the table with his restless fingers. "You are treading on loose sand, Miss Mandel."

"Loose sand?"

"Yes. Those matters are classified."

"Ha! You can't keep your losses a secret. Why, new

crews are training at Tokyo International and Tsu-chiura." She waved a hand. "Why, every day flights of fighters and bombers can be seen by everyone."

"Our CAP is always patrolling and, true, our training is continuous, Miss Mandel. We are always training new pilots."

"Replacements, sir."

"New pilots, madam."

"It's a matter of semantics."

"No! It is a matter of what I just told you." The heat was rising again. He stabbed a finger. "You are here by the grace of the Emperor. I will see him tomorrow. If you distort what I have said, I will personally report you to the Mikado and have you barred from ever reporting in Japan again."

The woman swallowed hard, hunched forward, and her eyes narrowed. To Brent, she looked like a vulture eyeing carrion. She was not intimidated. "I assure you," she said. "I only report the truth."

Fujita rocked with laughter which was completely devoid of humor. "Truth! That is certainly a rare commodity with the 'Fourth Estate'."

Alistair Cunningham's timely interruption broke the hostile mood. "Admiral, you've got a brace of Brits, sir."

Fujita stared at the Englishman as if he had just heard a foreign language. Cunningham offered some aid, "Ah, two of our lads, sir, Flying Officer York and Captain Willard-Smith. The captain had a distinguished record during the unpleasantness in the Falklands."

The admiral gestured at Commander Yoshi Matsu-hara. The air group commander said to the Englishman, "Captain Colin Willard-Smith and Flying Officer Elwyn York are my wingmen. They are two of the finest fighter pilots in my group. I could use more like them."

"Just smashing! Capital!" the Englishman exclaimed, beaming. "Rumor has it scores are in training and five more will soon be reporting aboard *Yonaga*."

The officers were silent for a moment. They all knew six of the RAF's best had graduated from the RAF's college at Cranwell and were now completing their training with new, more powerful Seafires. However, Yoshi responded with a noncommittal, "We hope you are right, Mister Cunningham."

Lia Mandel said to Yoshi, "You have French, German, and Greek pilots."

"True," Yoshi agreed. "And we expect more from all over the world. The love of freedom is not limited by nationality."

"And your American squadron, it took heavy losses."

Yoshi sighed. "Yes. It has been reported. We had a complete squadron of twelve Grumman F-6-F, Hellcats. They intercepted a huge Arab raid. We lost half of them."

"They've been replaced?"

"That is correct."

Lia scribbled on her pad and then looked up at Admiral Fujita, her square jaw set in a determined line. She breached a subject that had troubled the free world for years. "What do you intend to do about Kadafi's poison gas plant at Rabta? You know it is reported they make both mustard and nerve gas there."

Again, the officers exchanged a knowing look which did not escape the reporters. The Rabta plant, which was sixty miles south of Tripoli, had been a source of heated debate among the staff, and no clear-cut plan to destroy it had yet been developed. It was an enormous problem; the distances vast, the plant ringed with anti-aircraft guns and fighter bases. Lia read the looks and spoke sarcastically, "I know I'm treading on loose sand."

"No, madam," Fujita said. "You are an insufferable boor."

Lia gasped and her face flushed. However, before the exchange could continue, they were interrupted by the communications man who had a phone to his ear. "Admiral! Lieutenant Jimpei Yashiro is prepared and all is ready in 'The Shrine of Infinite Salvation.' Captain Arai respectfully requests your presence."

The old admiral placed both hands on the desk and pushed himself to his feet. He glared at Lia Mandel who stared back with the eyes of a cobra. "Now you shall see for yourselves the essence of my samurai. The heart and soul of Bushido." He glanced at his officers, "White gloves and swords, gentlemen."

Silently, the ancient sailor left the room followed by the others.

Chapter Six

The officers hurried to their cabins to don Number One blues, white gloves and swords. Fujita's tunic, gloves and sword were brought to him by an orderly. Then, the party moved forward toward the pilothouse where the ship's passenger elevator was located. Actually, the *Yamatos* were built with three passenger elevators, however, only one was incorporated into *Yonaga's* design.

With Fujita leading, Hakuseki Katsube, Yoshi Matsuhara, Alistair Cunningham, Lia Mandel, Arlene Spencer and Brent Ross moved slowly forward in the single passageway that ran the length of the flag bridge. The pace was very slow, dictated by Katsube's arthritic joints. Fujita was uneasy as if he were leading a group of enemy spies through the covert labyrinths of his most secret sanctum sanctorum.

They first passed through the chart house where two quartermasters were busy hand correcting charts. The two ratings came to attention and then bowed. No salutes were exchanged. Similar to the British navy, salutes were never given below decks and the Japanese considered the bridge "below decks." Fujita returned the bows with a cursory nod. Katsube nodded but the effort threw him off stride and only a quick hand from Yoshi kept the scribe on his feet. The enlisted men eyed Arlene with long stares. Lia was regarded with curiosity.

Leaving the chart house, they passed a door leading into a room dimly lit with red battle lamps. A number of green scopes glowed and men crowded around banks of electronics equipment, their flesh cast a ghoulish hue of yellow-green like days-old corpses, lips appearing blue and the veins of their necks and foreheads standing out like meandering purple lines. Arlene, who had worked her way to Brent's side, took his arm and gestured questioningly.

The touch hit the American lieutenant like an aphrodisiac. He managed to explain in calm tones, "Radar, ESM. I mean Electronic Support Measures."

"A-band and S-band?"

"Why yes, Miss Spencer. You know those things?"

"A little. But why do you have your S-band searching in port? You can't see anything except harbor clutter."

"Not quite true, Miss Spencer. Our surface search can pick up individual vessels moving in the bay and our air search is highly efficient."

"State of the art?" she remarked, leaning close to his ear.

"Sorry, Miss Spencer. Classified."

She laughed, the soft refreshing sound of a gentle breeze through the first growth of spring. "That equipment isn't fifty-years-old, Mister Ross."

"Madam," Fujita interrupted, turning his age stiffened neck with difficulty. "Do not pry into matters that are of a sensitive nature."

"Sorry, Admiral," the girl said contritely. "But everything seems sensitive on this ship." Lia laughed, a sound like a rutting hog. Brent felt his stomach turn and the aphrodisiac vanished.

130

At that moment a seaman guard opened the door of the elevator which was just abaft the pilothouse. The party filed in and the door closed.

The elevator exited just forward of amidships. The opening of the door ushered in a noisy world of pounding hammers, rumbling steel-wheeled bowsers being pulled across the armored deck, machine-gun bursts of pneumatic tools, and the shouts of hardworking men.

Almost as if obeying a signal, the three reporters stopped in their tracks and stared in awe at the cavernous compartment. Just under a thousand feet long and 140-feet wide, it was one of the largest single compartments ever to put to sea, not equaled until the nuclear-powered carrier *Enterprise* was launched in 1961. Although most of the aircraft had been flown off to Tokyo International Airport and Tsuchiura when *Yonaga* was a hundred miles at sea, fifteen Aichi D3As, Nakajima B5Ns and Mitsubishi A6M2s were segregated into groups where busy mechanics worked on engines, tested controls and made adjustments on the hundreds of systems upon which a pilot's life hung: But two new elements had been added: three Grumman F6Fs and a pair of Seafires were clustered in a separate bay on the port side. Here, a mixed crew of British, American and Japanese mechanics worked.

"Good Lord," Alistair Cunningham muttered. "You could jolly well get Wembley Stadium in here. Soccer match, fans, constabulary. The whole lot."

"Or three football games end to end," Arlene offered. Still at Brent's side, she pointed back over her shoulder at the starboard side at what happened to be a long balcony built midway between the hangar deck and the overhead.

Brent answered the unvoiced question, "The gallery

131

deck. Pilots' briefing rooms, pilots' quarters, junior officers' quarters." Then Brent noticed a silence creep into the compartment, shouts, the sounds of tools and of steel wheels on the steel deck suddenly ceasing. The enlisted men had come to attention, and with the exception of the British and Americans, were bowing toward the admiral. However, all eyes were on Arlene Spencer; hot, disrobing eyes that probed with the intensity of X-rays. Showing exceptional aplomb, the young woman seemed not to notice, walking with a casual swinging gait that moved her remarkable buttocks with sinuous catlike undulations. The woman definitely moved with a lyrical kind of beauty.

Led by Admiral Fujita who waved the mechanics back to work, the group moved to the starboard bow where The Shrine of Infinite Salvation was located. Built of unpainted wood, it was a large square room with a single door opening into the interior. A combination Shinto-Buddhist shrine, the front was decorated by two huge sixteen-petalled imperial chrysanthemums which flanked the door. A golden torii of rough hewn beams built like a post and beam doorway stood just outside the entrance. Every shrine had at least one torii, most three.

Admiral Fujita waved at the chrysanthemums. "The sixteen-petalled chrysanthemum. It represents the Mikado—the chrysanthemum throne. We have two on the bow of *Yonaga,* and on every aircraft, every weapon, you will find this sacred flower. We believe it enlists the aid of the gods in our most perilous moments." He looked at Lia Mandel. "Put that in your notes."

The woman glared back, but remained silent.

As the group approached the entrance, Arlene whispered into Brent's ear, "I've only been in Japan for three weeks, but I know to pass under the torii is the first step in purification. right, Mister Ross?"

Yoshi overheard the girl and before Brent could answer, the pilot said, "Correct to a point, Miss Spencer."

"To a point?"

"Yes. We believe the torii banishes the night, announces a new day much like the crowing of a cock. So, you see, the torii prepares the heart of the pious worshipper for his purified appearance before our gods."

"I see," said the girl. "In a sense, passing under the gate drives darkness from a worshipper's heart just like the darkness of night is lifted by dawn's light."

"Very good," Yoshi said, plainly impressed. "You are a poet, Miss Spencer." Fujita turned and eyed the girl with what appeared to be respect. Brent stared at her with new interest. There was a big brain behind that "Miss America" face.

When the party entered the shrine, the Westerners found a strange place of worship. There were no naves, benches or seats of any kind. At least a hundred officers standing in ranks snapped to attention. All were dressed in Number One blues, wearing white gloves, and swords hung from every belt. Fujita acknowledged their bows with his own and then proceeded to a place at the head of their ranks. He gestured at Brent, Yoshi and the reporters to remain at a place near the door where Rear Admiral Whitehead, Minister Shizuki Kaushika, Lieutenant Tadayoshi Koga, Captain Colin Willard-Smith and Flight Officer Elwyn York already stood in a smart military line. Standing behind them Brent recognized two of the new American pilots; Lieutenant James Bender and Ensign Don Hoeffler. Both were young, superb pilots. The minister, rear admiral, Self Defense officer, the Englishmen and the Americans all eyed the women but remained silent. To Brent it was obvious the mysterious ship's "telegraph" had informed every man of the presence of the reporters; especially of the women.

Arlene, Lia and Alistair began to look around and scribble on pads. Arlene gestured to the far wall, actually the starboard side of the ship, where there were rows of shelves holding hundreds of white boxes covered with ideograms. "Ashes of the dead," Brent said in a soft voice perceptible to the three reporters. "Mostly of original members of the crew who had no families left when *Yonaga* returned."

Yoshi pointed to an altar positioned in the center of the shelves which were cluttered with icons. "A golden Buddha from the temple at Ise."

"The other figures?"

Yoshi's finger moved to a large robed figure of green jade carved with singular perfection and said, "The Shinto god Hachiman. She is a heroic oracle in our history. In the eighth century she saved the Empress Shotoku from the ruthless grasp of a monk named Dokyo." He tugged thoughtfully on his chin with a thumb and forefinger. "Their relationship was much like that between the Tsarina and the monk Rasputin in imperial Russia. Both empresses were captivated by what they thought were holy men. Fortunately, before Dokyo could seduce the Empress Shotoku, Hachiman interceded and Dokyo was banished to a monastery and the purity of the imperial line preserved." He pointed to a row of gods, some done in jade, some in gold and silver, and still others carved in ivory. "Some of our most important *kami*. Onamochi, the god of the sea, Ame no Mihashira 'the August Pillar of Heaven,' Homosubi who we call 'Growth of Flame,' Kukumochi known as 'Father of the Woods,' Inari who represents the fox. Perhaps, the

134

most important kami of all to *Yonaga* is Kompira who is the protector of sailors."

The reporters scribbled and then Lia looked up and pointed to a platform covered with white silk which was located directly in front of Admiral Fujita and the senior officers who flanked him. "That platform? What's it for?"

Before Brent could answer, the ranks of officers nearest the altar parted and Lieutenant Jimpei Yashiro stepped into view. He was dressed in flowing white robes of the finest silk. The collar blended into wide hempen wings and his waist was pulled in with a white *obi*. White sandals were on his feet. He walked slowly to the platform followed by the old Chief Engineer, Lieutenant Tatsuya Yoshida. A frail, bent "plank owner," Yoshida was carrying a dagger on a silk pillow much like a ring bearer at a wedding. However, no festive mood filled the chamber. In fact, a harsh silence, oppressive with its weight, bore down on everyone, filling not only the shrine, but the entire hangar deck as well. Not one tool or mechanic could be heard. No shouts. No mumbling of men conferring in groups. No rumble of auxiliary engines. No whine of blowers. Nothing at all.

"I say, something's twisted here," Alistair Cunningham said suspiciously.

"I don't like the looks of this," Lia added.

"The bloody bastards," Rear Admiral Whitehead muttered.

"Nineteenth century," Minister Shizuki Kaushika hissed.

"The Emperor did not expect this nor ask for this," Maritime Defense Force Lieutenant Tadayoshi Koga said.

Arlene glanced at Whitehead and Kaushika, and

135

then clutched Brent's arm and looked up into his eyes. "Something horrible is going to happen."

Brent stared down into the deep blue of her eyes for a long moment before answering. "It depends on your viewpoint."

"It's going to be bloody," she countered.

Yoshi Matsuhara gestured at the door. "The admiral told me to inform you that you are free to leave." His wave indicated all three reporters. "All of you can leave."

Alistair shook his head. "No," Lia said.

"I'm a reporter. This is my story. I'll stay," Arlene said with determination. Then with her face crossed by both curiosity and confusion, she looked up at Brent and gesticulated at Yashiro. "That man doesn't look very Japanese. He looks different."

"He *is* different," Brent answered. "He's from the Bonin Islands. One branch of his family descended from Yankee whalers."

"Oh, I see," Arlene said, scribbling furiously.

"A Yank!" Cunningham declared.

"Buggeration!" Elwyn York sputtered.

"Watch your tongue, Pilot Officer York," Willard-Smith scolded.

"Sorry guv'nor."

Followed by Yoshida, who walked with stiff knees, Lieutenant Jimpei Yashiro slowly mounted the platform, faced the altar and then prostrated himself. Yoshida stood patiently by his side. The heavy, enveloping silence returned.

Fujita's voice, suddenly surprisingly deep and showing new strength, broke the stillness. He directed his words at the reporters. "Some of you have mistakenly accused Lieutenant Yashiro of some kind of heinous crime. True, his guns sank a boat and killed some

136

people. This is of no consequence." He stabbed a bent finger at the altar. "Understand, the gods look down on the samurai and judge him only on his honor, loyalty and obedience to orders. There was a breach of discipline and Lieutenant Jimpei Yashiro has chosen to redeem himself through *seppuku*."

Arlene gasped and pressed the back of her hand over her mouth.

Lia said, "Well I'll be goddamned."

Brent could hear Elwyn York's voice, "I'll be stuffed. The bloody bugger's gonna cut 'is guts out."

Fujita continued speaking to the three reporters with an occasional glance at Koga, Kaushika and the British and American pilots. "To appreciate fully what you are about to witness, there are some things you *must* know about us. First, samurai means to be on guard against your enemies and your own weaknesses. We samurai are taught to strive for supreme moral character. This is how we serve our Emperor and set examples for the Japanese people and, at this moment, send a message to the entire world." He moved his eyes to the supplicant who was still prostrate on the platform. "And you must understand that we are committed to maintain the integrity of our karmas." He moved his eyes back to the reporters, explaining, "Karma is strengthened by one's honorable actions in this life and its purity determines one's fate in the next life. Dishonor sullies a samurai's karma and atonement can be only attained through *seppuku*. There is no other way." He pounded a tiny fist into his palm. "The samurai not only must master the vicissitudes of life, but he must also master death itself." He glared at Lia Mandel and spat, "Put that in your notes."

Every head turned to the reporters and shouts of "Banzai!" echoed from the massive bulkheads like the waves of a tsunami smashing against the shore. Lia Mandel stared back venomously at the admiral while Alistair Cunningham shuffled his feet awkwardly and muttered, "I say, that wasn't sporting." Arlene looked wide-eyed at Brent, her expression one of both hurt and anger. Brent took her arm and whispered, "It's Lia, not you."

Fujita silenced the bedlam with raised hands and then took a leather-bound volume from Katsube's trembling hand. He held the book over his head. "This is the *Hagakure*, the samurai's bible. *Hagakure* means 'Under the Leaves.' It dictates the way we live, the way we die. It defines the Code of Bushido." He lowered the book and clasped it prayerfully in both hands before him. "Bushido teaches the samurai he must perceive the moment of his own death, and, if there is a choice, it is always preferable to die quickly. This concept is ancient, the first *seppuku* performed by the great warrior Minamoto Tametomo in 1170. Since then untold thousands have followed, including the famous *seppukus* of the forty-seven Ronin in the eighteenth century, General Nogi in 1912 and Yukio Mishima kept the tradition alive in 1970." The black eyes swept over the entire assemblage. He raised the book in both hands as if he were trying to hand it to the gods. His strident voice filled the compartment, "The samurai must die with honor and find death quickly. There is nothing else worth recording."

Again, "Banzai!" filled the shrine and Arlene stared at Brent in wonder as he added his own "Banzai!" to the others.

Silence fell again as Lieutenant Jimpei Yashiro came slowly to his feet. He faced the admiral and the senior officers. However, Fujita's eyes were on the reporters. He said directly to Lia Mandel, "Lieutenant Jimpei

138

Yashiro has agreed that every detail of the ceremony should be explained to you in English." At that moment, Lieutenant Tatsuya Yoshida dropped slowly and painfully to his rickety knees and offered up the dagger. The condemned man lifted it reverently and removed a sheet of transparent rice paper wrapping. Yoshida dropped the pillow, placed both hands on the deck and tried to push himself to his feet. His scabbard caught on a line holding tufts of silk to the platform and the old man almost tumbled off the platform. Yashiro grabbed his arm, which was little more than bone wrapped in thin parchment, and pulled him to his feet.

Fujita continued speaking to the journalists. "We call the ceremonial dagger *wakizashi*. It is nine-and-one-half inches long with its point and both edges as sharp as a razor." Brent saw Arlene's pencil tremble as she took notes. Fujita's voice droned on as if it were resonating in the hollow confines of a great steel tube. "Lieutenant Yoshida is Lieutenant Yashiro's *kaishaku*. When Lieutenant Yashiro completes his ceremony, Lieutenant Yoshida must behead him with one clean stroke and if Lieutenant Yashiro falters in his procedure, the *kaishaku* must behead him immediately." Taking the cue, Yoshida clumsily tugged on the handle of his sword. It took Yashiro's help to free the blade.

Yashiro said to the admiral, "Sir, with utmost respect to you and to my best friend, Chief Engineer Lieutenant Tatsuya Yoshida, I would like to choose another *kaishaku*. I do not think the lieutenant is feeling well." The ranks of officers stiffened with shock at the unprecedented request. However, the frail chief engineer looked at Admiral Fujita imploringly. The old man obviously was not up to his task and everyone knew it.

Fujita stared at the applicant silently. And then asked,

139

"Who would you choose?"

"Do I have your permission, sir?"

"Yes."

Yoshida sighed a great sound of relief, sheathed his sword and was helped from the platform by a young ensign. Yashiro's eyes began to search the faces of the throng that stared back expectantly. Brent was gripped with a sudden mystic sense of predestiny, a distressing apprehension, a sense of unease and disquiet. As Yashiro's eyes met his, Brent's stomach churned wildly and he choked back the sudden sour taste that burned in his throat. Yashiro wanted him. He knew it as surely as he knew his feet were planted on the steel deck of *Yonaga*. He knew it as surely as he knew all eyes had followed the condemned man's stare to finally come to rest on him. He knew it as surely as he knew Arlene Spencer gripped his arm. He felt like an amateur performer suddenly thrust into the limelight, exposed to the stares of thousands of leering spectators.

Lieutenant Jimpei Yashiro's words made Brent's suspicions a reality, "I have Yankee antecedents in my ancestry." His tone became bitter. "Some of you have hated me for this." The Americans stirred and shifted their feet. "I choose the strongest, one who has rendered this service twice before with great strength and skill. One with the same blood as that which flows through my veins." Watching Yashiro raise his hand, Brent felt his stomach drop and his heart became a hammer trying to pound its way through his ribs. The finger was pointed directly at him as Jimpei Yashiro declared, "I choose Lieutenant Brent Ross!"

"No!" Arlene Spencer cried, tightening her grip.

"He's off his wick," Cunningham said.

"Bonkers," Willard-Smith agreed.

140

"Insanity!" Rear Admiral Whitehead said. Koga and Kaushika nodded agreement with him.

"It is his right," Yoshi Matsuhara declared.

"Could be interesting," Lia Mandel smirked. Clearly, the woman was enjoying the moment. "What a story," she added.

Lieutenant James Bender spoke for the first time, "They're all mad. This is the wrong century for this and you're of the wrong race. Don't do it Mister Ross."

Flight Officer York stabbed a finger at the giggling Lia. "This 'ag's gettin' 'er bags off over this. She's balmy."

"Silence!" Fujita shrieked, the single word bouncing from the bulkheads and overhead like a ricocheting missile. The blue ranks stiffened into a rigid, expectant silence. Fujita said to Brent Ross in a calm, controlled timbre, "Lieutenant Ross. You have been honored by Lieutenant Jimpei Yashiro."

Brent felt the grip of indecision. The thought of *kaishaku* repulsed him; yet, he was a member of the ship's company, honored by the title, "The American Samurai." He was respected by every member of the crew. He liked the officer from the Bonin Islands and knew to refuse him would be the ultimate insult. "You are the strongest, Mister Ross," Fujita persisted.

"Is this an order, Admiral?"

"You know me better than that, Mister Ross."

Brent heard whispers. "Don't do it," Whitehead said. "No! No!" Arlene Spencer said softly in his ear. And he heard Koga, Kaushika, Cunningham, Bender and Hoeffler all whisper their objections. Yoshi, Lia and the cockney held their silence.

Lieutenant Jimpei Yashiro stared directly at the young American. "Could you refuse me this, my friend?" he said, raising his arms imploringly. "The last

141

request of my life. The way to find an honorable death and perhaps add my spirit to those of so many of our comrades in the Yasakuni Shrine? Where is your *Yamato damashii?* Does it still live?" He stabbed a finger at Brent. "You sent Lieutenant Yoshiro Takii into the next world with one swing of his own sword. You removed him from his worldly misery and allowed him to join the ranks of heroes where he belonged. Can you not do the same for me?"

Takii's name dragged the entire horror from the dark recesses of Brent's subconscious where the American had tried to suppress it. It all came back. The crash of the bomber on the flight deck. The pilot burned like a piece of meat forgotten in a broiler by a careless house-wife. He had no nose, no lips, no ears. Lidless eyes sightless in charred hollows. His continuous, hideous pain relieved only by the intravenous flow of drugs. The old pilot begged for death, begged for an honorable sa-murai's death instead of the living hell. Brent grasped the sword. The single swing that dispatched Takii-san and nearly cut through the bed as well.

Jimpei Yashiro continued, "And Brent-san. Have you forgotten that you dispatched Lieutenant Nobutake Konoye in the same way? I saw you do it on this platform when he committed *seppuku*. Konoye, a man who hated you, fought you with his fists out there," he waved, "on the hangar deck. But he respected you and knew you would be the best *kaishaku* on the ship." He pointed at the sword hanging at the American's side. "You carry his sword." He raised both arms upward from his sides in a reverential manner as if invoking a *kami*. "And I am your friend. You have known me as long as you knew Lieutenant Takii. Can you deny me? Can you deny your duty?"

142

Brent gripped the leather wrapped *tang* of the fabled Konoye blade, his by the right of *kaishaku*. Four-hundred-years old, it had fulfilled its destiny of blood and honor many times over. The Konoye sword was extraordinary, fashioned by the master swordsmith Yosumitsu in 1581, it was a "pedigreed" blade, a Stradivarius of Japanese killing steel. Its curved cutting edge had been fashioned much like the famous Damascus blade. Of layered and tempered metal, folded and drawn eleven times, it was as finely wrought as a polished gem, as sharp as Bodhidharma's wit. Gazing up at Yashiro who stared down at him beseechingly, Brent felt a force emanating from the black eyes as if he were hypnotized and drawn to a sorcerer. He stepped forward. The move was met with wild yells of "Banzai!"

"No!" Arlene shouted. He pulled away from her grasp stiffly like an automaton and walked toward the platform.

Whitehead's voice joined the uproar, "This is insane! Stop!"

Fujita's voice cut through the noise and silenced it. "Lieutenant Ross has made his decision. Please observe military silence or leave this shrine!"

Brent mounted the platform and faced Lieutenant Jimpei Yashiro. The supplicant bowed. Brent returned the bow. Yashiro gestured and the American pulled his sword from its jeweled scabbard. The hard thin metal rang out with a high chime-like sound as if it were joyously celebrating its freedom and anticipating its task. Yashiro sank to the platform, knees on a white silk pillow. He raised the *wakizashi*, examined it carefully and placed it on the platform before him. Brent stood to his right side, sword at his side. He felt a strange calmness, as if he truly belonged on the platform.

Yashiro addressed the onlookers with the mandatory confessional speech. "I and I alone was responsible for the destruction of the boat and the deaths of twenty-seven innocent people. I and I alone am responsible for disobeying the orders of our commanding officer. I ordered my mount to fire. For this crime, I disembowel myself." His eyes moved over the entire group. "I am pleased that so many of you are here to be my witnesses."

He pulled a slip of paper from under his *obi*. He looked at the Americans and British. "My death poem," he explained, holding up the paper. He read, "All of nature, the sea, the sky are one, merging into an infinite now as does life into death. Joyfully, I go to join the captain of the black ship." He dropped the paper, glanced up at Brent. The American nodded his readiness and gripped the *tang* with both hands. Yashiro stripped his upper garments, tucking his sleeves under his knees. He nodded at the admiral.

Fujita addressed the Westerners. "He did that so that he will not fall forward, giving the *kaishaku* a difficult stroke."

"My God," Whitehead muttered.

"Can't be happening," Arlene whispered back.

Yashiro picked up the knife and held it in both hands. He turned it, stared at it wistfully with an amalgam of curiosity and near affection. There was no fear to be read there. Gripping the handle tightly, he placed the point to the left side of his abdomen. He held his breath and stared at the admiral.

Casually, Fujita's voice rang in the chamber as if he were describing a new book, the cuisine of a fine restaurant. "First will come the horizontal cut from left to right. This will release the 'seat of the mind.' Then, the blade must be turned to cut upward to complete the dis-

144

embowelment. Finally, the *kaishaku* will consummate the *seppuku* with a single swing of his killing blade. Ideally, the *kaishaku* would leave a sliver of flesh intact to prevent the head from rolling. However, Lieutenant Yashiro has requested this convention not be observed. Lieutenant Ross is to swing with all his power and execute a clean beheading." Brent raised the blade over his right shoulder and crouched in the classic samurai killing stance.

There was mumbling and gasps from the Americans and British. Fujita waved them to silence. Lia Mandel leaned forward, eyes wide, face flushed, leering like a spectator in the Roman Coliseum waiting to see lions devour Christians. Arlene choked back a sour welling and took notes with a hand that almost defied control. She felt Whitehead's hand on one shoulder, Matsuhara's on the other. All stared at the condemned man in silence.

The expression on Yashiro's obdurate face changed. His jaw tightened, lips became a determined slash. Perspiration like a beaded curtain ran down his forehead. He pushed on the blade with both hands. With agonizing slowness the point of the blade penetrated and released a gush of blood, staining the white robes and dripping onto the platform. Then with new resolve, lips pulled back from clenched white teeth, Yashiro pushed the blade in deep, pulled hard to the right and stopped, breathing in gasps like a poorly conditioned runner trying to complete a marathon. Blood poured from the cut like water from a broken dam. His face was red, veins on his forehead and neck bulging as if they were trying to burst through the skin. A hesitation. Brent raised the blade. Stopped. Then the cut upward followed by intestines, assailing Brent's nostrils with the sour stench of gastric juices. Incredibly, Yashiro actually pulled the blade from his body and dropped it into the gore piled on the deck. Deliberately, he stretched out his neck.

Staring down at the knobs of vertebrae bulging through the skin of Yashiro's neck, Brent tensed the muscles of his arms and stood transfixed as if frozen by a sudden Arctic blast. This was his moment. Something inside of him screamed, "This is wrong! Wrong!" Or was it Whitehead? He could hear Arlene crying and then Whitehead definitely shouted, "No, Brent!" But his duty was stretched out before him. His honor as an officer, a samurai, a man, was on the line. He could not fail now. And the sword became a live thing in his hands, eager to slash and kill. It had done this before with Konoye and Takii. It had its own mind, its own destiny and he was only an instrument in its fulfillment. Still, he hesitated.

Fujita broke through. "Now, Lieutenant. Now!"

The voice of command banished all conflict. Suddenly, he wanted to feel the impact of sharpened steel on Yashiro's neck. His ears hummed with the rush of blood and he felt the flush of it on his face as a killing lust gripped him. He was suddenly a killing machine. He swung the blade with all his great power. The thin steel edge hummed almost gaily through its arc, hitting the neck with the sound of a cleaver striking beef in a butcher shop. The blade was sharp, the swordsman strong, the big neck offered little resistance. The razor-like edge sliced through skin, bone, cartilage and muscle like a knife through warm butter. Blood sprayed upward, sprinkling Brent's face and the front of his tunic. There was a thump as the head hit the platform, twisted awkwardly to the edge, fell to the deck and dutifully rolled across it until it finally came to rest at Admiral Fujita's feet. Both eyes stared up at the admiral.

Relieved of the weight of the head, Yashiro's body

146

straightened bizarrely as if still alive and trying to rise to its feet. Jugulars hosed blood like twin red geysers from a still beating heart. Then, as if made of rags, it tumbled onto its side, arms outflung, jerking spasmodically in the usual autonomic spasms of the newly killed.

Breathing hard, eyes wide and unblinking, Brent stepped back from the headless body, finally stilled by the embrace of death. The bleeding was diminishing, but quarts of blood had flowed across the platform and spilled onto the deck. Brent wondered that a human body could hold so much blood.

An ensign stepped close to the platform and offered up a towel. Brent took it and stared at it dumbly. Then slowly he wiped his face, dabbed at his uniform and finally cleaned the blade. He replaced the sword in its scabbard and came to attention facing the admiral.

"Banzai! Banzai!" rang through the chamber. Brent bowed to the admiral and turned to the group of visitors. Whitehead was holding his head, Cunningham was talking to York, Koga and Kaushika stood transfixed, Bender and Hoeffler just stood quietly staring with disbelief. Arlene Spencer was clutching her face in both hands. Lia Mandel stood as rigid as a statue, eyes big and round like saucers, face the color of a ripe apple. Her lips were twisted into a sensuous leer as if she were in the final throes of an erotic experience.

Slowly, the young American descended from the platform. His emotions were as conflicting as the wild seas in the eye of a hurricane; triumph and distress, joy and melancholy rushing in waves to dash against each other in a mad sea without coherence, defying logic and rationale. True, he had pleased his Japanese comrades, but, just as truly, he had shocked and disgusted his countrymen. He knew he had to leave this place; find privacy, solace, a bottle. He walked to the door through ranks of cheering officers. He seemed to be in a tunnel of blue, his ears assaulted by the shrieks of wild animals.

As he left, he heard Fujita's voice ring through the shrine, "Put that in your notes!"

Chapter Seven

Just minutes later Yoshi Matsuhara caught Brent in "flag country" at the moment the American reached the door to his cabin. "This way, my friend," the pilot said, grasping Brent's arm and steering him to his own cabin.

Slowly Brent entered Yoshi's cabin and sank into a chair pushed next to the room's one small table. His eyes wandered over the Spartan furnishings of the small compartment; narrow bunk, writing desk folded against the bulkhead, bulkhead mounted telephone, a door leading to the tiny head, a small table and two chairs, and bookshelves. Jammed with books, the shelves lined every available inch of wall space. Yoshi had a great intellect and insatiable thirst for knowledge. But, tragically, the driving force was his search for some reason behind the brutal murder of his beloved Kimio Urshazawa that afternoon in Ueno Park. His quest was still concentrated on the teachings of Bodhidharma, advocating the path to enlightenment was found through contemplation. Yoshi spent hours with his body locked in the lotus position, unblinking eyes fixed on an invisible spot on the bulkhead. No one would ever know what he found, or, if he found anything at all. He did emerge from the sessions somewhat relaxed and occasionally Brent thought he actually detected a trace of peace on the stern face. For this, Brent was thankful to Bodhidharma. But it was only a momentary thing, for their work of preparing and carrying out the killings of other men erased all traces of tranquility from every one of them.

"Chivas Regal straight up," Matsuhara said, pouring two drinks and seating himself opposite Brent. He placed the bottle on the table and held up his glass, "To Lieutenant Jimpei Yashiro. He honored us all." The men drank. Brent tabled his drink and then brought it to his lips again, draining it with one gulp. Yoshi recharged it.

"I didn't honor him."

"You were splendid, Brent-san."

"I fucked up."

"Nonsense."

"I stopped. I made him wait."

"A second or two. I've seen it happen before. It is a natural reaction, Brent-san."

"I didn't hesitate with Konoye or Takii."

Yoshi shrugged. "It may have seemed like an eternity to you, but to us, it looked as if you took a moment to gather your strength and isolate the target. Remember, Yashiro was moving and the blow must be delivered precisely in the center of the neck. I have seen horrible miscalculations by *kaishakus* who hurried their strokes. Some hit shoulders, others the skull. But you struck with great accuracy. It was a beautiful beheading."

"Yeah, gorgeous." Brent drained his glass. The pilot refilled it. Brent continued sarcastically, "The Americans and British were delighted with my performance. Koga and that Minister Shizuki Kaushika, too."

"That bothers you?"

"Of course."

"Lia Mandel showed no lack of enthusiasm, Brent-san."

Brent snickered, the spreading warmth of the fine scotch finally beginning to relax his bunched muscles. "She has the heart of a cannibal. I expected to hear her yell, 'Bravo! Encore!' Maybe, she'll give me a good write-up." He sipped his drink while his friend studied his face. The sarcasm became caustic, "Maybe she'll get me on the Johnny Carson Show. 'America's finest *kaishaku*. If you want a head chopped off, call on good old Brent Ross, beheader par excellence'."

"This moment will pass. Brent-san." The pilot stared over Brent's head, eyes squinting as if he were examining an object in the far distance. "Always remember, each moment follows another like beads on a string, blending with the others until it is lost in the past."

Brent looked up at his friend with admiration in his eyes. "Always the poet, the philosopher, Yoshi-san."

"I try."

Brent knuckled his forehead. "I hope you're right."

"You know I am right." The pilot palmed an annoying strand of black hair back from his forehead. He waved at his massive library, "Goethe said, 'The present moment is a powerful goddess'." He sipped his drink. "Don't let her overpower you."

Brent smiled at his friend's uncanny knowledge and retorted with one of his own favorite quotes, "Dostoyevski said, 'The soul of a poet is in his aching tooth'."

Yoshi chuckled. "You really believe that?"

Brent rubbed his palms together as if he were trying to warm the flesh. "Not really, Yoshi-san. I think it's in his aching ass."

Yoshi did not laugh. His voice took on a grave timbre. "Wisdom is a repeatedly appearing and disappearing

151

mirage on the road of learning. Men with knowledge but lacking wisdom are like a blind man with a lantern."

Brent's forefinger tapped his glass restlessly with a high ringing sound and his voice sharpened. "It's not necessary to quote Bodhidharma to me. I have never claimed to be a 'wise man'."

"I meant no offense, Brent-san. I meant to say that through Zen, through meditation, you can find enlightenment. It is your individual quest and will come to you in intuitive flashes like the sun bursting through a thick cloud cover."

"You have told me this before, Yoshi-san." The restless fingers found his ear, tugged on a lobe. He stared into his friend's intense black eyes. This was the only man privy to his innermost thoughts. He shifted his gaze and spoke to the far bulkhead almost wistfully. "You know, Yoshi-san, I really believe that all men are almost totally ignorant about their place in this mad universe, if there is any reason to be found."

The pilot nodded encouragement. Brent pushed on. "I think that any child knows as much of the cosmic truth as Einstein did."

"But we can seek modesty, new perspectives, which to me are the definitive wisdom, and try to see the part or the moment in the light of the whole. Perhaps, here, we can find what you and all men seek."

"But have you found it?"

The pilot shook his head. "I have not lived long enough and, perhaps, never will. No man ever will. But I have had flashes and caught glimpses. You are right about Einstein. Western science hides behind his formulas. I am convinced that only meditation allows us to reach cosmic truths that Western science can never reach. Modern science is nothing but the disintegration of certainty in a cold, empty cosmos."

Brent sighed. "I know, Yoshi-san. Remember, I have studied Zen, too."

"You believe?"

Brent sipped his drink. "I don't know what to believe, Yoshi-san."

The pilot hunched forward. "Give Bodhidharma a chance."

"I have. Along with Jesus, Allah, Izanami, Izanagi, Osiris, Isis, Zarathustra and the rest of them. There's quite a smorgasbord out there." He grinned at his friend.

They both chuckled. Yoshi, encouraged by his friend's improving spirits, opened a new topic. "You are disturbed by Arlene Spencer, Brent-san?"

Not quite sure of how to interpret his friend's double entendre, Brent toyed with his drink, swirling the amber liquid until it peaked almost to the lip of the glass. "I'm not quite sure of what you mean, Yoshi-san," he finally admitted.

"Any way you want it, Brent-san."

The American shrugged at his friend's intransigence and reached into his pocket and removed Arlene's business card. "I was to phone her tomorrow for an appointment." He laughed bitterly. "Fat chance now." He flipped the card toward a wastebasket in the corner. The card sailed across the room and over the basket like an errant Frisbee. "Can't even hit the fuckin' basket," Brent groused.

"She's that important?"

"Yes."

"You have only known her for a few hours."

"True." Brent's blue eyes caught and held the steady, perceptive stare of his best friend. He bared more of his soul. "In our business life goes by at double time and you know it, Yoshi. We live it wherever we can find it. That woman liked me and I wanted to see her again."

"You would put a woman before duty?"

"You know me better than that." The young lieutenant sipped his drink. "Yashiro's parted company from his head, hasn't he?"

"Of course, of course, my friend. That is not what I meant." He entwined his fingers and his thumbs began to duel each other. "I mean we should not be swayed from the righteous path of Bushido by anything, especially a pretty face."

Brent nodded. "Of course, Yoshi-san. But it wasn't just Arlene Spencer. It was Admiral Whitehead, Bender, Hoeffler. They thought I was a butcher."

"Let them," Yoshi bristled. "Let them! You are a samurai. You have earned this honor by deeds of great valor. If they do not understand, they are not worthy of you. Don't forget that the *Hagakure* tells us, 'A warrior is a man who does not hold his life in regret'."

Brent nodded his understanding of his friend's quote. "I have studied the book and I believe the truth in those words, old friend." He held up his glass in a salute. Yoshi returned the salute and they drank.

Brent studied the pilot. He looked tired and haggard. "Take liberty with me tomorrow, old friend. We'll find a good restaurant, get drunk, chase broads."

Yoshi smiled warmly. He was pleased with Brent's brightening demeanor. "Sorry, Brent-san. I must be at Tsuchuira first thing in the morning. In fact, I will leave within the hour and stay at the airfield tonight. All group commanders must meet with their new pilots and supervise training. And don't forget, besides Americans, we have two Frenchmen, a Greek and two Germans and more foreign pilots are coming." He sighed. "I like having them, but we are presented with a new set of communications problems."

"I thought they were all fluent in English."

"They are. But, still, they are not familiar with our methods; our radio calls and procedures, terminology, tactics." He took a drink. "Why, the Germans still expect to use the old *schwarm* tactics."

"Why, that dates back to World War Two. Hugo Sperrle developed it during the Spanish Civil War. The British called it the 'finger four.' Two elements of two fighters operating as a unit. Actually, our American pilots have copied it, but won't admit it."

"You amaze me, Brent-san. How did you know?"

Brent shrugged. "Open any history."

"Any history," Yoshi repeated sarcastically, but obviously impressed by his young friend's knowledge.

Yoshi reached for the bottle and tilted it toward Brent's half-empty glass. Brent pulled his drink back, shaking his head negatively. He had had enough and another question had entered his mind. "Yoshi-san," he said. "You have one helluva big operation going on at Tokyo International and Tsuchiura."

The pilot pursed his lips and then released them with a small popping sound. "I'm training three-hundred-seventy fighter pilots and more new men arrive every day. Iwata has over two-hundred new dive bomber crews and Yagoto is training nearly the same number of torpedo bomber crews."

Brent scratched a spot behind his ear thoughtfully. "I know we need replacements, but we still can only handle one-hundred-fifty aircraft. Why so many?"

The pilot shrugged. "Orders, Brent. Admiral Fujita has some —" He was interrupted by the shrill ring of the bulkhead-mounted phone. With the ship's telephone system patched into Tokyo's massive network, Brent expected his friend to be called from Tsuchiura or Tokyo International Airport. He soon discovered he was wrong.

"Commander Yoshi Matsuhara here," the pilot said. Yoshi shifted his eyes to Brent. "Yes, Admiral. Immediately, sir."

Brent knew the nature of the message before Yoshi could open his mouth. "The admiral wants to see me," the American said with resignation.

"You are clairvoyant, my friend. He wants to see you immediately."

Brent rose on steady legs despite the effects of the liquor. In fact, he was surprisingly clearheaded and steady. The only effects he realized from the scotch was a relaxation of his tensions. He turned toward the door but was halted by Yoshi's voice. "Brent-san, I suggest you wash your face and remove your gloves."

Brent looked at his gloves. They were stained with blood and he could see blood still remaining on his sleeves despite the cleaning he had done in the Shrine of Infinite Salvation. How did he miss the gloves? Obviously, he had been in such a state he had done a poor job of it. He walked into the tiny head and stared into the mirror. There were still bits of coagulated blood clinging to his face like freckles. Pulling off his gloves, he scrubbed his face with a wash towel and wiped the blood from the sleeves of his tunic. He threw his gloves to Yoshi. "Take care of these, Yoshi-san," he said.

The pilot slapped him on the back. "You have done well, today, Brent-san. Remember that."

Brent smiled and left the room.

The old admiral was seated behind his desk. Compared to Brent's and Yoshi's cabins, the admiral's was very spacious. The desk was of polished oak, deck carpeted. Similar to Yoshi's cabin, bookcases were prominent, but not as dominant. The admiral's incredible library was jammed into an adjacent cabin of a long dead flag officer. It was a storehouse of military knowledge, especially histories of The Greater East Asia War. Charts occupied most of the bare bulkhead space above the books. However, a portrait of Emperor Akihito was mounted behind the old sailor's chair. A small shrine in the usual log cabin configuration hung next to it.

The admiral looked up from some documents, removed his old-fashioned steel-rimmed glasses and waved a single seaman guard out of the room. He gestured for Brent to seat himself in one of four leather chairs bolted to the deck in front of his desk. The old man's face was grim. "You were upset today, Brent-san."

"True, sir. But I had a long talk with Commander Matsuhara and I really feel better about it." He did not mention the liquor.

"You honored Jimpei Yashiro."

"He honored me."

The old man's smile showed obvious relief. "Spoken like a samurai." Then his smile vanished, "The Americans and British do not understand the samurai." He shrugged and turned his palms up in a gesture of hopelessness. "I tried to explain, but their minds are walled off by their own dogma and prejudices. It is impossible for truth to penetrate." His smile returned, "But you understand. You are one of us."

"Thank you, sir. But, sometimes, I am not sure that I understand myself."

The old man nodded solemnly. "Of course, Brent-san. You are a mixture of both Occident and orient. Christianity, Buddhism and Shinto all dwell within you side-by-side. This mixture of values and dogma have given you enormous strength."

Brent was taken aback by the compliment. The old admiral was stingy with praise and, suddenly, he was lavishing it on him. Staring at the face cut by time into deep crevices and ridges like a countryside ravaged by a vicious storm, Brent was seized by a queer pang, almost of conscience, to see the evident pleasure Fujita experienced at the sight of him. It was odd to know he was considered a valuable aide, admired as a warrior and, at times he felt he was regarded with genuine affection. Brent answered with a simple truth. "Sometimes they clash, sir."

Fujita's answer was what he expected from the oriental mind. "Only to make you a more complete man, Brent-san. Enhance your karma." He tugged at a single white hair dangling from the point of his narrow chin, his mind changing direction in its usual mercurial fashion. "You have liberty tomorrow?"

"Yes, sir."

"Take a five day leave. You know we must take on stores, bring the Engineering Department up to top efficiency. You can have the time."

Brent knew what was behind the admiral's largesse. The old man was convinced his junior NIS liaison man had been pushed to the edge and needed rest. He had seen this in the old man before. He had an uncanny mind that could probe and evaluate you almost as if the old man could climb into your head. Strangely, Brent felt resentment. The offer could be construed as preferential treatment. "Respectfully, sir. I have a new cryptographer and I must supervise his training. And, sir, my absence would leave the entire burden on Admiral Whitehead. With your permission, I will remain on port and starboard liberty."

A rare smile rearranged the wrinkles. The ancient sailor was pleased with his subordinate's devotion to duty. "You have liberty tomorrow?"

"Yes, sir."

"Good."

They were interrupted by a knock. Brent opened the door and two intelligence men were in the passageway; Horace Mayfield of the CIA was in the doorway and Colonel Irving Bernstein of Mossad, Israel's intelligence service, stood behind him. The pair had been dispatched by Admiral Fujita ten weeks earlier on secret missions to Washington and Tel Aviv. Brent suspected their missions had been concerned with the Libyan poison gas works at Rabta. Fujita had been terribly disturbed by the plant for over a year. He had vowed to "take it out." The admiral waved the two newcomers to a pair of chairs. Seating themselves, both agents placed attaché cases on the carpet.

Brent did not like Mayfield, and the CIA man showed his own dislike by shouldering past the American without any greeting or even sign of recognition. In turn, Brent ignored him. Traditionally, the CIA distrusted and was jealous of NIS. Beyond that, it was well-known the man was an alcoholic and a libertine, picking up trollops on any street corner, in any country. Brent had returned from many long cruises as horny as a "hound sniffing a bitch in heat." But he had never ever considered paying a professional for her services. It was not just pride at stake, but Brent felt his manhood was on the line as well. Anyway, he had never found it too difficult to find his way to bed with an enthusiastic volunteer.

The evidence of Mayfield's alcoholism was written across his face like a billboard for everyone to see: purple veins ridging in his bulbous nose; cheeks a mass of broken blood vessels; hazel eyes puffy and bloodshot. He was a short fat man, not even his expensive three-piece Brooks Brothers suit could conceal the extent of his dissipation. Mayfield's slumped shoulders and beefy chest angled out to a huge stomach which Brent suspected was not only layered with fat but gorged with organs swollen by the man's consumption of liquor as well. Only a few strands of brown remained in the sparse white hair vainly combed across the nearly bald pate in a futile attempt to hide the ruinous hair loss. Brent knew Mayfield was about fifty, but he appeared to be at least ten years older. The admiral distrusted Mayfield, but he was the only liaison Washington would send. Fujita had no alternative but to keep him on staff.

The Israeli Intelligence officer, Colonel Irving Bernstein, was everything Mayfield should have been. He grasped Brent's hand and said, *"Shalom."* Brent returned the friendly greeting with a smiling, *"Shalom aleichem,* Colonel."

Although he was at least ten years older than the CIA man, Bernstein's sparsely bearded face was unlined, brown eyes clear and alert. Dressed in his usual Israeli Army desert fatigues, his slender build still appeared muscular and athletic. The man defined the word survivor. He had survived the Warsaw ghetto uprising in 1942. He had survived three years at Auschwitz where his mother, father and sister were gassed and incinerated. He had survived the Arab-Israeli wars of 1947 and 1948, the Six Day War, the Yom Kippur War, innumerable skirmishes and ambushes. The six blue numbers

160

the Germans had tattooed onto his right forearm the day he entered Auschwitz were visible anytime he wore a short-sleeved shirt or rolled up his cuffs. "Jew number nine-hundred-sixty-two-thousand-four-hundred-twenty-one," he would tell anyone foolish enough to ask.

While the newcomers seated themselves, the admiral picked up one of three phones on his desk and called Rear Admiral Byron Whitehead and asked him to report immediately to his cabin. Obviously, an important conference was about to begin. Brent knew nothing about it and expected to be dismissed. However, the admiral remained silent, examining some documents on his desk.

While the four officers waited, Horace Mayfield examined Brent from head to foot. "Heard you chopped off another head today, Mister Ross," he said sneering. "What's the count now? Four?"

Brent stared at the florid face and could not conceal the revulsion he felt. "No, three."

"I counted four men. Konoye, Takii, Yashiro and Haj Abu al Sahdi. I saw you lop off Haj Abu al Sahdi's head. Remember?"

Bernstein and the admiral stared at Brent Ross. As Brent expected, the admiral remained silent, curiously staring, and Brent suspected, anticipating some pleasure in what might develop into a rancorous exchange.

"Haj Abu al Sahdi was an Arab. He didn't count," Brent said matter-of-factly.

Colonel Irving Bernstein guffawed. "Never have I heard a truer statement."

The CIA agent ignored Bernstein and said to Brent, "You have a way with a blade, young man."

"Like to try me sometime?"

Fujita and Bernstein chuckled.

"Now see here, that was out of line," Mayfield blustered. "I knew Yashiro. His death was a waste of a fine officer. A terrible, tragic death." He stabbed a finger at Brent. "That's what I mean, young man."

Fujita broke his silence. "That is not really true, Mister Mayfield."

"Not true?"

The old man's fingers found the single white hair hanging from his chin. "No," he said. "The greatest tragedy is not in dying, but in never having lived. Lieutenant Jimpei Yashiro had lived fully and died gloriously." Both scabrous hands found the desk and the fingers spread in a crooked pattern. The old man hunched forward on his elbows. "When I was just a child, Emperor Meiji personally issued a rescript to the Sendai Division. It has become a sacred axiom for the samurai." He leaned back and his eyes found the overhead. "The Emperor's words were, 'Death is as light as a feather, duty is as heavy as the mountain'." His gaze returned to Mayfield and silence filled the room.

Mayfield said, "Yashiro found his feather."

There was a knock and Rear Admiral Byron Whitehead entered. He greeted the intelligence officers and quickly found the last empty chair and stared expectantly at the admiral. Then he glanced at Brent and was about to speak when the admiral preempted him. "We are not here to discuss the recent demise of Lieutenant Jimpei Yashiro." He glanced at Brent. "In fact, that topic is closed. There are far more important matters to occupy this group."

Whitehead sank back. Bernstein and Mayfield stared at Brent Ross. Fujita sensed their unvoiced question. "Lieutenant Brent Ross will remain for this discussion."

"I object, sir," Mayfield said. He patted his attaché

162

case. "These matters are of the utmost secrecy. Most sensitive, sir. The fewer who know—"

"Please do not try to dictate to me, Mister Mayfield," Fujita bristled. "I have made my decision." His eyes moved from Mayfield to Bernstein and back to Mayfield. He spoke impatiently, "Your reports, gentlemen." He gestured to the Israeli.

Bernstein stood and pulled a sheaf of papers from his attaché case. He spoke in a deep, strong voice. "The poison gas works at Rabta is operating again. Apparently, Admiral, you were right when you suggested the reports of a great fire were nothing but a smoke screen to conceal the fact the plant is still in production."

"Mustard and nerve gas?" Fujita suggested.

"Correct, sir. Mustard gas sears the skin and lungs and can cause hemorrhaging. A man drowns in his own blood. Nerve gases attack the central nervous system, inhibiting breathing and usually causing a quick death."

"I know," Fujita said, waving a hand impatiently. And then with a voice ladened with sarcasm, "Of course these weapons were banned by the 1925 Geneva Convention. I was there. I helped write it."

"Everyone ignores it," Bernstein said.

"Naturally," Fujita agreed. "It was only a solemn international agreement made by men of honor and integrity." His laughter rang hard as steel.

Mayfield glared at Bernstein. Not only was the CIA jealous of NIS, there was sometimes near open hostility with Mossad, an organization that operated on a minuscule budget, yet still managed to outperform the CIA in nearly every part of the world. "How in hell do you know so much about Rabta?" Mayfield spat. "Your aircraft don't have the range to overfly the goddamned place."

Bernstein smiled benignly. "We have agents working

in the factory. They smuggle their reports out to Chad. From there they are relayed to us by French operatives. No wireless. Couriers only."

"Production? Production?" Fujita interjected impatiently.

Bernstein glanced at his documents and sighed. "We estimate three-thousand tons of mustard gas can be produced a year and two-thousand-five-hundred tons of nerve gas."

"Sacred Buddha," Fujita said. "Why, that is enough for thousands of bombs and artillery shells."

The Israeli nodded his agreement. A new thought furrowed across Fujita's brow and brought a gleam to his eyes. "Storage? Do you know where they store it?"

"Most of it is stored in four large warehouses within a kilometer of the plant. We have reports the ordnance is assembled in one of these buildings and stored in the other three. Two brigades of paratroopers guard the facility and they have built a defense in depth; guard towers, barbed wire, tanks, sensors connected to automatic weapons. It would be impossible to storm by anything less than an armored division, perhaps a corps." Bernstein clutched the back of his neck and tightened his jaw. "Of course, it is totally impossible for Israel to mount an assault of this magnitude. And, for good reason, the Libyans don't fear air raids. Our aircraft don't have the range and *Yonaga* is on the other side of the world. They feel very secure."

Fujita pulled on the single hair so hard, he grimaced with the sharp pain. "We shall see how secure they are," he muttered, turning to Horace Mayfield and gesturing with bent fingers as if the CIA man were a mannequin and he was pulling him to his feet.

Clutching a number of reports, Mayfield stood while

the Israeli seated himself. Modulating his husky, whiskey-addled voice into a low-pitched authoritative timbre, he began, "I can get you your sixteen North American B-25s, Mitchells."

"B-25s?" Rear Admiral Whitehead and Brent blurted.

Mayfield ignored the two officers and said to Admiral Fujita, "The first will be flown to Betio Island in the Tarawa Atoll in about a week. They should all be there fully manned and ready for operations within three weeks. Every security precaution has been taken. In fact, even the natives have already been evacuated to neighboring atolls."

Fujita said to Rear Admiral Whitehead. "You were on the *Hornet* when the Doolittle raid was launched against Japan in 1942?"

"I was Assistant Air Operations officer. But I don't understand—"

"The first aircraft, General Doolittle's, had the shortest run and had no trouble taking off."

"They had extra fuel tanks in their bomb bays, Admiral, and they were stripped down to compensate. No radios, only twin fifty-caliber machine guns in the upper turret and a single thirty-caliber in the nose. They had five man crews and only carried a ton of bombs and, also, we were steaming into a stiff head wind which helped to get them airborne. It lifted them right off the deck."

Fujita again amazed everyone with his knowledge of World War II minutia. "It was a force eight wind on the Beaufort Scale, thirty-nine to forty-six miles per hour, and Doolittle used exactly four-hundred-twenty-seven feet of flight deck." He struck the desk with a tiny fist. "There is no reason why the B-25 cannot take off from *Yonaga*'s flight deck. We can give it another one-hundred

165

feet and if necessary, make thirty-two knots. Give them all the wind they need."

Every man now suspected what the admiral planned; every eye found the chart of North Africa attached to a bulkhead to the left of the admiral. Whitehead pointed, "You're not thinking of attacking Rabta? Why you'd have to enter the Med with a deck load of medium bombers." He slapped his head in a gesture of frustration. "You'd be seen by a million eyes, draw bombers like flies to honey. And with a deck load of bombers, you couldn't launch a single fighter. Even if you had catapults, you could only operate a few fighters." He dropped his hands in a hopeless gesture. "No chance. We'd lose everything."

Admiral Fujita slowly pushed himself to his feet. It seemed to Brent the old man moved a little faster, had an almost youthful gleam in his eyes and bounce to his step. This always happened when the old man smelled action or sniffed blood. He had a plan to attack Rabta, but on the surface, it appeared impracticable. He had deliberately goaded Whitehead to use him as a sounding board; to play his attack scenario off of him like a straight man in an old vaudeville act. He picked up a rubber-tipped pointer and stabbed it at the chart. "We will take on the B-25s and steam around Cape Horn, staying well clear of shipping lanes." Everyone stared wide-eyed as the tip traced the journey around the South American continent, into the South Atlantic and then north. However, it did not head for the Straits of Gibraltar. Instead, the tip traced a line well west of the Cape Verde Islands, split the thousand mile gap between the Canary Islands and the Azores and then turned sharply east and stopped just off the coast of Morocco. "We will launch the B-25s here, one-hundred

166

miles off the coast of Morocco and north of Agadir."

Whitehead rose to the bait. "Impossible, Admiral," he declared. "My God, the Doolittle mission only had a six-hundred-mile run-in." He waved at the chart. "Why, here, in this mad scheme, your run-in would be well over a thousand miles. Over Morocco and Algeria."

"Fourteen-hundred miles," Fujita corrected him. "We will fly over the interiors of Morocco and Algeria and over the Sahara Desert. These regions are virtually uninhabited. There is very little chance of detection."

Whitehead would not remain silent. "The B-25 only has a range of fifteen-hundred miles, Admiral." He glared at the chart and spoke with a voice loaded with irony, "What are they going to do? Bomb the plant and then land at the nearest friendly field?"

"Precisely."

"Precisely?" Whitehead exploded in exasperation. His voice rose, "It's a one way mission. You'll throw away sixteen aircraft, their crews and probably *Yonaga*, to boot."

Fujita dropped the tip of the pointer to the deck. "I wanted your reaction, your opinion, and there is validity in what you say. However, we will not lose the crews." He returned to the chart and stabbed the Mediterranean just north of Libya. "We have an agreement with the Italian government for any of our aircraft to land in Italy. The B-25s will carry Japanese markings and will land in Sicily."

Whitehead punched a finger at the chart. "That's still at least a seventeen-hundred-mile mission. They'll run out of—"

"Negative," Fujita interrupted. "These aircraft have been modified." He beckoned to Mayfield. "Give us the B-25's specifications, Mister Mayfield."

167

The old sailor returned to his chair.

Pleased to be the center of attention, the CIA agent cast a triumphant glance at both Bernstein and Brent Ross before he read. "We will take aboard a collection of B-25s, a mix of 'B' and 'C' models. All were manufactured during World War II, but are in mint condition. Seventy-three of these bombers have been preserved by flying clubs and museums all over the United States. It is estimated two-hundred more are scattered all over the world in various states of repair and disrepair." He glanced at his notes. "The wingspan is sixty-seven feet, nine inches, length fifty-three feet, height fifteen feet, maximum speed three-hundred-twenty —"

"Three-hundred-twenty?" Whitehead challenged. "That plane can't do over two-hundred-eighty."

The CIA man waved the rear admiral off imperiously like a man chasing an annoying gnat. He droned on, "Take-off weight thirty-five thousand, forty-four pounds." There were whistles from Whitehead and Brent Ross. "Ceiling twenty-eight-thousand feet. Armament, six fifty-caliber Brownings, crew six men. Bomb load three tons."

"The speed, weight, bomb load, ceiling, not to say anything about range, are all increased over the World War II bomber."

Mayfield's expression was more of a superior smirk than a smile. He spoke down to the two Americans and the Israeli, "New engines. Wright has developed a new R-Thirty-Three-Fifty power plant, eighteen cylinders in two banks, two turbo-superchargers, thirty-two-hundred horsepower, methanol injected . . ."

"Commander Yoshi Matsuhara has that Thirty-Three-Fifty in his Zero. It's always overheating. It's nothing but a reworked engine from the old Boeing B-

29. Too much magnesium and the cooling system is poor," Brent exclaimed, half-rising.

"True," Fujita added, obviously disconcerted. "It is not a dependable power plant."

"You're talking about the Sakae-43, built by Nakajima on license from Wright." Brent and the admiral nodded. Mayfield held up more papers. "According to these reports, Wright engineers have solved that problem. Some of the magnesium has been replaced with a titanium and aluminum alloy and a new cooling system installed. The new engine has been tested over hundreds of hours and shows no signs of overheating. It is fuel-efficient and with this enormous power, the bombers can carry their full loads to Rabta and then they should have enough fuel to make it to Caltagirone in southern Sicily." He turned his hands up and shrugged. "They'll be cutting it close, but they should make it."

"I want more of these new engines," Fujita said. "All of our aircraft should have them."

"Production is limited, sir," Mayfield answered. "The United States is hard put to equip its own new Grumman FX-1000 fighters. Why, we had a fight on our hands obtaining enough for the sixteen B-25s. We were only able to get them because the Pentagon wants the Rabta plant taken out as much as we do. But I know the new modifications are being sent to Nakajima."

Whitehead said to Admiral Fujita, "Sir, there is a chance this plan could succeed. But what are we to do for fighter cover while our decks are crowded with B-25s? On the Doolittle raid, the *Enterprise* provided air cover." He pointed again at the chart. "Why, it must be ten-thousand miles from Tarawa to our launch point. With no CAP?" He slapped his head.

Fujita turned to the CIA man. Mayfield read the gesture and spoke directly to Rear Admiral Whitehead, "We have another carrier."

"Another carrier?" Excitement filled the room.

"Yes. The CIA bought the *USS Bennington,* CVS Twenty, through a front. It was dubbed 'The Bay Area Warship Museum'."

"I thought she was to be broken up," Whitehead injected.

Again, the smug smile. "CIA efficiency, sir," Mayfield gloated, staring at Bernstein. "As you know, she is an *Essex.*" He stared at a sheet of paper, "Displacement thirty-five-thousand tons, length eight-hundred-ninety-nine feet, beam one-hundred-one feet, four shaft Westinghouse geared turbines, one-hundred-fifty-thousand shaft horsepower, thirty-two-point-five knots, ninety-eight aircraft, twelve five-inch guns, sixty-eight forty-millimeter Bofors, seventy-two twenty-millimeter Orlikons, range seventeen-thousand miles at twenty knots." He looked up. *"Bennington* is in superb condition. She has been moved from Bremerton to Mare Island and rebuilt and restored to her World War II configuration. She has an American skipper and a crew recruited from America, England and France with a sprinkling of other nationalities. She is ready for sea and her air groups are almost complete."

"Security?" Whitehead said. "Why, you can't conduct such an operation without serious chances for leaks."

"True," the CIA agent conceded. "The crew is restricted to the base at Mare Island and not one man knows what the mission is. In addition, so that they won't attract too much attention, the pilots are training in Florida, Texas and Southern California. They are also restricted and are unaware of their mission. They don't even know they're going to fly from *Bennington.*" He stared directly into Admiral Whitehead's eyes. "We've taken every precaution."

"Still risky. The Russians and Arabs have probably sniffed her out by now."

"Possible. But keep in mind, The US Navy has the right to arm her and use her and every man who volunteered hates tyranny and is willing to put his life on the line to help bring down the *jihad*." Mayfield leaned forward on his knuckles, eyes hopping from face to face. "As soon as she puts to sea, she will be officially transferred to the Japanese National Parks Department, but she won't fly Japanese colors until she engages the enemy."

"Escorts?"

"Five *Fletchers*. We bought them from Pakistan, Turkey and Greece. Completely rebuilt and we've berthed them in five different ports. Seattle, San Francisco, Long Beach, San Diego and Pearl Harbor."

Whitehead seemed somewhat placated, but Brent was not. His questioning mind was not satisfied. "The New Grumman fighter, the FX-One-Thousand? Will *Bennington* be equipped with them?"

"Yes. Yes," Whitehead said, "the FX-1000?"

"Sorry, gentlemen. Not enough are available. She will be equipped with F-Six-F Hellcats, Grumman TBF Avenger torpedo bombers and Curtis SB-Two-C Helldiver dive-bomber. Even a few Douglas SBD Dauntless dive-bombers were scraped up for her." He glanced at his notes. "Her biggest group will be her fighters; perhaps, sixty. The remainder of her aircraft will be split evenly between the bombers." He looked up. "She will rendezvous with *Yonaga* off Tarawa. You will have continuous air cover."

An exuberant mood filled the room. "I think

we can do it," Brent said to himself, thumping his armrest with his fist.

Fujita waved Mayfield to his chair and brought the high spirits crashing down with his next words. "Gentlemen, it has been confirmed by the CIA, Mossad and British Intelligence that the Russian government has sold the carriers *Minsk* and *Kiev* to the 'Trans-Arab Iron and Salvage Works' which is nothing but a front for Kadafi. In fact, both ships are underway and were seen in the Faeroe-Iceland Gap yesterday. We expect them to make Tripoli within a week."

"But why, sir, I don't understand," Brent anguished.

"Glasnost," the old admiral replied as if his mouth were filled with acid. "America has agreed to lay up her seven nuclear carriers and the Russians agreed to scrap their two nuclear carriers, mothball the *Novorossiysk* and *Baku* and scrap *Minsk* and *Kiev*."

"It's a fraud and a sham. The Russkies cheated before the ink was dry on the treaty."

Fujita smiled sardonically. "That is an excellent definition of international diplomacy, Mister Ross, and, of course, the two carriers steaming the North Atlantic prove your point."

Whitehead entered the exchange with a new thought. "Our *Kitty Hawk* class, the *Forrestal* class, two *Midways* and two *Essexes* are all conventionally powered carriers. Why, that's twelve ships."

"True," Mayfield said. "They may remain in commission. That is why the US entered the pact. The US navy will be able to maintain a powerful carrier force even if *Midway* and *Coral Sea* and the two *Essexes* are laid up. They are all World War II carriers, you know, and are long in the tooth. To the Pentagon, it was a good deal."

Bernstein broke his silence. "I disagree. It's a stupid

172

treaty. The Americans knew going in the Russians and Arabs never honor any agreements. They have the ethics and integrity of Adolph Hitler." Solemn glances of concordance were exchanged.

Brent Ross said, "The *Kiev* and *Minsk* are hybrid ships. They are Vertical Take Off or Landing (VTOL) carriers with cruiser armaments on their bows. Why, they each even carry ten torpedo tubes."

"That's right," Whitehead said. "They're not 'attack carriers' on our model. No indeed. They're designed to carry out long-range antisubmarine operations. The Russians' original concept was to design a class that could engage surface ships or land targets at long range with SS-N-Twelve missiles and attack aircraft at significantly greater distances with the Forger VTOL fighter bombers. Why, the flight deck is only about six-hundred-feet long."

Mayfield smiled and held up a document. "True, the flight deck was six-hundred-seven-feet long. However, both ships have been rebuilt at Severodvinsk and the flight decks lengthened to the full length of the hull about eight-hundred-ninety-five feet." There were whistles. "We figure each ship of this class is capable of operating over sixty conventional aircraft."

Whitehead scowled in frustration. Brent muttered, "Jesus." Bernstein groaned and spat a Hebrew oath. Fujita just nodded. The expression on his face was impassable, but Brent knew the old man was churning inside.

The CIA man glanced down at the table, scanning a document. "This is the latest on the class. Thirty-seven-thousand tons with a full load, length eight-hundred-ninety-five feet, beam one-hundred-seven feet, draft twenty-nine feet, four-shaft steam turbines generating one-hundred-eighty-thousand shaft horsepower, thirty knots, sixty-plus aircraft." Fujita looked up. "As far as we know, both ships are equipped with the latest radar. 'Top Sail' Three-D, D-band, range three hundred nautical miles. Surface search is 'Top Steer,' three-D, D and E band, so both radars are capable of air search." He looked around and his glance was answered by silent grim stares. He continued, "We're not sure of her AA batteries. But there are rumors of one-hundred-twenty-seven-millimeter dual purpose cannons, numerous twenty-millimeter and forty-millimeter installations, but no Gatlings."

"Fire control radar?" Whitehead asked.

Mayfield shook his head. "None, according to our information. Apparently, the Russians are honoring the Geneva restrictions on fire control radar, their latest quick-firing AA guns and passive and active guidance systems on their five-three-three, 21-inch, torpedoes."

Fujita said, "That's not honor, that's fear. They don't trust the Arabs."

Bernstein's chuckle interrupted. "Why, of course, during the Six Day War, we captured their latest Surface to Air missiles (SAM) complete with radar control and their latest T-Fifty-Four main battle tanks (MBT) from the Egyptians. The Russians have never forgotten or forgiven." And then bitterly, "That is the only restraint they feel."

"Your David Ben-Gurion Line. You have improved it?"

"We have, indeed, Admiral." The Israeli rose and walked to a chart of the Middle East. He raised the pointer and tapped a point on the Mediterranean. "We have connected our strong points, here at Gaza." The pointer began to trace a continuous line, "to Sedom on the Jordanian border and then north to Al Khalil,

Ariba, the Syrian border and from the Golan Heights to Al Khushniyah." The pointer paused and then struck west to the coast along the Lebanese border until it reached the sea. "And it is anchored here in the north at Achzib."

Whitehead leaned forward. "You said 'connected'?"

"Yes. The line is now a continuous four deep wall of concrete blockhouses with interlocking fields of fire. It is reminiscent of World War I style fortifications which is ideal because the Arabs have been using human wave attacks supported by armor. And remember, we have the old Japanese battleship *Mikasa* to use as a monitor. She's almost ninety-years-old, but she has four new twelve-inch guns with a range of ten miles."

"She has the latest sabot charges," Brent noted.

"Right," the Israeli answered. "With sabots, she can fire six-inch shells over twenty miles. Half the bore, twice the range." He tapped his forehead. "Twenty miles covers a lot of geography in the Middle East."

Whitehead broke in, "Still a stalemate on all fronts?"

"Yes."

"They could use their gas weapons on you," Whitehead warned.

"We have our 'nukes'," Bernstein said softly, avoiding Fujita's eyes. He turned to his chair.

Brent saw Fujita twist with a touch of horror at the suggestion of the possible use of nuclear bombs. Quickly, the old sailor rushed back to naval matters. He said to Mayfield, "You did not mention air groups for the Arabs' two new carriers."

"Unknown," the CIA agent said.

Bernstein looked up and said, "I may be of help, sir." Fujita nodded, Mayfield glared, but remained silent. The Israeli continued, "Our operatives have been reporting large formations of Messerschmitt Bf One-Oh-Nines, Junkers JU Eighty-Sevens and North American AT-Sixes practicing short landing and take-off procedures on nine-hundred-foot rectangles marked in the desert southwest of Tripoli." He waved at the chart of the Mediterranean. "Please note, gentlemen, Kadafi's training areas, his yards at Tripoli are fourteen-hundred miles from our bases, well out of the range of our bombers."

Whitehead looked down at the table and muttered, "Oh, Lord. We'll be in a helluva bind if those carriers sortie just as we close on Morocco. Remember what happened when our dive-bombers caught *Kaga*, *Akagi*, and *Soryu* at Midway with their decks loaded with planes? They didn't have a chance."

He had used the worst possible example. The massacre of Japan's finest carriers and air groups in 1942 was still a running sore with all of the older Japanese. Fujita's tiny fist met his desk with an audible thump. "We Japanese have learned to not repeat our mistakes!" he retorted harshly.

Obviously flustered, Whitehead said, "I meant nothing personal, Admiral. After all, you weren't there." His attempt at rapprochement fell flat on its face.

Fujita waved him off with a dismissive gesture. "I'm sure the two carriers are destined for the Western Pacific." He thumped a stack of papers and glanced at the two intelligence officers. "We did a tremendous amount of damage to the Arabs' *Essex*, the *Al Kufra*. She took two torpedoes, four bombs and when Lieutenant Joji Kai rammed her island, the fire spread to the flight deck which buckled. Ready fuel was ignited and spilled down into her hangar deck through bomb holes. Her own ready ordnance exploded and the hangar deck was torn apart, too. She had to be towed to Surabaya." Bernstein and Mayfield nodded and smiled.

"The Indonesians have a good yard, there, Admiral," Bernstein warned, tugging on the tip of his beard that hung from his chin like a gray spade.

"True. But her repairs may take as long as eight months."

"Eight months?"

"Yes, perhaps longer. Some new armor plating must be imported from the Ruhr and her air groups were almost wiped out and you know rebuilding her flight and hangar decks will take time." He stared first at Mayfield and then back to Bernstein and the old parchment cracked with the semblance of a smile. "I have my own operatives working in the yards. They keep me informed."

Bernstein nodded, face showing relief. He continued, "Then, you expect the two new carriers to steam to the Western Pacific?"

"Without a doubt. Their air strength in the Marianas has been greatly reduced." He looked around the room at each intent face. "Why do you think I ordered that last fighter sweep?" He moved back to his desk and squinted down at a document. "According to our observers on Aguijan and reports from natives, Major Kenneth Rosencrance only has fourteen serviceable fighters."

"The Super Constellations. I hear they have six of them," Bernstein said. "They could bomb this whole area when we are off in the Atlantic." He waved to demonstrate the size.

"True," Fujita acknowledged, "there is that chance." He tapped gently on the document. "All six are operating from Tinian," he said. "Our troops on Aguijan will make a commando-style landing and attempt to disable the Constellations."

"And if they fail?"

Brent could see Fujita was tiring. But he was carried by his enthusiasm at the thought of the approaching action; the destruction he would wreak half-a-world away, the men he would kill. "We have been training over three-hundred extra fighter pilots and an equal number of bomber pilots."

So that's it, Brent thought. *A fighter screen to defend the islands while* Yonaga *was in the Atlantic. A well-kept secret. Not even Yoshi Matsuhara had known.*

Fujita walked stiffly to a chart of the Western Pacific and picked up the pointer. "As you gentlemen know, we have two survivors of the Maritime Self Defense Force, the frigate *Ayase* and the destroyer *Yamagiri,* which served us well as radar pickets during our battle with carriers *Al Kufra* and *Ramli al Kabir.*" He stabbed the chart. "During our absence, *Yamagiri* will patrol a station here." He tapped the rubber tip one-hundred-fifty miles south of Kyushu. "*Ayase* will patrol here, two-hundred miles southeast of Tokyo Bay. They both have excellent sea and air search radar." He dropped the pointer to his side and smiled with satisfaction.

"Sir," Brent Ross said. "Where are the fighters and bombers to be based?"

A mask of confusion passed over the wrinkled face like the shadow of a squall. Brent felt a pang of apprehension. It seemed now and then the old sailor's mind misfired; recalling incidents in the distant past ucidly, yet, hazy on recent events, or forgetting them completely. "Oh, yes, yes. Of course," Fujita said, recovering quickly. "We will base squadrons of our new Zero-sens here." He stabbed the southern tip of Kyushu. "Here!" the pointer moved to Kobe. "And here." The tip came to rest on Tokyo. "All fighter groups will be supported by bombers for attack, but primarily for reconnaissance."

"Our PBMs and PBYs?" Whitehead asked. "Twelve are operational."

Fujita's eyes widened. "Of course. They will maintain long-range patrols in the vicinity the Marianas and to the east of Japan." He returned to his chair and sank into it in obvious weariness. "You see, gentlemen, the Arabs have given us a window of at least three months. We will grab it," he said.

Brent was still troubled. He addressed himself to Horace Mayfield, "Can we still depend on American nuclear subs to give us reports of Arab ship movements?"

"Why of course, son," the CIA man shot back as if he were a schoolmaster addressing a slow-witted student.

Brent felt a small fire flare in deep in his viscera. "I'm not your son and don't give me any crap!" he retorted angrily. "Just give me the goddamned facts."

Mayfield winced as if he had been slapped. "See here, young man—"

"Enough!" Fujita shouted, squelching the argument. "We have Arabs to fight, not each other. That luxury can come later." He waved at Mayfield and then pointed to a Mercator projection of the entire world. Mayfield waddled to the chart and picked up a pointer. "American nuclear submarines are on station here," he indicated the Gulf of Aden, Straits of Gilbraltar, Strait of Malacca, South China Sea and a point in the Sea of Japan near Vladivostok. He looked at Admiral Whitehead. *"Yonaga*'s NIS officers have the cryptological input to decode their sightings. With the sensors these boats mount, not even a sardine can slip past them without being detected."

179

Bernstein spoke up, "We know there are twelve transports in Tripoli and a full infantry division appears to be preparing to embark."

"Why haven't they?" Mayfield asked.

"The Israeli army had been massing as if to mount an offensive and our air force has been very active, bombing and strafing Arab positions."

"All this to take pressure off the Japanese?"

"Of course." The Israeli looked at Admiral Fujita. "*Yonaga* saved us in 1984." His fingers found his beard. "And Admiral, as you requested, the High Command is prepared to mount ground and air offensives when *Yonaga* approaches her launch point. They will await your signal. That should turn Arab heads."

"Very good," the old admiral said. "In addition, we will fabricate the rumor that *Yonaga* will move against *Al Kufra* in the yards in Surabaya. That should send the *Minsk* and *Kiev* rushing to her aid."

"Excellent. Good plan," everyone agreed. But Whitehead still showed reserve. "Fuel, Sir." He waved at the Mercator projection. "Not even *Yonaga* can steam to Morocco and back without refueling."

Fujita indicated Mayfield with an open palm. The CIA man said, "A tanker will refuel the battle group after the B-25s are taken aboard and another one will refuel the group in the Atlantic." He looked down at his notes. "I can give you the exact latitude and longitude, if you wish."

The men were impressed. Every contingency seemed to have been evaluated and met. Fujita eyed the officers silently. Finally, he spoke to Rear Admiral Whitehead, "You approve of the plan, Admiral?"

The American rubbed the hard bone behind his ear. "There are a lot of contingencies, sir. Rarely in war do the pins fall as neatly into their holes as the planners would wish. Why, in the Great War, the British planners for the Battle of the Somme had the objectives of each company plotted, shelled the German lines for a week with one-and-a-half-million rounds, went over the top, and lost sixty-thousand men on the first day, alone. Thousands were shot down before they reached their own wire. It went on for months. They gained nothing but a few hundred yards of moonscape and hundreds of thousands of widows." A funereal silence filled the room. Whitehead had resorted to one of the most horrifying examples of incompetence in military history. Historians were still sickened by the carnage along the Somme. In academies all over the world the attack was used as an example of the worst possible battle tactics.

"Very true," Fujita said, breaking the silence. "There are the imponderables, chance, blind luck and in the case of the Somme, the unsurpassed stupidity of General Douglas Haig. Haig used American Civil War tactics against the twentieth century fire power of Maxim guns and rapid fire field guns. The man had no imagination and was incapable of learning. In fact, he repeated the same stupid mistake made by Robert E. Lee at Gettysburg, attacking fixed positions with masses of infantry." He toyed with the single whisper and his eyes moved over the men. "There are no 'Haigs' on my staff. However, we can only make our plans, execute them with all of our skill and courage, and then trust in our gods." His eyes found Rear Admiral Whitehead. "Do you have any comments, Admiral Whitehead?"

Whitehead rubbed his pate and narrowed his eyes meditatively. "I would suggest *Yonaga* not begin this mission until *Minsk* and *Kiev* are transiting the Red Sea. Our nuclear subs can track them and we can be sure they won't embarrass us when we appear off the Moroccan coast with a deck load of B-25s."

Fujita turned to Brent Ross. "And you, Mister Ross?"

Brent came to his feet. "Great idea and great planning, sir. Let's take it to the bastards and kick butt."

There were cheers. Fujita smiled warmly and then silenced the men with raised palms. And then, wearily, he pushed himself to his feet and faced the shrine. The men rose. The admiral clapped twice to attract the attention of the gods. Odd numbers were considered bad luck. It was either two claps or four. Brent also clapped twice. The old man called on the creators of the islands of Japan.

"Oh, Izanagi and Izanami, be with us in our efforts to destroy the enemies of *Yamato*." He waved a hand and his voice took on a hard edge. Brent recognized some ancient passages from the *Hagakure*.

"Let us teach the enemy that the samurai does not sleep on logs, eat stones or drink gall. Instead, he welcomes being ripped apart by arrows, rifles, spears and swords, always facing the enemy, even in death." His eyes wandered over the silent group, his mind now occupied with the teachings of Buddha. "Let each of us follow the Noble Eightfold Path to strengthen our karmas with righteous acts, thoughts and resolve."

And then to appeal to the Christian-Judaic belief in life after death, "Remember, The Blessed One would never teach that on the dissolution of the body the saint who has lost all depravity is annihilated, perishes and does not exist after death." He gestured to the sky with a dramatic flair, "There is a refuge for that which is born, becomes, is created, is caused." He stopped to catch his breath. Brent knew he was in a deep emotional state although his face was petrified wood.

182

He continued, voice still firm and strong, "Let no man rest until the forces of evil are wiped from the face of the earth." He turned to his companions, "Do any of you have prayers to offer in your own religions? A pantheon of three of the world's greatest are gathered in this room. It would be wise to mass all of the power of our gods in a great ecumenical force. In the near future we may be in dire need of the combined might of all of our gods and *kamis*." Mayfield was the only one who smiled at the absurd statement. A glance from Fujita wiped his face clean.

Bernstein touched his chest several times. Fujita nodded and the Israeli pulled a linen yarmulke from his pocket and placed the skullcap on his head. He spoke to the far distance.

"Blessed art Thou, O Lord our God, King of the universe, Who didst choose us from among all thy peoples, Who has restoreth the land You promised the Israelites in Your words in the holy Pentateuch. O Lord God smite those who would strive to drive the Chosen from their rightful land and bless those who would stand at our side at this moment of our greatest peril."

Brent noticed a distasteful twitch cross Mayfield's face. Bernstein caught it with a sidelong glance.

Bernstein continued his solemn chant, "Help us follow the Laws of Moses and vanquish thy enemies and send his walls tumbling to dust as those of Jericho."

He pulled a worn *Book of Psalms* from his pocket, stared for a moment at Mayfield who smirked back and then read the third and fourth verses of the "Twenty-Fourth Psalm." " 'Who shall ascend into the mountain of the Lord . . .' " Brent raised his head and saw Mayfield staring at the Jew who droned on " '. . . He that is of clean hands and pure heart; who hath not lifted up his

183

soul unto falsehood, and has not sworn deceitfully'." He looked up and closed the small volume, indicating completion.

Staring at the Jew, Mayfield stepped forward. He held out his hand in a silent demand and Bernstein placed the *Book of Psalms* in his palm. The CIA man raised his head and narrowed his eyes. "Jesus Christ our saviour," he said, stealing a glance at Bernstein's face which appeared set in concrete, "look down on us and help guide us in this hour of trial." He paused and thumbed through the book, finally finding a page and studying it for a moment. He smirked, glanced at Bernstein and then read, " 'Why, Oh God, hast thou cast us off for ever? Why will thy anger smoke against the flock . . .'" Bernstein turned, his face a book of rancor.

Fujita raised a hand and spoke angrily, "The Seventy-Fourth Psalm." He gesticulated at Bernstein. "It angers Jews. It speaks of their destruction. That was unconscionable."

Brent and Whitehead looked at each other, shocked again by the incredible breadth of Fujita's knowledge and what appeared to be Mayfield's deliberate challenge of the Israeli. The subtle slur had gone right past them; but not Fujita.

Everyone was jarred by Bernstein's blunt rejoinder, "If you're anti-Semitic," he spat at Mayfield, "just come out and admit it." The Israeli chuckled mirthlessly. "Believe me, you could only be an amateur. I have dealt with professionals."

Mayfield drew himself up in a defensive posture and sniffed ruefully. "I meant no offense. I was speaking about the anger of God being directed at the Libyans. They are our Philistines."

It was a weak ploy and fooled no one. Fujita spoke bitterly. "We will dispense with prayers. This meeting is closed."

Walking silently past Brent, the men filed through the door. He stared at the intelligence men. Mayfield's face was twisted by a sneer that hooked up the corner of his mouth and exposed his yellow teeth. Bernstein's jaw was cemented into a hard set and his lips were resolutely pressed together. Now Brent knew the antipathy between the two men was not just based on their professional competition. It was deeper, profane, foul as a decomposing corpse and was part of the poison that infected the entire world. As he left, the young American's stomach was suddenly soured and upset as if he had been struck by a sudden virus.

Chapter Eight

The next morning Brent had no incentive to go ashore. Instead, he donned his number one blues and made his way to the quarter deck. Here he stood at quarters with dozens of other officers and at least two-hundred enlisted men awaiting Admiral Fujita's departure from the ship for his audience with Emperor Akihito. Brent smiled when the old sailor made his way slowly to the accommodation ladder. He was literally swallowed by his finest blue uniform.

The admiral was dressed for the old Imperial Navy. His tunic was single-breasted with stand collar and slash side pockets, old-fashioned hook and eyes fastening the front. Fine black silk lace trimmed the top and front edge of the collar, the front and skirt of the tunic and the pockets. Four gold cherry blossoms on his shoulder straps and ruffled cuffs indicated his rank. His peaked field cap proudly displayed the gold chrysanthemum worn only by *Yonaga*'s officers. All other officers of the old Navy had worn cherry blossoms on the front of their caps. Splendid on his emaciated chest was his most illustrious possession: the Grand Cross breast star of the Order of the Rising Sun, resuscitated and awarded to him by Emperor Hirohito just two days before the Emperor's death.

There were ruffles and flourishes from drummers and boatswains' mates pipes as Fujita reached the ladder followed by Executive Officer Captain Mitake Arai and a young yeoman carrying an attaché case. The old scribe, Commander Hakuseki Katsube, was too infirm to accompany the party. Instead, supported by a young ensign, the rickety old scribe clung to the rail, staring at the admiral reverently as if Fujita were a *kami* suddenly come to life.

After Fujita and the officer of the deck exchanged salutes, the old man faced the stern and saluted the colors. Then, after brushing off aid proffered by a guard, the old man slowly descended the ladder to his waiting limousine. Mitake Arai and a group of guards carrying Arisakas followed him. There were shouts of "Banzai!" from hundreds of men lining the quarterdeck rail, the flight deck and the upper works. They waved their hats, pounded each other on the back. Brent added his own shouts. Preceded by a truck loaded with guards and mounting a pair of Nambus and followed by another similarly manned and armed, the limousine drove off.

"Dismissed!" was shouted and the men slowly melted away. Brent turned toward the elevator. He missed Yoshi Matsuhara, but not one pilot was aboard. They had all left before dawn for the training facilities at Tokyo International Airport or Tsuchiura. Slowly, the young American walked down the passageway, mind filled with memories of the beautiful but unattainable Arlene Spencer. He tried to force her out and think about the qualifications of the new cryptologic technician he must train. However, the girl persisted like a specter in a haunting dream. He cursed under his breath and jammed his hands into his pockets. He was

187

in a nasty mood.

Brent disliked the oppressive red-blue glow that filled CIC. Today it was far too close to his own mood. The large compartment was crowded with men reflecting the ghostly light like ghoulish characters painted on the cheap pulp pages of a cartoon horror magazine; skin a sickly amber-green, dead blue lips, purple veins maundering across faces, necks and hands. The plotting boards were unmanned, but ratings sat before banks of electronics equipment studying green-glowing radar scopes and waterfall displays on CRTs. Both "A" and "S" band radar were searching. The new technician, Cryptographer Second Class Stan Fleishman, a short, fair athletic young man, sat before the fabulous Raytheon SLQ 38 ESM unit. Behind him, the experienced Electronics Technician Martin Reed stood to one side while Rear Admiral Byron Whitehead stood on the other.

Reed was talking to the new man. "Three-hundred-sixty-degree azimuth, instantaneous frequency measurement, threat library which can be accessed in thirty-two milliseconds, scan analysis by period and frequency . . ." Reed stopped in mid-sentence when he saw Brent.

"Carry on," Brent said. "I have some work with Fleishman when you finish."

"I can handle it, Lieutenant," Rear Admiral Whitehead said. "I thought you had liberty today?"

Brent shook his head. But before he could utter a word, an enlisted man holding a wall mounted telephone called, "Mister Ross. For you, sir."

188

Brent walked to the end of the compartment and put the instrument to his ear. His heart leaped when Arlene Spencer's voice filled the earpiece, the depressing light brightened. "Lieutenant Ross," she said. "I thought we had an appointment today?" Not even the raspish tinny tone of the phone could hide the soft warmth of the completely feminine voice. "Did you forget?"

Brent felt like a small boy who had rushed to the Christmas tree on Christmas morning and found it surrounded with packages with his name on them. He caught his breath and then forced a firm, well-modulated tone that still failed to completely conceal the excitement he felt. "I . . . ah," he stumbled in confusion. "I, ah, thought you had seen enough of me in the Shrine of Infinite Salvation yesterday."

The voice was all business. "That's not the point. You're a story, a big story, and you are my story. You promised me an interview and my editors are waiting for it. I thought I could depend on you."

"Of course you can. When can I see you?"

"How about lunch?"

"Today?"

"Yes."

The way she said *"yes"* sent a tremor through him. He felt momentary disgust for himself. *Christ, I'm a horny son-of-a-bitch,* he said to himself. He managed to mutter, "Where?"

"My apartment at one o'clock."

"But where?"

"I'm staying at the Tokyo Hilton Hotel in the Western Shinjuku District. Do you know where it is?"

Brent knew the Shinjuku District well. Actually, the Hilton was in the heart of the new downtown of the city,

189

the home of most of Tokyo's new skyscrapers. "Yes,"
Brent said. "You're just north of the Meiji Jingu
Shrine."

"I didn't know that."

Brent chuckled. "What's your room number?"

"1410."

"See you at one." He glanced at Fleishman who
stared back expectantly. "But I must leave by eighteen-
hundred hours. I have a new man to train."

"Fine. I'll expect you at one p.m."

Arlene's apartment was actually a suite including a
large sitting room, small kitchen and bedroom. A large
picture window gave on the concrete and steel mundan-
ity of the sterile downtown area. Fortunately, to the
north and east respite was found in the lush greenery of
Shinjuku Gyoen Park and the elysian gardens surrounding the Meiji Jingu Shrine. In the far distance,
the Imperial Palace and the congested Ginza were visible. Backdropping it all was the blue stretch of the harbor. An ugly pall of polluted air hung over everything.
It made a man long for the clean air of the high seas.

The long ride from Yokosuka had been uneventful.
Not even a single member of the *Rengo Sekigun* was to be
found demonstrating outside the gates. Brent had been
provided with a Mercedes staff car and a driver, Seaman First Class Haruo Iketa. Not more than twenty-
five-years-old, Iketa was squat and powerfully built,
always wearing a stoic, solemn expression. He was
armed with an Otsu pistol and Arisaka rifle.

Brent had traded his Otsu for the Beretta M951
Brigadier, nine-millimeter automatic pistol. Cham-

bered for the tissue-destroying Parabellum cartridge, Brent liked the Beretta's balance, high rate of fire and ten round magazine. The first time he palmed the vicious little weapon he had chuckled to himself, *If it's good enough for James Bond, it's good enough for Brent Ross.* He wore it in a shoulder holster, only a small bulge showing in his left armpit.

When he had appeared at Arlene's door, Iketa was standing behind him, rifle slung over his shoulder. Arlene looked over Brent's shoulder at the glowering seaman and said, "You don't need him, Lieutenant. I have no intention of ravishing you." Smiling incongruously, her eyes ran over his massive shoulders and thick neck.

Brent had been pleased with the young woman's mood. "Admiral Fujita's orders," he said. "Seaman Iketa will remain on guard here, at the door."

Shrugging, she ushered him in and preceded him to the window. She was wearing blue silk pants and a white satin blouse. The spectacular outfit was so tight, it fit like another layer of skin. Her body was truly magnificent. Brent's eyes widened as he watched the perfectly balanced, wonderfully easy action of her buttocks.

"Great view," he said, staring out the window but thinking of her body. He wondered about her cordial attitude and if she could really put the horror of the Shrine of Infinite Salvation behind her.

"You mentioned the Meiji Jingu Shrine," she said, gesturing at the city.

He pointed to the east at a swatch of green breaking the concrete welter. "You can only see part of the grounds from here. The shrine is magnificent. It's a memorial to Emperor Meiji who was responsible for the modernization of Japan. He was . . ." Conscious of another presence in the room, the lieutenant stopped and turned. Lia Mandel had entered from the kitchen. She was wearing slacks, a white shirt and tie. It was a deliberate attempt to appear masculine. He felt his stomach scalding and he could not hide the distaste that spread across his face.

"Well, well. 'Chopper' Ross," she said, extending a hand.

Brent would not raise his own. "I didn't come here for any crap," he said. "Put a civil tongue in your mouth or the interview is off." He turned to Arlene. "I thought your story was between you and me?"

"It is," the young woman pleaded.

"I was just leaving," Lia said. "So don't get your balls in an uproar." She walked to a closet, grabbed a coat and left.

Arlene gestured to a luxuriously overstuffed satin couch with a long glass-topped oak table in front of it. "You'll have to forgive Lia," she said, leading him to the couch. "She is a highly capable and intelligent reporter, but, she sometimes lacks tact and diplomacy."

Brent laughed. "To put it mildly." He seated himself next to the girl. The blue eyes caught his.

"Would you like a drink? Coffee? Tea before lunch?"

"You have scotch?"

"Haig and Haig."

"Straight up, please . . . ah, Arlene."

"And you're Brent," she said rising.

Again he watched the magnificent display of chiseled and molded buttocks as she walked to the kitchen. In a moment she returned carrying a silver tray with two glasses and a bottle of Haig and Haig. She poured generous portions of the whiskey into the glasses and handed him one. Holding up her drink, she touched his. "To a good, in-depth session."

His eyes widened as he wondered about the statement. Was there a Freudian side to it? "In depth," he repeated with a straight face. They both drank and then sank back with a new feeling of relaxation loosening both of them. He raised his glass and studied the dark amber fluid as if he were a scientist searching a test tube for an elusive microbe. Something was troubling him. He took a deep breath and finally blurted it out. "Arlene?"

"Yes."

"Does Lia live here with you?" Brent knew he had tread on dangerous ground. He could be told to "mind your own business!" But he had to know if this maddeningly sexy creature was lost in the quagmire of homosexuality.

Arlene smiled broadly. "No. She does not live with me. She has her own suite two floors above." She took a drink and tabled the glass. "We're not a 'pair', an 'item', if that's bothering you."

"I didn't mean to pry."

"Yes, you did. And I'm pleased."

Brent beamed at the subtle compliment. They held up their glasses, saluted each other with smiles, and drank. "I shocked you in The Shrine of Infinite Salvation?"

She nodded. "Yes, it was unlike anything I had ever seen; anything I had ever experienced."

"You were disgusted with me."

"I'm not sure," she said sincerely. "Remember, the

193

good reporter tries to be detached, objective. You live in a different world and in that different world of yours, you were doing your duty. The right thing." She looked up at him, blue eyes wide, the deep color of the clear sky at dusk. "Does that make sense?"

"Yes. And I hope you can keep it in that context because that is precisely what you saw. I was a man doing his duty." He emptied his glass.

"A samurai doing his duty," she corrected him. She refilled both their glasses.

"Correct, in a way, Arlene." He sipped his scotch. "My friends told me Lia had a weird reaction to the whole thing; highly excited."

"She had an orgasm."

The bluntness of the statement, the choice of words by this sweet, angelic girl took Brent aback. "Not really," he sputtered.

She laughed, a high lilting sound. "She told me you could probably make her go straight."

Brent groped for words. None were available. He finally managed, "I can't believe that." He waved a hand in a gesture of confusion. "And she called me 'chopper'."

"I know she did, but it's true, Brent. Why should I lie?"

"Don't get me wrong, but I've got to admit I'm not really overwhelmed at the prospect of trying to straighten her out."

She giggled. "You won't really break her heart, Brent." She tapped the table with a perfectly manicured nail. "She has other interests." The nail continued to drum and was joined by another. She reached to a side table and pulled a recorder from a drawer and placed it on the table in front of them. "Do you mind if I turn on

194

this recorder, Brent?"

He nodded his approval and she threw a switch. Then he noted, "It's a Mitsubishi."

"Why? Is that important?"

He laughed softly. "They built the Zero fighter."

"It was famous. Everyone knows *Yonaga* still uses it."

"Right, Arlene. *Yonaga*'s are modified." He took a drink. "In the early years of World War II the Zero was the best fighter in the Pacific. It inflicted a lot of punishment on the Allies. Nothing could dogfight with it."

Her laugh had a touch of irony in it. "Well, Brent, I'll just bet you Mitsubishi has done a lot more damage to America with this recorder, VCRs, tvs and the rest of it. It's laid waste to a lot of industry."

He held up his glass. "You're a smart girl. Can't argue with that." Another thought intruded. He drank and then put the glass aside. "You work for Nippon Press?"

"Correct."

"It's a news gathering agency?"

"Yes."

He rubbed his cheek with an open palm. "*Yonaga* is news, battles are news, but Brent Ross?"

"You're news. They want a feature story."

"There's more to it, isn't there, Arlene?"

"Now I'm beginning to understand why Fujita admires you so much. You have a shrewd, insightful mind. Yes, there is more." She leaned forward to pick up her glass and then settled back closer to her guest. Her thigh almost touched his. He took another drink and felt a pleasant warmth begin to seep. But it was not just the liquor. "Yes, I free-lance for *Personalities Magazine,*" she said. "They've bought six of my articles about

195

unusual people all over the world."

"I'm unusual?"

"Very."

"I could be a source of income for you."

"Do you mind?"

"No. I like you." His big hand closed over hers. It was tiny and soft like fine silk. She made no attempt to pull it away.

"You've been at sea for a long time."

"You mean I'm horny." He released her hand.

She giggled. "You're blunt."

"No more than you. Remember Lia's orgasm?"

"Touché!" She touched his glass with hers. They both sipped their drinks. "I've made a great seafood salad for lunch with genuine Italian garlic bread. Are you starved?"

He shook his head. Fascinated by this beautiful girl, he was enjoying her closeness, the warmth and near intimacy of the moment. He wanted to preserve the mood. "Later. Go ahead with your questions. You've put me into a good mood and I'll probably talk too much."

"You think I'm setting you up?"

"Probably. But I'm enjoying it."

She laughed and ran her hand up his arm, not stopping until she grasped his bicep. He could feel her fingers digging into the hard muscle. She leaned close to his ear, "You're cute, Brent." Her warm breath caressed his cheek. It started a fire deep down. Gritting his teeth, he stared down at the table. He dared not turn toward her. He knew he would do something foolish and it was far too soon. The hand slipped down his arm and found the couch. Then, leaning back, her

196

voice became businesslike. The first question took him by surprise. "This *Hagakure*?"

" 'Under the Leaves.' What about it?"

"It's very important to the samurai . . . important to you. Admiral Fujita had it on his desk in his cabin. He carried it into the shrine and waved it at us like an icon and quoted it. He held it close to his chest with affection."

"With love, Arlene."

"Yes. Love. Like a mistress."

"If a mistress commands a man's life," he turned toward her, "then, yes."

"And you?"

"I'm not sure."

"But you follow the dictates in that book."

"Yes."

"It's like the Bible?"

"People will say that, but actually, no."

"Then what's it like?"

"Itself."

"That's no answer."

"That's the only answer."

"Explain." She leaned closer.

Brent took a drink, gathered his thoughts and stared at the table as he spoke. "First, you must understand there is no modern pragmatism or materialism in the book. Its appeal is to a man's intuition, not his rational side. It's this intuitive nature of the thing; the book's emphasis on sincerity and moral guidance gives it its power."

"It must be highly philosophical?"

"Not really. There is no organized philosophy in arguments or subject matter in the *Hagakure*. Actually, it contains anti-intellectual or anti-scholastic sentiments."

"Then, what in the world is it?" she asked in frustration.

"Plain and simple, it's a record of the utterances of Yamamoto Tsunetomo, a famous Buddhist priest who lived in the eighteenth century. A young samurai lived with Tsunetomo for seven years and recorded all of the old man's thoughts. Most of it is in the form of anecdotes and aphorisms."

"That's it?"

"Yes. That's it."

"Subject matter?"

"As broad as the *Torah* or the *Koran*. That's where you can get your comparison." He stared out of the window and focused on a puffy white cloud above the harbor. "It ranges from duty, death, loyalty, to the implements of the Tea Ceremony or how a certain village got its name. But through it runs the Confucian ideal of the complete man as being both warrior and scholar."

"And death? It exalts dying well. The death of Lieutenant Jimpei Yashiro showed that."

Brent felt a sharp pang of discomfort. But the girl's intense, fascinated visage told him no offense was meant. He continued, "Death is the supreme act the samurai can perform for his master and for the preservation of his honor." He looked up at the ceiling and half-closed his eyes. "It actually says, 'The way of the samurai is the practice of death and as everything in the world is but a sham, death is the only sincerity'."

"It's a grim book."

Brent chuckled. "It contains some very frivolous things bordering on the ridiculous."

"Oh?"

198

"Yes." He smiled down at her. "It teaches that when faced with a crisis, the samurai should put some spittle on his earlobe and exhale deeply through his nose so that he can overcome anything."

"And there are more passages like this?"

"Many more." He took a small sip from his half-filled glass. "Well, this one's a little raunchy, but you asked for it." He leaned back and organized his thoughts. " 'If you cut a face lengthwise, urinate on it, and trample on it with straw sandals, the skin will come off'."

"Good heavens!" she giggled. "I must admit I'm not overwhelmed by its charm. But it's a fascinating piece of work, isn't it?" She brought her glass to her lips, paused, and returned the glass to the table without drinking. "Does it say anything about women?" she asked suddenly.

He rubbed his chin and found the beginnings of his afternoon bristle prickling like fine sandpaper. "I remember one but I don't think you'd like it."

"Please," she pleaded.

He sighed, "All right. It goes something like this, 'Reason is four-cornered and will not move even in an extreme situation. Woman is round and she does not distinguish between good and evil or right and wrong and tumbles into any place at all'."

"Terribly chauvinistic."

"That's how they were."

"That's how they still are, Brent."

"I know, Arlene. But, the *Hagakure* does help one understand the Japanese. Past and present." He waved a hand in a broad gesture. "Its power is still here. I think you can find it in Japanese business practices. I've heard Japanese businessmen still study it." He took an-

199

other small drink. "If you wish, I'll get you a copy."

"I'd love that."

Then the questions began about Brent's personal history. He told her about his father's glorious war record, his mother's tragic death by cancer, the Naval Academy, his father's breakdown, his return to sea and capture by *Yonaga*.

"He committed suicide."

"Yes, Arlene. The day before I came on board *Yonaga*." He went on to describe his first duty as a liaison officer between *Yonaga* and NIS, the attack on Libya, the great sea and air battles in the Mediterranean and the South China Sea, the raid on Arab North Korean bases, his growing friendships with the crew, his involvement with Bushido, Shinto, and Buddhism.

"You became a samurai. 'The American Samurai'."

"That name stuck."

"But you're still a Christian?"

"Yes."

"You're many contradictory things."

Brent chuckled. "You sound like Admiral Fujita."

"You've flown, had duty on a submarine."

He told her about his duty as a gunner, his assignment to *Blackfin* and her tragic loss with all hands.

"Yes, I know. It was well reported, especially in the Arab press."

"I didn't know any of them could read."

She laughed. "Some."

"Remember Salman Rushdie's *The Satanic Verses?*"

"Of course, Brent. Tehran went absolutely bonkers after it was published. There is still a death sentence on Rushdie's head."

Brent snickered humorlessly. "They rioted in the

200

streets, screaming for Rushdie's blood and none of them had read the book. They couldn't read anything. Their mullahs and that dear humanitarian the Ayatollah Khomeini had *told* them to riot." He struck the table with a big set of knuckles. "They're sheep. That's all they are, sheep."

"That's the way of Moslems and of Arabs. They follow a prescribed course like a river in its bed."

"You're very astute," he said, impressed by the girl's incisive intelligence.

"Thank you." She took his hand. "Now let's get astute about personal stuff."

"Like what?"

"Women. You've known a few. You haven't been at sea that much."

He looked at her out of the side of his eye. Her face was slightly tinged with rose and she was leaning very close. "Is this for *Personalities Magazine* or for Arlene Spencer?"

The rose turned to fuchsia. She giggled like a young girl. "Both."

He spoke frankly, "I have known several women, but at the present I'm in love with only one old girl."

"Oh?"

"She calls herself *Yonaga*."

"Spoken like a sailor."

"That's what I am."

"You're also modest."

"I am?"

"Yes. You were an All-American fullback at the Academy and you have shot down a number of Arab aircraft."

"Four. Maybe five."

"Well, my readers want to know about these things and the carrier you sank."

"It was the *Gefara* and one man doesn't sink a carrier. It's a team function. Every man on *Blackfin* shared in the kill." He looked away. "And now they're all dead."

"I'm sorry."

"I wasn't looking for that."

"I know." And then she persisted, "You were attack officer, weren't you?"

"True."

They continued to talk for over an hour. Brent described daily life aboard a carrier, the boredom, the excitement, the tragedy. She nodded and listened quietly. Both nursed their drinks, both forgot about lunch.

Finally, he sank back, still holding his third drink. She shocked him with her next question. "Will *Yonaga* attack the poison gas works at Rabta?"

His jaw became tempered steel and his eyes glared into hers. "Do you actually expect me to answer such a question? If such a plan was in the works, do you think I would discuss it with you, with anyone?"

She bit her lower lip. "Sorry. That was stupid of me, but you do know there has been a lot of talk about this possibility."

Brent resorted to simple logic as his smoke screen. "Think of the distances involved, the logistics and the fact Fujita will *not* take *Yonaga* into the Med. She'd be easy meat for Arab bombers." He shook his head. "It's simple enough. It's a tactical impossibility for *Yonaga* to attack that plant."

"Can I print that?"

A deep rooted feeling of satisfaction brought a smile

202

to Brent's face. This was precisely what Fujita would want. "Of course."

She turned off the recorder. "Would you like some of my famous seafood salad?"

"I'm famished."

"You should be. It's almost time for dinner." She rose and walked to the kitchen.

Standing very close to him just inside the door, she looked up with the captivating blue depths of her eyes arresting his. "You enjoyed lunch?"

"Superb."

She smiled slyly. "And you still have your maiden-head."

Again, she had managed to jolt him and he wondered about this ethereal yet earthy girl and her audacious sense of humor. However, he came back with a quick rejoinder, "I was terribly worried."

She pointed at the door. "You didn't even have to scream for your chaperone."

Now, catching the spirit of the girl's humor, he threw it back at her. "Once, when you held my hand, I almost cried out."

"I controlled myself."

"I'm very proud of you, Arlene. You're a tower of strength." They both laughed.

She glanced at her watch. "It's only five. I mean it's only seventeen-hundred hours. Only a lousy date leaves this early."

The sound rattling deep in his throat was more of a disappointed grunt than a sigh. "I know. Believe me, I don't want to leave, but I told you I have a new man to train." He reached for her hands and she yielded them eagerly. Now she was so close the tips of her breasts

203

pushed against his tunic. "The day after tomorrow, Friday, I have liberty again, Arlene."

"Can I see you?"

This time he did sigh. "I can't think of anything I could want more and I won't be a lousy date."

"Dinner?"

"Better than that. The theater first and then dinner."

"Theater?"

"Kabuki. Have you ever seen one?"

Now she was the delighted child on Christmas morning. "Oh, no. I told you I've only been here for three weeks. I haven't seen anything. I'd love it." And then with a wry smile, "That evil sorcerer Fujita won't turn your coach into a pumpkin at midnight, will he?"

He laughed. There was nothing mordant in the jest, and he accepted it as an innocent joke. "No. I won't be due back until zero-eight-hundred hours Saturday and all evil *kamis* are off duty for the weekend."

"Good."

He touched her soft lips with his finger and spoke with mock theatrics like a Shakespearean actor slicing ham. "Then it shall be yours, from the gloaming until the moon's waxing crescent." And then with seriousness, "I'll be here at eighteen-thirty. Ah, I mean six-thirty."

"Six-thirty," she repeated. Reaching up, she brushed his cheek with her lips and then placed her cheek against his. He ached to crush her to him, smother her lips to his. But, somehow, he knew it was too soon. It would be wrong. Instead, he only touched her ear with his own light kiss and then reached for the doorknob.

As he opened the door, her voice stopped him. "Brent."

"Yes."

"It's about Friday."

"What about Friday?"

An elfin grin slowly enveloped her face. "Please shave closer."

"I'll put that in my notes," he said, stepping into the hall.

Following the American to the elevator, Seaman First Class Haruo Iketa wondered why the big lieutenant's shoulders were shaking. He concluded that all Americans were inscrutable.

When Brent returned to the ship, he hurried to CIC. Cryptographer Stan Fleishman was not there. He had the man paged and in a few minutes the cryptographer walked into the room, bleary-eyed and obviously fatigued. Brent gestured to a small alcove and the young cryptographer followed him into the area where rows of shelves held banks of electronics equipment. He gestured to a chair and the two men sat side-by-side. Brent indicated a computer, "Did Admiral Whitehead show you our Control Data CYBER one-seven-six?"

"No, sir. I spent all of my time on the ESM with Martin Reed. Admiral Whitehead said he'd give me a quick run-through tomorrow."

Brent nodded. "You have a lot to learn, Fleishman. I know you're tired, but I'll give you a quick course now." He pointed at the computer. "Of course its language is military, 'Ada' and it has a six-hundred-megabyte hard disk memory. Its Read Only Memory (ROM) has built-in software that encrypts and decodes signals. It's formatted to interface main frames in Washington and

Tel Aviv."

Fleishman pointed to a small box connected to the computer. "That's not a modem," he said. "It must be an encryption box interfaced with the CYBER."

Brent was pleased with the young man's knowledge. "Right. The encryption box is hard wired by both the CIA and Israeli Intelligence. It encodes and decodes the CISRA code which is used exclusively for transmissions between those agencies and COMYONAGA."

"COMYONAGA. That's Admiral Fujita."

"Right on. The box is seeded with a new pseudo-random sequencer, a Pulse Code Modulator (PCM)—"

"You mean it frequency hops, Mister Ross."

"Right. And it time hops its transmissions in random bursts. Some in milliseconds." He pointed at a Hewlett-Packard LaserJet III printer. "You'll know CISRA because the first group will always be five Cs followed by groups of numbers. The only thing you'll recognize will be the Greenwich Civil Time of the transmission. You will immediately call Admiral Whitehead or me."

"There's another whole layer of decoding which cannot be accessed here."

"Right, Fleishman."

"The rest is up to the admiral and me." Thinking of the extraordinary complexity of the system, Brent allowed the air to escape his lungs in a long sighing sound. At first CISRA had been based on an eight figure sub routine which in turn was based on random combinations and permutations of a ten figure master. The data had to be fed into another small computer— usually a NEC lap-top—along with an eight figure digital control code predicated on the phase of the moon and the Greenwich Civil Time of reception plus three.

Only then, would the message flash on the screen in plain language. Now, that routine, too, had been modified because the CIA got word that main frames in Tripoli and Moscow were "chewing" on the code and would soon break it. The eight figure sub routine was increased to twelve and the ten figure master became sixteen. The combinations and permutations of the master now exceeded 2 to the ninety-sixth power. They were safe for a few more months.

Fleishman toyed with the keyboard. "I should be able to handle it, sir. After all, this electronic genie does most of it." He grinned, a likable boyish smile. "All you have to do is teach it to print-out, brew coffee and carry the message to you. Then I'll be out of a job."

Brent laughed and patted the young man on the back. "There's a lot in what you say." He waved at the equipment. "Some day these computers may put us all on the same shelves where we keep them." He indicated the door. "I think that's enough for today, Stan. Get some rest."

Both young men stood and walked to the door.

Chapter Nine

Although the next day was a busy one for Brent, it passed slowly, his mind occupied with thoughts of Arlene Spencer. A short staff meeting was called by Admiral Fujita in the morning. In buoyant spirits, the old admiral reported on his meeting with the Emperor. "The Mikado," he said, "has been pleased with *Yonaga*'s operations and gives his blessings to whatever new operations we may undertake. He has pledged the continued support of the chrysanthemum throne." There were shouts of "Banzai!" and *"Tenno heiko* Banzai!"

Brent noticed the admiral did not mention the poison gas works at Rabta or any other specific target. Only the admiral, Brent, Bernstein, Mayfield and Whitehead knew of the plan to attack Rabta with B-25s. And that was how it would remain. Then the old man waved his hand over the group as if he were giving a benediction. "And then the Son of Heaven prayed with me. We implored the help of Jimmu Tenno." Jimmu Tenno was the first Emperor and direct descendent of the goddess Amaterasu. Everyone knew his power was great and if he gave his blessings, the chances of success were greatly enhanced.

Fujita reported on the commando attack on the Tinian airfield. Thirty men from the garrison on Aguijan landed in the dead of night. Although most of the attackers were killed, they managed to destroy four Super Constellations and damage two more. There were more shouts of "Banzai!" After a short prayer, the meeting was dismissed.

Brent spent the remainder of the day with Rear Admiral Byron Whitehead, Electronics Technician Martin Reed and Cryptographer Stan Fleishman, studying CISRA and Purple Alpha which was given the old NATO phonetic alphabet designation "Foxtrot" for "Fleet Code." In addition, every man in CIC was expected to be able to function at all stations. Consequently, Fleishman was checked out at every point. Whitehead tired quickly, and the bulk of the training was left to Brent and Martin Reed.

It was sunset before Brent left the irritating glow of CIC. That night dreams of Arlene Spencer jarred him awake several times. "Tomorrow night I'll see her," he told himself. But it seemed time had almost come to a halt.

Despite Brent's impatience and the slow crawl of time, the next evening the young lieutenant finally found himself at Arlene's apartment door at precisely eighteen-thirty hours. However, the redoubtable Seaman First Class Haruo Iketa was not at his side. He and another seaman had pulled a sturgeon from Tokyo Bay and eaten it raw. They were both in the sick bay suffering from vomiting and diarrhea. Brent had hurried from the ship to the motor pool before another seaman guard could be assigned. He was smiling with self-satisfaction when he drove the staff car out of the gates. He was free at last and he was going to see Arlene.

When Arlene opened the door, Brent caught his breath. She was lovelier than ever. Her knee-length dress fit her body perfectly as if it had been tailored by an expert seamstress. Ivory silk, woven gossamer fine, it appeared to float about her body whenever she moved. Swept up severely, the profuse mane of long blond hair was cropped and folded into a flossy chignon. When she turned her head, the penumbra of light behind her played upon it, changing its color from burnished iridescence of argent to the rich gold of a polished necklace. Without the soft folds of her hair framing her face, the shape and size of her eyes were emphasized, the planes of the bone structure of her cheeks and jawline seemed more finely chiseled, lips fuller and even more alluring. There was a soft blush in her eyes as if the warming glow of the morning sun was blooming just behind them. "I'm ready," she said softly.

Brent was not sure of what she meant, his mind snagged on the reef of the possible double entendre. He finally muttered, "Of course." Then glancing at his watch, "You'd better hurry. We're going to the Kabukiza Theater in the Ginza and the traffic's heavy, even with the gasoline shortage."

She glanced to both sides of the lieutenant. "Where's your shadow?"

"He's been eclipsed by a bad fish."

"Serious?" she asked, reaching into the guest closet and pulling a coat from its hanger.

"He'll live."

"We'll be alone."

210

"I'm for that."

Hand in hand the couple walked to the elevator.

The Kabukiza Theater was already crowded when they arrived. Pulling Arlene by the hand, Brent hurried through the throng. He flashed his tickets at the door, grabbed a program and pushed through, leading Arlene across a small foyer to the main auditorium. By American standards, it was quite small. He led Arlene to a pair of chairs which were next to an aisle.

Arlene waved down toward the stage. "There are no chairs down there."

"No," Brent answered. "Most of the Japanese prefer to sit on *zabritons*."

"They're nothing but flat cushions."

"Right, Arlene. It's their way."

"You've been here before?"

Brent smiled. "Many times. I enjoy Kabuki. There's nothing on earth like it."

She bared a subtle needle, "You usually bring your women here?"

Ready for her, he dodged artfully, "No. I usually drag them into the nearest bedroom, bind them with leather thongs, chain them to the bed, beat them with whips, burn the bottom of their feet with cigarettes, twist the nipples from their—"

Giggling, she waved a hand in surrender. "Okay. Okay, I get the picture. That runway," she said, pointing to a long platform that projected from the stage into the audience, "is like a strip joint."

"You've been to strip joints?"

"That's how I worked my way through college. I was the feature act at 'Fat Jim's T and A Emporium'," was the deadpan response.

211

Brent nodded solemnly as if he actually believed her and indicated the platform. "That's the *hanamishi*. A lot of the action will take place there."

The girl at last appeared serious. "*Hanamishi* means 'the flower path'."

"Right. You're good at this language."

"Thank you, but the program . . . what are we going to see?"

Brent pulled the program from his pocket, studied it in the dim light and then turned to his companion. "*Shibaraka*, Arlene. It's a play that dates from the seventeenth century. I can assure you that it hasn't changed much."

An usher passed, offering headsets for five dollars. Arlene shook her head. "I understand Japanese."

"I know you do, but they talk very fast," Brent warned.

"I listen fast."

Brent shrugged and continued his explanation, "*Shibaraka* is mainly pageantry, a spectacle of flashy costumes and absolutely mad makeup jobs."

"Aren't you describing all of Kabuki?"

Brent nodded, pleased the quick mind was at work. "Right. In all of Kabuki you'll find amazing combinations of elements and skills. Music, song, choreographed movements, vivid sets, incredible costumes, wild makeup, all synchronized like the high kicks of the Rockettes. Yet, it still produces the most dramatic and captivating fairy tales. And you must keep in mind Kabuki is an escape from realism. It does not try to imitate life. Its emphasis is on unbelievable characters and emotions." He wrapped a hand around her thin arm. "You're going to see acting so extreme, so intense, it

212

will appear to be hammy and amateurish." He waved a hand. "But it's the style. They make a meal out of everything. When someone cries it can take twenty minutes." He ran his hand down her arm and took her hand. "So be prepared. It's an incredible experience."

"You love it."

"You could say that."

"*Shibaraka* must have a plot."

"Of course. It's basically a good guy against bad guy yarn."

"Like an old John Wayne western."

"Good comparison, Arlene."

"The actors are all male."

"Right. The female impersonators are called *onnagata*. Some are gorgeous."

"They turn you on?"

He felt his face flush, but maintained his composure. "Except for one notable similarity."

She laughed so loud several heads turned. And then she changed moods as quickly as the wind in the doldrums. "Tell me more, Brent," she said seriously. "It's fascinating."

"It's all male now, but, at first, Kabuki was an all female theater."

The girl seemed surprised. "I didn't know that. Why the big change?"

"Too many of the women were accused of prostitution and they were banned." He shrugged. "It stuck."

"The Japanese hate to change tradition."

"Like no other people on earth. I found—" He was interrupted by clacking of wooden blocks being struck together. Lowering his voice, he leaned close to her ear, "Those are *hyoshigi*. The play's about to begin."

A stagehand cloaked in black hauled back the curtain revealing a small village situated on a tinfoil river. In the distance a huge castle crowned a ridge. Musicians crouching at one side of the stage began to pluck three-stringed samisens and a narrator started his chant.

"A Greek chorus," Arlene noted in a whisper.

"Same idea."

Then the action began, the actors storming onto the stage. The costume of the lead actor, playing the part of the villain, was macabre, terrifying, while at the same time, ludicrous. Ten prongs like exaggerated spider legs protruded from his cheeks, a pointed black topknot gave him the aspect of a walking temple devil. From the back of his head, two stiffly starched white wings spread upward, suggesting that he might be able to fly. Brent guessed the costume must have weighed at least a hundred pounds.

The faces of all of the actors were painted a deathly white. Eerie black lines of mascara outlined the eyes while tiny mouths of vermilion were grotesque. As the play unfolded, the action spilled onto the *hanamishi* where long dramatic soliloquies were shouted at the audience. Through it all, stagehands dressed in black wove through the action dangling birds on strings, dragging papier-mâché animals across the stage, and sometimes, actually straightening the actors' ponderous costumes.

Finally, came the denouement with the villain vanquished by the hero. However, the deed was accomplished by a laser-like stare, not the violence so typical of an American western.

"Astonishing," Arlene said, leaving the theater on Brent's arm.

"I'm glad you enjoyed it," he said honestly. "Now for dinner."

The *Toyo-Yamato* restaurant was one of Tokyo's finest. The old man who opened the door looked as small and twisted as a two-hundred-year-old dwarf pine. *"Irasshai,"* he wheezed, bowing. He welcomed his honored guests in the traditional way. He gestured for the couple to follow.

Followed by the couple, the old man hobbled down the center of a small room flanked by separate chambers for each party. Waitresses in colorful kimonos hurried by carrying trays loaded with food. The atmosphere was heavy with the savory aromas of steaming food, talking and laughter.

The old man stopped in front of a compartment with the characters *So-Yo* above the door. "Send the sun," Arlene said, pointing at the ideograms. The old man turned, smiled at the girl and gestured. Arlene and Brent entered and the old man slid the wood and paper *fusuma* shut behind them.

The room was small with an interior of paper, straw, and wood. All wooden surfaces were carefully planed and untreated. There was no paint to hide the grain. Not one scrap of metal was to be seen. In the center of the room was a low table with two *zabutons* on opposite sides. Brent gestured to one cushion and Arlene seated herself.

"This is a 'three mat' room," Brent said. He went on, answering the quizzical look on his companion's face. He gestured at three mats of woven rushes covering the floor. "Tatami mats. Each mat is exactly eighty-four centimeters by one-hundred-seventy-four centimeters,

215

and the proportions in classic Japanese rooms from bowls to flowers and even to the patterns in a woman's kimono will be in harmony with the tatami mats."

"I can't believe it."

Brent laughed. "They call it harmony. You can see it in the architecture of their temples, gardens, the perfect proportions of the roofs of country houses, in their art, poetry."

"I'd like to get in harmony with a drink, Brent."

Brent clapped twice and immediately a young, beautiful woman in a colorful silk kimono walked in with the short mincing steps forced by her tight garment. Upswept and ornamented with jeweled combs and cherry blossoms, her lacquered hair glistened like newly mined coal. She was carrying a tray with two porcelain cups. She placed one in front of each diner.

"You've ordered already," Arlene said, looking at the cup.

"Yes. Hot spiced sake. They call it *sakazuki*." A slight smile turned up the corners of his lips. "But I haven't ordered everything."

"What do you mean?"

"The dessert will be up to you."

"I usually skip dessert."

"Usually?"

She held up her cup and stared at him over the rim. "Not always." They touched cups and drank. "Excellent," she said.

"You're sitting in the place of honor," Brent said, nodding to an alcove behind Arlene. She turned her head. "It's the *tokonoma*," he explained, pointing at a small table with an old vase that appeared to be from the Heian period. Behind the vase were two woodblock prints of countryside scenes. "The guest of honor always sits with his or her back to the *tokonoma* so that it provides a frame." Brent pointed to a small banner hanging above the prints. There were four characters on it.

"I can read it," Arlene said. She pondered a moment, *"Hoge jaku* which roughly translates into, 'Break the bonds of useless things'."

Brent was impressed. "Very good," he said. "It's an old Buddhist maxim."

She nodded. "I'll drink to that." They drained their cups. There was a flash of a colorful kimono and the cups were refilled. "I don't like drinking on an empty stomach, but that's the way the Japanese do it. Right, Brent?"

"Right. They do all of their serious drinking before eating."

"I'll get smashed, Brent." Again the sly smile. "Or is that your plan? Get me drunk, violate my body, fate worse than death, ruined for life, that damned scarlet letter on my left boob, no other man—"

"Alright! Alright," he pleaded through his chuckles. "We'll eat now."

He clapped twice and in a moment the waitress entered carrying a tray with two rectangular black lacquer boxes. For the first time, the waitress spoke, "Good food must please the eye as well as the palate," she said, bending very close to Brent's ear. A box and *hashi* were placed before both diners.

Brent and Arlene lifted the lids and peered into the boxes. Brent smacked his lips. "Sushi garnished with seaweed and bean curd," he said.

"You mean raw fish and mine's still moving."

217

"They take pride in the freshness of their fish."

"This one can swim down my throat."

"Bite him to death first." Brent expertly pulled a piece of fish from the box with his *hashi* and downed it, and then smiled at his companion.

Slowly, Arlene followed his example. "Hmm, not bad," she said.

After the fish they were served a fish and mushroom soup followed by a salad of pumpkin, more fish, cucumber blossoms and chestnut leaves.

Arlene looked up. "I've been eating in the hotel or at American-style restaurants. I can't believe this. It's so tasty."

"You ain't seen nothin' yet," Brent quipped, just as the waitress brought sea bream, roe and abalone roasted with onions and ginkgo nuts and baskets of tiny crabs. "Eat the basket, too," Brent said. "It's seaweed combined with cherries, peas, noodles and potatoes. Marvelous stuff."

Arlene shrugged and attacked her meal with her *hashi*. She seemed to have no trouble with the wooden sticks.

When the meal was finished, Brent was pleased with his companion. She had genuinely seemed to enjoy her meal. "Dessert?" he asked.

She pondered for a moment. "I'd rather have a nightcap. Why not at my place?"

Silently, they rose together.

❧

They sat close together on the couch, sipping their Haig and Haig. Her closeness, the smell of her perfume, her sheer femininity — they worked like an aphrodisiac on the young lieutenant. He wanted to hold her, kiss her, make frantic love to her. But there was an aura of tension about her, an undefinable barrier that said to him, *this is not the time*. He felt it in the stiffness of her hand, in the looks she avoided when he glanced at her. He opened with an innocuous question, "Where did you go to school?"

"Cal-Berkeley," she said.

"Lot of radicals there."

"There are people interested in change, in justice there, if that's what you mean."

He sipped his drink. "No, that's not what I mean. I mean radicals, the raw material for traitors and terrorists."

"You're thinking of the sixties."

"The reputation is still there."

"But, undeserved."

He shrugged and returned the glass to his lips. She took a large drink and then tabled her glass, making a ring on the table. She lifted the glass and made an interlocking ring, and then another. He wondered at her silence. This was not like her. "You know a lot about me," he said. "But, you know, I know very little about you."

Animation returned with a chuckle. "I'd bore you to death."

"Try me."

She refilled both glasses, took a deep drink, and said, "I was born in Burbank, California. My father was a high school teacher, mother an alcoholic. I was the only child." He listened intently as the story unfolded. Undergraduate work at the University of California. A graduate degree at Columbia followed by her first job;

a reporter for a small Greenwich village paper. Her beat had been Chinatown.

"Where did you live?"

"I had a small place . . ." she laughed, "I mean a room in the Lower East Side."

"That's dangerous."

"Tell me. I was mugged twice."

"Romance?"

She smiled wryly. "My share."

"The first time?"

"I was nineteen-years-old, and I lost it in the backseat of a Buick."

"No! I meant the first time you were truly in love."

She tossed off a large part of her drink. "There was one, an artist in Greenwich Village."

"You still love him?"

She emptied her glass and poured another drink. "He's dead."

"I'm sorry. He died young."

"It was AIDS."

He jolted upright as if a thousand-watt circuit had raced up through the springs of the couch and charged his spine. He felt his scalp tingle and he was sure his hair was standing on end. "Good Lord," exploded from his lips.

"I'm HIV negative."

"I didn't ask."

"I know. But you sure as hell want to know." She took another drink and her speech was slightly slurred. "You've wanted to lay me from the first time you looked at me."

He had to collect his wits. He had never met a woman like this. Taking a drink, he worked the liquor around his teeth and gums, forcing himself to savor the charcoal flavor before he swallowed it. He turned to her and she stared up at him. "My mind wasn't the only one occupied with the bedroom, Arlene."

She smiled. "You're attractive. I'll admit that." She moved closer and lifted her lips.

Tabling his drink, he slipped an arm around her narrow shoulders. Her mouth was open, hot, wet, and hungry. As he crushed his mouth on hers, a burning force seemed to control his body, clenching like a hot coil in his groin, and he felt a trip-hammer pounding furiously against his ribs. His tongue found hers, a slithering, darting creature with a life of its own. Her arms were around his neck, a hand clawing at the back of his head, fingers furrowing his hair. Then, pulling him back onto the cushions, she raised her body and stretched full-length on the couch. He pressed down on her, lips still glued to hers, their kiss growing wetter and hotter, tongues dueling furiously. She began to make small sounds in her throat like a tiny animal in the throes of happiness.

Her maddening body. His hands began a quest as old as mankind, snaking down over her breasts, dipping in at her tiny waist, flaring out with the perfect hips and buttock, down further, finally finding the hem of her skirt and pulling it up. Then the journey upward. The hand moved slowly over the perfect thigh. Twisting, she clutched him tighter, her hands running over the bunched muscles of his back, kissing, gasping muttering into his ear. Finally, he reached his goal, tore frantically at the panty hose with numb fingers. Then the panties were pulled aside and he finally found the hot well of her essence.

She cried out incoherently, thrust her hips up in short thrusting movements and then suddenly twisted away, pushing his hand down. "No! No! No!"

"No!" he repeated incredulously. "After all that?"

Pulling away, she sat up. "I'm sorry, Brent. I want to as much as you do." She straightened her dress.

"Then why not," he spat bitterly.

"It's too soon."

"My God, Arlene. Let's not be sophomoric."

"I'm sorry, Brent, dear. That's how I am." She kissed him on the cheek. "Please forgive me. That was rotten of me."

He tossed off his drink and leapt to his feet. "I've got to get out of here."

She was at his side both hands on his shoulders. He looked away. She kissed him on the cheek. "Please don't be angry. Give me time, my darling. Don't rush it."

He looked down into the earnestness on the girl's face and he felt his anger begin to fade. "I've still got to leave." He walked to the door.

She grabbed him again, held him. "I'll see you again?"

Sighing, he looked down into the blue of her eyes heightened by moisture. "I suppose so."

"I need another interview, Brent." She toyed with his lapel. "You will have liberty the day after tomorrow?"

"That's right."

"Then spend it here. I'll broil you a steak and bake a potato."

He shook his head. "I can't go through this again."

"You won't have to."

"That's a promise?"

"A promise."

222

She pulled his head down and her kiss was again filled with passion. Holding her close, he could feel her pelvis begin to move as if she were trying to grind herself into him. "A promise," he said, breathlessly.

"A promise."

Walking to the elevator, his head spun with thoughts of the bizarre, undefinable workings of the female mind. She had promised for the next night, but refused this evening. It made no sense whatsoever. Forty-eight hours. What difference could forty-eight hours make? Somehow, it was significant to Arlene. Was there a vestige of Victorianism in this strange girl? In all women? This had happened to him before. He was still puzzled when the elevator doors opened.

Chapter Ten

"Never will the samurai hesitate to raise his sword for honesty and truth and compassion against injustice, tyranny and greed," Admiral Fujita said, his eyes roaming over the members of his staff who stared back at him from the long table in Flag Plot. "If good men all over the world, in thousands of rooms like this would emulate those brave men who fight for *Yonaga,* the world would be changed and tyrants would find their graves."

Brent Ross added his own "Banzai!" to those shouted by the Japanese. And they were all there. Even the aviators added their voices: Air Group Commanding Officer Commander Yoshi Matsuhara, the new torpedo bomber leader, Lieutenant Commander Iyetsuma Yagoto, and the C.O. of the dive bombers, Commander Takuya Iwata. All had been summoned from their training duties. All looked very tired.

The admiral squelched the high spirits by telling the staff about carriers *Kiev* and *Minsk.* Because of reports in the media, the sale of the ships to an Arab front and their course for Tripoli were well-known to all hands. However, their conversion and remodeling was still secret. The officers remained grimly silent as the admiral gave the details of operational aircraft, radar, armament, speed and range.

"We will engage them, destroy them!" the old scribe Katsube screeched, waving a fist and spraying his neighbors with spittle. There were a few halfhearted shouts of "Banzai!" while several officers pulled handkerchiefs from their pockets and wiped their faces.

Brent wondered if the admiral would now disclose the entire plan for the attack on the gas works at Rabta. And he had not mentioned carrier *Bennington*. However, the old man spoke only of *Minsk* and *Kiev* and the prospect of engaging them. "We will destroy them, of course, if they dare venture within striking range of our sacred islands."

Now the "Banzais!" were shouted with enthusiasm.

A gesture from the admiral, and Captain John "Slugger" Fite rose. Silence returned to the room. A veteran destroyer officer dating back to World War II, Fite was the bravest, most knowledgeable escort commander Brent had ever known. Under air attack, his ships always closed on the carrier, adding their vast fire power to that of *Yonaga*. Twice Fite had led his slim *Fletchers* in near suicidal torpedo runs on enemy cruisers and destroyers. On both occasions, he had bought time for the damaged *Yonaga* to escape. However, the price had been paid with the blood of his men and the loss of five ships. The escort commander appeared tired and although he had lost weight, he still had the hulking, burly look of the stalking bear. The sharp, strong contours of his face still showed the determination of the fighter to whom defeat was a stranger. He was a man who would not ask for or give quarter. Crowned by a shock of unruly white hair the color of an Aspen ski slope, his countenance showed new lines driven into the flesh by the sun, wind, salt spray, and time. There was suffering there, too; terrible suffering stamped irrevocably when his only son was murdered.

Assigned as an interpreter to the American ambassador in Damascus, young Fite had been kidnapped and tortured to death by terrorists in 1981. The torture had been inflicted with consummate Arabic artistry. He was skinned alive, fingernails and toenails pulled, eyes gouged out, teeth and tongue ripped from his mouth with pliers and, finally, in Arab tradition, penis cut off and stuffed into his mouth. Driven by unbounded hatred, "Slugger" Fite only took prisoners when ordered. His favorite method of execution was to drop shallow-set depth charges among swimming enemy survivors. The terrific concussions drove water up their rectums and burst their intestines. It was a horrible death. Fite laughingly called it "the salt water enema." Yet, despite the relentless killer who lurked in the hell within, the leprechaun still dwelled in the blue Irish eyes. Brent was sure his big laugh could still be found. But not often; especially this day.

Fite spoke in deep sonorous tones like Laurence Olivier filling Carnegie Hall with *Othello*. "Admiral, two of my DDs are still laid up with fouled boilers."

"When will the descaling be completed?"

"Six or seven days." He ran a finger over a ruddy cheek. "But I need thirty twenty-millimeter barrels, the same number of forties and a dozen five-inch barrels. Some of my barrels are so worn they're spraying shells like lawn sprinklers. I'm a menace to our own ships."

"How many of your *Fletchers* are battle-worthy?"

The big man sighed. "Six, but, again, their gunnery is not what it should be."

"We need at least seven," Fujita said, turning to the executive officer, Captain Mitake Arai. "The gun barrels, Captain. When will they arrive?"

Before Arai could answer, the gunnery officer, Commander Nobomitsu Atsumi, who was one of *Yonaga*'s "plank owners," interrupted. Miraculously youthful with black hair and clear skin, his voice was sharpened by the hard edge of impatience. "*Yonaga* needs twenty-seven twenty-five-millimeter barrels and at least fourteen one-hundred-twenty-seven-millimeter barrels."

The harried Arai retorted quickly, "We have a new supply of barrels due tomorrow. They were shipped yesterday from Nakajima."

Fujita returned to Fite. "Your crews, fully manned and trained?"

"I have some new men, but they're the best. We have given them all the dock-side training they can take. But they need to be underway, on the high seas, not in classrooms. That's the best training." The officers all nodded agreement. Fite seated himself.

Fujita turned to the chief engineer, Lieutenant Tatsuya Yoshida who was another "plank owner." He was as old and gray as Commander Nobomitsu Atsumi was youthful. Fujita said, "One of the main bearings on number three shaft overheated during our last run at flank speed." Brent looked at Rear Admiral Whitehead. Both men remembered the fearsome vibrations that had come up through the deck gratings on the bridge. Both had been convinced terrible damage had been done to the drive train.

Yoshida placed both hands on the table and pushed himself to his feet. His arthritic spine prevented him from straightening completely. He spoke with his head slightly hunched forward and down, and he eyed the admiral over his glasses like a gambler trying to steal a glance at his opponent's cards. His voice was high and squeaky. "It was a matter of lubrication, Admiral. We were able to reduce speed before irreparable damage was

227

done. As you know, two of my watertenders hand lubri-cated the bearing until we docked. We have corrected the problem."

"Boilers one, six and nine are still down?"

"Yes, sir. The descaling will be completed by tomorrow."

Brent felt a charge in his pulse. Tomorrow, Sunday, he would see Arlene. Would she honor her promise, or would he experience more hell of frustration? But it was more than that. He liked her. He felt a deepening attachment. He knew that sex-starved sailors were easy prey for instant infatuations, easily mistaken for something far more serious. He was no different, but, still, the girl had a special kind of attraction completely divorced from her erotic appeal. She was clever, witty and utterly charming. He yearned for her company the way a starving man hungers for a scrap of bread.

Fujita's voice broke through the musings, "Evaporators, auxiliaries?"

"All overhauled and ready, sir," Yoshida answered.

"And if I had to put to sea within the hour?"

"I could give you seven-hundred-fifty pounds of pressure in all boilers except one, six and nine."

"Twenty-eight knots," Fujita said.

"Yes, sir," the chief engineer agreed. "With three boilers off line, twenty-eight knots."

Fujita seemed satisfied, but Dive-Bomber Commander Takuya Iwata was not. "Sir, when will my Alchis get the new Sakae Forty-Three *Taifu?*" Iwata waved a hand in a gesture of frustration. "The F-6-F Hellcats have a new twenty-eight-hundred-horsepower Pratt and Whitney engine, our Seafires have three-thousand-fifty horsepower Rolls Royce Griffons." He glared at Yoshi Matsuhara. "Our enemies boast of their new three-thousand-horsepower Daimler-Benz *Valkyrie* and yet," he stabbed a finger at the air group commander, "only our fighter leader's Zero mounts the new Sakae Forty-Three *Taifu* with its great power of three-thousand-two-hundred horsepower. The rest of us are still under-powered with the Sakae Forty-Two."

It was the old *horsepower* argument. Brent had seen it many times. All pilots craved more power. Power meant speed, armor, altitude; all of the things that spelled survival for those who fought in the skies. The Sakae Forty-Two was a two-thousand-horsepower engine and now lagged far behind the others.

Yoshi came out of his chair as if fired. "That is not of my choice," he shot back. "You know very well the engine is not perfected. It runs hot when in overboost."

"All engines do."

Brent watched Fujita for a sign of concern, of anger; a sign that the old admiral would bring the mounting argument to a halt. He saw only the usual benign complacency; the look of the interested observer who was fascinated by the growing acrimony. Perhaps he was amused. The two flyers hated each other and everyone knew it. Brent was convinced the old man would let the exchange run its course. He felt the old man would find some pleasure in witnessing the vindictive broadsides.

Yoshi slapped the table with an open palm. "They don't over-heat like the *Taifu* and you know it. Must I remind you that mine is a Nakajima experimental engine."

"Remind me of anything you like, but my bombers still need more power."

"All aircraft need more power," Yoshi retorted.

"Gentlemen," Fujita said, gesturing at Horace Mayfield, "the CIA has reported that Curtis Wright has redesigned a new version of the *Taifu*. The R-Thirty-

Three-Fifty. It will be made available through license with Nakajima, but not for this operation. We must use what we have." He made a small temple with his bony fingers and then tapped his fingertips together, narrow brown eyes boring into the aviators. "Your new pilots are ready?"

"Negative, sir," Yoshi answered while Iwata and Yagoto nodded their heads in agreement. "We need more time."

"We do not have it." The aircraft commanders looked at each other in frustration.

Fujita's eyes swept the entire room. "Our magazines are full and our bunkers topped off." He began to pound the table with a fist to emphasize each word. "We must be ready to put to sea in seven days!"

The officers looked at each other in surprise. Finally, Atsumi said, "Sir, may I inquire as to our mission, our destination?"

"No! You may not."

The weighty silence that fell on the room was pregnant with suspense, frustration, hostility, expectancy and uncertainty. There was also an element of fear Brent could feel in the looks, the body language. He knew what his fellow officers were thinking. Were they to raid Arab bases? The Tomonuto Atoll? Hunt down and engage *Minsk* and *Kiev?* Everyone was wondering why the objective of the operation was kept secret from the staff. This level of secrecy was unprecedented. It could only mean the risk-taking was of extraordinary proportions. Only four officers and Fujita knew the details of the operation. All other members of the staff were unaware of this. Obviously, they all believed only the admiral was privy to the plan.

Fite broke the silence, "Seven days. That's cutting it

close, sir."

"I know." In a deliberate effort to change the subject, Admiral Fujita gestured at the new torpedo bomber commander. "Only a few of you have had an opportunity to meet our new torpedo bomber commander, Lieutenant Commander Iyetsuma Yagoto. He is the replacement for Lieutenant Joji Kai who died so splendidly when he rammed carrier *Al Kufra* with his bomber."

"Banzai!" roared through the room.

Fujijta gestured and the young pilot stood self-consciously. Slender and tall, the lieutenant commander had a square jaw and bright eyes. Although he shifted from foot to foot in this awkward moment, Brent knew he was quick-witted, tenacious and resourceful. The pilot nodded at the curious faces, but before he could return to his chair, Yoshida rapped out, "Yagoto?"

"Correct, sir. Yagoto."

The chief engineer persisted, "The Yagotos of Komokiri?"

The young officer answered with his chin high, eyes flashing defiantly, "Yes. I was born in Komokiri."

There were whispers and hard looks were exchanged. Brent sat bolt upright, confused by the galvanic shock of hostility that filled the room. Then he heard the despised word *eta* whispered, and he understood. Lieutenant Commander Iyetsuma Yagoto was an *eta*. Often called *burakumin,* the *eta*—literally translating to *much filth*—were outcasts. They were the harijan caste of Japan. Hounded by an ancient bigotry whose origins were lost in antiquity, the million people who constituted the *eta* class were no different religiously or genetically from other Japanese. Only their jobs distinguished them from their neighbors. The *eta* were midwives, executioners, undertakers, tenant farmers, peddlers, day laborers,

231

butchers, tanners, sandal makers, all of which were considered "unclean." In centuries past, they produced saddles and weapons, invaluable in wartime. Yet, despite their talents, they were despised by the masses. Much of this abhorrence was rooted in religion. Shintoism with its obsessive devotion to cleanliness and purity, and later Buddhism, with its strictures against the slaughter and cleaning of animals, played major roles in the lowering of their station. Although they had been allowed to die in Japan's wars since the turn of the century, they were still singled out, segregated and detested.

Iwata, the haughty aristocrat, spoke up with obvious distaste, "You expect samurai to serve with *eta*, Admiral Fujita?"

The old sailor tugged at the single whisker dangling from his chin. He spoke slowly and deliberately, "I am well aware of Lieutenant Commander Yagoto's background. He is a fine officer and served with distinction with the Self Defense Force for ten years. His great-uncle served with me on board *Mikasa* in the war with the Russians. He died gloriously for the Mikado. I will tolerate no discrimination against him." His black eyes searched every face. "Remember, a five-hundred-kilogram bomb discriminates against no one. All corpses are equal." His black eyes searched every face. "If any of you find you cannot serve with Lieutenant Commander Iyetsuma Yagoto, see me privately and I will cut orders for your transfer."

Iwata glared at Yagoto who had returned to his chair and stared back unflinchingly. Brent and Yoshi caught Iwata's eye and the looks shifted. Hatred filled the room with an icy force felt by everyone. Again, Brent recalled Iwata's hatred for the black commanding officer of submarine *Blackfin,* Lieutenant Reginald Williams, calling him "nothing but another filthy Pakistani." He recollected the near fist fight between the pair. And now more bigotry. He would stop Iwata if he had to pound sense into him with his fists. He had done it once on the hangar deck and would do it again. In addition to sore knuckles and a tender jaw, he had derived a deep sense of satisfaction from the pounding he had given to the big dive-bomber commander. Iwata had never forgotten or forgiven and was hungry for revenge. The venom would be vented on Brent or his best friend, Yoshi Matsuhara.

Eager to cool the tension, the admiral searched for a distraction, a unifying device. He struggled to his feet and gestured for the others to follow. Staring at the little admiral, the officers came to attention. Brent expected a prayer which was de rigueur at the end of an important meeting. However, in a high brittle voice, the admiral began to sing the "Kamigayo," the old Imperial national anthem. Brent and the Japanese joined in: "Corpses drifting swollen in the sea depths, corpses rotting in the mountain grass. We shall die, we shall die for the Emperor. We shall never look back."

There were shouts of "Banzai!" and back slapping. Fujita raised his hands and said, "This meeting is closed."

The officers began to file from the room. Iwata, with his usual dramatic flare, shouted, halting the men, "Admiral, 'The Naval Lament', sir, before we leave!"

Fujita tucked his lower lip under and nodded his approval. Iwata's voice led a booming chorus of the old lyrics sung generations ago by men of the Imperial Navy: "If I go to sea, I shall return a corpse awash. Thus for the sake of the Emperor I shall not die peacefully at home."

More shouts of "Banzai!" and the officers began to file through the door. Brent whispered into Yoshi's ear loud enough for Iwata to hear, "Anyone for a chorus of '*Auld Lang Syne*'?"

Yoshi's laughter turned a half dozen heads. Iwata's stare was the quintessence of hatred.

Brent heard the PA command him to report to Admiral Fujita's cabin just as he reached the door to his own cabin. When he entered the admiral's quarters, the old man was already seated at his desk. They were alone. Fujita gestured to Brent to take a chair directly in front of the desk.

His opening was blunt, "You went ashore unguarded on your last liberty, Brent-san."

"True, sir. Seaman Haruo Iketa was very ill."

"Did you attempt to replace him?"

"Yes, sir. None was available."

"My standing orders are that no officer is to go ashore alone."

Brent tightened his jaws and pulled his lips into a slash. "I know, sir."

"You have liberty tomorrow?"

"Yes, sir."

"A woman. The reporter Arlene Spencer?"

The old man missed nothing. "True, sir. Dinner at her place."

"The Tokyo Hilton Hotel, room 1410."

"Correct, Admiral."

The old man sighed and sagged back. His face softened. "I was young once, Brent-san. The burdens of age are numberless and many old men spend their last years lamenting their lost powers. But there are blessings, too." Brent raised an eyebrow. It was not often the old man spoke his innermost thoughts to anyone.

"Yes, Brent-san, the desires of youth can bring exquisite joy when realized, but can inflict frightful pain when thwarted. I know watches at sea can be long, lonely, and painful. I know you must be fond of this woman. She possesses great beauty." He tapped the shiny surface of his desk with his knuckles. "But do not allow your emotions to replace good judgement. You have been ambushed four times by the *Rengo Sekigun,* fought gun battles in the Imperial Hotel and Ueno Park, had two fist fights out here," he waved, "on our own perimeter, shot Kathryn Suzuki dead not a hundred meters from here." He punched an open palm with his fist for emphasis. "You know how dangerous they are." He pointed at the young American, "You are 'The American Samurai'. There is no member of my crew they would enjoy killing more."

"Am I restricted, sir?"

The old man pulled on the single white whisker. "That would be appropriate." Brent felt his heart sink. "However, you need your liberty and the company of a woman." He ran a hand through the thin film of white hair that failed to cover his pate. "You said you were to have dinner with Miss Spencer?"

"Yes, sir."

"You will not leave the hotel?"

"If that is a condition of liberty, we will not leave the hotel. We will remain in her apartment."

"I will have a staff car drop you there, a guard escort you to her door and then the guard will return here. We are short handed." Brent nodded. "When you are ready to depart, you will phone the duty officer at the main gate and request a staff car."

Brent sighed and a warm feeling of happiness spread through him like a double shot of scotch. He had escaped punishment. He would see Arlene. "Thank you, sir. You are generous."

"Not generous, Brent-san. Only practical. We have a long perilous voyage ahead. Every man needs 'R and R'."

Some troubling thoughts entered Brent's mind. "Sir, at the staff meeting four days ago, you said we had a window of three months, that carrier *Al Kufra*'s damage would take at least eight months to repair and that we would wait for *Minsk* and *Kiev* to commit themselves to the Red Sea before we began our operation against Rabta." He waved a hand. "And, now, you tell us we will get underway in seven days."

Fujita stared at the young American over the temple of his fingers. Then, flattening his palms on the desk, he leaned forward. "I said that we *must be prepared to get underway in seven days,* not that *we would get underway in seven days.*"

"Then it is indefinite?"

"Not really. The CIA and Mossad suspect leaks. They fear that the Arabs suspect our operation against Rabta." He sighed. "And Rosencrance and the Fourth Fighter Squadron have vanished from the Marianas, yet, enemy reinforcements have been landed, infantry, tanks and artillery."

"But *Al Kufra* will be in the yards in Surabaya for at least eight months."

The old man grimaced and drew his fingers down over his sunken cheeks as if weariness were a mask he could pull from his face and discard. "Not true, Brent-San. The Arabs have flown in German, Russian and, yes, American technicians. They are working around the clock and she could be ready for sea in four months. We must be prepared to engage her then. That is our latest intelligence."

Brent felt his stomach sink. "The Fourth Fighter

236

Squadron assigned to *Al Kufra?*"

The old man shook his head. "Not reasonable. We suspect they have been pulled back to Libya. As you know, we inflicted heavy casualties on them. They need to be retrained and rebuilt as a fighting unit."

"They haven't been replaced?"

"No."

"And Rosencrance and Vatz are still alive."

"The world's misfortune."

"Then *Al Kufra, Minsk* and *Kiev* could all intercept us when we return from the Rabta operation."

"It is possible. So, now, you can see why I must preempt the Arabs with our own strike as quickly as possible."

Brent sank back, his own broad shoulders sagging with the burden borne by Admiral Fujita. He asked himself about the old man's readiness to discuss sensitive matters with him, matters he was sure had not yet been discussed with senior staff members. Obviously, the admiral sought his opinion with the same trust he had placed in the fine tactical minds of his father, Ted "Trigger" Ross, and Admiral Mark Allen. This high regard in which the storied old warrior held him brought feelings of gratification. Yet, the awesome responsibility of command demanding decisions that could kill thousands and lead to the destruction of a nation came home with the crushing impact of an avalanche. Brent rubbed his chin for a long moment. "You want my opinion, sir?"

The old man nodded affirmatively.

"Tough decision, sir. But I can't see any options." He pointed at a chart of the Atlantic mounted on a bulkhead. "We can make for the Moroccan coast with our B-25s but keep our fighters ready on the hangar deck by both elevators. We can build ramps and if the Arabs sniff

237

us out, we can push the bombers over the side in minutes and launch our Zero-sens. Along with *Bennington*'s F-6-Fs, we should be able to handle anything the Arabs can throw at us."

"Good thinking, Brent-san. You remind me of your father more every day. We will proceed with the operation." The old man tapped the desk. "If we get underway in ten days, I have been assured the B-25s will be ready at Tarawa and the *Bennington* will be on station."

Brent punched his arm rest. "Good, sir. We'll bomb their gas plant and if their carriers try an interception, we'll whip their butts."

The old man chuckled into his hand. "Your attitude is that of the samurai. However, sometimes your use of American idiom can be confusing. We will thrash more than their posteriors."

Brent laughed at the old man's dry wit. "Right, sir."

"You are dismissed, Brent-san. I know you have a new man to train."

Brent began to rise.

"Brent-san," the old man said as an afterthought. "Remember, Arlene Spencer is a reporter and truth is the first casualty when reporters enter the arena. You are only one of five men who knows of our mission. Now you know much more. Watch her questions and mind your tongue. Tell her nothing. Remember, clever people can put obscure, disconnected facts together and sometimes produce correct deductions. It is the old game of intelligence."

"She is not a spy, sir."

The old man nodded. "She is a journalist, Brent-san; a purveyor of information, not necessarily one who seeks the truth. There is a difference. She knows how to gather information and she is clever and beautiful. Be cautious."

"Of course, sir."

The old man looked up at the big American for a long silent moment. For an instant Brent felt the admiral was looking right through him, perhaps into the past and seeing someone else in the dark archives of his memories. Yoshi had said that Brent reminded the old man of his long vaporized son, Kazuo. At this moment, Brent felt that the air group leader might be right. Finally, Fujita averted his eyes and spoke in thick tones, "You are dismissed, Lieutenant."

Brent turned and left the room.

Chapter Eleven

Although Seaman First Class Haruo Iketa had lost seven pounds, his color had returned and he still looked formidable with his Arisaka slung over his shoulder. He followed Brent to Arlene's door and stood ramrod straight behind the American while the lieutenant knocked. When the smiling young woman opened the door, Brent dismissed the seaman with a gruff, "I'll call the duty officer at the gatehouse when I'm ready to be picked up."

"Aye, aye, sir." The sailor turned toward the elevator.

Eagerly, Arlene pulled Brent into the dimly lighted apartment with both hands to his shoulders. Brent kicked the door closed. Pulling her to him, he could feel her arms circle his neck. She was all warmness and fullness and sweet smelling softness. Deep, wet, and soft, her mouth was open for him to probe and she pushed her body hard against his. She was amazingly pliable, molding herself to him like plastic. His mood thickened with lust and he began to steam with the stirrings of sexual fury. Sliding his hands slowly down her back, he explored her tiny waist, the flare of her hips. Then he clasped a buttock with each hand and pulled her against his arousal. He could feel the heat of her through his uniform. There was a volcano building inside him and his heart was a trapped animal trying to batter its way through the cage of his ribs.

"Whoa, cowboy," she said breathlessly, pulling away.

"Not again?"

She laughed and looked away. "Don't hurry things." She gesticulated toward the couch and the table where a bottle of Haig and Haig and glasses waited on a silver tray. "A couple drinks, then that steak I promised you — American style."

She led the grumbling young man to the couch but remained standing as he seated himself. He looked up expectantly while she smiled down. Then, raising her arms, she began to turn in a burlesque of a high-fashion model showing off a Parisian couturier's latest creation. "I bought this outfit yesterday, just for you," she said, looking back at him over her shoulder.

It was a breathtaking ensemble, obviously selected to show off her superb body. Short and tight, the skirt was black satin, blouse white silk that clung to her breasts like plastic. And her hair was swept up. This time, instead of a chignon, it was coiled into a rope the size of Brent's thumb and wound in a pile on the back of her head. Jeweled combs held it all in place. The perfect face was slightly flushed either by the subtle application of makeup, or the rush of excitement. His eyes dropped to her legs. Her knees were flat and dimpled, artfully formed as if by a renaissance sculptor, the muscles of her calves curved with a sinuous flair. "You like my legs?" she said, watching his eyes, a slight taunting smile touching her lips.

He sighed. "I approve, if that's what you mean." She giggled. He continued, "You must have done some dancing."

She stopped in mid-pirouette, arms akimbo, facing

241

him. "I took ballet lessons when I was a little girl and then I danced with an amateur ballet group when I lived in Greenwich Village."

He gestured for her to take the cushion beside him. She shook her head and walked across the room to a corner where an expensive stereo system sat on one of a row of shelves that reached almost to the ceiling. She slipped a disk into a Sanyo CD player. Immediately, the opening, hypnotic strains of Ravel's "Bolero" softly throbbed through the room from hidden speakers like ominous stirrings of the wind preceding a storm.

Walking back to the couch, she slowly settled beside him like a bright, beautiful bird alighting. She kissed him on the cheek and then avoided his lips, leaning forward and pouring two drinks. She handed him his glass and then touched her glass to his. "To Maurice Ravel," she said, staring up into his eyes, "he could write romantic music." They drank.

Brent listened to the mounting, repetitious strains. "Sex on a disc," he said.

She nodded. "How true. Its rhythm does pound and pound. Ravel himself said, 'It's a work for orchestra without music'." And then she managed to shock him again, "I hear that at the climax, the whole orchestra had a collective orgasm." She giggled into her glass and then emptied it. She poured more scotch into her glass and Brent's.

Stumped for words for a moment, he finally managed a retort, "And then they all have a cigarette and go home."

"After they shower."

"Of course," he said solemnly. "After they shower."

She touched her glass to his. "This one's to *Yonaga*," she said seriously. "Success on your next mission."

"Whatever that may be," he said cautiously. They

drank. He took her hand and she squeezed back.

Holding up her glass, she studied the rim as if she were searching for an imperfection. "You know *Minsk* and *Kiev* have been spotted by two merchant ships in the Atlantic," she said to the glass.

"Oh?"

She tabled her drink. "Yes, it came in over the wire an hour ago. Rumor has it they're headed for Tripoli."

"Bon voyage," he said, holding up his drink.

She pulled his hand onto her lap. He could feel the rapid rise and fall of her abdomen under his hand. Escaping her grasp, he began to rub lower and lower.

"Don't. Please," she pleaded, pulling his hand up but leaving it on the hard flat plane of her stomach. "I'm afraid I'm going to lose you, Brent," she said, eyes moist. She kissed him fervently and released his hand. Again, sliding his hand down, he rubbed her thighs, her buttocks. The volcano began to boil and churn again. But, she pulled away. "There are all kinds of wild rumors, Brent. The *Bennington,* North American B-25s training on short strips in the Mojave Desert, huge pilot training programs right here on Honshu."

The hand stopped. He pushed her back, hands on her narrow shoulders and stared deep into her eyes; his ardor suddenly cooling. "I don't know a thing," he said icily.

"But you do."

Anger replaced passion. "You ask too goddamned many questions."

"It's my job."

"You're not working tonight."

She kissed his mouth, his cheek, stroked his hair with spread fingers. "Please, darling," she said contritely. "I didn't mean to offend you." She took another drink. "I guess I'll always be the reporter."

243

"Sorry, there's no scoop tonight."

A small chime sounding in the kitchen turned her head. "The potatoes are done." She tabled her drink. "I've got to put the steaks on and then we'll eat. I've prepared a feast for you that's fit for Olympus." She kissed him again. "And I promise, no more questions."

He smiled and kissed her back. "No more questions," he repeated.

"None at all," she reassured him.

He watched her walk to the kitchen, her buttocks moving under the tight satin in perfect rhythm to the throbbing, melodic and harmonic monotony of the music which was growing in volume. His desire was now tempered with irritation at her persistent questioning. Fujita was right. All reporters sought information. And with enough information, a clever person could put apparently disassociated facts together and, perhaps, make an accurate guess as to *Yonaga*'s next mission. She had asked him about the Rabta works when they first met. And the whole world would soon know about *Minsk, Kiev, Bennington* and the B-25s. If she was suspicious, what did Arab intelligence sources suspect? He shuddered and emptied his glass.

His thoughts were interrupted by the crashing climax of the "Bolero" and Arlene's call from the kitchen. He rose and walked to the small dinette.

They sat side-by-side on the couch staring at the big picture window in a nearly darkened room. She had rheostated the indirect lighting down to a bare glimmer. Both were fascinated by the spectrum of light reflected from the glaring signs of downtown Tokyo. Hitachi, Nissan, Sanyo and many others, burning and pulsing in garish neon signatures, were refracted by the thick panes into myriads of glorious colors, bathing the room in

244

eerie, unearthly hues. It was an astonishing sight.

Brent was content. The dinner had been superb: filet mignon, light, airy broccoli souffle, and potatoes he had called "au gratin."

"Not really au gratin," she had said. "They're prepared more in the 'Delmonico' style." And then she explained how the potato had been baked, scooped out, mixed with butter, crushed cornflakes, flour, milk, sharp cheddar and placed back into the skin and layered with more cheese. "Truly gourmet," he had said.

She even thought of the perfect wine, a ruby-red, Chateau Lafite-Rothschild Bordeaux whose delicate flavor she described as "understated and indefinable." He agreed.

Now they sat in the weird light, sipping a delicious liqueur. He held up his drink and stared at the thick, reddish liquid. "It's *framboise,*" she said, answering his unvoiced question.

"Raspberry," he said.

"Very good, Brent. You know French." She held up her glass to his. *"Dieu vous garde,"* she said with a sly smile.

"God keep you," he translated.

"Very good."

"Mazel tov," he said, touching her glass with his.

She stared over her glass at him. "That's Yiddish."

"Right. It means 'good luck'."

"That's a dead language. It died with the Jews of Poland during the Holocaust."

"Not really. Colonel Bernstein grew up in Warsaw. He has taught me a few phrases."

"Bernstein is the Mossad agent?"

"Right. Israeli Intelligence."

"He wasn't at the *seppuku?*"

"That's right."

245

"You like him."

"We're very good friends."

"I hear the Israeli agent Captain Sarah Aranson was your very good friend, too. In fact, she taught you quite a few things in her apartment in Tel Aviv," she said, an enigmatic smile twisting her lips impishly.

Heat came to his face and he cursed the woman for tying his tongue into a knot again. He sipped the thick, sweet liqueur. "You know one hell of a lot about me," he finally managed.

She laughed, a light trilling sound of a bird awakening to a bright spring morning. "You're notorious, Brent. Don't you know that? So you want to know about Kathryn Suzuki, Dale McIntyre, Mayumi—"

"No, thanks," he said, throwing up his hands defensively. Of course she knew about the women. Every move of "The American Samurai" had been followed by the media. He had even made the tabloids in American markets. She was a reporter. She had access to it all and she was doing a story on him. "You must have a file on me," he noted.

"I told you I'm doing an article."

He placed a finger on her soft lips. She kissed it. "But not tonight."

"Not tonight," she whispered, pulling his head down and kissing him. Clumsily, she tried to place her glass on the table without turning from him. Brent heard it topple and roll across the table and shatter on the floor. It was ignored. Her arms were around his neck, mouth open, tongue at work, searching his gums, teeth, slithering over his tongue. His hand found a large, swelling breast, felt the nipple under the silk. His fingers began to toy with it. Then the buttons were pulled free and he cupped the hard mound with a hand that trembled. She began to

246

make small sounds deep in her throat.

But, again, she pulled away, struggled from his grasp and stood up. "Oh, no," he cried. "Not again. This isn't human."

She smiled down. "You know I was a dancer."

"But what the hell—"

"Would you like to see me dance?" There was a hot promise in the blue eyes that looked black in the weak light.

"Yes. Yes, dance for me."

Quickly, she walked to the Sanyo CD player. "Do you like Khachaturian? His (Spartacus) ballet?" she asked.

"Anything," he said.

In a moment the romantically eloquent strains of the love duet between Spartacus and Phrygia filled the room. Compared to the earthy "Bolero," it was restrained and discreet, but intensely romantic. As Arlene glided toward Brent, she loosened her hair, shook her head and her golden tresses tumbled to her shoulders, shimmering softly in the eerie light. She kicked off her shoes and began to sway and turn to the music. Slowly her fingers found the buttons on her blouse Brent had missed. She pulled it free and threw it into a corner. Her large breasts, heaving with her hard breathing, strained against the white lace of her brassiere. Brent felt something hard clogging his throat and he was incapable of swallowing. He followed the swaying, twisting girl, eyes big like blue marbles.

Next, the skirt was unzipped, dropped to the floor with a quick movement of the hips, and she stood dressed only in her brassiere and panties. Standing in a shaft of light slashing into the room from the kitchen's partially open door, the skin of her tanned, perfect legs, calves and ankles shone like carved and polished ivory. Then she began to whirl with professional grace from one part of the room to another, breaking one plane of light and moving into another. Gliding through the arcane aura, her lustrous flesh at times glowed like porcelain and at other times gold, marble and pearl. It appeared a magus wielding magic lanterns was doing tricks with her body and her entire being seemed to light up with some inner illumination. Spellbound, Brent watched. She was as bright and beautiful as a flame and as a flame she could not be held.

Lust roared to life and blood sang in his ears. Brent could not believe it was all real. It must be a mid-watch. He was fantasizing again. Or he was asleep, having one of those maddening dreams.

Swaying to the music, she stopped in front of him, eyes riveted to his. She raised her arms, her hands moving gracefully like two love birds in a mating ritual. He could no longer restrain himself. He came from the couch slowly, eyes boring into hers fiercely. The look pulled them together like magnet and metal. In a moment, he was crushing her to him, hands running over the hot bare flesh of her back, pulling at the brassiere, running down to her hard buttocks, tugging at the elastic of her panties, groping under. The lower he reached, the hotter the flesh became. There was so much of her to want, to love and he wanted all of her at once. Finally, he found the short hair, rubbed, reached further down with trembling fingers as a slight spread of her legs gave his hand the room it sought. She cried out when he touched her, parted her.

"No, not here darling," she hissed. She gestured at the hall.

He picked her up and carried her to the bedroom.

* * *

He was on his back, breathing slowly after the fierce exertion. She was in the crook of his arm and she snuggled against him like a contented animal making its nest. Serene and radiating contentment, her face reminded him of a Raphael painting of the Madonna. But only moments before, it had been twisted into a mask of passion as she writhed, whimpered, cried out, butted and thrashed to meet his frantic onslaught. Her passion had been unbounded like nothing he had ever known before. There were scratches on his back where her fingernails had left tracks when she had reached her final shrieking climax, crying, "Oh, Jesus! Jesus! Jesus!" Then she fell limp and moaned like a mortally injured kitten. And his ear was tender where she had bit him at that unbelievable moment when he had exploded, convulsed and collapsed, enmeshed in the rood of her arms and legs, drained and destroyed. It had been the most complete and devastating moment of his life.

Sighing and stretching, he listened to the music. The love duet between Spartacus and Phrygia was still playing. She had programmed the player to repeat the band, and she had been right. The romantic theme had been perfect for the moment, enhanced their lovemaking. He would never tire of it; never forget it.

She grunted a small sound of happiness in his ear. For the first time in months, he felt relaxed; felt content.

" 'Spartacus' is still playing," he said.

"I know."

"You prefer it to the 'Bolero'."

"Savages make love to the 'Bolero'."

"I agree," he said, kissing her cheek.

She ran her hand over the thick mat of hair covering his chest. "That was really 'in depth', darling," she giggled.

"The 'in depth' interview you really wanted?"

"From the very beginning." The hand continued its exploration of the mat of hair. Found the two bare tracks crossing his chest and ran fingers along them. "What are these?" she asked.

"Seven-point-seven-millimeter slugs leave tracks. They were tracers. Phosphorus destroys the hair follicles."

"Good Lord, you've been shot?"

He chuckled. "Almost. Actually, grazed."

"Can I put it in my story?"

"If you like." She would never stop perplexing him; she was either the nosy investigative reporter or *Alice in Wonderland*.

She ran her fingers down to his hard stomach. "You have a stomach like a washboard," she said.

"Like it?"

"You have a magnificent body, the kind of body all girls fantasize about." She snickered. "But I like this better." She slid her hand lower until she took him in her hand. "I'm glad they didn't shoot this off. It's a big, beautiful target."

He almost laughed, but felt the flames begin to fan. He pulled her close, molding her body to his. He kissed her neck, her shoulder, cupped her breast and tongued the areola of her swollen breast, spread a big hand across her buttocks and jammed her hard against him. She moaned and rolled to her back, pulling him with her. He lowered himself between her knees and the hand guided its prize.

In a moment, she gasped and cried out incoherently. There were no more giggles.

Chapter Twelve

The next week flashed past like the blur of a passing Japanese commuter train. Admiral Fujita held staff meeting after staff meeting in which every detail of battle readiness was discussed without disclosing the objective. Besides the admiral, only Brent Ross, Irving Bernstein, Horace Mayfield and Byron Whitehead still knew of the plan to destroy the poison gas plant at Rabta.

To the delight of everyone, the six long-awaited new British pilots reported aboard. Captain Colin Willard-Smith and Pilot Officer Elwyn York were particularly pleased, greeting the newcomers — all graduates of the RAF college at Cranwell — like members of a fraternity at a reunion. To a man, the new pilots were young, bright and expert pilots. Within hours, the roar of the mighty 3,050 horsepower Rolls Royce Griffon echoed like thunder over Tokyo Bay as eight Seafires streaked overhead.

The morning after the new British pilots arrived, Brent was standing with Admiral Whitehead on the signal bridge when a mock dogfight broke out overhead. It sprawled across the skies, leaving vapor trails like webs spun by mad spiders: Zeros, Hellcats and Seafires twisting, turning and plunging in their tight, desperate maneuvers. Although the Zero was powered by the smallest engine, the bigger, heavier British and American fighters were incapable of turning with it. "Hasn't changed in fifty years," Whitehead said, staring upward. "Nothing can turn with a Zero."

Rumors and speculations filled the media. *Minsk* and *Kiev* made Tripoli and were immediately renamed *Daffah* and *Magid*. No attempt was made to continue with the deception that the ships were to be scrapped. No one had believed it, anyway. The crews of both vessels were well trained, boarding in Archangel and having their shakedown cruise while steaming the carriers to Libya. Experienced seamen, they represented cutthroats, terrorists, opportunists and mercenaries from all over the world. Although the majority were Arabs, large numbers of Germans, Englishmen, Russians, Americans and even a few Japanese could be found on their musters. They were exorbitantly paid, experienced and vicious. Both vessels took aboard air groups just before they made the port of Tripoli.

The flyers were the usual collection of hired assassins. The early German dominance had been replaced by an "internationalizing" which matched the amalgamation of nationalities of the seamen. Their numbers counted Rosencrance and Vatz who had been sighted by Israeli agents frequenting some of Tripoli's most prominent brothels. It was generally accepted that the pair and their crack Fourth Fighter Squadron had been assigned to one of the carriers.

The movements of *Bennington* did not go unnoticed. She was seen putting to sea late in the week and two Mexican fishing vessels and the captain of a Liberian tanker reported large formations of fighters and bombers rendezvousing with her off the California coast. Then she vanished.

The media never tired of speculating about the B-25s which had disappeared early in the week only to reappear at Hickam Field on Oahu. One newsworthy item that had escaped the inquisitive eyes of reporters was the installation of extra tanks in the bomb bays. After a short layover, the sixteen bombers took off and vanished to the northeast in the hopes of misleading curious eyes as to their true destination. Once over the horizon, the echelons of bombers made a big sweeping turn to the southwest and headed for Johnston Island for refueling before making their final run to Tarawa. The orchestration by the US Navy, the CIA, Mossad and Admiral Fujita seemed to be moving well and in near perfect harmony. However, the Arabs seemed to be tuning up their instruments as well.

The orchestration fell into discord on Wednesday night when the CIA man, Horace Mayfield, vanished. The disappearance would not have been of great concern, especially since the man was a known alcoholic and libertine, but repeated calls by Colonel Bernstein to the CIA cover at the Imperial Hotel resulted only in anxious questions being hurled back by the agent who was actually the assistant manager. Mayfield had missed his check-in time at two thousand hours. Perhaps he was in a drunken stupor in a bordello or had fallen victim to Red Army assassins and would never be found.

Brent and Rear Admiral Whitehead were called into Admiral Fujita's office for a conference with Colonel Bernstein. It was a tense meeting. Brent could see the concern on the admiral's face. Mayfield was one of five men who knew the details of the Rabta attack plan. The other four sat in that office.

"He has not been heard from since last night, Admiral," Bernstein said.

"The *Rengo Sekigun* could have him. They could torture the plan out of him." The admiral punched the desk.

"It's possible. The worst scenario. It would be a rare plum to kidnap a CIA man. And Mossad suspects leaks, Admiral. The Arabs are acting suspiciously as if they may expect an attack on North Africa."

"You are sure, Colonel Bernstein?"

"No, sir. But according to our intelligence, they have pulled back some of their best fighter units, concentrated them along the Mediterranean coast. I have informed you of this."

"Yes. But remember, they have *Daffah* and *Magid* to man."

"True, sir. It is possible we are misreading their intentions. It would not be the first time." He shifted his eyes to Brent and continued, "Mayfield was last seen . . ."

Forever the warrior, strategic and tactical considerations diverted the old admiral's mind from the missing Mayfield. He interrupted Bernstein in mid-sentence, "What do you know of Morocco's neutrality, Colonel." He gestured at a chart mounted on the bulkhead. "Arab air bases on the Atlantic coast could be a grave menace when we approach with our decks loaded with B-25s."

Obviously not finished with the topic of Mayfield's disappearance, the Colonel suppressed his frustration. Yielding to rank, he turned to the Admiral's subject which every man in the room had heard haggled over many times, "Morocco is still neutral, sir. And as you know, Mauritania, Mali, Niger, Chad and the Sudan all

254

despise Kadafi and his *jihad*. But, they are all weak and are afraid to anger the Arabs." He looked at Whitehead and Brent and indicated the chart, "However, you are all aware Algeria is part of the *jihad* and our B-25s must overfly that country."

"Any new fighter bases in Algeria?"

The Israeli shook his head. "No, sir. Still the two bases at Oran and Alger, maybe twenty-four fighters, a thousand kilometers north of our B-25s projected flight plan."

Brent knew this discussion had been held between the two men many times. It was almost as if the admiral was reviewing for a final exam. But this test could spell life or death.

The admiral continued. "The Algerians have a mixed bag of Messerschmitts, Spitfires and a few Curtiss P-40s."

"Yes, sir."

"And we can be assured that most Arab fighters are still concentrated on the Mediterranean coast of Libya, Egypt, the Sinai, Jordan, Syria and Lebanon."

"According to our latest intelligence and as much as one can be sure of anything in wartime, sir." Bernstein looked around the room. "And as I have told all of you in our previous meetings, our land sea and air forces will go on the offensive forty-eight hours before the B-25s are launched."

"Yes, yes, I know," Fujita said as if he were assuring himself for the twentieth time.

The Israeli tapped his armrest, threw an uneasy glance at Brent, and turned the discussion back to the missing CIA man. Brent had known the Israeli for years and it was obvious something was gnawing at him, something that involved Brent. This time, the admiral allowed him to complete his sentence. "Mayfield was last seen in a cheap Ginza bar with a woman," the colonel said bluntly.

"Woman?" Fujita said.

"Yes. Lia Mandel."

"Mandel? Why?" Brent blurted out and then his throat froze.

Bernstein eyed Brent with a steady stare. "We don't know why or for what reason. We don't think they're in love." His hard black eyes stared into the Lieutenant's without flinching. "You've been seeing Arlene Spencer?"

Now Brent knew what had been bothering the intelligence agent. The lieutenant's defensive shields went up. "Why do you ask?"

"You didn't discuss the Rabta attack?"

"Are you out of your goddamned mind?" Brent roared, leaping from his chair. Fujita raised his hands and shook his head in a disapproving gesture. Glaring and with Whitehead's hand tugging on the back of his tunic, Brent sank slowly back into his chair.

Undaunted by the young man's anger, the Israeli bored on, "You saw Lia Mandel at Arlene Spencer's place at the Tokyo Hilton?"

"Once, the first time I was there."

"Not again?"

"No, and what's all this about Mandel? She's a reporter."

Bernstein nodded grimly. "Yes, a reporter." But there was far more meaning and suspicion in the timbre of the man's voice than in his words. Brent was convinced Bernstein knew more than he indicated and Fujita was very concerned. Bernstein said to Admiral Fujita, "With your permission, sir, I will begin an intensive search for Mayfield. Three of my men and five CIA agents are on the case and we are deploying some new high-tech surveillance equipment."

"By all means that would be my order and, if necessary, you are to remain here even when we put to sea. Communicate your findings to us by CISRA." He drummed the desk. "Under no circumstances are you to notify the Tokyo Police. They are a bunch of bumbling buffoons riddled through with *Rengo Sekigun* informants."

"I will under no circumstances notify the police, sir, but I hate to miss this show, Admiral."

"I know, Colonel. You have been on board for every major engagement. However, for now, the missing CIA man takes precedence. The security of our entire operation may be at stake."

Bernstein nodded grimly and then the officers were dismissed, but not before the admiral warned, "What has been said here remains here. Not one word of this discussion will be repeated."

"Aye, aye, sir," the trio chorused. Bernstein and Whitehead left, but a wave from the admiral held Brent in his chair.

"You have liberty tonight?"

"Yes, sir."

"You will see the woman Arlene Spencer?"

Brent stirred uneasily. "Yes, sir." He palmed an irritating wisp of hair back from his forehead. "I could ask about Lia Mandel, if you wish. Perhaps gain some intelligence."

"No, Brent-san. Say nothing. Ask no questions.

257

Questioning Miss Spencer could alert Lia Mandel. That is, if she is involved in the disappearance of the CIA man. And remember, Colonel Bernstein is keeping all parties under surveillance. He has some new, ah, insects."

Brent smiled. "You mean bugs, sir."

"Insects! Bugs!" He shrugged his bony shoulders. "All the same, Lieutenant. Microphones as small as my finger."

Brent controlled his impulse to chuckle. "As small as postage stamps, tacks, nails, sir."

"Yes, yes. These new devices are very baffling, indeed." He tapped the desk impatiently. "But keep your silence."

"You know I will, sir."

"Yes, Brent-san. I know you will."

Brent was dismissed.

Port and starboard liberty ended on Friday when all liberty and leaves were cancelled. Brent saw Arlene only twice during the week, the last visit being made on Thursday evening, the night before the end of liberty for all hands. She could see the tension in his eyes. She read him like a primer. "You're leaving," she rued, curled up close to him on the couch.

Brent's mind was on Horace Mayfield, but he could not and would not ask one question — not even about Lia Mandel. Instead, he reacted to the question directly, "It's no secret. A million eyes will see us stand out."

"When?"

"Classified."

"Sorry."

258

She kissed his cheek, pressed a breast against his biceps. "I'll never see you again." Her voice broke. "I know it."

"Don't say that."

"You're going to attack the Arabs."

"That's no secret either. Someday we will. That's what they pay us for."

"The Marianas, Tomonuto, Surabaya, the Mediterranean?"

He pushed her away. "You can't be serious."

"I am. I want to know where I'll lose my love." She began to cry into a clenched fist.

He put an arm around her trembling shoulders. "Darling," he said, softly, resorting to his usual subterfuge. "I don't know. Fujita doesn't tell anyone. Sure, we're putting to sea." He turned her face to him with a finger to her chin and tenderly kissed the tears from her cheeks. He continued with his lies, "Rumor has it we're going to conduct exercises with our air groups, simulate attacks on the Kyushu coast. You know we have thirty foreign pilots and they need to practice and learn our systems, tactics, radio procedures." He smiled. "So, don't worry so much about me."

She was unconvinced. "Arab fighters are concentrating along the coast, and *Daffah* and *Magid* are exercising in the Med," she said, surprising Brent with her knowledge of facts he assumed were confidential, if not secret. "And everyone knows the carriers were never intended for scrap. Athens radio reported the Israelis tried to attack them. They lost twelve bombers and didn't score a single hit." Brent had heard of the abortive attack but did not know of the details. Only that Radio Tripoli had been gloating about massive Israeli losses. Arlene knew

259

more about the incident than he did. He felt outplayed and outwitted. It was demoralizing. She had some excellent sources, indeed. Apparently, Nippon Press had eyes and ears everywhere.

She threw her arms around him with frantic urgency, her emotions of fear suddenly channeled into passion. There was a demand in her kisses, the thrust of her pelvis. Eyes locked with his, she came to her feet slowly, pulling him from the couch. His feelings of inquietude withered, replaced by the passionate thoughts of her bedroom.

They walked to the bedroom for the last time while "Spartacus" played softly in the background. Soon, her moans, sighs and cries of "Jesus!" mingled with the music.

The morning *Yonaga* stood out was cold and dreary, gray mist and black sea blurred into each other, endless, changeless, featureless. Following seven *Fletchers* led by Captain Fite's destroyer with a huge pennant number "1" painted on its bows, the carrier entered the narrows of the Uraga Straits. Dressed in a lined foul weather jacket and with his Zeiss binoculars hanging from his neck, Brent was at his usual Special Sea Detail station on the flag bridge at Admiral Fujita's side. Rear Admiral Whitehead stood on the admiral's other side, while the talker, Seaman Naoyuki, manned the phones. Four lookouts were stationed at the rail.

The sea was restless, mirroring Brent's mood, a feeling of spiritual exhaustion, an ominous mood of despondency and a premonition that left him shifting from foot to foot in his unease. "I'll never see you again,"

Arlene had said, the last time they had been together. Over and over his mind's eye had reviewed the events of that last night together. The white, hot body; under his hands, under his body. The writhing, thrashing, the moans, and her cries for her savior at that explosive moment that devastated them both. And then they spoke of love and as lovers always do, made pledges they both knew would never be kept.

When he left, the look in her eyes was chilling. Almost as if she were staring into the future. But something more than words had struck an intangible, a deep despair that was greater than anxiety. It was icy fear that tied his viscera into a frozen knot. For one chilling moment he felt the big blue eyes were examining a corpse.

Brent's thoughts were broken by Fujita's command, "Execute to follow, left to one-eifht-sero, speed sixteen. Repeat the command to the escorts on bridge-to-bridge."

"Execute to follow, left to one-eight-zero, speed sixteen. Repeat command to escorts on bridge-to-bridge," came back through the tube.

In a moment, the tinny voice from the pilothouse resonated again, "All escorts acknowledge, sir."

"Very well. Execute!"

Brent felt the beat of the great engines pick up and the ship heel slightly as the helm was put over. Then the voice piped up from below, "Steady on one-eight-zero, speed sixteen, eighty-three revolutions, sir."

"Very well." Fujita shouted at the lookouts, "Keep a weather eye out for the sea buoy. It should be visible at any moment hard off the port bow."

Nearing the widening mouth of the channel, the mists began to thin and withdraw into the overcast and the

261

first surging power of the North Pacific swell gripped the great vessel by the head. The bow began to rise and dip with the harbingers of the power to follow once the channel was cleared and the protective shield of the land mass was left behind.

"Sea buoy, bearing three-three-five, range two-thousand meters," a lookout shouted.

"Very well."

With the rounded point of the Boso Peninsula's *Suno Saki* close to port, Brent raised his binoculars and studied the shore. Here, the land was wide open to the onslaught of the sea. Under the thick overcast, the water was gray, nearly leaden and it came up to the land in one charging swell after another and bit at the rocks. Spume as white as egg white leaped into the air and then splattered back. There was so much power there, Brent was sure he could hear the growling boom like artillery even at a distance of almost a mile. It was a great show, one of the many rewards a man could only find at sea.

A roll of his thumb changed his focus and he could see the hills of the peninsula cresting sullenly through the haze like rows of silent blue-gray sentinels. Arlene Spencer was there, staring up at him from her pillow, hair a golden halo, framing her beautiful face. He gulped at the air, let his breath hiss out slowly between his teeth. He knew he was incapable of putting her out of his mind. If he had nothing more than memories of the girl for the rest of his life, he was a fortunate man, indeed.

With the sea buoy left to port, there was a flurry of flags and pennants ordering the escorts to standard steaming stations. Fite led eight hundred yards ahead of the carrier, two destroyers off the carriers bows, two off the beams and two more off the quarters. The entire

262

force settled on course 135, speed sixteen. Finally, the old man shouted. "Secure the Special Sea Detail, set the port steaming watch, condition of readiness three." There were the sounds of boots on ladders and steel decks, shouts as the watch was relieved and the daily, monotonous routine of a ship at sea began.

But Brent did not leave the bridge. The air groups were due within the hour. Yoshi was up there in the flat, gray clouds and so were Willard-Smith, York, Bender, Hoeffler and so many of the men who had become close friends. He sighed wistfully. A man should not make so many close friends in wartime. There would be less pain when they died.

Twenty minutes later, radar reported large formations of aircraft approaching from the west. Fortunately, the rising sun broke through the mists and scattered the clouds like sheep pursued by a pack of predators. The bright beams struck the sea in a dazzling display of reflected light like gleaming chrome and stainless steel interspersed with burnished copper. The solid shafts of golden light that struck through the roof of the clouds raised Brent's spirits. And his best friend would soon be aboard. He filled his lungs with the clean, invigorating air. It was like nectar; it gave a man a rare kind of high. He raised his glasses. Nothing yet.

In a few minutes a great rumble could be heard and Fujita drifted to his side like a wraith, Rear Admiral Whitehead on his heels. "Navigator, wind?" Fujita shouted down a voice tube.

A voice came back, "Zero-eight-zero, force three."

As Brent expected, now that the channel was cleared and the battle group was headed into the open sea, the old man would remain at radio silence. Big electronic ears could be listening. "Very well. Flag bridge, make the hoist, execute to follow, course zero-eight-zero, speed twenty." Within seconds, there was the sound of bunting whipping at the yardarm.

Brent scanned the destroyers. "All escorts answer at the dip, sir."

"Two block!"

"All hoists two-blocked."

"Execute!"

The flags and pennants whipped down and Fujita shouted into the voice tube, "Left standard rudder, steady up on zero-eight-zero, speed twenty!"

The entire force turned and changed speed in perfect unison as if the escorts were marionettes tied to the flag ship with strings. More orders: "Prepare to receive aircraft, two block Pennant Two!"

As the command, "Prepare to receive aircraft," boomed through the ship's speakers, hundreds of men rushed to their stations. Within minutes, Naoyuki turned to the admiral and reported, "All stations manned and ready, sir."

"Very well."

Brent cast a glance astern. The lifeguard destroyer had dropped a thousand meters behind the carrier.

Now the huge formations of fighters and bombers were visible low on the horizon. Led by the dive-bombers, the formations began to make their usual counterclockwise orbits of the carrier. Everyone watched anxiously. The only carrier landings made by the new pilots had been on simulated decks at Tokyo International Airport and Tsuchiura. Luckily, the sea was comparatively calm with only a small swell running from the northeast. Still, the deck of a moving carrier was a far more difficult landing platform than the rock-solid thousand-foot rectangles painted on the tarmacs.

Hook extended, the first Aichi approached, caught the second cable and bounced to a safe, if not perfect, three-point landing. Then bomber after bomber landed without incident, was towed to the forward elevator and struck below. Following the bombers, Seafires, Hellcats and Zeros rushed over the stern like charging corrida bulls only to be caught and pulled to jarring halts by the great cables. Amazingly, there were no accidents.

Rear Admiral Whitehead turned to the admiral as the carrier returned to her base course of 135 and cruising speed of sixteen knots. "Astonishing, sir. Commander Matsuhara, Lieutenant Commander Yagoto and Commander Iwata have done an extraordinary job of training." He raised a hand in a sweeping gesture that encompassed the flight deck. "Not one casualty, sir. And this was the first, actual carrier landing for at least forty of them. God was good to us."

"A good omen, indeed," the old admiral declared. "May Amaterasu, the Blessed One and the sea *kamis* continue to smile on us for the rest of the operation."

"God willing and amen, sir," Whitehead said reverentially.

Struck by the head-on collision of theologies, the two old men stared at each other for a quiet moment, and then chuckled. Brent added his own laughter. Naoyuki and the lookouts stared curiously.

And, in fact, it did seem the variety of gods believed in by the disparate crew had allied themselves to aid *Yonaga*. True, there were feelings of anxiety and trepidation that all men suffer before a battle. However, Brent sensed a confidence in the crew, not only in their training, belief in their courage and righteousness of their cause, but in the security of their bases. All fighting units, whether afloat or on land, must feel their rears are secure. With *Ayase* and *Yamagiri* stationed as radar pickets to the south and east of Japan and fighter squadrons ringing the base at Yokosuka, there was little chance an Arab bomber could sneak in and carry out a successful attack. Of special concern was the safety of the great graving dock at Yokosuka which was the only dry dock in Japan capable of handling the great carrier. On four different occasions, battle damage had been repaired in this cavernous facility that yawned like a concrete canyon. It was the one support unit that was irreplaceable. Now, in their absence, land based radar, radar afloat, and continuous CAP protected the precious dock.

Yet, only five men still knew of their mission. Only five knew of the remote place on the planet where some of them could die, possibly most of them. It was time to inform the crew. When the last plane was struck below, Fujita brought the bridge microphone to his mouth and his voice boomed through the PA. "Samurai and our valued allies," he began, "we are destined for *Yonaga*'s most important and most perilous mission."

He went on to describe the plan in detail: the B-25s awaiting them at Tarawa, the rendezvous with *Bennington* just to the south and east of the atoll, the daring plan to launch the B-25s off the coast of Morocco for their bombing run on the poison gas works at Rabta. He even gave the locations of the two tankers which were to rendezvous with them and refuel the force enroute. He, also, informed the men of the threat of the two new Arab carriers, *Daffah* and *Magid*. When he finished, he began to sing the song the Japanese expected; the "Naval Lament."

He was immediately joined by over three thousand voices that reverberated through the ship, intoning the mournful, sacrificial dirge. When the last words, "I shall not die peacefully at home," rang through the ship, a bedlam of "Banzai" and the thunder of boots on steel rumbled and pounded through every compartment, every deck. Brent looked at Admiral Whitehead and the two men nodded silently to each other. "Better to join 'em than to fight 'em," the rear admiral said.

"I already have, sir." Then Brent shouted his own "Banzai!"

Whitehead shook his head and muttered, "I guess you have." Both men raised their glasses and stared off into the distance.

Quickly, Fujita restored order and the crew returned to the business of steaming the ship to whatever fate awaited them on the other side of the world.

On a southeasterly heading, the following days found the force plowing through one of the world's greatest wastelands. The sea was endless and capricious: sometimes flat and docile, sometimes stirred by endless rows of gentle swells that passed in smooth weighty majesty beneath the hull. However, at other times, it was hostile and challenging, charging cliffs frothing with spume attacking the ships angrily. "As unpredictable as a woman," Fujita said one day to Brent while both men clung to the windscreen as a particularly aggressive sea slammed into the carrier's port bow with a collision that shot lacelike spray as high as the flight deck and caused the hull to shudder and heel with a sick dead motion.

And the sky put on its show, too. There were times when not one cloud marred the crystalline clear aqua-

267

marine luminescence of the heavens. Now and then, especially as they approached the lower latitudes tiny thunderstorms appeared on the horizon, opaque curtains of gray rain slanting into the sea in tiny squalls not more than a hundred yards in diameter. Occasionally, small puffy clouds like layers of cotton balls would fill the sky in a vast layer that blended into a solid sheet on the circle of the horizon. There were times when high cirrus stretched across the sky, their undersides washed with purple and shot with gold. And there were days when thick gray blankets hovered over the ships as if all of the world's dirty linen was stretched overhead.

Crossing the Tropic of Cancer, there were uneasy times when the barometer "pumped" or dropped, and threatening thunderheads loomed over the horizon, lightning flashing, thunder growling a warning to the flimsy man-made machines that dared intrude. On these occasions, the sea and wind would rise and the ships would roll and pitch. The CAP would be recalled and lashed to the deck. However, good fortune held and no great storms were encountered.

As they steamed further to the east and south, they began to pass through a realm of ghosts. The first impact was felt by the old warriors. One evening when the sky was thick and dark, Brent, who was standing his first watch as officer of the deck, was on the bridge with Rear Admiral Whitehead and Admiral Fujita when the old men revived the phantoms.

"Back there, maybe seven, eight hundred miles to the northeast Wake Island," Rear Admiral Whitehead said.

Fujita nodded. "Your marines put up a good fight," Fujita conceded, black eyes sparking as the old man entered one of his favorite topics.

Whitehead said, "There were only about four hundred marines . . ."

"Three-hundred-eighty-eight marines, twenty-two Grumman Wildcats, some three-inch guns," Fujita said, startling everyone again with his encyclopedic knowledge of World War II.

"Sank a couple of your ships."

"True. We had stupid captains, too. The destroyers *Hayate* and *Kisaragi* came in too close."

"Our garrison held out until December twelfth," Whitehead said.

Fujita waved over the starboard beam. "Truk is down there."

Whitehead chuckled. "Japan's 'Gibraltar of the Pacific'." There was no sarcasm in his voice.

The two old warriors were warming to the topic. Brent moved his eyes from man to man as the exchange continued with Fujita's prideful remark, "You never took it."

"But we sure as hell trashed it."

Fujita's voice took on a grim timbre, "You mean the attack of February sixteenth and seventeenth, 1944?"

"Yes." Now it was the turn of the American to show off his detailed knowledge. "The planes of Task Force Fifty-Eight destroyed over two-hundred planes, sank two cruisers, three destroyers and over thirty support and merchant ships. We figured we bagged over two-hundred-thousand tons."

"But you never took Truk."

"No. We never took it," Whitehead conceded.

Fujita waved to the west and south, "But we took Guam, the Netherlands East Indies, Hong Kong, Malaysia, Singapore, the Bismark Archipelago, even invaded New Guinea."

"We retook Guam. Drove you out of New Guinea and the Bismark Archipelago."

"True, but you never took Rabaul, either."

"Bypassed. We bypassed Truk, Rabaul," the American waved in a big arc from the northeast to the south, "Ponape, Wotje, Mili, Jaluit."

"I know. I know," Fujita interrupted. "Left the garrisons to 'wither on the vine'. One of the few smart things you did. But, generally, your tactics were ill-advised."

Brent was surprised by the casual tone in both men's voices, the respect that approached camaraderie. It was as if two old athletes were discussing a soccer match they had played against each other long ago.

"What do you mean, Admiral Fujita?"

"Why did you continue to attack on Saipan until every last Japanese soldier was dead or captured? Why the same stupid, wasteful tactics on Tinian, Guam, Okinawa, Peleliu, Angaur, Iwo Jima?"

"You mean we should have taken the airfields, set up perimeters and held."

"Why, of course. General Douglas MacArthur used those tactics with great success in the South Pacific. But in the Central Pacific, your Admiral Nimitz used tactics inherited from your own Civil War. The man was either stupid or let himself be influenced by bloodthirsty Marine officers." He circled a finger overhead. "You had control of the sea and air, superior firepower. You should have held and let us waste ourselves attacking. That is the way of the samurai and you knew it. But, instead, on island after island, you threw away thousands of your fine marines and soldiers in useless campaigns of extermination."

"I know," Whitehead said softly, but not without bitterness. "You're very knowledgeable, Admiral. There was the drive by the brass to wage campaigns, gain recognition, with medals, promotions, power."

Fujita sighed. "You know, Admiral Whitehead . . ." The two old men stared at each other with an intimacy only old warriors who have waged war against each other can feel, especially years after the fighting when the fires have cooled. Fujita continued, "You Americans were not the only ones afflicted with bloody ambition. We Japanese had our share of those who sought their glory at any price, especially in the Kwantung Army." He sighed a deep sad sound. "Many white boxes were filled with the ashes of brave boys sacrificed for some officers' ambition."

"It's a universal disease endemic to our kind, Admiral Fujita."

"Indeed it is."

Then they talked of Kwajalein and Eniwitok, two magnificent atolls they would soon leave close to port and starboard. Fierce, short, bloody battles that were decisive in the outcome of the war. They talked late into the night until both old men finally tired. Then they walked side-by-side to their cabins.

"Mister Ross," the junior officer of the deck, Lieutenant Junior Grade Tokuma Shoten, called softly.

"Yes, Lieutenant."

"The war is never over, is it, sir?"

"Not for the old warriors, Lieutenant Shoten."

Both young men chuckled.

The morning they made their landfall on the Tarawa Atoll was overcast as if a giant burial shroud had been pulled over the sky. A low-flying PBM, a Martin "Mariner" flying boat, circled the force which had been shadowed constantly by PBMs or PBYs (Consolidated "Catalina" flying boat) for the past six-hundred miles of their run-in. Although the intruders' IFF (Identification Friend or Foe) showed friendly on the scopes and recognition signals exchanged by flashing light, two fighters of the CAP always flew slightly above and behind the flying boats. Discreetly, the Mariners and Catalinas circled the force at a range of at least ten kilometers.

Fujita took the deck as the battle group approached the huge atoll which was seventeen miles long and nine miles wide. Brent and Rear Admiral Whitehead leaned into their binoculars and studied the great atoll fringed with tiny islands, dense with profuse growths of coconut trees. The admiral turned to his executive officer and navigator, Captain Mitake Arai, and thumped a chart tacked to the navigator's small table, "The entrance is on the southwest side." It was not a question. The old man was reaffirming his knowledge of the navigation problems about to be encountered.

Arai stabbed a finger at the chart, "Here, sir."

"About five kilometers north of the biggest island, Betio," the old man said to himself. He ran a finger over the chart and then turned to Rear Admiral Whitehead, "You claim the CIA has blasted and dredged the channel to nine fathoms?"

"That is correct, sir."

"Very well, but we will send in a DD first with its Fathometer taking continuous soundings before we stand in."

"Good idea, sir," Arai said. Whitehead grunted his approval.

"Radar, range to nearest point of land," Fujita shouted down a voice tube.

"Northwest coast bearing one-seven-zero true, range ten kilometers."

"Very well." Fujita ordered a course change to one-eight-zero and after hurried hoists and shouted commands, the battle group came to the new heading that took them on a course just three miles off the west coast of the atoll. Arai kept his track by plotting periodic tangents shouted out by his assistant, Quartermaster First Class Ryo Rokokura, who hunched over the gyro repeater, squinting through the gunsight of the bearing repeater.

"There's the entrance and there's Betio," Whitehead said, waving over the bow.

"Signal bridge to the escort commander, have DD-Two stand in. I want continuous Fathometer readings in the channel. I am to be notified if it shallows less than eight fathoms. Then have DD-Two move into our anchorage and our turning basin which is marked by yellow and black striped buoys and monitor the depth. He is to scout for the same conditions."

There was the clatter of a signaling searchlight, flashes of light from Fite's DD-One and then the *Fletcher* off *Yonaga*'s port bow turned sharply and headed for the entrance. The entire force reduced speed.

Fujita said to Arai, "According to our charts we should enter on course zero-eight-seven."

"Correct, sir. Another fifteen-hundred meters." There was the sharp clacking sound of parallel rules moving across the chart and the navigator turned to Rokokura, "Tangents on the north coast and south coast."

The quartermaster shouted the bearings and Arai

273

The quartermaster shouted the bearings and Arai plotted them. "Twelve-hundred meters before we make our turn, sir," the navigator said.

Fujita glanced at DD-2 which was entering the channel at a slow speed. "All stop, escorts screen to seaward."

Brent felt the throb of the great engines cease and there was a sudden, strange feeling of something missing, like a heartbeat. Whitehead was standing rigidly, staring through his binoculars at Betio. "There are still some obstacles and blockhouses visible on the seaward side."

Every man raised his glasses at the same time. Brent's Zeiss lenses brought in one of the world's most hideous killing grounds with precise clarity. It was very small; he estimated about half the size of New York's Central Park. Over four decades after the massacre, trees had grown back, but evidence of the holocaust still remained. Beach obstacles like railroad tracks and concrete pyramids jutted from the water, concertinas of rusting barbed wire still connecting some of them. Twisted junk protruded from the sand, and he could see an eight-inch gun tilting precariously on its wrecked mount, muzzle pointed toward the sea. Two blockhouses showing hits from large caliber shells or aerial bombs were visible in spite of encroaching sand and bushes. Not one human being was in sight.

Whitehead's voice, "If you think this side looks bad, wait till we enter the lagoon. That's where the main assault was made."

Fujita's voice showed unusual emotion, "Admiral Keiji Shibasaki was in charge of the defenses. I knew him well. He said, 'A million men cannot take Tarawa in a hundred years'."

274

Whitehead nodded. "And Rear Admiral Howard Kingman said, 'We will not neutralize Betio. We will not destroy it. We will obliterate it'." He dropped his glasses. "They were both wrong."

"But you took it," Fujita said.

"We lost over a thousand dead in seventy-six hours and never made much use of the place. The taking of Eniwetok and Kwajalein made this assault unnecessary and useless." The voice was bitter. "Another strategic blunder and boondoggle that served nothing. Why, the planners assumed five feet of water almost to the beach; an LCVP (Landing Craft, Vehicle/Personnel) needs about three-and-a-half feet. They got their information from a handful of Britons, Australians and New Zealanders who had lived here or sailed these waters. You won't believe this, but they actually used hydrographic charts made during an American Navy expedition in 1841 — over a hundred years old." He punched his palm with a closed fist. "They never figured on the shallowing effect of the growth of coral."

"Yes. Stupid," Fujita said. "I read about these unbelievable miscalculations."

Whitehead continued, "Of course the LCVPs hung up on the reefs and the troops had to wade in. They were nothing but targets. They were shot down in the water. You'll see the wreckage of landing craft when we stand in. A lot of it is still there. LCVPs and LVTs (Landing Vehicle, Tracked.)"

"You know a lot about the battle, Admiral Whitehead," Fujita said.

The American rear admiral laughed bitterly. "I helped plan it." Shocked eyes turned to Whitehead. Brent had no knowledge of this painful chapter in his

275

friend's past. He stared in awe. "I warned them, told them the coral would have grown and shallowed the lagoon!" Whitehead struck the windscreen with a clenched fist. "But they wouldn't listen to a mere lieutenant J.G. 'Our bombardment will obliterate everything, and there's plenty of water,' they said. Ha! And we lost over a thousand fine boys."

"And we lost four-thousand-eight-hundred young soldiers. Our very best men of the Special Naval Landing Force," Fujita said in a chilling matter-of-fact tone.

A funereal silence fell on the bridge. Everyone breathed easier when a signalman broke silence. "DD-Two has cleared the channel. She signals Fathometer readings all exceeding eight fathoms, sir."

"Very well." Fujita glanced seaward where six destroyers were patrolling at slow speed. He said to Arai, "Course, navigator. I want to split the channel."

With short, jerky movements, the navigator worked his parallel rules across the chart to a compass rose and read a bearing. "I suggest course zero-eight-seven, sir."

"Very well. All ahead slow, left to zero-eight-seven."

The beat of the engines came up through the deck and the great ship began to swing toward the entrance.

Chapter Thirteen

From *Yonaga's* anchorage, Betio's beaches were only seven-hundred yards away. Although the Special Sea Detail had been secured, Brent, Captain Mitake Arai, Rear Admiral Whitehead and Admiral Fujita remained on the bridge. There were two large tankers, four supply ships, a yard oiler, a seaplane tender and a half-dozen seaplanes anchored in the huge lagoon. But every man on the bridge had his back to the lagoon. All seemed hypnotized by the small stretch of tragic sand before them.

Brent's lenses took him almost onto Betio's shore. Evidence of the carnage that had strewn the island and the shallows with corpses was everywhere. On the coral shelf leading up to the beach, rusting wreckage of LCVPs and LVTs protruded from the blue, clear water like carapaces of enormous long-dead beetles. More wreckage littered the beach, and a half-dozen block-houses, some still showing the searing black blasts left by flamethrowers, jutted out of the sand. Here and there, the remnants of a log seawall could be seen. Brent winced involuntarily as he stared. A garden of hell. A Gethsemane of the Pacific.

"You could smell it for miles when you were downwind," Whitehead muttered, standing between Brent and Admiral Fujita. His glasses were to his eyes. "Rotting meat, decay, death. There's nothing like that smell. It comes on fast and strong in the tropics. It sticks to your throat like glue."

"The defenders had four eight-inch Vickers guns captured at Singapore," Fujita said, "and ten more coastal defense guns."

"Correct, Admiral," Whitehead acknowledged. "And we found over forty more pieces — one-oh-fives, seventy-fives, thirty-sevens. They zeroed-in on every possible approach to every beach." He swept a hand down the long stretch of white sand, "There was a four-foot-high coconut log seawall that lined this entire side." He jerked a finger at mounds of shattered logs buried in the sand. "You can still see parts of it. We figured in our after-battle analysis there were at least one hundred machine guns emplaced to fire over the lip of the wall at approaching men and boats." He dropped his glasses to his waist, "And when the landing craft hung up on the coral shelf, it made it very easy."

"You had naval fire support and control of the air," Fujita said. And then the mind that had studied every aspect of the great conflict showed its great depth of knowledge again. However, this time there was a hint of the chagrin and frustration he felt in missing the great battles, "You had bombers from carriers *Essex*, *Bunker Hill* and *Independence*. You had the fourteen and sixteen-inch guns of battleships *Tennessee*, *Maryland* and *Colorado*. Cruisers and destroyers. Why, I read you fired three-thousand tons of shells into the island. According to my calculations, that is over ten tons for every one of the unit you call acre."

"I know, sir. But Admiral Shibasaki's pillboxes were built like no others I have ever seen. They were dug deep into the coral, lined with steel and concrete, overlaid with coral and coconut logs, and then sand was pushed up on top of them to give the appearance of small hillocks." His jaw altered into a granite-hard line. "Bombs and shells would glance off and do very little damage. They had to be taken by men . . . ah, boys with satchel charges, grenades, flamethrowers and guts." He gripped his glasses so tight his knuckles showed through the thin flesh like white marbles. "And it was all for nothing. Nothing!"

Captain Arai spoke up for the first time, "The defenders had great courage, too, Admiral Whitehead."

"Why, of course, Captain."

"And you say it was all for nothing?" Fujita said.

"Yes, for nothing. Kwajalein and Eniwetok were captured with comparative ease. Very light casualties. Majuro and Ulithi were taken without resistance. They were all better placed strategically than this. . . ." He punched a closed fist at the beach, "Than this hellhole, slaughterhouse."

"But it was not for nothing," Fujita said curtly.

"What do you mean?"

Fujita dropped his binoculars and extended both arms, palms toward the island like a crucifix. "I mean they died for honor, glory, their beliefs, love of country, Admiral Whitehead." Fujita's narrow eyes were black slits. "What better way is there to die?" He dropped his arms.

Whitehead would not back down. "I don't see it that way."

Brent expected an angry retort, a blast from superior rank. Perhaps it was the cemetery-like atmosphere of the place, or, possibly, the genuine respect the old man had for Whitehead. In any event, the response was uncharacteristically conciliatory. "That is your privilege,

Admiral Whitehead," Fujita said simply, raising his glasses.

Arai distracted the two old warriors by gesturing at the southeast end of the beach where a ramp had been built out into the lagoon and a newly dredged and blasted channel marked with buoys. A lighter had tied-up at the foot of the ramp and three more were anchored nearby in the lagoon. Each was loaded with a North American B-25. A crawler crane of at least thirty-ton capacity squatted on the beach over another B-25. Men were seen securing the crane's sling. A hundred yards off the beach, a huge floating crane clutching a B-25, like a dead housefly, was moving slowly toward the carrier.

"They are ready to load, sir," the executive officer and navigator said.

At that moment, a light began to flash from the small signal tower next to the landing strip. Naoyuki said, "From the signal bridge, sir. 'COMTARAWA to COMYONAGA. Ready to load bombers. Request instructions'."

"Crane to anchor off my port quarter. Commence loading procedures immediately," Fujita said.

The talker spoke into his mouthpiece and in a moment reported, "They 'rogered', sir."

"Very well." The old admiral turned to Captain Arai. "Captain report to the flight deck and personally take charge of the work party. I want those bombers firmly secured. Double the lashings. You know we may hit some heavy weather when we round Cape Horn."

"Aye, aye, sir." The navigator left the bridge.

The next two days were hectic. The loading of the bombers was a very slow procedure. Although four lighters shuttled to and from the beach to the anchored floating crane, it took almost an hour to lift each bomber to the flight deck where deckhands grasped the slings with boat hooks and guided them to the deck. The yard oiler came alongside and *Yonaga*'s fuel tanks were topped off. The destroyers moved alongside the tankers and drank their fill of the black life's blood. So that they, too, could fill their bunkers, the two *Fletchers* patrolling outside the entrance were relieved.

"Got to give credit to Horace Mayfield and the CIA," Rear Admiral Whitehead said to Brent while both men leaned on the windscreen of the flag bridge. "They really got their act together. They've come through with everything, so far."

"Yes, Admiral," Brent agreed. "But where's *Bennington?*"

That question was answered by a signaling searchlight flashing from the tower. Soon, a message came down from the flag bridge: "A PBM reports *Bennington,* a tanker and five escorts three-hundred miles to the southeast. She will remain on course zero-three-five and reciprocal at approximately latitude thirty-minutes-south, longitude one-seven-eight-east until rendezvous with *Yonaga.* A six plane patrol enroute."

As if to hyphenate the message, three F-6Fs and three Vought F-4U Corsairs swept out of the east and roared over the anchorage. Each had a large "B" painted on its vertical tail fin. *"Bennington! Bennington!"* was shouted from a thousand throats. The joy felt was that known only to men at war facing mortal risk who suddenly find a powerful comrade-in-arms at their side.

Fujita stepped onto the bridge and chuckled. Obviously in high spirits, he pointed at the gull-winged Corsairs and delighted Brent and Whitehead with one of his rare quips, "You Americans can not even put your wings on straight."

Both Americans laughed. "They had to 'gull' them, Admiral, or have an extra-long undercarriage," Whitehead explained. "The F-4U's original power plant was the two-thousand-horsepower Pratt and Whitney R-Twenty-Eight-Hundred Double Wasp. It took an enormous four-bladed prop, over thirteen feet in diameter, which would have torn up flight decks without the 'bent' wings."

Fujita raised his glasses and followed the six fighters as they made a sweep around the anchorage and then shot low over the strip. "The Corsair has a wide wing. Must be hard to land one of them on a carrier."

"You're very perceptive, sir. I'm surprised to see them. However, they are excellent fighters. One of our best. It's actually the first American production fighter to exceed four-hundred-miles-per-hour in level flight."

"A powerful weapon," Fujita acknowledged.

Late that afternoon when the last B-25 was being loaded, Colonel Irving Bernstein surprised everyone by coming aboard. The Israeli Intelligence agent had been flown in on a PBM. Brent and Yoshi greeted him with hand clasps, back slaps and joyful quips. "Couldn't miss the show, Colonel," Brent said, smothering the slender Israeli's hand in his own big hand. "Our big play."

"According to the 'Bard', 'the play's the thing'," Bernstein punned back.

"Why didn't you radio us your ETA? You could've missed us."

"I would have had to use CISRA or Purple Alpha." The colonel cupped his ears like an eavesdropping child. "Big Arab ears are listening, you know. It's best to maintain radio silence." He tugged on his spade-like beard. "Remember, I helped plan this operation. I knew your ETA Tarawa."

Before they could continue, the PA boomed an order for the colonel to report to Admiral Fujita's cabin. Bernstein hurried to obey the order. In a few minutes Brent Ross and Rear Admiral Whitehead were summoned.

When Brent entered the admiral's cabin, Fujita and Bernstein were grave. After the newcomers seated themselves, Fujita gestured to the Israeli. "I found Horace Mayfield," Bernstein said.

"You didn't come all this way to tell us that," Rear Admiral Whitehead said.

"Of course not." Bernstein's knuckles drummed on his armrest. "It's our plan to attack Rabta. It may have been compromised."

There were rumbles of distress and anxious looks were exchanged. "It's Mayfield. Remember he disappeared with Lia Mandel?" Everyone nodded. "Well, they went on a four day bender together."

"Dope, too?"

"Maybe cocaine. We don't know for sure."

"Good Lord," Whitehead said.

"He's been relieved?" Brent speculated.

The Israeli sighed deeply and shook his head. "I'm afraid not."

"Why not?"

"His uncle's a senator. Holds a key position on the Armed Services Committee, that's why. Now do you understand?"

"Damn!" Whitehead spat. He hunched forward. "But I still don't understand. A CIA man on a binge with a reporter who seems to be a, ah . . ."

"A dyke," Brent said, "that's what she is." He tugged at his ear. "And Mayfield likes young girls, has a punch card at every bordello in Tokyo. Why Mandel? It doesn't make sense."

"They're both bisexual," Bernstein said. "Mayfield also likes boys."

"That can lead to a lot of interesting complications," Whitehead suggested.

"And maneuvers," Brent added. Then to Bernstein, "You're suggesting they're having an affair? I thought you were going to set up surveillance equipment?" Brent asked.

The Israeli's lips nibbled on each other like a nervous horse before a race. "They have some kind of relationship. We have bugged all concerned. We did this before you left." He turned to Brent and then averted his eyes. "This includes Arlene Spencer's apartment. I'm sorry."

"You mean you were listening in when I—"

"When you last visited her? Yes. It was duty, Brent. Please understand," Bernstein pleaded.

"I can't believe this."

"You're clean, Brent."

"I can't believe you actually know . . ."

"Will this convince you, Brent?" The intelligence officer placed a small tape recorder on the admiral's desk.

Brent's stomach was suddenly hollow and sick. "No! I don't want to hear it."

Fujita took command: "But I do."

Clenching his teeth and throwing an imploring look at Brent Ross, the Israeli leaned forward and threw a switch. Strains of "Spartacus" filled the room and Brent heard his own voice, and the lies he told Arlene when she asked about *Yonaga*'s mission. The denials and subterfuge were clear for everyone to hear. Brent dropped his head into his hands when the thrashing sounds began; the sighs, the moans and shouts of "Jesus!"

"Secure that damned machine!" Fujita shouted. "But how? Where were the recording devices?" He waved at

284

the recorder. "It is like a miracle."

Brent sat back seething as Bernstein continued, "Every nail holding every picture was a microphone transmitting on eight-point-five-gigahertz or better."

"The bedroom?" Brent rasped deep in his throat.

Bernstein turned his lower lip under. "The seascape."

"Over the bed?"

"Yes."

Fujita said, "And the others?"

"We installed a hook-switch bypass device in her phone. It not only picks up telephone conversations, but conversations within twenty feet as well, even when it's in its cradle. We even hid a bug under the stamp on a fashion brochure we mailed her and another in the cap of her bottle of Haig and Haig, the only liquor she had in her place. We rented the apartment next door and attached a suction cup with a thousand-ohm supersensitive microphone on it. It had its own computer enhancement, amplifier and tape recorder. All recording and enhancement transmitted from all our bugs was done in this apartment. We also rented an apartment across the boulevard and focused a laser on Arlene's windows. She loves the view and always keeps her drapes pulled open."

"I know," Brent muttered.

"Laser?" Fujita said, obviously fascinated.

"Yes, Admiral," Bernstein said. "We beamed a laser light from a generator no larger than a flashlight onto her windows. Sounds within the rooms cause the windows to vibrate like a mirrored modulator or the diaphragm of a telephone, if you can visualize that better. The returned signal was fed into a computer for digital signal processing which removed extraneous sounds. Then a photo-amplifier reproduced the words or whatever sounds were desired."

"Why in hell didn't you bug Lia's apartment?" Brent asked in exasperation.

"We did."

"Then you sure as hell must have intelligence on her and Mayfield."

"No. Nothing."

"Nothing?"

The Israeli nodded solemnly. "She moves around. She and Mayfield seem to rent places on impulse, and they always pull the drapes."

"This hurt your laser surveillance?" Fujita asked.

"Drapes, screens, that's all it takes."

"But you had agents watching," Brent persisted.

"True, and on two occasions another woman was observed joining them. We were never able to identify her."

Fujita tugged on the single white hair dangling from his chin and said to Bernstein, "Do you believe this Mandel woman is a spy?"

The Israeli shrugged and turned his palms up. "We're doing a complete check on her. It will take time. So far, we've found nothing." He punched his armrest. "On the surface, she's just a reporter. But she and Arlene Spencer are too damned nosey."

"Then the Mandel woman's relationship with Mayfield may be completely innocent," Rear Admiral Whitehead said.

"Not innocent, Admiral Whitehead, but possibly free of security leaks."

Fujita said, "However, you are obviously suspicious, Colonel."

"Yes. It's part of my job. I've left a good man in charge. Arnold Greenberg."

"He will continue the surveillance?"

"Yes, Admiral. And he'll have a complete report for us when we return, and in an emergency, he will communicate with us by CISRA."

"The CIA is cooperating? Spying on their own man?"

"Yes. That's nothing unusual. They do it all the time. And they're digging into Mandel and Spencer back in the States."

"You said our plan may be compromised, Colonel."

"It's very possible, Admiral, even without informants in Tokyo. The whole world knows *Yonaga* is not on a romantic tropical cruise." No one laughed.

Whitehead said, "According to our latest intelligence, *Daffah* and *Magid* are still in the harbor at Tripoli."

"True," the Israeli said. "We have two subs monitoring all traffic in and out of the port. The carriers have been training with their air groups in the Med."

Fujita gestured at a chart of the Mediterranean and said, "There is an American nuclear submarine stationed off the Straits of Gibraltar."

Whitehead moved his head in assent. "The *Ohio*."

"Her captain is Commander Norman Veal," the admiral noted. "A good man. He gave us excellent intelligence off Vladivostok." Brent was amazed by the old man's memory. He could recall details of events of years past and, yet, sometimes completely forget recent occurrences. As all good commanders, Fujita was mulling over the plan again, looking for weaknesses, unforeseen perils, possible traps. The young lieutenant watched closely as the old Japanese tugged meditatively on the long white hair. Fujita continued, "Then with the two Israeli submarines and *Ohio* on station, we should be informed when the Arab carriers stand out, their course, and, if they are headed for the Atlantic, the moment they exit the straits."

287

"Correct, sir."

"And, in addition, we will have *Bennington*'s scouts." Tiny fingertips beat out a soft tattoo on the desk. "If necessary, we can jettison the B-25s, bring up our air groups and engage the enemy without risking *Yonaga* any more than necessary." Every man was aware of these options, but all nodded gravely as if hearing them for the first time. The fingers of one of the tiny hands balled and struck the desk. "At this moment, there is no conclusive evidence the enemy anticipates our attack."

"At this moment, Admiral Fujita, he has shown no evidence that he intends to commit himself to the Atlantic," Whitehead said cautiously.

"We will be prudent," Fujita said. "However, remember, the good samurai rushes in with his sword raised and attacks." He raised a clenched fist over his head. "Our sword is bared and we will not sheathe it until it tastes blood."

"Banzai!" Brent roared.

Whitehead and Bernstein stared silently. Both faces were troubled.

The bomber crews came aboard the next morning. With sixteen bomber pilots, Commander Yoshi Matsuhara, Lieutenant Brent Ross, Rear Admiral Whitehead, the executive officer Captain Mitake Arai, the doddering scribe Commander Hakuseki Katsube, Colonel Bernstein, the torpedo bomber commander Lieutenant Commander Yagoto, dive-bomber C.O. Commander Takuya Iwata crammed into Flag Plot, there were not enough chairs for everyone. Nine of the bomber pilots stood against the bulkheads while their commanding officer, a full colonel, answered Fujita's gesture by standing at the far end of the table.

Although the colonel was not tall, his massive build gave the impression of size and power. Strength shone from his face, too, a broad, square-hewn visage with flinty hazel eyes and his mouth a thin gash in the square jaw. "My name is Latimer Stewart," he said, in a deep, confident voice. "And these are my pilots." His eyes moved around the room, focusing on each officer who snapped to attention as he was introduced: "Sparling, Hennessy, Woodford, Dunne . . ." and the other names rolled from his lips; too fast for Brent to absorb and remember. It would take days to become acquainted with them all and remember their names and then, in a few weeks, they would all be gone; maybe dead.

Fujita introduced each staff member who came to attention when his name was called. As usual, Katsube almost fell and only a hand from Arai saved the scribe from disaster. Fujita struggled from his chair, picked up a pointer and moved to a chart. He stabbed North Africa. "You know your mission and its risks." It was a statement of fact, not a question.

"We're all volunteers, sir."

"How well are you briefed on the target, Colonel?"

"We have reports from Israeli and CIA operatives and aerial photos taken years ago by American satellites before they were blasted by the Chinese lasers. The satellite photos are still valid. The only change we can detect is the construction of several new warehouse-like buildings." Stewart swept a hand over his pilots. "Each aircraft has a specific target. If surprise is complete, we should take out the entire plant." He palmed a shock of brown hair back from his forehead. "Remember, the entire free world is as concerned about these works as you are, Admiral. No telling what a madman like Kadafi would do with that poison gas."

"Your flight plan still calls for you to land in Sicily."

"Yes, Admiral."

Bernstein spoke up: "Israel will provide you with two lifeguard submarines instead of only one."

"We appreciate that, Colonel," Stewart said. "Hear! Hear!" his pilots shouted, smiling and nodding at each other.

"You understand we may be forced to fight our way in?"

"We have our 'fifties,' our gunners, sir."

"No, Colonel." Fujita tapped the table with the pointer. "You do not understand. I mean the Arabs are suspicious. *Yonaga* and *Bennington* may be under attack even before we reach your launch point off Morocco. We may be forced to jettison your aircraft. We cannot operate our own air groups as long as your bombers are on our flight deck."

The pilot straightened as if he had stepped on a spike. "No, not that. Throw away our aircraft, our training, all the planning!" There was a frustrated, angry rumble from the Americans.

"Be assured, Colonel, no one would regret that action more than I." The old man placed his hands on the table and leaned forward. "However, remember, Colonel, the survival of *Yonaga* is the paramount issue here. Without her, there would be no free world."

Stewart's Adam's apple moved as if the flyer found difficulty in swallowing. "All right," he said hoarsely. "I understand, Admiral." He looked around at his men. "No one could expect you to take unnecessary risks with *Yonaga*."

"And understand this, Colonel Stewart, we will jettison only as a last resort." He pounded the table. "I want that poison gas plant as much as you do!"

The American smiled and his pilots nodded in approval.

Fujita sighed and his bony shoulders sagged. The timbre of his voice was a deep rasp. "You will be flying over the Sahara Desert, over Arab lands. If you are shot down, forced down, you can expect no mercy."

Latimer Stewart squared his shoulders. "None of us took on this mission with any illusions. We are aware of the risks." He patted an old Colt 45 hanging from his belt. "In fact, we are quite aware of the Arabs' humanitarian ways with prisoners." His face became very grim. "None of us will be taken alive. Besides our automatics, each man will carry a cyanide capsule concealed in his . . . ah, concealed in a body cavity." Everyone squirmed.

"You have the spirit of the samurai," Fujita said, obviously pleased. "Your American markings are now being painted out and you will take off with Japanese insignias." The ancient sailor smiled. "You know *Yonaga* is officially classified as a public park. That is the only way the Diet can support her without violating Article Nine of the constitution."

"We know, sir."

"Well, then, welcome to the Japanese Department of Public Parks. You are now all official employees."

"I was always great with a lawn mower," one of the pilots said.

"Yeah. I just love to putter with daisies," another added. Boisterous laughter filled the room.

"We'll sow a few seeds of discontent on old Kadafi's ass," a third pilot said.

"Yeah, five-hundred pounds of high explosives seeds," another piped up. More laughter.

Fujita raised his hands and turned toward the shrine.

Brent expected a prayer. Instead, after invoking the blessings of *Amaterasu,* the old Japanese turned and scanned the Americans. "The history of the samurai is seven-hundred-years long," he said. "The story of Kagemasa illustrates the spirit of the samurai. This incident took place during what was called the 'Later Three Years War', in the fourteenth century on your calendar. Kagemasa, who was only sixteen, was shot in the left eye with an arrow. With the arrow still protruding from his eye, Kagemasa closed with his adversary and killed him. Then he fell. A friend, Tametsugu, came to his aid and placed a foot against Kagemasa's cheek and grasped the shaft of the arrow to withdraw it. Kagemasa leapt to his feet and declared, 'I am ready to die from the arrow wound, but no man will ever place a foot on my face.' Then he attacked Tametsugu who managed to escape."

The old man's watery eyes searched the young faces while a thick silence filled the room. Then, the old man drew himself up to his near five-foot height. Despite his diminutive size, his voice was that of a giant. "Kadafi has placed his foot on our face. No man can do this and live!"

There were cheers and cries of "Banzai!"

Latimer Stewart's voice pierced the shouts, "Sir, may I say something?"

Fujita quieted the officers and nodded approval. Stewart said, "Our own Thomas Paine, a great and brilliant patriot, wrote, 'Tyranny, like hell, is not easily conquered . . .' and 'the harder the conflict the more glorious the triumph'." He held up his fist. "We will conquer hell, sir. Hell!"

He was drowned out by cheers. Fujita smiled.

Chapter Fourteen

Yonaga met *Bennington* at latitude zero-degrees, forty-five-minutes south, longitude 178-degrees, twenty-minutes east. After a flurry of signal flags and flashing lights, *Bennington* fell a mile astern of *Yonaga* with her five *Fletchers* on standard screening stations. A CAP of six fighters ranged in wide sweeps around the battle group. Fujita preferred the term "task force," but acquiesced to the American use of "battle group" along with an almost complete shift to English units of measure. He even abandoned the old international phonetic alphabet in favor of the NATO system used by the Americans and the multinational crews manning *Bennington* and her escorts. Eight TBMs, SB2Cs and SBDs armed with depth charges fanned out ahead of the force, searching for Arab submarines. It was known the Arabs had at least six old *Whiskies* armed with Semtex-tipped torpedoes.

At a cruising speed of 16-knots the force steamed slightly south of east in order to split the gap between Howland and Canton Islands. Although the sea appeared empty and void, there were hundreds of islands to the north and south. Palmyra Atoll and Jarvis Island were left to the north, the Marquesas and French Polynesia to the south. None was ever sighted, their presence known only by examining the charts and occasional blips on radar. These were the rear areas of World War II and the old warriors found little to talk about during the long boring watches on the flag bridge, a place where nervous officers tended to congregate.

A half-dozen inter-island steamers were sighted by scouts. All were easily avoided except one which bored on persistently despite low passes by two TBMs. Finally, at a range of only twenty-two miles, a burst of fifty-caliber machine-gun bullets across the bow suddenly caused her captain to decide on a change in course.

Well clear of the Marquesas Islands, Fujita ordered a course change that pointed the bows of the ships on a southeasterly heading; a heading that would take them six hundred miles east of Easter Island and five hundred miles west of the Juan Fernandez Islands. The course was altered again to near south so that the force would steam five-hundred miles off the Chilean coast and far to the west of Cape Horn. The use of the Straits of Magellan was unthinkable. Instead, the carriers would steam well south of the southern tip of South America and transit the Drake Passage. Here curious eyes could not find them and there was little chance they would encounter other vessels.

On his long deck watches, Brent was fortunate in having Lieutenant J.G. Tokuma Shoten in his section as JOD. The young lieutenant usually kept his watch on the navigation bridge where he constantly monitored the positions of their escorts with bearings and ranges taken on the radar repeater and bearings read from the gyro-repeater. He was very efficient, continuously relaying information to Brent through the talker, Seaman First Class Nobunaga Oda. During his day watches, Brent enjoyed watching the fighters and bombers taking off and landing on *Bennington*. When he tired of watching the aircraft, the sea and sky were always ready to provide a show, and so were his memories.

Arlene was always there, particularly at night. Warm, soft, reaching for him with eager arms. He would gnash his teeth and grind them in frustration, sometimes wince and groan like the victim of a medieval torture chamber, trying vainly to purge her from his mind.

Now and then, especially before they crossed the Tropic of Capricorn and when they still bucked the southeasterlies and the South Equatorial Current, sudden line squalls would burst on the battle group. Like a gray-black slug, a cloud would wall the horizon and rush down on the ships, its base trailing a glistening white slimy line where the wind frothed the surface. There would be the sudden downpour, wind, and then it would be past in a matter of minutes, sunlight like bright crystalline shafts rebounding from the sea to overload a man's retinas with their brilliance.

South of Capricorn, the clouds changed, the sky *kamis* seeming to bring on all of the variety in their inventory: low scudding dirty gray clouds and occasional fog banks so thick it seemed a man could cut it into chunks like cheese. And the sea changed its face as readily, sometimes flat and satiny, other times assaulting the ships in rows of running cross seas that advanced threateningly. *Yonaga* would roll and dip, never wooing the attackers, instead, striking back with all of her 84,000 tons, smashing the crests into streaming lace and fragments like bits of white porcelain, crushing the frothing crests ruthlessly under her keel. But there was a price. The new pilots, especially the bomber crews, lost control of their stomachs. There were hilarious stories of seasick airmen nearly falling over the lifelines as their stomachs rebelled against the unaccustomed roll and pitch.

"Wait until we make Drake's Passage," Brent said to Admiral Whitehead one particularly rough afternoon.

"It can be rough," the rear admiral agreed.

Moving further into the southern latitudes, the temperature dropped steadily. Foul weather jackets and parkas began to appear on the bridge. At latitude forty-four-degrees, thirty-minutes south, longitude ninety-two-degrees west, they met their first tanker, the *Sequoia Pines,* which was flying the Liberian flag. Although Brent had been to sea for seven years, he was always amazed at how a rendezvous could be made so precisely with no sign posts, no landmarks.

By contemporary standards, the *Sequoia Pines* was not a huge tanker; not more than 30,000 tons. But it was capable of almost twenty knots and was much more sturdily built than the giant, clumsy supertankers nearly ten times larger. First the escorts and *Bennington* were fueled in the usual side to side fashion favored by the Americans. *Yonaga* was fueled last, bow to stern in typical Japanese style.

As the hoses were cast off, Brent was standing at his usual station on the flag bridge with Whitehead, Fujita and a curious Bernstein. Brent chuckled and said, "An American tanker, under the Liberian flag and chartered by the CIA has just fueled a Japanese battle group."

"Strange times, indeed," Rear Admiral Whitehead concurred, watching the tanker secure her hoses and turn north. "But a necessary operation, of course. Besides mandatory logistics, it's good seamanship to fuel now instead of waiting until we make the South Atlantic."

"Mandatory?" Bernstein asked.

"Yes, Colonel," Whitehead answered. "The DDs need the ballasting effect of full tanks in heavy weather. It lowers their center of gravity. Admiral "Bull" Halsey lost three cans, the *Monaghan, Hull* and *Spence* in a typhoon off the Philippines in December of 1944 when they ran low on fuel. They were high in the water with nearly empty bunkers and rolled over. Over seven-hundred men were lost." He stabbed a finger south. "Drake's Passage can be just as rough, very nasty."

Fujita nodded and glanced at Brent. "We know about Drake's Passage, Mister Ross," he said. "Remember, we steamed these waters in 1984 when we bloodied Kadafi's nose in the Mediterranean."

"Yes, sir," Brent agreed. "We gave him a good introduction to *Yamoto damashii*, Admiral."

"Tanker sends the signal, Admiral. 'Good luck from your friendly petrol dealer. I will be at the same corner when you return. Just give me a buzz'."

"Send him a 'Well done'," Fujita said, untroubled by the American idiom. "And we will give him a 'buzz' before we return to his corner."

The officers dutifully chuckled at the admiral's clever retort.

Boring deep into the southern latitudes, the battle group did not turn east until latitude sixty was reached. Four-hundred-fifty miles south of Cape Horn and 540 miles north of the Antarctic Circle, the ships were well south of the shipping lanes. The thermometer plunged below freezing. Watches on weather decks and lookout platforms were stood by men clad in boots, heavy trousers, foul weather jackets over layers of sweaters, gloves, wool watch caps pulled down over ears or fur-lined caps with earflaps like poodles' ears secured by lines under their chins. Hands jammed into their pockets, the men stood like statues, the vapor of their breath ripped from their lips in steaming banners by the wind. Some lookouts wore ski masks.

The lashings on the bombers were checked and reinforced by more lines secured to engines, fuselages and wing tips. The heavy tarpaulins were snugged down under steel beams bolted to the deck. "Not even Force Twelve winds can damage those planes," Fujita said confidently, when Arai reported the new precautions to him.

Now the ships were in the only sea lane that circumnavigates the entire globe. They were, also, in an area that bred some of the wildest and most treacherous storms on earth. Here two vast air masses—the cold, heavy Antarctic air, and the warmer, lighter air of the subtropics—collide violently. Hurled together by the centrifugal force generated by the earth spinning on its axis, the violence of the conflicting fronts is exacerbated by the enormous torque of the Coriolis force: right in the northern hemisphere, left in the southern hemisphere. Out of this devil's brew of tortured air, swarms of warring masses spin off into gigantic whirlpools of revolving air, moving with great speed, gaining strength, momentum and velocity.

Everyone watched the barometer. At first the ships sailed in a high pressure area of 1033 millibars. But in these latitudes the barometer could "pump," readings changing with unbelievable speed. The sea was relatively calm, but not for long. A sudden drop to 995 millibars presaged a storm that struck with frightening swiftness. Luckily, the depression was relatively small—only about seventy miles in diameter—but while it lasted the seas were huge. Tops were ripped in snowy plumes like white down from a molting bird by winds that gusted to Force 11 on the Beaufort Scale (64 to 72 miles-an-hour.)

The frozen wind struck a man like an ax. It was so cold, the lungs tried to refuse it. Men gasped, gulped and grimaced, turned their heads when frozen spray pelted them like icy flechettes. Rain poured down like dense gray smoke; cold rain in torrents thickened by water clawed from the surface by the wind. The other ships of the force could only be seen on radar. Then mourning, whipping and sighing, the wind backed into the east.

Arai and Fujita estimated the storm was moving from east to west at about twenty knots. Combined with the speed of the battle group, it would take about two hours to cross through the heart of the storm. It took three. Three hours of hell that saw the barometer drop to 980 millibars and the wind cannon and thrum in gusts up to eighty miles-an-hour. The clamorous assault of the seas smashed into *Yonaga* with great booming sounds, waves slogging into her bow and shooting up explosions of blue water that the wind immediately shredded into white driven spray. The great ship shuddered after each furious blow; the superstructure creaked, popped and groaned with the strain.

Brent, nearly blinded by the downpour, tears streaming from his eyes and running across his cheeks, gripped the windscreen and wondered about the escorts. The narrow destroyers must be gyrating wildly, rolling nearly on their beams' ends. But despite the interference of the storm, radar showed the *Fletchers* still on station. Ragged, true, but the doughty little ships still maintained their formation.

The storm vanished as quickly as it struck. Notwithstanding, the force did not emerge into an area of clear skies and calm seas. Instead, the wind took a sudden drop, the rain stopped and the black storm clouds gave way to high scudding dirty gray clouds streaming long filmy scrolls of white cirrus.

Finally clearing Cape Horn, the battle group turned to a course just east of north—032 true on the gyro-repeaters—thus splitting the thirteen-hundred-mile expanse of water separating the Falklands and South Georgia Island. Steaming steadily on this heading, the ships paralleled the east coast of South America at a distance of over a thousand miles. They were safe from curious radars, but not free from accidental encounters with ships plying the South Atlantic shipping lanes. Course was changed four times to avoid being sighted by merchantmen.

Continuous monitoring of international frequencies brought no new information about the enemy carriers. *Daffah* and *Magid* were still exercising their air groups off Tripoli and Arab build-up of fighter strength along the Mediterranean coast appeared to be completed. Fujita, Whitehead and Bernstein had expected the two carriers to be underway for the Far East. They viewed the intelligence with growing unease.

The battle group crossed the Tropic of Capricorn twelve hundred miles east of Rio de Janeiro. Three days later, Natal, the "hump" of South America, was left far to the west and the ships entered the South Atlantic's narrowest area. Several more ships were sighted by the scouts and avoided. Then, just north of the Tropic of Cancer, they met their second tanker for a final fueling before the run-in on the Moroccan coast. She was British and had been sent north from the Falklands ahead of the battle group. Every ship drank its fill, and then, with a flurry of signals, the tanker headed south.

Brent became better acquainted with the crews of the B-25s. All of the pilots and copilots were Americans.

However, the gunners and radiomen included three Greeks, four Frenchmen, a Rumanian, a Russian and two Germans. Most had had loved ones killed or maimed by terrorist acts. All hated terrorism, all were determined to carry out their mission, and all realized their chances of survival were slim. Yet, they presented bold, brave, determined faces.

When not talking with Yoshi Matsuhara in his cabin or watching the pilot while he tinkered endlessly with his fighter, Brent spent his off-duty time in the wardroom. Here most of the pilots and copilots of the North American Mitchells could usually be found. Without watches to stand, these officers had hours to kill and spent most of it in *Yonaga*'s spacious wardroom reading, playing cards or becoming acquainted with the carrier's other pilots. Most had been wretchedly seasick during the transit of Drake's Passage and were thankful for the comparatively calm seas in which the carrier was now steaming.

The faces became names. To Colonel Latimer Stewart, Captain Charles Dunne, Lieutenant Paul Woodford, Lieutenant Jacob Sparling, Captain Michael Hennessy, all of whom Brent had met at the staff meeting before departing Tarawa, were added more names — names that stuck because the young faces were bright and cheerful and intelligent. Lieutenant Merle Brooks, Lieutenant Thomas Getty, Captain Al Gordon stood out. And there were two dozen more, all congenial and eager to ask Brent about *Yonaga* and her tumultuous history.

Brent was struck by the potpourri of nationalities represented in the fighter group. Never had there been so many foreign pilots flying *Yonaga*'s fighters. Eight Englishmen, twelve Americans, two Frenchmen, an

Italian, two Poles and a German. In all, twenty-six for-eigners were flying fighters. These were picked men Yoshi Matsuhara had deemed the quickest, the dead-liest, the most efficient killers. And these men, along with the bomber crews, were *Yonaga*'s claws, teeth and muscles. They would die in the greatest numbers. They always did. Often, when surrounded by the chattering pilots so filled with life, Brent would be seized with a great sadness.

The pilots and air crews of the B-25s were treated with unusual respect by *Yonaga*'s crew, a patronization that Brent realized was very close to that shown by men who realize their comrades-in-arms were condemned men. These were the men who would be at greatest risk, flying fifteen hundred miles unescorted over enemy turf at only one hundred feet or less to avoid radar. Cer-tainly, some of these fine young men would die. That was obvious to everyone.

As the days wore on and the battle group drew closer to its date with fate, tension mounted in the wardroom, mess halls, hangar deck; every compartment, every deck. The tarpaulins were pulled from the bombers and the ground crews swarmed over them. Bowsers hosed a small amount of fuel into their tanks; bombs were se-cured to their racks; pilots and crew chiefs tested con-trols and instruments; armorers and gunners oiled, loaded and checked weapons. The great Wright Cy-clone R-3350 engines were tested, blasting blue smoke in clouds to leeward. Then, two days from launch point, the signal to begin the promised Israeli offensive was sent by Bernstein by both Purple Alpha and CISRA.

The moment the bomber's engines blasted to life, the crew began to experience a strange phenomenon all men about to face the horrors of combat know intimately. Everyone became friendlier. Men who were nearly strangers smiled at each other, stepped aside in passageways, helped each other with burdens, shared cigarettes and candy. Arguments over cards, chess, and checker almost disappeared. Brent had seen this growing camaraderie many times before on the eve of *Yonaga*'s battles. It never changed.

The dive-bomber commander, Commander Takuya Iwata, was the exception. The arrogance continued unabated. His treatment of the *Eta*, Torpedo Bomber Commander Lieutenant Commander Iyetsuma Yagoto, was still harsh and filled with scorn. Although he was of inferior rank, Yagoto was made of stern stuff. With the attack now only hours away, Brent was on the hangar deck with Yoshi when Yagoto whirled on Iwata after a sharp reference to "antecedents like donkey's shit." Screaming an oath, Yagoto charged Iwata with balled fists. Only the intercession of Brent Ross and Yoshi Matsuhara prevented a brawl in front of a crowd of wide-eyed, excited enlisted men. Both officers vowed to finish the encounter after *Yonaga* dealt with the Arabs. "And then your turn will come," Iwata spat at Brent. "I owe you a debt, long overdue."

"At your pleasure, Commander," Brent smiled back. "I took care of you once and I'll be happy to accommodate you again." He held up his fists and turned them like two big clubs. "I've always been interested in freelance dentistry. You've got the big mouth for it."

"We shall see if your heart is as big as your mouth," Iwata retorted hotly. Then, glowering with the quintessence of hatred flashing from his eyes, the dive-bomber commander turned his back and stalked away.

Midway between the Canary Islands and the Azores and thirteen hundred miles due west of the coast of Morocco, a red flare from Fite's DD-1 sounded the submarine alarm. Every ship went to battle stations and *Yonaga* began zigzagging violently. Through his glasses, Brent could see DD-1 and DD-3 converging on a tiny vacant patch of ocean. Soon, the seas were ripped and torn by the gigantic blasts of shallow-set six-hundred-pound depth charges. No wreckage was seen, no oil, no evidence that a submarine had really been stalking them. However, Fite signaled that a periscope had definitely been sighted. This left everyone uneasy.

"Did the submarine get off a message?" Fujita asked Naoyuki anxiously.

"Radio room reports nothing, sir," the talker replied.

The old admiral punched the screen and grumbled to himself in Japanese.

"If he's still alive, he'll wait until we're over the horizon and then transmit his sighting, Admiral," Byron White-head said.

"If he is smart," Fujita said. "And if he managed to evade those depth charges, he is a bright one indeed. He will wait." He glanced astern where DD-1 and DD-3 still raced back and forth over the same patch of ocean like hounds sniffing lost game while two TBMs circled overhead. No depth charges were rolled or fired from the DDs' K-guns. The aircraft made repeated passes low on the water, but appeared as frustrated as the destroyers. Fujita looked at the sky and muttered to himself, "Amaterasu stay with us."

But Amaterasu had been looking away. Fujita recalled the destroyers and the torpedo bombers returned to their patrol. Then, he had just ordered a course change to 090 and speed increased to twenty-eight knots for the final run-in on the coast of Morocco, when the news they all feared came over on CISRA. *Daffah* and

Magid and ten *Gearing* class destroyers were headed for the Straits of Gibraltar at flank speed. "The sub," Captain Arai said flatly from his usual station next to the chart table on the flag bridge.

"Yes. But I think they knew from the moment we left Tokyo Bay," Fujita said. "They just were not certain of our time of arrival. I'm sure we've been betrayed."

"I agree," Bernstein said. "I think they sniffed us out back in Tokyo. I'll wager the Arabs got their verification there with the sub." He gestured over the stern.

Fujita nodded and stabbed a finger at *Bennington*. "I will detach *Bennington*. She will steam to the entrance to the Straits of Gibraltar and engage the enemy." He glanced at a chart tacked to the chart table. "She will have an eight-hundred-mile run while *Daffah* and *Magid* must make fifteen hundred. She will welcome them when they exit." He turned to the talker: "Signal bridge, by flashing light to *Bennington*, 'Execute Plan *Baker*. I mean execute Plan *Bravo*'."

There was a clattering of signaling searchlights and the big *Essex* class carrier began to turn north with her five escorts. Midway in the turn, the American flags of all six warships were struck and the Japanese battle ensign run up. Thousands of voices rose in hoarse cheers and cries of "Banzai!" The cheers faded as the force disappeared over the horizon at a speed of at least thirty knots.

Whitehead seemed to be free of the emotion that gripped every man on the bridge. Always the pragmatist, he asked bluntly, "You won't jettison the B-25s, Admiral Fujita?"

"Negative, Admiral Whitehead. We will proceed at top speed and launch our Mitchells."

"A terrible risk, sir. *Bennington* is outnumbered two-to-one in every department except aircraft. Even there, the Arabs will have an advantage in numbers. And we'll have no CAP or scouts." The American waved over the bow. "Kadafi could've bullied the Moroccans into allowing him to base aircraft on their coast." He gripped the windscreen with both hands. "It could be an ambush and we'd be cold meat, sir."

Fujita's expression was unreadable, but there was a hint of a smile in the crosshatch of wrinkles that gullied his face. "No one has ever said war was safe, Admiral," he said, matter-of-factly. And then pounding the chart table, "I want Rabta!"

Chapter Fifteen

Brent, Irving Bernstein and Yoshi Matsuhara were in the admiral's cabin when he called a conference with Colonel Latimer Stewart. "We feel the integrity of our mission has been compromised, Colonel," the admiral said.

"I've heard, sir," Stewart replied. "The sub."

"Perhaps far more serious than that." A thumb and forefinger found the dangling hair beneath the admiral's chin. "We may have been betrayed in Tokyo."

"Christ!"

"We must launch you from two-hundred-fifty miles instead of one-hundred."

"I'll lose the whole squadron," the American colonel said, half rising, eyes wide.

Fujita shook his head. "I have already given the order to remove two five-hundred-pound bombs and to install a fuel tank in your bomb bays." Stewart winced and twisted in his chair, but remained silent while the admiral continued, "This will give you more than the additional range you need and you will still have two-and-a-half tons of bombs." The old man ran a hand through the few surviving white hairs on his glistening pate. His eyes searched every face. "If the enemy has intelligence of our plan, we could be attacked at any time. However, with the limited range of the Messerschmitt

109, I would expect him to coordinate his attack to our expected launch point, one-hundred miles off the coast of Morocco. He still does not know *Bennington* has been detached." He moved his eyes back to Colonel Stewart. "We will preempt them, launch you, put up our CAP and steam to support *Bennington* at forced draft."

Nodding, Stewart sighed and sank back. "I understand, sir."

Fujita became very somber. "If Kadafi knows of our plan, you can expect to be under heavy attack. You may suffer heavy casualties."

"I know."

"The Arabs' first priority will be to protect their poison gas works. *Yonaga* would be second."

"That's reasonable. If I were an Arab commander I would have the same priorities."

The old man's fingertips opened hostilities with the desk top. "If you are attacked by large formations of fighters, you can abort and land in Morocco which is technically neutral, or, I will provide you with point option data. You can rendezvous with the battle group and ditch, and my escorts will pick you up—providing we are not engaged." He stabbed a finger at a chart mounted on a bulkhead. "Or, the best plan is for you to fly to the Canary Islands and land on Tenerife. There is a fine airstrip on the island and it is only six-hundred miles southwest of Morocco. Easy range for your aircraft. It is Spanish, neutral, and you would be interned."

Yoshi Matsuhara interrupted the exchange, "Admiral Fujita, I have never heard of bombers flying with fuel tanks carried in a loaded bomb bay."

"Then this will be the first time, Commander Matsuhara."

"But sir," the Japanese pilot persisted, "those auxiliary tanks are not self-sealing. A tracer round could set off the tank and the entire bomb load. You are adding a terrible risk to our bombers' mission."

The old admiral's narrow eyes shifted back to Colonel Stewart. "Not self-sealing? Why did you not tell me this?"

"There is no such thing as a safe war, Admiral."

"You are quoting me, Colonel."

"Not really, sir. It's an axiom all fighting men know. We'll empty the bomb bay tank first and drop it. The fumes are the dangerous thing. We'll vent the aircraft and, if necessary, we can even crack open the doors and blow them out until we drop the tank." Stewart's brow suddenly ridged with rows of furrows, eyes narrowed to slits. He rubbed the bridge of his nose. "We will proceed with the attack, sir. Distance, fuel tanks, fighters, AA be damned." He pounded his armrest. "I want Rabta as much as you do. Not one man, woman or child in the free world can sleep in safety as long as those poison gas works exist." He brought his open palm down in a short vicious chop like a karate fighter delivering the coup de grace. "If Kadafi gets the chance, he'll throw gas bombs at the world like handfuls of marbles."

There were no cheers, no shouts of "Hear! Hear!" The truth was too daunting to elicit rejoicing. A heavy, weighty silence filled the room. The only sound was the faint throb of the main engines seven decks below and the whine of blowers. Then a soft thumping sound could be heard. Fujita was absentmindedly pounding on the copy of the *Hagakure* which always occupied a corner of his desk.

Latimer Stewart nodded at the book. "I know about

that book, sir." Fujita arched an eyebrow quizzically. "Yes, Admiral, and I know one of your favorite sayings which has become mine."

The pounding stopped. "And what is that?"

" 'Duty is as heavy as the mountain, death is as light as a feather'."

This time Brent and Yoshi shouted "Banzai!" Bernstein added his, "Hear! Hear!"

Admiral Fujita straightened and the old parchment cracked with what appeared to be a warm smile. "Indeed, Colonel, you have a stalwart heart, the heart of a samurai," he said softly. He turned to Colonel Bernstein, mind shifting in its usual mercurial, unpredictable manner, "You said you had news for me concerning the Israeli offensive?"

"Yes, sir." Bernstein rose and walked to a chart of the Middle East. "You know we monitor Radio Tel Aviv continuously," he stated. The old sailor nodded. "It's the only reliable source of information in the Middle East." The Israeli turned to the chart and with a single finger traced a red ink line on the overlay that marked the David Ben-Gurion Line. "We have taken the offensive with armor and infantry here, here, and here." The finger stabbed at Gaza, Al Khalil, Ariba and the Syrian border along the Golan Heights. "We are making good progress because of the lack of Arab fighters. We have information that the Arabs are pulling some of their squadrons back from their bases along the coast to the west."

"Good. Good," Fujita said, rubbing his hands. "Have they recalled their carriers?"

"Negative, sir. One of our subs sighted *Daffah* and *Magid* off the Tunisian coast making for the Straits of

Gibraltar at at least thirty knots."

The old man nodded and turned his thin lips under. "May the gods be with *Bennington*," he said prayerfully.

"Sir, if there is nothing else," Stewart said, "may I be dismissed? According to my calculations we'll be taking off at dawn about twelve hours from now. Is that correct?"

"Correct. I have adjusted the speed of the force to do just that."

"Then, Admiral, with your permission, I'll meet with my pilots immediately and brief them on the changes in our flight plan."

Fujita nodded affirmatively. "Of course, Colonel, you are dismissed and so are Colonel Bernstein and Commander Matsuhara. However, Lieutenant Ross, please remain."

In a moment, the door closed and Brent and the admiral were alone. The fingers found the whisker. "We may be engaging enemy aircraft and enemy carriers very soon, Brent-san."

"I know, sir," Brent answered, wondering what was troubling the keen mind across the desk.

"You wish to fly as a gunner?"

"I enjoy flying."

"I know and you have a remarkable record as a gunner." The Admiral's hand dropped to his chest and he began to rub the fine wool material of his tunic over a collarbone that protruded from the bony chest like a small bridge. The next question from a man filled with surprises still managed to catch the young lieutenant off guard. "Do you seek your dragon, Brent-san? Is that why you seek the most perilous duty? The greatest risks?"

Despite occasional lapses in recalling recent events, the old man's astonishing mind was eclectic in its tastes, and still encyclopedic in its ability to store facts. Over the years, Brent had been startled many times by Fujita's incisive knowledge of western mythology and theology. He guessed these interests were fanned by Fujita's stay in the United States and his graduate studies at the University of Southern California when he was a young officer. Regaining his composure quickly, the lieutenant rose to the challenge, "Like Saint George?"

"Yes." The old man tapped his desk. "Or is it your white whale? Ahab's fatal quest, Jason's golden fleece, Galahad and the Holy Grail?" He knuckled the desk top for emphasis, "Western myths are filled with fruitless quests."

"Aren't we all driven to seek those things, sir? Our fate, our destiny?"

"Yes. As long as we do not stop to fight windmills on the way."

"I've never attacked a windmill, sir, and, respectfully, Don Quixote's lance would not fit in the rear seat of an Aichi D-3-A."

Fujita chuckled. "I know, Brent-san, I know. I enjoy your knowledge. Your wit." He became serious, "Commander Iwata has requested you again as his gunner," he said, revealing his true concern.

Brent had expected it. "He is the finest bomber pilot I have ever flown with. He planted a five-hundred-kilogram bomb in the center of *Al Kufra*'s flight deck. The flak was so thick a man could walk on it. He never wavered, never hesitated, dove so low he couldn't miss."

"He has courage. It is not all in his mouth which can be of considerable size." The hand moved up to his ear

312

and he began to tug on a withered pea of an earlobe. "You have had your differences with Commander Iwata."

"He is a bully and a boor. He's aggressive and can be violent. He thinks he's another Yukio Mishima."

"You had words with him on the hangar deck over Lieutenant Commander Yagoto. You promised to settle your differences physically after the coming battle."

The admiral's knowledge was not unexpected. His eyes and ears were everywhere. Nothing escaped him. "That is true, sir, and he is no windmill or windbag, for that matter."

Fujita did not smile at the jest. "You know I never stand in the way of these . . ." he waved a hand, "these resolutions so long as *Yonaga* is not jeopardized."

"I know, sir. That's why we agreed to wait."

"But you wish to fly with him?"

"Yes, sir."

Fujita had no trouble with the incongruity. A single finger traced an ellipse on the highly waxed surface of the desk while he thought. "In the past, I have allowed you to make these decisions," he said, black eyes catching the blue of Brent's and holding them as if tied together. "I am sorry, Brent-san. I cannot allow you to fly on this operation."

"Why, sir?"

"It makes no sense for a line officer, a lieutenant and a valued deck officer and cryptologist, to be flying as a highly expendable gunner. Now we have an abundance of gunners, all enlisted men. You flew against *Al Kufra* and the Arab bases in North Korea and the Marianas because we were short of gunners." He waved a hand. "But now, we have more men than cockpits. This would

313

truly be nonsense, the dragon, the white whale, the fleece, and the rest of it."

"But sir . . ."

Fujita waved him off. "You have become a highly competent deck officer. You are one of my best and you know my decisions are always based on the best interests of *Yonaga*." The tiny knuckles tapped out an accompaniment to the next words, "I want you as my JOD at General Quarters. In fact, I am ordering it." The fist came to rest and the fingers spread like bent roots. "I respect you and want you to know why I've made this decision, Brent-san."

Brent was not finished. "But, sir. You have Admiral Whitehead, one of the most experienced and—"

Fujita interrupted, "He has been sunk five times, helped plan the disaster at Tarawa. The gods have their backs to him and he brings ill omens with him."

"But his battle station is still on the bridge with you!"

"True. And he is a valued aide. However, Hachiman San, the god of war, smiles on you. You have survived a half-dozen air battles and two wounds that would have killed lesser men. I believe Hachiman San and O-Kuni-Nushi, ruler of the invisible, watch over you." He stabbed a finger at his young companion. "Brent-san, you carry good fortune with you."

Brent knew he could only lose if he grappled with the oriental logic and the Japanese myths which were not myths to the admiral but truisms based on historical facts. "But Whitehead will still remain on the bridge?" he argued.

"You will cancel whatever evil fortune follows him."

Of course. The circle was complete and it was impregnable to western logic. Anyway, it did make some sense to the young American. Good fortune and bad would be balanced like an assayer's scale in equilibrium. Why not? "I understand, sir."

The old face cracked with a smile that still revealed nearly a full set of teeth. Holding Brent's eyes with his, the old man spoke softly, "I knew you would, Brent-san. Truly, you have earned your title of 'The American Samurai'."

Brent returned the smile and said, "And, sir, be assured. It's not dragons and windmills I seek."

"The white whale?"

Brent sighed. "Perhaps, sir. I believe there's a Moby Dick out there for all of us. But I think we are all closer to Ulysses' quest than Ahab's fixation on the whale."

The old man's face brightened. "Homer. *The Odyssey*. It took Ulysses ten years of wandering before he finally returned home."

"Yes, Admiral. This is the eighth year of *Yonaga's* odyssey since I came aboard."

The old mariner smiled into the young man's eyes. "You know your mythology, Brent-san."

"There is much to be learned there, sir."

"True. But keep in mind, Brent-san, this is the fifty-eighth-year of *Yonaga's* quest."

"You've outdone Ulysses by more than five-times over."

The old man chuckled. "And our journey is not nearly complete, is it, Brent-san?"

"No, sir. The odysseys of men of our profession are never over. Never completed. The world will not permit it."

There was new respect, almost awe, in the old man's eyes as he nodded agreement.

The eastern horizon glowed with a malevolent jaundiced yellow when the flight deck whined and wheezed with the sound of energizers. Then, one after another, thirty-two great R-3350 engines gasped and coughed to life. *Yonaga* was three hundred miles off the coast of Morocco and the B-25s were warming their engines.

"Wind?" Fujita shouted at Captain Mitake Arai.

"Force six from the northeast."

"More precise, please."

"Gusting to twenty-seven knots, from zero-four-seven, sir."

"Very well." Fujita turned to Naoyuki, "Signal bridge, by masthead light, *alpha, alpha* (all ships and stations) execute to follow, course zero-four-seven, speed thirty-two." The talker spoke into his mouthpiece and the two lights at the end of the signaling yardarm began to blink. Within seconds, every escort was answering with his own *alpha, alpha*.

Brent nodded his approval. Radio silence must be maintained. It was still too dark for flag hoists to be used. Masthead signaling was the best option.

"All escorts answer, sir."

"Very well. Execute!"

Somewhere on *Yonaga*'s signal bridge, a signalman held down his key for a long dash.

"All answer."

"Very well. Left standard rudder, steady up on zero-four-seven. Speed thirty-two."

Brent could feel the throb of the engines pick up through the soles of his boots and the carrier heeled slightly as she turned.

"Steady on zero-four-seven, sir." And then in a moment, "Speed thirty-two, one-hundred-seventy revolutions, sir."

Fujita clapped his hands together. "Excellent. We'll have almost sixty knots of wind over the deck."

"Good, sir," Rear Admiral Whitehead agreed. "Plenty of wind and only a moderate chop. A stable platform. The Mitchells should have no trouble."

Fujita returned to Naoyuki, "Hangar deck. Stand by the aft elevator with our CAP and scouts. I want six fighters and four bombers brought up as the B-25s are launched and deck space becomes available. They will be launched as the last bomber clears the deck." The order was relayed and Fujita spoke to the talker again, "Signal bridge, send the signal, 'I am launching aircraft'!" There was a flurry of lights and a destroyer began to drop astern in lifeguard station. "Two-block Pennant One!"

The sun was a ball of dark satanic red balanced on the string of the horizon when Colonel Latimer Stewart gunned his great Wright Cyclone engines in their final test. Belching clouds of blue smoke, the big bomber trembled as it strained against its brakes like a great bird impatient to return to its natural habitat. Then, with a flash of illuminated yellow wands from the control officer, the brakes were released and the big bomber fairly leaped forward as over six-thousand horsepower accelerated it down the deck. Catching the breeze, the Mitchell lifted easily from the deck and soared up to almost two hundred feet as if caught by the hand of an invisible giant. Immediately, the colonel brought the aircraft down to under one hundred feet and skimmed the ocean as he banked to the east into the strange dawn of clouds painted red like hemorrhaging blood by the rising sun.

Great day for killing men, Brent thought. *The sky's even decorated for it.*

Quickly, the remaining fifteen bombers roared down the deck and banked to the east. All hugged the surface.

"They'll never get them on radar that low," Whitehead said confidently, gesturing at the fast disappearing bombers. "And flying low is less fatiguing on the engines."

Fujita nodded. "He said he would 'stay on the deck'. He certainly is doing just that."

There was new activity on the flight deck as two fighters were already being wheeled to the flight line by their handlers while a third could be seen rising to deck level on the aft elevator. Fujita glanced around at the sky which was now quite bright. "Make the hoist, execute to follow, speed twenty-four."

Within minutes, the first fighter — Yoshi Matsuhara's Zero-sen with the distinctive red cowling, green hood and white fuselage — shot from the deck. Its enormous R-3350 engine rocketed it into a nearly vertical climb. The two Seafires, three more Zeros and four Aichi D3As followed.

Fujita turned to Naoyuki and ordered a course change that headed the battle group for the Straits of Gibraltar. Speed was increased to thirty-two knots. Then he spoke to the other officers on the bridge, "Now we will meet *Daffah* and *Magid* — sink them, kill them." Everyone nodded and muttered agreement. And then aside to Brent Ross, "Perhaps the odyssey will be finished, Brent-san."

Brent shook his head grimly, "Never, sir."

Standing side by side, hands gripping the windscreen, the two officers stared stoically over the bow of the carrier, searching the northern horizon. There was nothing there but a reddish haze.

The first word of the Arab battle group came from Commander Norman Veal, the captain of the American SSBN, *Ohio*. Patrolling off the Straits of Gibraltar, the nuclear submarine's sensitive sonar picked up the enemy's screws. *Ohio*'s threat library identified the cavitations as the signatures of carriers *Daffah, Magid* and ten escorts. They were entering the straits at high speed. Then a commercial radio station in Gibraltar broadcast the news on a regular newscast and within minutes most of the world's networks were transmitting the same information. *Bennington* still maintained radio silence.

Four-hundred miles due west of the straits, *Bennington*'s patrol put her within easy scouting range of the straits yet left her with limitless sea room for maneuvering. To give her fighters maximum time over target, ideally she would send her air groups into the attack when about two hundred fifty miles from the enemy, unless she was spotted and attacked first. The best option was to avoid engaging the two carriers until she was supported by *Yonaga*. Only four-hundred miles to the south, the Japanese carrier was within thirteen hours of her consort.

Only two hours into her dash to the north, *Yonaga*'s receivers picked up plain language transmissions from *Bennington*. The news was shocking. She was under attack from an overwhelming force of at least 40 Junkers, 87 Stukas, and 20 Heinkel 111s escorted by at least six squadrons of ME 109s. A half-dozen Douglas DC-3s

319

were also reported. She gave her position as latitude thirty-six degrees, ten minutes north, longitude sixteen degrees, twenty minutes west. Much closer than anyone expected.

"DC-3s, the Heinkel 111! That is a medium bomber. The Douglases and Heinkels did not come from the carriers," Fujita exclaimed on the crowded flag bridge. He, Brent and Rear Admiral Whitehead crowded around the chart table while the old admiral measured distances with dividers. He thumped the chart with the knobbed end of the instrument. "Oran! Their closest land base. They could not come from Oran. It is eight-hundred-fifty miles from *Bennington*."

"Right! The JUs and MEs don't have that range," Whitehead agreed.

Fujita nodded. "Then they flew from Spain or Portugal."

"The Portuguese. Those spineless bastards gave in to Kadafi's oil blackmail."

"We do not know, Admiral Whitehead. Anyway, the only thing of importance is that *Bennington* is under attack and by land based aircraft! They could have come from Morocco."

"It's an ambush."

"A clever ambush. While we concentrated on *Daffah* and *Magid* they lured *Bennington* in close enough to attack her from a land base. They seem to know our moves before we make them." He turned to Yoshi Matsuhara. "Arm all Aichis and Nakajimas with bombs and torpedoes. We may be engaging the two carriers without support. You have *Bennington*'s position. Take twenty-four fighters, 'Fighter One' and 'Fighter Three' and support her." He stabbed the chart, "For your point option data,

320

I intend to steam northwest on three-one-five at twenty-four knots. This will open the range on any land base and still keep us in position to support *Bennington* and intercept the Arab carriers."

While Yoshi Matsuhara dashed off the bridge, Fujita shouted at Naoyuki, "Sound the general alarm. Prepare to launch 'Fighter One' and 'Fighter Three'! Pilots prepare to man your planes!"

Whitehead's voice rose over the sounds of klaxons, shouting men, the thump of thousands of boots on steel decks and ladders. "Admiral Fujita! You would send only two squadrons of fighters to support *Bennington?*"

"She has sixty fighters of her own. I can spare no more than twenty-four. I am sending our best: Commander Matsuhara's own squadron and our American F6Fs. Remember, we may be engaging two carriers alone. We," he punched the windscreen for emphasis, "cannot allow those carriers to break out into the open sea. They may be armed with gas weapons. Do you understand?"

Whitehead shook his head. "But, sir, you know she will probably be under attack from *Daffah* and *Magid*'s air groups as well. You'd sacrifice *Bennington,* one half of your force without a major effort to save her. This is not a good tactic."

"I would sacrifice you, myself, anything for *Yonaga.* Without her, Japan is doomed. Perhaps, the free world."

There was a roar of engines as twenty-four fighters began to warm up on the flight deck. Fujita returned to the voice tubes. Glaring, Whitehead leaned on the windscreen. His jaw was rigid and the muscles of his cheeks bulged as his teeth ground against each other.

Suddenly, Naoyuki cried out in an unusually high, tense voice. "Admiral, the radio room reports a plain language transmission from Colonel Latimer Stewart!" Every head turned. The talker seemed tongue-tied.

"Out with it, boy," Fujita demanded. "Speak, *shonen*."

"The colonel reports his command is under attack by at least two squadrons of fighters. He has lost two bombers but will not abort the mission!"

"Amaterasu, where are you?" Fujita pleaded, moving quickly to the chart table. He grasped the dividers and speaking to himself said, "They have been in the air for over two hours." Standing behind him, Brent could see one needle end of the instrument stab a point in Algeria. "They should be here, about one-hundred miles south of El Golea and under attack by fighters that should not be there!" He threw the dividers down with so much force they bounced across the chart table and clattered onto the deck. A rating quickly retrieved them. Brent had never seen the admiral in such a state. The cold, inscrutable exterior had melted for an instant.

"Mother of God," Whitehead breathed. "They know everything. We've been betrayed."

Filled with anger and despair, Brent turned back to the flight deck. Pilots were running to their aircraft, the Japanese in their brown flight suits and with *hachimachi* head bands wrapped around their helmets, the two Englishmen and the Americans in heavy trousers and leather lined jackets. All of the pilots wore life jackets and their parachutes hung low and bounced against their buttocks as they ran. Then with shoves from their crew chiefs, they heaved up onto a wing, swung their legs in big arcs to clear the cockpit coaming, and settled down into their bucket seats, using their parachutes as cushions. Fussing like old hens, the crew chiefs leaned over them, helping connect oxygen and radio leads,

322

checking safety harnesses and instruments. Some patted their pilots affectionately and shouted last words of advice into their ears.

Then the engines were gunned, chocks pulled and the ground crews raced to the catwalks, leaving only two men to steady the wings of the fighters. The yellow wand dropped. Immediately, the first fighter, Yoshi Matsuhara's, raced down the deck and shot into the sky.

From 24,000 feet, Commander Yoshi Matsuhara saw the smoke long before he sighted *Bennington*. It was a huge, oily-black pall that billowed high into the sky like a filthy thunderhead. At 350 knots, the fighters closed the range quickly. Then he saw *Bennington*, racing over the horizon and headed south, a great fire raging from her quarters to her stern. She was doing at least thirty knots and her speed kept a strong wind blowing down the deck, forcing the fire to blow over the stern. But Yoshi knew her bombs, fuel and magazines could explode at any instant. At this moment, her fate rested in the hands of her AA crews and damage control parties.

Bombers were circling her and diving like vultures tearing at carrion. But she was fighting back with her forward mounts. The black flowers of AA bursts blooming in the sky while glowing, smoking tracers rose in streams, leaving white phosphorous trails. Her *Fletchers*, crowding in close, added their own enormous fire power. But the bombers were piloted by courageous, determined men. Despite the deadly garden of black flowers and streaming ropes of tracers, the Heinkels, Junkers and Douglases bored in, seeking to deliver the coup de grace.

323

Below him and to the northeast, a handful of F6Fs and F4Us were dueling with at least a squadron of Messerschmitt Bf 109s. There was no sign of Rosencrance and Vatz's garishly painted 109s. Obviously, the MEs had managed to keep *Bennington*'s fighter screen at bay while the bombers drove their attacks home. Yoshi guessed there had been terrible attrition on both sides. Why so few fighters?

Yoshi threw the transmitting switch on his oxygen mask and spoke into his microphone, calling "Renga Leader, this is Edo Leader. Engage enemy fighters and maintain top hat. Edo will engage enemy bombers."

Renga Leader, young Lieutenant James Bender who was the senior American pilot on board *Yonaga*, answered, his voice showing not even a trace of anxiety or nervousness, "Roger, Edo Leader. Will engage."

Immediately, twelve Hellcats broke their "V" into elements of two which in turn blended gracefully into three flights of four. Then the entire squadron turned as one, banking sharply toward the dogfight to the northeast. Yoshi spoke into his microphone, "Edo, this is Edo Leader. Engage bombers! Follow my lead! Individual combat! Banzai!"

After punching his throttle open, but not quite into full overboost, Yoshi jammed his stick to the left and then down, sending the fighter into a screaming power dive, Captain Colin Willard-Smith off his port side, Pilot Officer Elwyn York his starboard.

In a near vertical dive, Yoshi's ears popped and his sinuses began to ache. He felt his nose run and he licked salty liquid off of his upper lip, never taking his hands from the control column spade grip or moving his eyes from the glowing bead of the new electric reflector sight that had replaced his old concentric range finder. His throat was raw from the pure oxygen and his neck and back ached from the tension in the muscles of his arms and shoulders. Charged with adrenaline, he shrugged it all off. Concentrated on his prey. He flipped off the safety cover and carefully placed a thumb that trembled slightly on the red button.

The bombers had seen the doom gathering like a storm cloud above them and now the cloud hurled a murderous lightning bolt their way, tipped by a Mitsubishi A6M2 with red cowling, green hood and an engine that appeared too large. Quickly, most of the enemy broke off the attack on *Bennington* and formed up into three boxes, one stepped up above another to give concentrated covering fire power. Most of them turned onto a course slightly north of east, a heading that would take them to Portugal. Two stragglers, both JU87s, ignored the defensive formations and began their dives. Immediately, both were hit by a storm of AA fire from the ships and tumbled into the sea.

Yoshi would have cheered the AA fire, but shells and bullets do not discriminate between friend and foe. Already, the Japanese planes were diving through hanging black puffs of exploding five-inch shells and rising fire beads of forty-millimeter and twenty-millimeter tracers. He would attack the last and highest box of bombers first. It consisted of twelve HE 111s flying in three rows of four, slightly stepped up from front to rear to give the gunners interlocking fields of fire.

The "tail end *ronin*" were the most vulnerable. Knifing in from above and from the side, Yoshi throttled back even more to reduce the flutter of the airframe. The red bead stopped jumping and he allowed a full length for

325

deflection, aiming ahead of the last bomber on the right. Suddenly, sparkling strings of tracers like fireflies in a windstorm raced to meet him from at least a half-dozen bombers. Ignoring the tracers, the Japanese pilot watched the Heinkel wobble about inside his reflector sight, growing fast until its wingspan stretched across the sight. When its wing tips touched the sight-bars, he jammed down on the button.

The massive recoil of the two twenty-millimeter cannons and the pair of 7.7 machine guns slowed the Zero like a stiff head wind. Harmonized for two-hundred meters, the guns shaped a pyramid of glowing yellow destruction. The commander was aiming for the cockpit, but his shells and bullets hit the right wing and he could see brightly colored flashes from his strikes on the wing and engine. Immediately, the starboard engine bled oil and then a bright red garland of flames tipped with yellow streaked back over the wing. Laying down a black ribbon of smoke, the big plane slipped off to its right in a slow descending turn that turned quickly into the brutally tight spin of the dying Heinkel.

"Banzai!" Matsuhara shouted, bolting past the enemy formation and pulling back on his stick. With centrifugal force sucking blood from his brain and driving him deep into the wicker of his seat, his vision was struck with a familiar fogginess and his peripheral vision blurred. Contracting his sphincter muscles to control his suddenly brim-full bladder, he watched the sea unreeling endlessly in his windscreen until it was finally replaced by the blue of the sky. He screamed to relieve the pressure, shook his head and when he "bottomed out" he jammed the throttle to the wall. Instantly, the great engine roared like an angry lion jabbed by a spear and he felt it try to tear itself free from its mounts, superchargers shrieking, water-methanol spraying into its eighteen cylinders, unleashing all 3,200 horsepower. The huge surge of power gave him a solid shove against the backrest and the needles on the instrument panel jumped and quivered. The little fighter fairly leaped upward, curving up beneath the second box of bombers which was made up of eleven JU87s led by a lumbering DC-3 gunship.

Yoshi shouted "Banzai!" again, glancing at the cataclysm that had struck the box of Heinkels. York and Willard-Smith had both scored; York's bomber cartwheeling across the sky, shedding great hunks of aluminum and parachutes. Willard-Smith had killed the cockpit crew of another. With little visible damage, the bomber was in a near vertical power dive. Another bomber, attacked by a pair of Zeros, dived off steeply, making smoke like an old steam engine. Hundreds of rips and rents tore its wings and fuselage, its antenna whipped in the wind, half the undercarriage dangled, the other shot off, the Perspex canopy and nose were shot to pieces. No parachutes opened as the big plane slowly rolled and flip-flopped toward the sea like an autumn leaf.

The slaughter had thrown the entire formation of Heinkels into confusion, and while the Zeros and Seafires dove through and past the formation, another bomber, trailing white misty glycol and unraveling a streamer of black smoke, did an abrupt half-roll and crashed into a Zero flashing past to its left. Like a pair of mating insects, the two locked aircraft spun and tumbled into the sea. Another Zero, with the inside of its canopy sprayed with blood, continued its full power dive as straight and unyielding as a taut rope. Plummeting into the sea like a berserk race car striking a brick wall, it shed its wings in a hundred-foot tower of water, its fuselage boring into the cold Atlantic waters like an express train plunging into a tunnel.

Pulling up under the Stukas, Yoshi's earphones were filled with the shouts of combat. He heard Elwyn York cry, "I pulled 'is bloody pisser for 'im, Edo Leader."

Willard-Smith's cultured voice was solemn: "Edo Leader this is Edo two. Krajewski and Itami bought the farm."

A hot reptile twisted in Yoshi's gut. Two of his most promising young pilots, one of his Poles, Stefan Krajewski from Warsaw, and Juzo Itami, a twenty-one-year-old from Kobe, were dead. He responded in a steady voice, "Roger. Edo flight, continue to engage!"

The Americans had their hands full with the ME 109s. The fighter frequency was filled with warnings, curses, questions and occasional whoops of victory: "Tinley this is Hoeffler. Look behind you, goddamnit, there's one on your ass!"

Another voice almost hysterical with excitement broke in. There was no identification: "Got him. He blew up like the Fourth of July."

"Bender this is Matthews. Two at three o'clock high."

"See 'em, Matthews. Break right and climb with me."

Hoeffler's voice: "Tinley, for Christ sake. Break! Break!"

"Turning right! Turning right! Get him off my ass, Hoeffler. I can't shake him!"

Yoshi saw a flash of orange flame spurt high in the sky like a broken necklace.

"Bail out! for Christ's sake, Tinley, bail out!" someone

screamed.

"Tinley's a dead man," another voice mourned.

Yoshi pushed the frantic voices from his mind and concentrated on the belly of one of the Stukas in the last rank. With the brute strength of the *Taifu* pulling him upward, the JU quickly grew in his sights. The enemy pilot tried to jink and bank to throw off Matsuhara's aim and give his gunner a shot. But speed, maneuverability, fire-power and geometry were all against him.

Watching the lumpy angularity of the Junkers grow to fill his sights like an insect under a microscope, the commander chuckled and his thin lips pulled back into a death's head leer. With a tingling warmth deep in his groin, he pressed the gun button and counted, "One, two, three, four." Hanging on his prop, vibrating from the aerodynamic strain and the buck of his weapons, Yoshi watched his converging streams of fire rage into the dive-bomber. Strikes blew off the radiator and the spatted undercarriage followed in the slipstream. The pilot did the only thing possible to prolong his life. He half-rolled into a dive.

Screaming curses, Yoshi followed. He gained quickly and dipped below the Junkers' slipstream to avoid the turbulence and the fire from the gunner that squirted past in short bursts. He eased his throttle just before firing. A two-second burst decapitated the gunner and sprayed Yoshi's cowling, hood and windscreen with flecks of blood. The pilot panicked. Pulled back on the stick and skidded into a turn. Yoshi laughed out loud as he cut inside the turn and closed in from above. He gave the JU a quarter length for deflection and pressed the button at only a hundred meters. It seemed every round of a three-second burst struck home. First the wing spun

329

away in three separate pieces, the fuselage bent just aft of the greenhouse like wet cardboard, and then the entire airframe came apart like a poorly assembled toy. There was no explosion, instead the aircraft simply dissolved into a corona of debris before Yoshi's astonished eyes and fell from the sky in a rain of bits and pieces. There were no parachutes. "Banzai!"

Pulling back on the stick, Yoshi added power and clawed for altitude. The sky was raining shattered and burning bombers. Shouts of triumph filled his earphones. Then Bender's voice came through, "Edo Leader, this is Renga Leader. The 109s are on the run on a northeasterly heading. We've inflicted casualties and taken some. We're running low on fuel."

Yoshi glanced at his fuel gauges. The needles were quivering low down on the black-faced instruments. Time to go home. "Disengage! Edo and Renga, this is Edo Leader. Disengage. Assemble on me at *alpha* two-four (altitude 24,000 feet) and return to base."

A series of acknowledgments and "Rogers" came through the earphones. Yoshi looked around at the few surviving bombers that were fleeing to the northeast and then down at the *Bennington*. It took him a few moments to follow the trail of smoke to the stricken vessel which was making for the western horizon on a course that would intercept *Yonaga*. Apparently, Fujita had broken radio silence and directed the carrier to a rendezvous. Four F4Us and two F6Fs with huge "Bs" on their vertical tail fins still circled above the carrier. Yoshi opened his fourth fighter circuit, "This is Edo Leader. *Bennington*'s fighters join my flight. *Yonaga* will take you aboard."

A tired voice scratched back, "Edo Leader, this is Carousel Leader. Thanks for the invitation, buddy. But we'll stay here with our own old girl until we run out of fuel. Could be a stray bomber around."

"You may all die, Carousel Leader."

"Comes with the territory, ol' buddy."

Yoshi choked a little. "Roger and out, Carousel Leader."

The commander checked *Yonaga*'s presumed position by glancing at the clipboard strapped to his knee and brought his fighter to a westerly heading, climbing at three-quarters throttle. Looking around, he saw only seven Zeros, two Seafires and seven Hellcats following. He choked back a swelling in his throat and thinned his mixture until the R-3350 backfired her objections. It could be a very long flight back.

Nearly five miles beneath them, the fighters passed over *Bennington* which still left a solid black carpet of smoke in her wake.

Chapter Sixteen

Brent was on the flag bridge when Fighter One and
Fighter Three returned. Every man's spirit was at low
ebb. There had been no more signals from the B-25s
and there were not enough fighters returning. Bernstein, Whitehead and Brent went through the counting
ritual together. "They took casualties," Bernstein muttered.

"Sure as hell did," Whitehead concurred.

"I count seven Zeros, two Seafires and seven Hellcats," Brent announced.

"Then we lost eight," Fujita said, staring through his
glasses. He turned to the voice tubes and gave orders
that brought the big ship into the wind. "Stand by to receive aircraft!" was ordered and Pennant Two hoisted.

Quickly the fighters landed and Yoshi Matsuhara reported to the bridge, still dressed in his flight clothes.
His goggles were up over his *hachimachi* headband, leaving their dark outline of exhaust and oil fumes on his
face. Even in the windy confines of the bridge, Brent
could smell engine oil.

"You took casualties," Fujita observed.

"The enemy pilots were good, Admiral. *Bennington* is
finished as a fighting unit. She's burning from her quarters aft and could blow up and sink at any time."

"I know, Commander. We can only hope to save her." He waved at the horizon. "She is only four-hundred-thirty kilometers . . . I mean, two-hundred-seventy miles to the east. We have a CAP over her now and we will cover her withdrawal to the south. She will lay to off the Azores until we destroy *Daffah* and *Magid* and then join her."

Brent, Colonel Bernstein, and Rear Admiral Whitehead exchanged a speculative glance.

Yoshi continued as if he believed every word of the admiral's optimism. "I saw no trace of the enemy carriers, sir. I believe all of the aircraft we met were land based. I know the Heinkels and Douglases were."

"True, Commander." Fujita stabbed a finger to the east. "Our scouts have sighted both enemy carriers. They are six-hundred-twenty miles to the east. We will close and destroy them. As you know all of our bombers have been armed with bombs and torpedoes. They are being fueled now. Get some rest, Commander. If the enemy maintains his course and speed, you will be in the air again within seven hours."

"Aye, aye, sir." But Matsuhara did not turn to leave the bridge. Instead, he asked a question about a subject that was tormenting every man on the bridge. "The B-25s, sir. Any word?"

"You do not know?"

"Know what, sir?"

"Just before you took off, we received a plain language signal from Colonel Stewart. The squadron had been intercepted by fighters over Algeria. They had taken casualties but were pressing on to their target."

"But sir, if any of them got through, they should have made Rabta by now."

333

"I know."

"Radio Tripoli should be screaming."

"I know that, too, Commander. We are monitoring Radio Tripoli."

"Nothing Admiral?"

"Nothing. They are silent and we have received no further transmissions from Colonel Stewart."

"Maybe they are all dead." Yoshi gripped the windscreen and pulled on it as if he were trying to tear the half-inch steel plate free. Brent could not look at the pilot. He was nursing his own private anguish over the Mitchells.

The old man said with resignation, "There is nothing we can do for Colonel Stewart's squadron now, except, perhaps, avenge them." A cold silence filled the bridge. Everyone knew something had gone terribly wrong with their carefully laid plans. The admiral leaned close to the air group commander and broke the silence with a voice softened to an intimate whisper, "Get some rest, Yoshi-san."

"Aye, aye, sir." The pilot punched the door open with a gloved fist and left.

Yonaga was spotted by the JU 87 four hours later. It dropped out of a solid blanket of cumulus and fled back into its vaporous shelter before the CAP could shoot it down.

"Radar!" Fujita screamed. "Why did you not report the intruder?"

"Turbulence, echoes from squalls, ghosts," came back through the voice tube.

"Sacred Buddha. Your 'ghosts' will sink this ship."

Anxiously, the flag bridge crew leaned into their glasses as if the power of their concentration could bridge the gap of hundreds of miles that separated the two forces and reveal the enemy fleet. They were steaming into a head-on collision. The insatiable angel of death would feast his fill this day. Deep in his viscera, Brent felt the usual sour churning begin to well. It was a near sexual excitement; the anxiety, the feeling of helplessness to halt the cascading events driving him like flotsam into the jaws of battle. The realization you are a pawn in other men's games: an expendable pawn whose death would mean nothing but a cold statistic to the faceless planners in Tripoli, Damascus, Baghdad, Moscow and Washington. A casualty is only a cipher to those who count the hideous calculus of war. It was the familiar sensation of utter helplessness to control one's own destiny that tortured the young American on the brink of combat. Turning his lower lip under, he bit down on it hard until he felt a sharp pain.

With the exception of Fighter Four and the depleted Fighters One and Three kept for the CAP, *Yonaga* launched all of her air groups an hour later when Fujita estimated the enemy force was 280 miles away. In the usual samurai tradition of the single massive stroke for victory, thirty Zeros, six Seafires, forty-three Aichi D3A dive-bombers and forty-four Nakajima B5N torpedo bombers roared into the sky.

As the last bomber took off, the shadowing *Ohio* reported *Daffah* and *Magid* were turning into the wind and beginning their own launch. Ominously, their capacities were far greater than the sixty aircraft each first reported. *Ohio* reported each ship was operating at least seventy-five aircraft and gave the enemy's position as much closer than Fujita's estimate. In fact, they were only 240 miles from *Yonaga*. Brent figured the enemy attacking force would probably number about 130 aircraft while, because of casualties, *Yonaga* could counter with air groups totalling 123. In numbers, it would be a very even match. In these circumstances, skill, bravery and luck were the decisive factors. It would be a savage, bloody battle.

Everyone knew that the enemy attack would arrive in less than two hours. Every gun was cranked upward, helmeted gun crews dressed in Number Two green battle fatigues clustered about the mounts, staring at the sky in uneasy silence. Six fighters of Fighter Four, radio call Kiba (Fang), were kept in the air constantly, flying in two elements of three. The British pilots called them "vics," and were sweeping in wide circles around the battle group. Brent Ross, Byron Whitehead and Irving Bernstein, wearing helmets, life jackets and binoculars dangling from their necks, took their stations on the flag bridge near Admiral Fujita. The admiral brought the force to course 180 to open the range on the enemy ships and move closer to the fleeing *Bennington*.

And *Bennington* did provide some good news. She radioed her fires were under control and she was proceeding to the rendezvous west of the Azores. She still had twenty-seven flyable fighters on board and her forward elevator and both catapults were operable. Repairs were underway on the twisted and warped after part of the flight deck and if enough of it could be cut away and repaired, she could be operating a limited number of aircraft in hours.

"I cannot believe it," Fujita said.

Byron Whitehead grinned. "Why not, sir? Those *Es-*

sex class carriers are tough. In March of 1945 I was with Task Force Fifty-Eight only fifty miles off Kyushu when *Franklin* took two bombs, one exploded on her flight deck right in the middle of an armed and gassed strike and the other penetrated to her hangar deck." He waved a hand dramatically. "I saw it all. Bombs, torpedoes, 'Tiny Tim' rockets, gasoline stores all went off. It was like watching an ammo dump and gasoline refinery all going up together. There was so much smoke the sun was actually blotted out. She lost all way and looked like a sure goner."

Fujita waved impatiently. "I know, Admiral Whitehead. She had a list of over ten degrees, flight deck and hangar deck blown into junk, over seven-hundred dead, but still made her way back to the U.S. on her own power."

No one was surprised at the admiral's knowledge. In fact, Brent had rather expected the rejoinder that showed the depth of knowledge of the walking encyclopedia. He knew that the old admiral secretly enjoyed surprising the experts with his own expertise. Fujita continued, "She took that punishment because your *Essexes* are not as tough as you say. They are not armored well enough. Five-hundred-fifty-pound bombs should not pierce their flight decks." He waved in a proud encompassing gesture. "They would not penetrate *Yonaga*'s."

Before Whitehead could respond, Naoyuki's voice cut them all off short, "Radar reports, many aircraft bearing two-two-zero relative, range eighty miles, closing at one-hundred-fifty knots."

"Very well." Fujita shouted down the tubes and at Naoyuki simultaneously. "Alert CAP! Start engines on

337

ready fighters, pilots man your planes. Engine room stand by to give me every knot on our engines, AA crews stand by to open fire on raid approaching from two-two-zero."

Looking down at the flight deck, Brent Ross watched Yoshi Matsuhara leading his pilots across the deck at a run. This time there were only nine.

At full throttle Yoshi led twenty-two fighters in a hard climb. Quickly joined by the six Zeros of the CAP, they made one orbit of the carrier, forming their squadrons. Yoshi led the nine aircraft of Edo, Lieutenant James Bender led his seven Hellcats of Renga, and the flamboyant Frenchman, Captain Jean-Claude Dubois, commanded Kiba's twelve Zeros. Turning on a northeasterly heading, the twenty-eight aircraft formed three "Vs," stepped up from Yoshi's leading squadron to Dubois's trailing fighters. There was about eight-tenths cloud cover; high cumulus and cirrus like rabbits' and lambs' tails, stratus faint chalk marks scrawled all over the sky.

The flat, unemotional voice of the control officer in *Yonaga*'s CIC filled Matsuhara's earphones, "Edo Leader, this is Saihyosen."

"Go ahead Saihyosen."

"Your vector is zero-five-seven. Raid at *alpha* eight, sixty plus bandits, range forty. And we have an escort of many more bandits, twenty plus, at *alpha* eighteen, range seventy. Intercept and destroy."

It was all so simple. Intercept and destroy. Over sixty bombers and more than a score of fighters against his twenty-eight fighters. Yoshi almost laughed. However,

338

he controlled his voice and repeated the information. Then he continued, speaking into his microphone, "This is Edo Leader. Kiba engage bombers. Renga engage bombers. Edo will give top cover."

The acknowledgments echoed back immediately. Bender's calm, unmistakable west coast inflection giving his words a hard cutting edge came first, "Roger, wilco, Edo Leader." Then Dubois's excited northern Picardy accent which put a heavy slant on every word he spoke, "Roger Commandant. *Voilà* Kiba! *Hourra!*" Although the Frenchman spoke acceptable English, he had a disconcerting habit of lapsing into his native tongue when excited and his radio discipline was almost as exasperating as York's. But he was one of the best and Yoshi would not trade him for anyone.

Seven Hellcats and twelve Zeros roared away on vector 057 while Yoshi pulled the stick back, enriched his mixture and pushed his throttle all the way to the next to last stop, grabbing his most precious commodity, altitude, in huge chunks. There was no chance he could stop all the bombers even if he led Edo into the attack against them. With fighters coming on hard behind the bombers, throwing his entire force against the bombers would be foolhardy and out of the question. They would kill a lot of bombers but would be easy meat for the diving 109s. He would deal with the fighters and then, if the gods were willing, he would attack the bombers. Luckily, the enemy fighters were trailing the bombers by thirty miles. Poor planning and execution. There were amateurs on *Daffah* and *Magid*. The thirty-mile gap would give Dubois and Bender a precious few seconds to attack the bombers without interference. Edo must buy them more time.

339

While Edo climbed on a heading of 057, Yoshi turned his head ceaselessly, as regular as an electric fan. Finally, far on the horizon, he saw a mass of specks. The raid . . . massive! He shuddered. Where were Bender and Dubois? Then he saw them. Streaking down out of the thin cirrus cover. Seven Hellcats and twelve Zero-sens. They fell on the bombers like wolves on sheep. He cursed. His wing and lumpy clouds blotted out most of the action. He moved his stick to the left and increased throttle. Balanced with rudder as his left wing dropped. Now he was climbing over the fight and he could see four JU 87s already burning and tumbling into the sea. But there were more than forty dive-bombers left. Then, spotting a flight of antiquated aircraft, Yoshi shook his head in disbelief.

The Arabs were still using the old North American AT-6, Texàn, as a torpedo bomber. He counted twenty with big, deadly torpedoes slung beneath their bellies. Although it was reported their Pratt & Whitney engines had been upgraded to nearly one thousand horsepower, laden with a torpedo, the old plane could only lumber at about 150 knots. Now the commander understood why the SOA of the raid was so slow. The North Americans were very low on the water while the dive-bombers were at about eight thousand feet. While he watched, two F6Fs plunged through the JUs and casually shot down a pair of Texans with short bursts in a single pass. It was like shooting target sleeves.

The fighter frequency was filled with whoops and shouts of triumph, punctuated with Jean-Claude Dubois's *"Hourra!"* But Yoshi knew Bender and Dubois would never shoot down all of the bombers. Even if they were left unmolested by enemy fighters, they simply did not carry enough ammunition to do the job. Some bombers would get through. Now clouds began to obscure the fight again and the commander pounded his padded combing in frustration.

They levelled off when his altimeter showed twenty thousand feet. The last layer of broken clouds was three kilometers below them and they seemed to be hanging motionless in a vast blue dome. His ears were still buzzing and popping from the change in pressure. He wiggled his shoulders to relax the cramped muscles and his glance flickered around the cockpit, checking his banks of instruments with their clumsy American calibrations; artificial horizon, airspeed indicator, rate-of-climb indicator were all normal. Engine RPM, turn-and-bank indicator, manifold pressure gauge, fuel pressure, oil pressure, oil temperature, magnetic compass were all working perfectly. Only his cylinder head temperature gauge gave him reason to feel uneasy. It was high from the strain of the climb, but not in the red. He shrugged, checked to make certain the gunsight was turned on and the gun-safety cover was off. He was ready and so was his killing machine.

Looking down, he changed focus, but it took his eyes a little longer to adjust now that time had stiffened his lenses. The last layer of clouds below was breaking up into small patches while above the sky was so blue and fresh that it looked as if the gods had just scrubbed it. However, Yoshi was not looking for beauty. He was looking for men to kill. He found them on the horizon.

They were only specks of sand on the wind when he first found them. Then, squinting, he brought his eyes to deep focus and saw sunlight playing off a row of prop-discs stuck on razor-thin wings. 109s. At least twenty-four of them. Two-thousand feet below and closing in on their harried bombers beneath them. He threw the switch on his oxygen mask, "Renga and Kiba, this is Edo leader. Twenty-four enemy fighters high and to the northeast. Closing fast at *alpha* eighteen. I will engage." Both Bender and Dubois acknowledged.

The planes grew and Yoshi's heart leaped to his throat and he could feel his pulse pounding against his temple. The enemy was led by a blood-red Messerschmitt with the familiar zebra-striped fighter off his elevator. The remaining Messerschmitts were solid black. Rosencrance and Vatz. *Vierter Jagerstaffel*. The Arabs' best squadron.

While he watched, twelve of the enemy fighters peeled off and dove toward the melee below while Rosencrance led the remaining twelve fighters of his own *Vierter Jagerstaffel* in a turn toward Edo. Yoshi switched on his microphone, "Renga Leader, Kiba Leader, this is Edo Leader. Twelve enemy fighters diving on you from *alpha* eighteen!" Bender and Dubois acknowledged and they shouted warnings to their men. But they did not regroup. The attack on the bombers continued.

Yoshi had to look out for his own squadron. "Edo, this is Edo Leader. Arm your guns!" Obeying his own command, he threw two switches on his instrument panel. "Engage enemy fighters closing from ten o'clock and two thousand feet below. Follow my lead and then individual combat. Pick your target. Watch your tails. Kill them! Banzai!"

He increased throttle and began a long sweeping turn that took his squadron past Rosencrance and brought him astern of the enemy. He had superior altitude and was behind the enemy. For once, he had the advantage.

He pushed the stick forward.

With the Zero steeply canted and accelerating in its plunge, he watched his air-speed-indicator creep toward four hundred. The airframe began to vibrate. He braced his arms and legs, felt the rudder stirrups against his insteps, gripped the spade, hardened his stomach muscles, sucked in pure oxygen and gasped. Now the bouncing red dot of the reflector sight was all over the red ME, and behind it, ahead of it, to the sides. But, in a blink, the entire enemy squadron turned to the left with amazing swiftness. He threw the stick over, balanced with rudder. Found the tail of the red machine. Eight-hundred meters. Then the wings and fuselage staggered into the orange reticle like a crucifix and bounced all over it. Too much speed and the enemy's turn had given him a tough deflection shot. Pulling back on the stick, he throttled back and felt the familiar onslaught of g-forces. His sight dimmed. His arms weakened. He stretched his mouth like someone testing a rubber band and screamed, "Amaterasu!" Eagerly, he watched the enemy's silhouette grow out to the sight bars. He tried to give the ME a full length for deflection but his vision was so blurred he could only guess. He punched the red button.

The fighter bucked like a stallion jabbed with a branding iron. His tracers sprayed out from the shuddering machine. He cursed. Two, three red flashes on his enemy's fuselage and tail and he vanished from the reflector sight. Instead of the expected dive, Rosencrance had flipped up and over into a tight loop and clawed for the sun. He knew the diving Zeros' enormous momentum would carry them past his squadron. But not all could escape the accuracy of the diving Japanese

343

squadron. All of the Zeros fired.

A black ME exploded in its final moment of glory like a new nova. Another dropped off unwinding a white trail of glycol like an endless bandage. Yoshi levelled off, bouncing and rocking. Although the temperature was near freezing, his shirt was drenched with sweat and his goggles began to fog. He pushed them up. Then hard back on the control column and the sea vanished and blue velvet of the sky swung across his windscreen. Where was Rosencrance? Then he saw him. Turning back and over at the top of his climb, but far to the right. Now the renegade American would have the advantage of speed and altitude. But he did not have the Wright R-3350. Yoshi jammed the engine into overboost and a wild stallion bucked and snarled like a mad animal. Horsing the stick back and kicking right rudder, Yoshi climbed and turned as if the fighter had suddenly sprouted after-burners. The cylinder head temperature began to climb.

The Zero's rocketing climb took Rosencrance by surprise. Yoshi actually zoomed up above the ME before Rosencrance could fire. Then a half-roll, flipped the Zero on its back and again, Yoshi was closing on his enemy from above. Half-rolling into level flight, he throttled back and the vibrations diminished. The ME filled his sight. He pushed the button while Rosencrance banked toward him and opened fire almost simultaneously.

The sky between the two aircraft was a blizzard of passing tracers. There was so much hate in Matsuhara's soul, he could only wish to kill the man by any means; even ramming. There were thuds. Bits of aluminum flew from his wing. He felt his controls tremble from strikes, saw his tracers bounce off his enemy's hood, rip the ME's wings, tear into the exhaust stubs. They were spinner to spinner. At the last second, Rosencrance dipped slightly, there was a bump as the Zero's belly carried away the ME's radio mast and Rosencrance was gone, diving at full throttle. Cursing, Yoshi split-essed into his own dive.

The clouds had broken below and Yoshi could see a great sprawling battle tumbling across the sky. Bombers and fighters were weaving, rolling, firing, embroidering the sky with tracers. An F6F was spinning into the sea while two burning Stukas tumbled and disintegrated as they fell. An ME 109 pulled up sharply, shed its starboard wing and then flipped and gyrated into the sea like a teal blasted by a shotgun. Four white parachutes were descending slowly and a half-dozen columns of smoke rose from the ocean like pillars to be whipped to shreds by the wind. Half of the enemy force seemed to have disappeared, but the number of Zeros and Hellcats had been whittled down, too. And four of the *Fletchers* were firing, AA puffs stationary in the sky like hanging snowballs. Soon *Yonaga* would open fire, adding her storm of firebrands to the hell above.

Suddenly, a Zero rose above the fight spouting orange flame and puffs of black smoke as if it were scrawling Morse code across the heavens. The zebra-striped ME of Wolfgang Vatz was hard on its tail, firing. Jean-Claude Dubois's shrieks filled Yoshi's earphones. *"Mon Dieu! Mon Dieu! Non!"*

Bender's voice: "Bail out! Bail out, Dubois!"

But Dubois would never escape his flaming fighter. Cannon shells smashed his instrument panel, his fire wall. Bullets and shell fragments shattered the bones in his legs, blew his left knee into his throttle quadrant. Blood splattered the cockpit and ran from the canopy. A cannon shell exploded his windscreen into a million shards, shattered his goggles, pulped the flesh of his face and blinded him with blood, gore and glass. He screamed again and again. Then the petrol flooded back into the cockpit from the shot-out fuel tank and ignited. He began to burn, first his legs and then the flames raced up to his genitals, groin, chest. His flight suit burned off in big patches as if it had been hit by a blow-torch. He could actually smell the sweet aroma of his own roasting flesh. He never conceived of such pain this side of hell. The screams became the howls of a tortured animal and it was all broadcasted from his radio which he had left open.

Vatz dropped off and the Zero flew itself almost level for a few seconds, now leaving a solid black streamer in its wake. The Frenchman groped for the cockpit release which he could not see and then grasped the quick release of his safety harness. He fumbled. Felt the straps fall loose. Tried to pull himself up, but he had no legs and his arms were weak. He fell back. Flames enveloped him, the flesh of his face peeling off, skin bubbling and smoking. Then he sucked in the flames which seared his tongue and followed his breath down his throat to his lungs. Then, mercifully, a darkness as black as the smoke pouring from the doomed Zero blotted out his consciousness. Slow rolling, the fighter arced down toward the sea.

With one bridge speaker carrying the fighter frequency, every man on the flag bridge heard the horror of the likable Frenchman's death. They could see his funeral pyre as well, his immolated Zero curving high over the fight, leaving its black shroud before falling into its final spin. It exploded in a display of spectacular pyrotechnics long before it hit the water.

When the shrieks had first started, Whitehead had cried, "Turn it off. In the name of God, turn it off, Admiral!"

Fujita did not even turn from his binoculars. "Negative, Admiral Whitehead," he said in a flat voice. Then waving at the approaching raid, he shouted at Naoyuki, "All guns that bear, stand by to open fire."

No one called the admiral's attention to the fact friendly fighters were mixed with the enemy aircraft and would be just as imperiled as the bombers. The pilots would have to take their chances. Everyone knew this; none better than the pilots.

Brent stared through his glasses with all the intensity he could muster. The dogfight had degenerated into a series of individual combats with the enemy MEs trying desperately to protect their bombers while Zeros, Seafires and F6Fs strove to fight their way through to the Junkers and North Americans. The enemy bombers had taken heavy casualties, but at least forty Junkers and eight North American Texans still pressed on. While the AT-6s drove on straight for *Yonaga,* the Stukas split into two groups; twenty continuing on a direct course for the carrier while about twenty more climbed and circled high above their attacking comrades. There were so many bombers, it appeared they were queuing up to await their turns to attack. They were immensely confident. Obviously, they believed *Yonaga* was doomed.

"Fire control reports raid to port in range, Admiral,"

347

Naoyuki reported over his mouthpiece.

"Main battery, all guns that bear, commence firing on raid to port. Commence! Commence!"

With a concussion that shook the bridge and brought a stab of pain to Brent's eardrums, at least twenty of *Yonaga*'s thirty-two five-inch guns fired simultaneously. All of the *Fletchers* were crowding close to the carrier and firing their five-inch thirty-eights, those outboard to port were already adding their twenty-millimeter and forty-millimeter batteries to the barrage. The result was awesome. The sky was splotched with hanging white, brown and black bursts while tracers rose in strings like festive holiday lights. Three JUs and four of the low Texans were shot out of the sky in quick succession while two Messerschmitts and a Zero were also destroyed.

Suddenly, four F6Fs broke through the Arab fighters and raked the Junkers which were forming up into their usual single line of attack. Some already had their dive brakes down and were throttling back. In one pass, three dive bombers were destroyed. Then four Messerschmitts led by a solid red machine, tore after the Hellcats. Bender's voice sounded in the speaker, "Hoeffler, on your tail. Two of 'em. Break right! Break right!"

"Breaking right!"

Brent watched as a single F6F pulled sharply to its right and climbed. But the red machine cut inside the turn and with a short two-second burst, blasted the cockpit into junk. With a dead man at the controls, the big fighter twisted, flipped and turned like a demented moth seared by a flame. At full throttle, it flung itself into the sea, vanishing in a great column of blue water and white spray. Hoeffler was dead. Brent felt rage, anger, and great sadness all flood through his

348

charged emotions.

Matsuhara! Where was Yoshi? raced through his mind. *Was he dead, too?* He searched frantically. Finally found the familiar Zero which was storming after the red Messerschmitt, when Bernstein's shout of "Here they come!" turned his head.

The young American dropped his binoculars and stared upward. Seven Stukas had broken through. All had their dive brakes down, and the pitch of the engines dropped to a deep-throated roar as the pilots turned their propellers' pitch controls to full coarse. Desperately, a Zero whipped in and hit the last JU's bomb. Both aircraft were annihilated by the gigantic yellow blast that for a millisecond eclipsed the sun.

"Secondary battery, commence firing. Commence! Commence!" At least fifty twenty-five-millimeter triple mounts fired. The gun galleries were alive with leaping flames. Clouds of dirty brown smoke trailed, searing Brent's nose and throat with the acrid stench of cordite. Tracers rose in clouds.

One after the other the dive-bombers dropped off into their dives and into the smoking barrier of twenty-five-millimeter shells. And five surviving North American Texans were boring in closer. By luck, perfect coordination of both attacks brought two problems. *Yonaga* could not solve them both at the same time. Fujita took the best course of action. He turned toward the torpedo planes.

"Left full rudder," he screamed. "We will turn in a circle until I change the command."

At thirty-two knots, the great ship heeled sharply into her turn. The leading Junkers had lost a wing and twisted into brutally sharp rolls until it corkscrewed into the sea. Another had its spatted undercarriage blown off and then its tail. It whipped round crazily, spilled one parachute and then screamed straight down to its grave. Another, caught by a five-inch shell whose proximity fuse detonated only five feet from the cockpit, flew into tiny fragments like chaff in a cyclone. But the three survivors shrieked down, straight down, their huge eleven-hundred-pound bombs looming larger by the second.

"Right full rudder!" The fifty-five-ton slab of the rudder driven by its powerful engines halted the turn to port with agonizing slowness. But the change in course was sufficient to throw off the aim of the first dive-bomber. With fascinated horror, Brent watched the crutch swing and the glistening black projectile plunged down. It hit off the starboard bow and shot a waterspout high into the sky. It seemed to freeze for a moment before collapsing and dissolving in a welter of ripples, spreading spray and mist.

A quick glance told Brent the torpedo bombers, which had been hugging the water, were leaping over the port *Fletchers*. At only two hundred feet and at a slow speed, three were shot to pieces by twenty-millimeter and forty-millimeter shells almost immediately. But two survived the gauntlet and bored in on *Yonaga*.

"Two torpedo bombers, port bow, almost in range, sir."

Fujita tried to look up and to his left simultaneously. "Sacred Buddha! Left full rudder! Secondary batteries two, four and six engage torpedo bombers!" Immediately, nine triple mounts on the port side depressed and began to fire at the pair of torpedo bombers. Some of the twenty-five-millimeter shells bounced off an escort. The fire never slackened.

Before the carrier could even feel the change in rudder angle, the wail of a hundred banshees turned Brent's head upward. Engine roaring, sirens howling the second bomber had released its bomb which screamed down almost vertically. It hit the bow. The blinding explosion of nearly one thousand pounds of high explosives battered like a thunderclap. Everyone ducked and clapped his hands to his ears. There was a great clanging sound, the tortured screeching sound of steel plates being ripped and bent like paper. Metal, debris, guns, men and parts of men shot skyward. At least three triple-mounts had been destroyed. The shock jarred the bridge and the young lieutenant grabbed Fujita's shoulders and steadied the old man.

As the Junkers pulled out, shells tore out its belly. With a dead crew, it crashed into the sea just as the next bomb hit *Yonaga* on the bow just forward of the elevator. The AP tip penetrated the 3.75 inches of steel plate but not the box beams, cement, sawdust and latex that were crammed into the thirty-three-inch box below. Torn plates, a fountain of latex, cement and sawdust erupted from the wound. But the bomb did not penetrate to the hangar deck. Fujita's brilliant design had been vindicated.

Miraculously, the JU escaped the tracers, flattened its dive, and fled low on the water, its propeller actually leaving a trail of dappled water like a terrified flying fish.

Fujita never even glanced at the bomber. He screamed, "Damage report!" at Naoyuki, but his eyes were on the two approaching torpedo bombers. One had been hit and its torpedo hung down crazily, held only by its rear crutch. The other dropped to about eighty feet and released its weapon. It dropped into the

351

water with a small splash.

Thousands of eyes watched the white track approach. The Texan suddenly reared up like a frightened animal, did a half-roll and twisted into the sea at full throttle. It flipped across the water, losing its wings and coming to rest only fifty feet from the carrier's side. The torpedo was just behind it. But *Yonaga* had begun to turn only slightly, but enough to dodge the torpedo which passed harmlessly across the carrier's bow. Cheers broke out. Screams of "Banzai!"

But the cheers were squelched by the second torpedo bomber. Staggering like a drunk, its torpedo still hanging precariously and flopping with the erratic movements of the aircraft, it charged down on the carrier's port beam, level with the superstructure. All of *Yonaga*'s port machine guns were firing. Brent stood transfixed. It seemed impossible that even a housefly could pass through that barrage. But the AT-6 bored in. Its wings were ripped, fuselage holed in a dozen places, top of its vertical stabilizer sliced off. A shell blew off its cowling ring and the cowling ripped off into the slipstream in two hinged pieces like the wings of a sea gull. The exhaust outlet clusters were shot off, and orange flame and puffs of black smoke belched from the hood. But it came on straight at Lieutenant Brent Ross. He could see the pilot's face, back of a partially shot out windscreen. His helmet was black, goggles up, face very white, eyes wide and staring. Perhaps he was mad. Dead.

Just as the bomber roared over the port galleries, its nose reared up and the torpedo broke free, dropping onto the flight deck. It fell flat, bounced, skidded and crashed into the island where it broke into hundreds of fragments. Brown HE spilled across the deck in chunks and clouds of fine powder. Terrified deck crewmen scurried like mice.

The plane was on them, pulling up sharply over the flag bridge. Everyone ducked. Hitting the main director with its port wing, the North American spun around, dropped half the wing and twirled far out to the starboard side like a flat rock thrown by a child. It hit the water, skidded, bounced twice in sheets of water and spray, flipped over and sank almost immediately.

"Banzai! Banzai! Banzai!"

Brent gripped the admiral's shoulder and pointed upward to the starboard side. While they had been diverted by the attack to port, the twenty remaining Stukas were circling high off the starboard side. They were free of fighter attack, every Zero, Seafire and Hellcat was occupied, fighting for its own life with the enemy 109s. Almost leisurely, the dive-bombers turned toward *Yonaga,* big slatted dive brakes dropping, slowing and forming up into two lines of ten. A lurch of fear sent Brent's heart sinking. His mouth tasted sour, his skull pressed down on his eyeballs. He was caught by the familiar atavistic dread of a man who knows he is doomed.

All of the escorts and the carrier were firing their 5-inch guns. Two of the Stukas were hit, but the others continued their approach. "We're doomed. Doomed!" Brent said to himself. His stomach jumped as if someone had poked it with a cold stick. He drew himself up. Stiffened his spine. Focused on the approaching aircraft. No man would see fear on his face. Out of the corner of his eye, he saw Bernstein, Whitehead and Fujita all stiffen into similar postures. The young American suddenly realized every man on the bridge felt the same fear, saw doom overhead, reacted in

353

the same way. He almost smiled.

Yoshi Matsuhara was the first to hear the strange radio call. He had pulled high above the carnage and was searching for the red Messerschmitt when it came into his earphones. "Edo Leader, this is Carousel Leader. Have you in sight. What are your orders?"

Then Yoshi remembered. Carousel Leader, the American who had refused to leave *Bennington*. He turned his head so quickly, he felt a sharp pain in his neck. Then he saw them. Twelve spinning disks, broad, blue gull wings, huge Double Wasp radial engines. Coming in from the south at well over four hundred knots and two thousand feet above him. *Bennington* had launched her fighters! But she was off the Azores. Damaged. He did not understand, but he did not care. Help had arrived. That was all that mattered. Yoshi cried out with joy, "The bombers, Carousel Leader. Destroy the bombers and maintain CAP over *Yonaga!*"

"It's a pleasure, Edo Leader. Glad to return the favor. I owe you one, ol' buddy."

Banking gracefully, the twelve great fighters formed the usual American style formation of six elements of two; a "top gun" with a wingman trailing to starboard and slightly below. As one, the F4Us plunged down into a shallow dive. As they came into range, the five-inch guns of the ships ceased fire. Panicked by the approaching Corsairs, the Stukas flocked together like frightened chickens. Two collided and spun down into the sea locked together like a pair of lovers.

The first pass was devastating. With each Corsair firing four twenty-millimeter cannons, six Junkers were

354

ripped and blasted by the big shells and tumbled into the sea in swirls of burning wreckage. Two more dropped off trailing glycol and smoke, The survivors dove for the sea and turned to the northeast. They all jettisoned their bombs. The F4Us made a big sweeping turn and came back for another pass. Four more of the fleeing bombers were splashed. There were cheers and shouts of "Banzai!" on the radio.

The Corsairs broke off the pursuit, climbed and began to orbit around the battle group protectively. Now, the damaged *Yonaga* should be safe.

Yoshi Matsuhara did not have time to celebrate. Although the bombers had been smashed, the enemy fighters fought on. Perhaps it was hate, professionalism, or the fact that each destroyed Japanese fighters brought a bonus to the renegade pilots. Perhaps all of these. Yoshi had fought Rosencrance and his *Vierter Jagerstaffel* before. The man was ruthless, killed with savage efficiency, but he was no coward. He wanted Yoshi, *"Yonaga's* Butcher,"* just as much as the Japanese wanted to kill the American. And it was common knowledge Kadafi had put a million dollar bounty on Matsuhara's head.

In the strange way of dogfights, the sky suddenly seemed almost empty of fighters. The few remaining fighters visible had drifted far to the south in a sky cluttered with cumulus and smeared with high stratus. Then, on the far horizon, Yoshi spotted a Seafire pursued by the black and white fighter of "Zebra" Vatz. The German was pulling into a killing angle on Pilot Officer Elwyn York. Yoshi jammed his throttle into overboost and shot after the pair. York was diving and jinking through small puffs of clouds while Vatz followed and tried to anticipate, firing short one and two second bursts. "The bugger's on me arse!" York shouted into his microphone.

Yoshi remained silent. Waited until the striped machine grew in his sights. He eased the throttle. Was it possible the German was so intent on his kill he did not see him? He began to tighten his thumb on the red button when both aircraft disappeared into a solid bank of clouds. Then he plunged in. Temporarily blinded, Yoshi cursed. Then he was in brilliant sunshine. Something was wrong up ahead. There were three planes instead of two. A red Messerschmitt, diving out of a ghost-white smear of cirrus made almost luminescent by the sun, had begun its firing run on York while Vatz and Yoshi had been concealed by the cloud. A murderous matrix. Both 109s were firing, the red Messerschmitt slashing in from high and to the right, trying a tough deflection shot. York slipped into a full-roll and then jinked from right to left and back, avoiding most of the tracers.

Yoshi roared with joy. Vatz never saw Rosencrance. His shells and bullets ripped huge chunks of fabric off Rosencrance's tail as the red machine plunged through his stream of fire. Immediately, Rosencrance sprayed glycol, half-rolled and steepened his dive, plummeting almost vertically like a fleeing gannet.

The striped 109 was in the center of Yoshi's sight. It was a perfect set-up on a confused, distraught Vatz who made the mistake of flying straight and level while he leaned over the combing, following his stricken leader's descent. One-hundred-fifty meters, zero deflection. Yoshi licked his lips and pressed the button. His shells and bullets caught the enemy fighter in the hood and then marched back, hammer blows making bright splashes of orange and tearing off huge chunks of aluminum like skin being peeled from an orange. The canopy vanished in a glittering stream of shattered Perspex. He held the button down until he heard compressed air hiss and his breech blocks clang on empty firing chambers. No ammunition. He cursed and pounded the instrument panel so hard the needles jumped. The German killer would escape. He wanted him more than ever, especially for Dubois. He would follow close on his tail, chew off his control surfaces with his propeller.

Vatz rolled, a poorly controlled flopping maneuver. A bullet from the first burst had grazed his spine between the fifth and sixth cervical vertebrae. His hands and feet went numb immediately. Perhaps that was why he had felt little pain when the next three slugs hit him. The first, passing from right to left through his abdomen, ripped his liver and carried off the lower half of his stomach. The next two struck his right arm and tore it off just above the elbow. Arterial blood squirted over his smashed instrument panel and he tried to grab the stub with his left hand while jamming the stick between his knees. The Messerschmitt flipped and tumbled and he seemed to be outside looking in on the horror and the blood that was saturating everything.

The Zero was still on his tail not more than fifty meters behind, but not firing. Thank God for that. However, he was weakening rapidly. Then the fighter suddenly had a mind of its own; rolling, thrashing, and diving. Blood soaked his flight suit and dripped from everything, was caught by the slipstream and whipped out in a red haze. But Wolfgang Vatz did not notice. Four liters of blood had shot out of his severed arm and poured from his ripped abdomen.

The final black curtain of the last act had closed.

There was jubilation tempered with anxiety on the bridge of *Yonaga*. The enemy bombers had been beaten off, most destroyed, and the carrier was still operational. Twelve beautiful F4U Corsairs orbited above. The fires were under control and, as a precaution, Fujita had ordered number one twenty-five-millimeter magazine flooded. Twenty-seven men had been killed and forty-one wounded. Four twenty-five-millimeter mounts and one five-inch gun had been destroyed. They had turned into the wind and the first fighters had begun to land. Most were damaged. The undercarriage on Bender's F6F collapsed and the fighter spun and whipped into the barrier where its port wing was bent straight up. The pilot was pulled from the wreckage uninjured.

Then the great news arrived. Just as the radar reported friendly aircraft approaching from the east, Commander Takuya Iwata's voice came through the speaker reporting *Daffah* sunk and *Magid* damaged and burning. And then somberly, "Our casualties have been very heavy." There was cheering, but it was restrained.

Then spirits were buoyed again when *Bennington* heaved over the southern horizon. She had put out her fires, repaired her deck and then turned toward *Yonaga* after broadcasting a false position report in plain language. The Arabs had bitten and swallowed the whole subterfuge. While Brent watched, *Bennington* launched twelve Hellcats to replace the twelve F4Us of the CAP which were running low on fuel. Through his glasses, Brent could see her stern and aft part of her flight deck. Most of her galleries from her quarters aft had been destroyed and the flight deck still showed some warped and twisted plates. But he could see new shining steel, and the aft elevator was operational. "Marvelous damage control," he heard Admiral Whitehead breathe.

"Remarkable," Fujita agreed.

Then to Brent's joy, Yoshi Matsuhara landed, followed in quick succession by Captain Colin Willard-Smith and Pilot Officer Elwyn York. York's Seafire was so full of holes it seemed miraculous that the fighter could still fly. But the Cockney brought her in for a perfect three-point landing. Only ten Zeros and four F6Fs of Edo, Renga and Kiba landed. Eleven Zeros and three Hellcats had been lost. Then the bombers and what was left of their escort were in sight. Some staggered low, out of trim, smoking. Two fired red flares. There were very few.

Everyone was counting. Brent heard Whitehead choke, "Only thirteen Zeros, three Seafires, maybe twenty Aichis and, my God, I see only eight torpedo bombers." He turned wide-eyed to Fujita, "Eight out of forty-four torpedo bombers. My God. My God."

The old man nodded grimly. "The spirits of many of our samurai have passed through the gates of the Yasakuni Shrine." He turned to Naoyuki, "Radio room, plain language to *Bennington.* 'I want a damage report and a count of your operable aircraft. Maintain twelve fighter CAP. I will put up twelve of my own as soon as I have recovered my returning strike. Well done! Well done!' " More orders followed, detailing course, speed and formation.

While Fujita was dictating to the signal bridge, Bernstein stormed through the door, clutching a message, his face a scarlet mask of anger and horror. "Admiral," he

359

sputtered, waving the sheet of paper. "Radio Tripoli reports sixteen North American B-25s piloted by gangsters have been shot down." He glanced at the document and read, "Twelve gangsters have been captured. They will be given a fair trial before they are executed."

"Oh, no!" Whitehead exploded.

"Goddamn!" Brent said, pounding the chart table.

"Amaterasu, who betrayed us?" Fujita implored the sky.

He was answered only by the wind that mourned through the rigging.

Chapter Seventeen

The return journey to Japan was uneventful. There was elation over the destruction of *Daffah* and the heavy damage inflicted on *Magid*. However, *Yonaga*'s losses of pilots and air crews had been grievous. Out of the strike on the enemy carriers, seventeen Zeros, three Seafires, twenty-three Aichis and thirty-six Nakajimas had failed to return. Two of the bombers landed with dead gunners and three with wounded pilots. Two fighter pilots had been wounded. The contingent of foreign pilots had suffered heavily. Three Englishmen, both Frenchmen, the German and the Italian had all been shot down. In addition, of the twenty-eight fighters of Yoshi Matsuhara's CAP, only ten Zeros and four F6Fs survived. Ensign Jack Matthews, Ensign Kuroi Ame and Lieutenant J.G. Masuji Ibuse of the CAP had been picked up by Fite's escorts along with four enemy pilots and two crewmen who were immediately transferred to *Yonaga*. However, most of the downed aircraft of *Yonaga*'s strike force had crashed among the enemy ships. Any survivors would have been killed or picked up by the enemy.

Commander Takuya Iwata had returned from the attack on the enemy carriers with a heavily damaged Aichi D3A and a wounded gunner. The torpedo bomber commander, Lieutenant Commander Iyet-suma Yagoto, had been killed. With his slow Nakajima B5Ns being shot down like clay pigeons at a sporting event, the Eta had bored in close, launched his torpedo and scored a crippling hit on *Daffah*'s stern, disabling her starboard screw and jamming her rudder. Yagoto's B5N was last seen hitting *Daffah*'s flight deck and vanishing in a long streak of burning gasoline and flaming wreckage. Then circling helplessly at no more than five knots and burning, *Daffah* had been easy meat for Iwata's dive-bombers.

"The Eta had the full, round balls of the hero, not the shriveled raisins of the coward," Iwata had grudgingly conceded at his debriefing. And then he waxed eloquently and for moment Brent thought the man was Yukio Mishima incarnate. "He cleansed his karma in the righteous act of giving his life for the Mikado. All the gods of heaven will shelter him. Truly, he has earned his place in the Yasakuni Shrine." Everyone agreed.

Brent was surprised at the haughty pilot's concession to the contemptible Eta. Notwithstanding the terrible losses and the shared mortal danger, hostility still lurked in the black depths of the man's eyes whenever he glanced at the young American. Despite his long tenure on *Yonaga*, Iwata was one man Brent could never understand. The showdown between them still appeared inevitable.

Long before the force had passed the Cape Verde Islands, Radio Tripoli was boasting of the destruction of *Bennington* and the heavy damage inflicted on *Yonaga*. Strangely, a female announcer was the most taunting, the most aggravating. She was quickly dubbed "Tripoli Tillie." In perfect English sharpened by a nasal New

York twang, she punctuated her broadcasts with American colloquialisms and idiom. With obvious pleasure she told of the preparations for the trials of Colonel Latimer Stewart and eleven of his men which would begin in about a month. She also gloated about the four pilots and eight crewmen of *Yonaga's* strike force who had been picked up by *Daffah* and *Magid's Gearings*. They, too, would be tried for "International Gangsterism." According to "Tillie," the Israeli offensive had been smashed and thousands of "kikes" killed. Actually, when the sea battle had begun, the Israelis had called off their attacks. Colonel Bernstein confirmed this. The loss of *Daffah,* the heavy damage to *Magid,* and the massacre of the Arab air groups escaped "Tripoli Tillie's" attention.

In plain language, Fujita had a message transmitted warning whatever punishment was inflicted by the Arabs on their prisoners would be duplicated by the Japanese on their prisoners. "Tripoli Tillie" taunted back, "Have fun, boys. You ain't long for this world."

Steaming southward at twenty-four knots, Radio Tripoli faded rapidly. However the powerful stations at Rio de Janeiro, Buenos Aires and Port Stanley relayed the news. Brent actually missed "Tripoli Tillie." Her voice had been sexy and her ludicrous claims of losses inflicted on the Japanese — especially of the sinking of *Bennington* — had been a source of amusement for all hands.

After the first refueling off the Falklands, the force steamed the Straits of Magellan and then cut a course directly for Japan. Refueling from tankers had been arranged before the battle group departed Japan, avoiding stops at either Tarawa or Pearl Harbor. Thus, the battle group eluded curious eyes and kept the use of radios at a minimum. Although the entire world was aware of the presence of the force, particularly after steaming the Straits of Magellan, Fujita resorted to these stratagems to keep their route on the remainder of the trip as secret as possible. Brent had vivid memories of their previous return from the Atlantic in 1984 when an Arab submarine torpedoed a tanker and then hit *Yonaga*. Fujita, too, had the horror of that afternoon burned into his memory.

Thirty-three days after the battle, *Yonaga* and *Bennington* steamed into the Straits of Uraga. Squadrons of fighters from Tokyo International Airport and Tsuchiura roared their welcome overhead. In the channel, bouncing like tiny corks, gaily decorated boats filled with delirious celebrants flocked around the slowly moving giants. However, when the terrible damage to the two carriers became clearly visible, the celebrants lost most of their boisterousness. In addition, all the ships' armaments were manned and levelled. This, too, dampened the enthusiasm. Before Fujita could make the remark, Brent did it for him, "As long as we keep their bellies filled with rice and their Toyotas brimming with petrol, we are their heroes."

Fujita dropped his binoculars and smiled, "Sometimes you are psychic, Brent-san. You can see into my mind."

The young American laughed. "Sir, we have served together for over seven years."

The old man nodded. "True, Brent-san. We are well-acquainted."

He turned to the voice tubes and gave his final orders for the ship's approach to her dock.

* * *

It was dark when the final line went over. The gangway had no sooner been lowered than the CIA man Horace Mayfield, Lieutenant Tadayoshi Koga of the Self Defense Force, the Minister of Agriculture and Forestry Shizuki Kaushika all trooped aboard. Quickly, Fujita convened a meeting in Flag Plot including his most trusted aides; Rear Admiral Byron Whitehead, Lieutenant Brent Ross, Colonel Irving Bernstein, Commander Yoshi Matsuhara, Captain Mitake Arai and the scribe, Commander Hakuseki Katsube.

Fujita opened the meeting with a blunt statement, "We were betrayed!" He eyed Horace Mayfield who stared back through puffy bloodshot eyes. "What does the CIA have to say about this?"

In a little more than two months, the man seemed to have deteriorated more than two years. To Brent, Mayfield appeared to have consumed too much liquor, and, perhaps, too much dope. His pudgy fingers were trembling and he pressed them down on the tabletop tensely like a concert pianist awaiting his cue. "Why, nothing, sir. As far as the CIA knows, security has been tight." Obviously, the man did not suspect he had been under constant surveillance by both the CIA and Mossad.

"You have not been associating with the reporter Lia Mandel?"

Mayfield's face turned from red to purple and the veins on his forehead and large nose bulged. "Why, yes, but only socially, Admiral."

He was interrupted by a knock. With the two seaman guards dismissed to stations in the hall, Brent opened the door. Two young men entered. With dark brown hair, black eyes that glinted like newly mined coal, sharp features and the muscular build of a Grecian prize-fighter, the first newcomer gave the appearance of a man who attacked life with a sledgehammer. The second man looked like a college freshman, with blond hair, pug nose, a smattering of freckles and flashing blue eyes that radiated a little message: a combination of Peck's bad boy and Jack the Ripper.

"Greenberg! Arnold Greenberg!" Colonel Irving Bernstein shouted happily, rising and rushing up to the first young man and grasping his hand. "We've been waiting for you. You have your report?"

"Yes, sir."

Bernstein introduced Greenberg as a trusted Israeli Intelligence officer.

Mayfield, too, came to his feet. Eyeing the second young man, his welcome was cool. "Terry Case, CIA counterintelligence. What are you doing here? I thought you were back in the states."

"I'm on special assignment," Case answered, in a deep strong timbre that belied his boyish appearance. Brent guessed he was much older than he looked.

Fujita waved the two men to chairs. However, only Terry Case sat. Greenberg remained standing. He placed a tape recorder on the desk.

"You have a report?" Fujita asked.

"Yes, Admiral."

"About leaks?" He waved at the other officers. "We all believe we were betrayed. The Arabs seemed to know our every move. They knew all about the B-25s and their target, even *Bennington*'s position when she was off Gibraltar."

Greenberg's black eyes found Mayfield and stared right through the squirming CIA man. "They should have, sir." He stabbed a finger at Mayfield, almost hitting the tip of Mayfield's bulbous nose. "I am loathe to accuse one of our own, but Agent Horace Mayfield gave it all away."

"Nonsense! Lies!" Mayfield shrieked, coming to his feet.

"No! True!" Terry Case countered. He waved at the recorder on the table in front of Greenberg. "We have it on tape!"

"What on tape?"

"You and the reporters in that apartment in the Imperial, two nights after *Yonaga* left."

Mayfield blanched. "Impossible!"

"What reporters?" Brent asked, stomach sinking as if it had suddenly been turned to lead.

"Lia Mandel and Arlene Spencer."

"No, no," Mayfield moaned. "You can't have anything! I told them nothing. We were just having a good social evening."

"You were having a good social *ménage à trois*," Greenberg scoffed.

Brent's mouth was suddenly as dry as Sahara sand and he thought he was going to be sick. He felt Yoshi's hand on his arm.

"Lies!" Mayfield screamed. He shook a finger in Greenberg's face and then turned to Case. "I'll have your job. Both your jobs for this smear." And then staring at the recorder, "You couldn't bug that apartment. You didn't have time. Lia just rented it that evening for our private party." He turned to Fujita, pleading, "That's all it was, Admiral, a party." Fujita stared back as implacable as a temple icon.

Greenberg and Case both laughed. Case said,

"You should've pulled the drapes, but Arlene and Lia love the view. Right?"

"Lasers!"

"Right, Mister Mayfield, lasers. We focused on the living room and bedroom windows," Case said. Mayfield looked like a condemned man staring at the electric chair.

Fujita nodded and Greenberg switched on the recorder. Immediately, the sounds of "Spartacus" came through. Brent squirmed and tried to withdraw into himself. Greenberg stared down at the table as if he knew all about Brent and Arlene. He explained, "Arlene Spencer loves to have sex to the love duet between Spartacus and Phrygia." Brent could only stare at his feet and grit his teeth so hard his jaw hurt. Greenberg continued, "Everything is computer enhanced. The voices will be so clear, you'll think you're standing in the room with them."

Lia's unmistakable booming voice came from the tape, "Have another line, Horry."

" 'Horry'?" Fujita said.

"She called Mister Mayfield 'Horry'," Greenberg explained over the sounds of the tape.

Mayfield's voice, "After another shot of booze."

"Have a double, Horry."

"Don't mind if I do, only my fifth. Just getting a little buzz."

Giggles. Arlene's voice purring, "Gimme another line."

Mayfield: "That's your third, baby. You won't be able to tell sex from a horseback ride."

"It's all the same. Lia's a bronco," Arlene giggled. "Nose candy gets me ready for the saddle."

"I know. I've had that ride and I've got the bruises to prove it," Mayfield said, slurring his words. "I need another snort of snow, too."

Raucous laughter filled the room.

Lia's voice, "Before we get to the gymnastics, *Yonaga*'s picking up bombers. Right Horry?"

"Shouldn't tell you, sexpot."

"You already have, but not where they're headed."

"I know, but you promised not to use any of it 'til after they come back."

Arlene's voice, "I promise. Rabta—isn't it?"

Mayfield's laughter was wild. "You really want to know, baby?"

"I'd give anything for the scoop."

"Then I ain't sayin' 'til we're on the mattress. After I scoop you." He roared with laughter.

"After me," Lia said.

"Okay, I'll watch. But I get my crack."

Everyone laughed wildly again. "Your crack at her crack," Lia quipped. Still more laughter.

Mayfield's voice with an edge of impatience, "Time for a little fun and games on the work bench." There was some rustling sounds and laughter which now seemed continuous.

Greenberg turned off the recorder and said, "We cut a little here."

"I refuse to hear this phony tape. It's been cut and spliced to disgrace me. I'm leaving!" Mayfield exclaimed, leaping to his feet.

"No you are not," Fujita said, gesturing to Brent and Yoshi Matsuhara. Before Brent and Yoshi could rise, Mayfield sank back into his chair with a sigh of resignation.

369

Greenberg threw the switch. Brent could hear the "Bolero" playing in the background. *Only savages make love to the "Bolero"* raced through his numb brain.

Mayfield's shout, "You're doing great girls! Go for it!"

Brent could hear Lia grunting, Arlene sighing and crying out her little whimpering sounds Brent knew so well. She was approaching a climax. Then Lia bellowed like a bull servicing a cow, Arlene shrieked, "Oh, Jesus! Oh, Jesus!"

The girl's ecstatic cries sent a hot knife twisting in the young American's heart. He moaned, *No. No,* softly to himself.

"Man, that looked good," Mayfield's voice said from the machine. "That really makes a guy horny. I almost got off watching you broads."

Every man in the room looked down and away from his companions. They were looking into other lives where they did not belong. It was not titillating. It was disgusting and repugnant, and they felt some of it for themselves as if the curtains had been ripped from their own secret selves as well.

"Rabta, isn't it?" Arlene asked.

"Spread 'em for me, baby."

"I want the story."

"I want your pussy."

"The story first."

"Okay, you're right. Rabta. Gotta bail out the kikes again. But don't print it 'til it's all over."

"I promise. Come and get it, cowboy," Arlene said.

Lia's voice. "Let me in on this. You know what I like, Horry."

"Just the three of us," Mayfield said. "Bring it up here, baby. Get your teeth into Arlene's butt while we're at it."

There were grunts, moans and finally Mayfield's hoarse shout and Arlene's cries of, "Oh, Jesus!"

Lia's voice, "Had enough, Horry?"

Mayfield laughed. "You know what John Paul Jones said?"

"What?"

"I have not yet begun to fuck."

The crude jest brought gales of laughter from the women. Brent choked back sour gorge.

"Turn it off," Fujita cried out, voice an amalgam of anger, anguish and revulsion.

"There's more. He tells them all about *Bennington*," Case said.

Fujita shook his head. "Enough! Enough depravity for one evening." He turned to Mayfield, "You are a traitor."

"You can't believe that phony tape. I've been framed." Mayfield pointed at Colonel Bernstein, "That Jew has always hated me!" The finger moved to Greenberg and Case, "And now those two are part of the plot." Sweat beaded his brow and he wiped spittle from his lower lip with the back of his hand.

"Would you like to see our videos, too, Mister Mayfield?" Greenberg asked casually.

"What videos?"

"We got some through the windows with telephoto lenses. Not as explicit as the audio, but, quite interesting, if you care for a double feature."

Mayfield's brow wrinkled with new thoughts, his face brightened. "Why those broads are just reporters. How in hell do you know they leaked the information?" He threw a baleful look at Colonel Bernstein and then thrust a finger like a dagger into Greenberg's face.

371

"You're just out to get me, goddamn you. A fuckin' plot to discredit me and the entire CIA." He looked grandly at Rear Admiral Whitehead and Brent Ross.

Case handed Greenberg a sheet of paper. The young Israeli glanced at the document and then looked up at Mayfield. "We have some information on both women which might prove interesting."

Mayfield's eyes narrowed in alarm. "What?" he finally asked.

After placing the document on the table, Greenberg said, "Lia Mandel, alias Beatrice Forbes, alias Toni Asch, alias Ramiza Karaish and several others. Her name is actually Cecilia Drummond. She was born in Cleveland in 1950, attended Ohio State University where she led student protests against the Vietnam war. She did graduate in journalism, traveled to Europe and immediately began to associate with known terrorists. She met Illich Ramirez Sanchez—"

" 'Carlos the Jackal'," Whitehead interrupted.

"Right, sir," Greenberg said. "She participated in two bombings of El Al and Pan Am offices that we know about. She helped in the assassination of a Swedish diplomat sympathetic to Israel. She fell into disfavor when she seduced Carlos's favorite mistress. Then the Middle East, first the PLO and then she switched to Arafat's enemy, Abu Nidal and his Fatah Revolutionary Council. She was sent to Libya for special training at Kadafi's Tinduf camp and became acquainted with the colonel. It was rumored she participated in some of his more imaginative sex orgies. In any event, she became trusted and was primed as a liaison agent with the Japanese Red Army. This is where her training in journalism proved an asset. She was given a set of beautifully forged pa-

372

pers, a magnificent resumé and through influence we have not yet pinpointed, given a position with The United Information Service—"

"Enough! Enough!" Fujita shouted. "She is a spy! There is no doubt?"

"Correct, sir."

"And the other woman?"

"She seems to be a dupe. She has had an affair with Lia for several months."

"But she has helped with the espionage, knowingly helped this Mandel, or whoever she is."

"That is correct, Admiral. Their contact was Hayao Miyazaki of The Japanese Red Army. We suspect details of your operation were smuggled out of the country in a diplomatic pouch carried by an Iranian embassy official. It was easy after that."

Mayfield's head dropped almost to the tabletop, and his breath came with the labor of a marathon runner approaching the finish line. His face was as pale as bone china, eyes wide and staring at his open palms. Catching Fujita with the corner of his eye, he pleaded, "Admiral, they caught me in a moment of weakness. They got me drunk. Loaded. Used every ploy. You heard it. I'm not a traitor." The admiral stared silently. Encouraged by Fujita's silence, the CIA man carried on. "I admit I don't like Jews." He gestured at Greenberg and Bernstein who sat expressionless, "But I wouldn't betray anyone deliberately. Not anyone, sir."

"The sentence is death," the admiral said matter-of-factly.

There was a long, stunned silence in which every man seemed to draw in his breath and then found himself incapable of releasing it. Minister Shizuki Kaushika and

Lieutenant Tadayoshi Koga broke it. "He's a swine, but you can't do that!" Kaushika shouted.

"He deserves his punishment, Admiral, but this is a police matter!" Koga added.

Rear Admiral Whitehead nodded his agreement.

Mayfield could only blubber into his open palms.

"I am the law here," Fujita added.

Even Terry Case leaped in, "This is an internal matter. The CIA will handle this case. He'll get what he has coming, sir."

"Yes, Admiral," Byron Whitehead agreed. "We Americans know how to handle this kind of situation. We deal very harshly with traitors and those with loose mouths. Let us have him, sir."

"All this man has done is cause the deaths of hundreds of fine men, the complete failure of our attack on Rabta, and you are concerned about where and by whom he is tried?" The old Japanese shook his head. "You Americans would confiscate his library card, and confine him for a week in a luxury hotel." He pounded the table. "No! My verdict stands and it will be carried out immediately."

Mayfield looked up. Tears streaked his cheeks and he had slobbered on his chin. "You'll cut off my head, you goddamned barbarian."

Fujita shook his head. "Beheading is an honorable demise. It must be earned. I will hang you from the yardarm like the offal you are."

"No! No!" Mayfield shot out of his chair. Brent, Yoshi and Captain Arai grabbed him and held the CIA man against a bulkhead.

Fujita pressed a button and four seaman guards burst through the door. The old man had anticipated everything. "Take him to the signal bridge. *Yonaga* will soon be flying a new hoist. Tell the OD to await my arrival. I will personally place the noose around his neck." Two of the guards dragged the crying and pleading Mayfield out of the cabin.

"It's not right," Whitehead said.

"You'll hear from the Diet about this," Kaushika shouted.

"And from the Self Defense Force and the police," Koga added.

"Suit yourselves, gentlemen," Fujita responded.

Bernstein and Greenberg chuckled and rubbed their hands. They were both obviously delighted.

Kaushika and Koga came to their feet. "We're leaving," Kaushika announced.

"No, you are not," Fujita countered. He waved at the two remaining guards. "Take these men to my cabin. Hold them until I order their release."

Both men cursed and muttered warnings as they were pushed through the door.

Fujita turned to the two young intelligence agents. "What is the status of the two women?"

Terry Case waved at a phone in the corner of the room. "Do you have a shore line yet, Admiral?"

"Yes. I have already consulted with the Emperor."

"May I use it, sir? We have men keeping Mandel and Spencer under continuous surveillance. The last report, just before we came on board, was that they were both in Arlene Spencer's apartment, apparently having an intimate party."

Fujita nodded and gestured at the phone. Case made a quick call, smiled, and returned to his chair. "They're still in her apartment, Admiral."

Moving his eyes around the table from man to man, Fujita rubbed his hands together like an executioner about to spring the trap on a condemned man. He gestured at Brent, Yoshi, Colonel Bernstein, Captain Arai. "You are to proceed to the apartment in a staff car. You will be followed by twenty seaman guards in five staff cars. No trucks. Trucks attract attention; they could give your approach away." He turned to his executive officer. "Captain Arai, you will be in charge of the guards. Seal off Arlene Spencer's floor before Commander Matsuhara, Colonel Bernstein and Lieutenant Brent Ross enter her apartment." He stared at Brent Ross. "You all know we do not have time for police, for conventional justice which is never just."

"What do you mean, sir?" Brent asked suspiciously.

"Yes, Admiral, what are your orders?" Yoshi asked.

"Execute them."

A thick, heavy silence enveloped the room.

Yoshi Matsuhara broke in. "How?" he asked quietly.

The old man's voice was bitter and so raspy Brent had a hard time hearing him, "I am not concerned with methods. Just carry out my orders." And then in a high pitch that grated with its intensity, "Kill the spies! Avenge our sacred dead! Kill them!" He waved a fist.

Terry Case spoke up, "Sir, Arnold and I should accompany them."

"Why?"

He held up a small transmitter. "We can contact our crews, verify that the women are still in the apartment before your men break in."

"I thought you objected to my justice."

"I did to Mayfield's, but these creatures are spies. Enemy agents. If you don't kill them, we will. And keep in

376

mind, we can be of great help." And then with obvious distress, "You may be right about American justice. It stinks. That's why, sometimes, the CIA applies its own brand of justice, its own retribution."

"You two could destroy your careers."

"We know, Admiral," Greenberg said. "But we have both been involved in the covert elimination of enemy personnel before. This is not new to us. And as Terry said, they've earned their deaths."

"Then, both of you are not to enter the apartment. Just confirm the presence of the women before Commander Matsuhara breaks in. Understood?"

"Understood, Admiral."

Fujita's eyes shifted to Brent. A new thought narrowed them. "If you feel that you should not participate—"

"I am ready, sir," Brent said.

"Then carry out your orders!"

Before the men could rise, Rear Admiral Whitehead addressed Fujita in a strident voice, "Admiral, I belong with Brent and Commander Matsuhara, too."

Fujita shook his head and a hint of a smile seemed to crack the plethora of wrinkles crowding his thin lips. "You too? And you objected, Admiral."

"True, but the situation with the women is different. I agree with Mister Case. I should be part of this operation, Admiral."

"Captain Arai and Commander Matsuhara will be in charge. Both officers are junior to you."

"I can accept that, sir."

"Very well. You will all carry small arms. Proceed and kill them."

The men stood quickly and left the room. Entering

the passageway, Yoshi turned to Brent Ross and whispered in his ear, "White gloves and swords, Brent-san."

Brent nodded silently. He did not question the order.

It was very late before Byron Whitehead, Brent Ross, Yoshi Matsuhara, Irving Bernstein, Arnold Greenberg, Terry Case and two seaman guards arrived outside the door to suite 1410 of the Tokyo Hilton. Arai's Arisaka armed guards had sealed off the entire floor and warned the few guests encountered to remain in their rooms. All passengers exiting elevators were herded at gun point into an apartment where they were told to remain until released. Four of Arai's guards took over the switchboard and disabled the hotel's telephone system.

Yoshi signaled Arnold Greenberg, but instead of speaking into his communicator, the Mossad agent tapped on the door of suite 1412. The door opened a crack, there were a few whispers and the Israeli returned to the expectant group. "We still have a surveillance team in 1412. The women are in the bedroom and have been quiet for about an hour. Could be sleeping."

All of the men pulled their pistols and stepped back from the door. The two seaman guards raised their rifles and held them butt-first over their shoulders like battering rams. Yoshi pointed. The two powerful young men smashed the butts of their rifles against the door. It splintered, but did not give way. It took repeated battering to finally smash the door free. Case leaped into the opening, Yoshi shouted, "No!" But the CIA man was through the door first and into the dark interior, brandishing his nine-millimeter Walther. He never had a chance to use it.

Rushing in on the agent's heels, Brent heard a series of shots so fast it sounded as if someone was firing an automatic rifle. There was the unmistakable sound of heavy slugs striking flesh and bone. Case stopped in mid-stride as if he had run into an invisible wall. He did not scream. Instead, he sighed a long "Aaaah" sound. Brent was splattered with bits of bone, gray-red mushy substance, and blood that fanned out in a circle as Case whirled and crashed to the floor. At least two slugs had blown off the top of his head.

Brent dove headfirst past the dead man who still jerked spasmodically like a victim of palsy. He scurried across the floor on elbows and knees until he had put the couch between himself and the hallway to the bedroom. The shots had come from that doorway.

"Stay out, Yoshi!" he screamed. The warning was not necessary. The other man remained outside. It was death to enter.

Lia's voice came from the interior, "Well, well, the 'American Samurai'. Welcome, imperialist pig. Come for a bit of your own *seppuku?*" She fired two rounds, one smashed into the couch, the other ricocheted off the marble top of an end table.

Arlene's voice came from far down the hall, "Brent! Brent! Go back! She'll kill you."

"Shut up, bitch," Lia shouted. "Why do you think they're here? They're going to shove a gun up your pussy and blow your guts out." She laughed mirthlessly.

"No. No." Brent could hear Arlene sobbing. Carefully and silently, he worked his way around the couch to the wall which was the darkest part of the room. Slowly, like a surgeon raising his scalpel for a delicate incision, he raised his Beretta and pointed it at the doorway. At that

379

instant, an Otsu fired from the door to the apartment, sending three rounds into the hallway where Lia hid. Immediately, Lia fired back, but she was low, obviously belly-down on the floor. The slugs passed over her. But not Brent's. He saw her muzzle flashes, pulled his trigger four times. The entire apartment lit up with the flashes and there was the sound of metal hitting metal. Lia shouted out in pain. A slug had hit her hand, or pistol, or both. Brent heard something metallic clatter across the floor.

Possessed by an ungovernable rage, caution thrown to the winds, he leaped to his feet, charging the doorway. A low, maddened bull met him just outside the entrance, hitting him chest high, knocking the Beretta from his hand. It was Lia, nude and screaming. The impact knocked him onto his back as if he had been hit by a linebacker on a full blitz. He could not believe a woman could be so powerful.

She was on top of him. Punching. Clawing. Salivating. Screaming like a rabid animal. He brought a knee up into her crotch, but women do not disable from that blow as easily as men. She grunted and she punched the side of his head until his ears rang and his eyes starred with a hundred galaxies.

He punched back, knuckles impacting her ribs, head, cheeks, nose. Felt the cartilage break and pop with the sound of a snapping twig. Blood and mucus sprayed his face. He elbowed her up. He grabbed a great sagging breast and twisted.

She screamed. Sank her teeth into his neck like a steel trap. He felt sudden fear. She was an insane animal who wanted his jugular. She wanted his blood. He heard Yoshi shout, "Push her away!"

He punched and twisted her breast until she cried out. He heaved up hard, leveraged with his elbows and knees. She reared up, bloody teeth releasing.

The lights went on at the moment the Otsu fired. Brent was staring into Lia's face when the first slug tore through her left scapula, smashed two of her ribs and punctured a lung. Her eyes widened and her body stiffened. Her screams sprayed blood. He pushed her up and away just as another bullet fired downward tore off most of her lower jaw and ripped out her larynx. Then the killing round entered her left temple and exited just behind her right ear. The expanding soft-nosed round blew out her ear and sprayed Brent with brains, bone, and gore. She sagged down on him, blood pouring from her mouth, brains oozing onto his face. He could hear Arlene screaming.

A hard shove and she rolled onto her back next to Terry Case's body like a sack of rice. Her arms were flung out, legs spread. They twitched and trembled in their last spasms. Head spinning and numb from her blows, Brent stood slowly, and stared down at the woman. The eyes were wide. He felt a sudden chill. They were still filled with hate. *Put that in your notes,* ran through his dazed mind. He almost chuckled at the irony of it.

Arnold Greenberg's voice jarred him out of his stupor and back to reality. "The other one. She's in the bedroom."

Whitehead's voice, "For Christ's sake. Be careful."

Yoshi moved cautiously toward the hallway. Brent could hear crying coming from the bedroom. "Let me. Please, Yoshi-san? I owe her something," he waved, "I owe all of you."

"You all right?"

"Yes."

The commander nodded. "Then be careful, Brent-san."

Both hands gripping the Beretta, Brent crouched in the classic shooter's stance and slid into the hallway, keeping his back to the wall. Nothing. The crying was definitely coming from the bedroom. He edged his way along the hall until he reached the door to the bedroom. The crying was loud now. He took a quick glance in. A light on one nightstand was on and Arlene was stretched facedown on the bed, nude. He entered the room followed by Yoshi, Byron Whitehead, Irving Bernstein and Arnold Greenberg. They all stood for a moment, staring at the magnificent form on the bed.

"Shoot her," Bernstein said matter-of-factly.

"Yeah. Finish her off," Greenberg agreed.

The girl howled, rolled over, and sat up. She looked at Brent. "Don't let them, Brent. I love you. You know that. I was no spy. Lia used me. I'm glad she's dead. Honest I am. You're the one I love." Tears ran down her cheeks and spittle covered her chin. She trembled violently like a cornered mouse facing a predator.

Yoshi turned to Bernstein and Greenberg. Both Israelis shook their heads and made throat-cutting motions with flat palms. Then he gestured to a seaman guard who was standing in the doorway, holding a roll of line. "Tie her up!"

"Tie her up!" Greenberg shouted.

"Get to it!" the commander said.

The guard, Brent, and Arnold Greenberg tied the sobbing girl hand and foot.

"Stretch her across the bed, her head over

he edge and pointed at that wall," the commander ordered, stabbing a finger.

For the first time, Brent could hear the clanging sounds of police vehicles outside. Everyone ignored them. Yoshi pulled his sword from its scabbard and stepped toward the bed.

"No!" the girl shrieked.

"Don't do it," Brent said.

"We're honoring her, Brent-san, an honor she does not deserve."

"I know, Yoshi-san."

"Cut her throat like the dog she is," Greenberg said impatiently. "You goddamned samurai are too goddamned filled with ceremony. Don't get fancy about it. Kill her! Let's get on with it!"

Brent ignored the Israeli. "Let me do it, Yoshi-san. I owe it to everyone."

"You can?"

"Yes." The Konoye blade leaped from its lair with a joyous ringing sound. Yoshi stepped aside and Brent raised the killing blade over his head and stepped close to the girl.

"Please. No. No, I love you, Brent. Lia was the one."

Brent began to recite a litany of the condemned and the dead: "Don Hoeffler, Latimer Stewart, Stefan Krajewski, Juzo Itami, Tinley, Sparling, Hennessy, Woodford, Dunne, Yagoto, Dubois . . ."

"I had nothing to do with it!"

"You killed them all and a hundred more. You deserve a more inventive death than this. We are being kind."

The girl was beyond words. She sobbed. She drooled onto the carpet, and lost bladder control

383

"For God's sake do it," Bernstein shouted.

With the blade high over his shoulder, Brent stared down at the slender, beautiful neck. The vertebrae seemed to bulge out with each sob. "Goodbye, Arlene!" he screamed, bringing the blade around in its arc with all his power.

The tempered steel, as sharp as a fine razor, slashed through the bone and tissue of the girl's neck as if it were paper. It cut into the carpet and stuck in the wooden parquet of the floor. The head dropped like a chunk of wood axed from a tree. It bounced on the floor, and rolled into a corner.

Breathing in gasps and suddenly perspiring, Brent pulled the sword from the floor, stepped back and stood next to Yoshi. Everyone was silent, watching the blood spurt from the jugulars. It hit the wall, splattered and ran down to the carpet. Gradually, the bleeding diminished and finally ebbed to a dribble.

Brent could not take his eyes from the blood-smeared wall. It looked as if it had been painted by a lunatic. He was numb, weak, and his mind a scrubbed slate. Suddenly, Yoshi was next to him.

His friend took the Konoye blade, wiped the steel on a bedsheet and returned it to its scabbard. Then a firm hand on the back turned the American toward the door.

"It's over," Yoshi said. "Finished — ended."

Slowly, like a father leading his injured son home, he guided Brent out of the apartment.